# THE COST

*Also by Morgan Cry*

*The Daniella Coulstoun series*

THIRTY-ONE BONES
SIX WOUNDS

*Novellas*

DEATH INSURANCE (with Douglas Skelton)

# THE COST

Morgan Cry

SEVERN
HOUSE

First world edition published in Great Britain and the USA in 2025
by Severn House, an imprint of Canongate Books Ltd,
14 High Street, Edinburgh EH1 1TE.

Paperback edition first published in Great Britain and the USA in 2025

severnhouse.com



Cover and jacket design by Nick May at bluegecko22.com



*British Library Cataloguing-in-Publication Data*
A CIP catalogue record for this title is available from the British Library.

ISBN-13: 978-1-4483-1542-0 (cased)
ISBN-13: 978-1-4483-1776-9 (paper)
ISBN-13: 978-1-4483-1543-7 (e-book)



*All Severn House titles are printed on acid-free paper.*

Typeset by Palimpsest Book Production Ltd.,
Falkirk, Stirlingshire, Scotland.
Printed and bound in Great Britain by CPI Group (UK) Ltd, Croydon CR0 4YY

The manufacturer's authorised representative in the EU for product safety is
Authorised Rep Compliance Ltd, 71 Lower Baggot Street, Dublin D02 P593
Ireland (arccompliance.com)

# Praise for Morgan Cry

"Told with trademark wit and flair . . .
a brilliant, pacey, riveting read. A roller coaster
of a Euro-thriller, it's Morgan Cry at his best"
Abir Mukherjee, author of the
Sam Wyndham series, on *Six Wounds*

"Dark, disreputable and hugely entertaining. I loved it!"
Marion Todd, author of the
Detective Clare Mackay series, on *Six Wounds*

"Just brilliant . . . Highly recommended. All the stars"
Helen Fields, author of the DI Callanach thrillers, on *Six Wounds*

"A tight, taut and totally terrific read from Morgan Cry.
Smart characters, smart dialogue and a smart plot"
Douglas Skelton, author of the
Rebecca Connolly series, on *Six Wounds*

"Certainly delivers . . . riveting"
*The Sunday Post* on *Six Wounds*

"Fans of . . . twisted plots might want to try this one"
*Library Journal* on *Thirty-One Bones*

"A complex and immersive thrill ride"
Denise Mina on *Thirty-One Bones*

"Hugely entertaining [and] deftly told"
*Irish Independent* on *Thirty-One Bones*

# About the author

Gordon Brown, also writing as **Morgan Cry**, has eleven crime and thriller books published to date, along with a novella and a number of short stories.

Gordon is a founding director of Bloody Scotland, Scotland's International Crime Writing Festival, and runs a strategic planning consultancy. He lives in Scotland (when Brexit rules allow, Spain) and is married with two children – who have long since flown the nest.

In a former life Gordon delivered pizzas in Toronto, sold non-alcoholic beer in the Middle East, launched a creativity training business, floated a high tech company on the London Stock Exchange, compered the main stage at a two-day music festival and was once booed by 49,000 people while on the pitch at a major football Cup Final.

gordonjbrown.com

For Mum and Dad. I miss you both.

# ONE

*'Rooze'*

'Blake, where the f' are ye?'

The dented CB speaker mushes up the words as I wrestle the handset from the plastic holder.

'Doddy,' I spit. 'If you bought a proper taxi system' – I pause – 'you know the sort I mean – the ones that come from the twenty-first century, not the Stone Age – then you'd know exactly where I was.'

*'Aye,'* comes the reply. *'And if ye want tae give me the folding tae purchase the system, I'll buy you one all to yersel. Now, where f' are ye?'*

Doddy Robertson runs the least reliable taxi service in Fraserburgh. Based out of his small flat on Mid Street, there are three drivers. Doddy's supposed to be one, although you've got more chance of seeing a great white shark at the fish market than spotting Doddy behind a wheel nowadays; three fish suppers a day aren't helping him fit well into his crumpled old Mondeo, and his addiction to The Macallan would put him square in the firing line of the local police if he touched a steering wheel. The other two drivers consist of me, a raw recruit of two months, and Conn, Doddy's girlfriend of ten years.

Between Conn and me, the business is just about keeping itself alive.

'I'm up at the Tesco,' I say. 'Picking up Mrs Lang. Remember, you sent me?'

*'That was ages ago. Ye should've drapped her aff by noo.'*

The supermarket car park is busy. The main entrance and exit a live conduit of Saturday morning shoppers. Most heads are down against the chill, with only the odd nod of recognition passing between acquaintances. A young couple stop near me, briefly, then move on. A family is bickering next to the hole-in-the-wall machine. Two young kids are huddled beneath the entrance canopy. A boy and a girl. Leaning towards each other. Chatting. Maybe a boyfriend and his girlfriend. Their parents inside giving them a chance for a little private time. Reminds me of when I was that age. Me and my girlfriend at the time, Carol Teach. I still think about her. Of what might have been had I not been forced to leave this town forty years ago.

The shoppers flow around me. It all adds up to the usual frenetic shopping experience that cold weather brings. People want out of the chill and into the warmth as quickly as possible.

I'm parked up at the spaces reserved for taxis, engine running to keep the hot air inside flowing. A sleek, minted Mercedes feeds my vents with exhaust. I flip the switch to recirculate. The Merc's catalytic convertor is doing the rotten egg thing. It smells like a bunch of kids have let off a stink bomb in my car.

'Well, she's not out yet,' I say to Doddy as I scan the supermarket entrance. 'She does know she's looking for a dark blue Accord?'

I'm beginning to realize why so many police – 'till recently, my profession – take up taxis. Beyond the ability to deal with drunks and skunks, there's merit in getting to know your regulars well. In a small town like Fraserburgh, it can be a real boon to the job. Take my next fare, Mrs Lang, for example. Doddy has told me she's 'a wee wifie with a face like sour porridge'. There are more than a few of them around, so I'm hoping the bright yellow 'Doddy's Taxis' sign stuck to the side of my car will alert Mrs Lang to my presence.

I knew Mrs Lang when I lived here as a kid, but people can change in so many different ways. Take me. I used to be a stripe of a boy, allergic to fat. I pat my stomach. A beach ball that's being inflated daily. I've swapped out my police diet for a taxi driver's fayre – and that isn't helping.

*'F's sake, Blake,'* comes the reply from Doddy. *'She's been usin' my taxi for years. Same journey. Tesco tae Broadsea. Same day. Saturday. Same time. Eleven o'clock.'*

The dashboard clock tells me it's twenty past eleven. No one fitting Mrs Lang's description is in sight.

I remember her as a small woman whose colour combination of choice was dark on dark. She spent hours hanging over the fence that separated our back garden from hers. A jet-black shawl flicking in the wind. Spindly arms resting on the wooden slats, conversing with my mother from the safety of her own property, unwilling to venture into our domain.

Our garden was a wasteland of dying grass and mud, hers a showpiece creation she rarely stopped tending. That's why, rain or sun, she was always there to dangle over the fence when Mum appeared. As they chatted, Mrs Lang would chew on mint humbugs. If I was in the garden, she'd give me one when she wanted me to scoot. Usually because she was about to divulge some juicy piece of gossip with content too adult for my ears. I didn't mind; I had a sweet tooth that needed regular feeding back then. It's never left me, and the taste of the mint I'm chewing brings back the sight of Mrs Lang's dirt-ingrained fingernails.

'Maybe she got a lift?' I venture to Doddy.

There's an exasperated grunt from the speakers. *'She's dropped aff at ten, Conn picks her up at eleven. Unless she's died, that's the way it has been every week since the pope wore shorts.'*

Conn is Mrs Lang's usual driver of choice. Today she's on another job. She usually gets the regular runs. I'm still the rookie. But with only two of us on the road, Conn can't get all the good pickings. There's a knock on my window. I jump a little. A woman with a face like sour porridge is staring at me. I hit the wind-down button.

'Mrs Lang?' I enquire.

It takes me a few seconds to connect the memory of this woman from childhood to the one standing in front of me. Her face has a river delta of wrinkles on top of plumped-up skin. Her hair is a severe bun, silver to the roots, tied back, tucked under a plastic Rain Mate. A black overcoat hides everything else.

'And where have you been?' she spits. 'I've been waiting and—'

She launches into a series of questions, 'Where's Conn? Why did no one come in and help me with my bags? Did Doddy not tell you about me? Are you—'

I throw my hand up and push open the car door. 'Sorry, Mrs Lang, I don't know the routine. Can I help you with your shopping?'

'I needed help ten minutes ago, *son.*' She mashes on the last word, crunching it under foot. Her voice is unchanged from my youth. The light brogue. The clipped words. Mum had said Mrs Lang was as sharp as a slice of ice. A woman not to be crossed. A widow before I was born, I often wondered if she had ever married again, but thick woollen gloves hide her ring finger.

She has six bags, all packed to bursting. I'm amazed she got them here without me spotting her.

'Why didn't you use a trolley, Mrs Lang?' I ask.

'Because Conn always comes in and helps me,' she replies. 'That's why. Any more stupid questions?'

I have none. I load the bags into the back of the car before opening the front passenger door to let her in. She belts up, and I do likewise.

'Where to?' I ask.

She turns to me, wiping sweat from her forehead with the back of her arm. 'Did you just come up on the fish truck? Where do I always go?'

'I know it's Broadsea, Mrs Lang – but what street?'

I'm utilizing my most diplomatic voice.

'My house,' is the reply.

Broadsea sits on the road out of Fraserburgh to the northwest; it was once an old fishing community and is peppered with terraced grey, granite homes – some dating back to the seventeenth century.

I exit the supermarket car park, wheeling the car around to enter the town from the main road that leads south. Mrs Lang is eyes front. We pass the old cricket ground and dive into the town proper. Bellslea Park rises on the right. It's the home of Fraserburgh FC – a team in the Highland League. When I was small, you could climb the chute in the playpark next to the ground and watch the games for free.

As we hit the top of Cross Street, I signal left to enter High Street.

Fraserburgh has a way of naming some of its streets that milks directly from the 'blindingly obvious functional' period of town planning. Mid Street, Cross Street, High Street, Broad Street, Main Street. Or there's the 'let's attach ourselves to royalty (sometimes vaguely)' convention: Victoria Street, Charlotte Street, George Street, Hanover Street, Albert Lane, Alexandra Terrace and, up there on the obscure link-meter, Denmark Street – I like to think it's a reference to Hamlet rather than just a boring nod to the country.

Around us, the town is bedding down for winter. The shoulder of Scotland that Fraserburgh clings to provides no protection from the cold that rolls in. Exposed to the North Sea and the last remnants of the Moray Firth, the town is built with its back to the water. Only a few hardy homes, down where Mrs Lang lives, brave facing the sea. The rest huddle down, like penguins in the Antarctic, backs to the elements, waiting for the maelstrom to pass.

When I used to play on these streets, we took full advantage of breaks in the weather, milking them for what they were worth. A few degrees was all it took to pull my mates from their lairs.

We would wear T-shirts when visitors were wrapped in thick sweaters, shorts when strangers revelled in thermal underwear. You learned to take pleasure when you could; the appearance of a weak sunbeam was a starting pistol for fun. At school, it took a hurricane to cancel playtime. My blood runs thick and hot because of that. It has served me well. No winter and summer wardrobes for me. Coat on or off is the only call I ever make as a concession to temperature. 'Coat on' requires thick frost on the ground.

As we slide through the town, the colour of many of the buildings, dark grey, is channelling the mood of the skies on to the streets, wrapping the people of the Broch in a sombre cloth that outsiders often fail to penetrate. As I drive, I watch the people scurry through the chill and smile. I may have been away for a long time but I'm still one of them.

The trip is short. Fraserburgh is compact; nowhere in the town is more than a five-minute drive from anywhere else.

Now that she is in the car, I have a lot I could ask my passenger. When Conn told me that she couldn't pick up Mrs Lang, I had sensed a chance. I've bided my time since I returned to Fraserburgh to talk to someone who knew my mother.

Mrs Lang knew her well.

'Mrs Lang. Do you know who I am?' I ask.

She doesn't look round, choosing to watch the passing scenery, but she replies. 'I ken fine who you are, Blake Glover. Rhona's boy. Back from Glasgow. Policeman. Just a constable, though. Thirty years a constable.' She shakes her head as if I've somehow wasted my life. 'A good woman, your mother. Tragedy the way she died. You'd think a son would have been back afore now. How long have you been away? When did you last visit her grave?'

I'm taken aback at her forthrightness. 'It's been a while.'

'Well, that's not right. Is it?'

'Look, Mrs Lang, I'd like to talk to you.'

'I'm sure you would. Why else would a son be back in this town if not to ask a few questions?'

'You knew Mum well.'

'We were good friends.'

I take a right when I should take a left, extending the journey. I had this conversation all planned out. The questions to ask. Now they're all jumbled up. As if someone has stuck a Kenwood in my head.

'I . . .'

She puts her hand up. 'You were there the day she passed away, weren't you?'

'Yes.'

'That was no way to go. None at all!'

'Cancer,' I say, my voice low.

'At least she was spared the worst of it.'

'Was she?'

'Aye. If it wasn't for . . .' She stops talking.

'If it wasn't for what, Mrs Lang?'

'Nothing.'

I ask again. 'Wasn't for what?'

She shakes her head. 'Nothing,' she repeats. She turns away from me.

*'Blake, I love you.'*

*I'm sitting on the edge of Mum's bed. The large iron frame dominates the room. I spend many nights in here, mostly when Dad is away. Dad tells me Mum's not well. But he also says she'll get better. She's been ill for a long time. She cries at night when she thinks I can't hear her. Her room is full of flowers. They smell nice. But there's another smell in the room. Something that I don't recognize. It's not nice. It's a bad smell. Like the rubbish bin that's been left too long.*

*The doorbell rings.*

*'OK, honey. Can you get that? It'll be Doctor Noble.' Her voice is so, so quiet.*

*Dr Noble has been here an awful lot. I suppose it's what doctors do when people are sick. I run downstairs and open the front door.*

*'Hi, Blake. How's your mum?' Dr Noble is a big man, with bright red cheeks and a large, ginger, bushy beard that always has traces of food in it.*

*'OK,' I say, knowing she's anything but OK.*

*'Let's go see.'*

*I follow him upstairs. When he gets into the bedroom, he takes Mum's hand. He bends down and kisses her on the head.*

*I'm sent from the room. Dr Noble comes out ten minutes later. I'm standing in the hall.*

*'I'll be back in the morning,' he says to Mum, before turning to me. 'Blake, your mum is very brave.'*

*I have nothing to say to this. I know she is. He leaves and I go back into the bedroom.*

*Mum has her head on the pillow. She's looking at me. 'Blake?'*

*'Yes, Mum.'*

*'In the bedside drawer. Could you get some of my sweetie jars out for me?'*

*I open up the drawer. There are many small glass bottles and tubs, all with labels that have words I can't read. Her pills, but she calls them sweeties.*

*'Which sweetie jars, Mum?'*

*'The ones with the green label.'*

*I scan the bottles. So many. She spots my confusion. 'Just take them all out. Lay them on the bed. I need to sort them anyway. I'll find the ones I need.'*

*I scoop the bottles out.*

*'On the bed, honey,' she says.*

*I drop them all next to her, and there are so many bottles on her bed that when I move, some rattle against each other, making a clickety-clack sound. I don't like that sound.*

*'Honey,' she says, and I take her hand.*

*'Can you do me a favour?' she whispers. 'Can you get me some cash from the corner shop? There's a cheque in the drawer. The shop owner will cash it. I owe Mrs Lang for the messages this week.'*

*Mrs Lang has been doing the shopping for us while Mum is ill. Sometimes I go with her. To help.*

*'Sure, Mum, but it'll take a while.'*

*The shop is on the other side of town.*

*Her yellow teeth show as she tries to smile again. 'That's OK. Take your time and buy yourself a comic.'*

*She tries to return my hand squeeze but can't. Her face tells me it hurts to do so. She looks at me. 'My wee Blake. You know why you're called Blake?'*

*'It's the name of a famous man from Fraserburgh.'*

*'A real hero. Thomas Blake Glover. He became famous around the world for what he did in Japan. Fought for what he thought was right. And that's what you need to do, Blake: always fight for what you think is right. OK?'*

*'OK, Mum.'*

*Her eyes close, and she whispers, 'Just remember that. I love you.'*

*I find the cheque in the drawer, run down the stairs, out of the front door. I turn left towards the town. Dr Noble's car is still there.*

*I return, an hour and a half later, cash in my pocket, the comic under my armpit, read from cover to cover while I'd sat in the park. There are people at my front door. There's also a police car and an ambulance. I spot Dad and run up to him. He grabs me around the arm to stop me going into the house. He looks down on me.*

*'What's wrong?' I say, looking at the ambulance.*

*Dad's eyes are red. 'Son, I've something I need to tell you.'*

*He leads me into the living room and sits me down.*

'Where are you going? I'm here,' shouts Mrs Lang.

I jump as Mrs Lang drags me back to the present. We are cruising by Bicocchis, my ice-cream haunt of choice as a child. I look for inspiration from Mrs Lang on locating her home. 'Sorry, Mrs Lang, here?'

She waves her hand. 'Yes, here.'

'You moved house?'

'It's allowed.'

'What number are you?' I ask.

'Eighty-two B. There.' She points across the road. 'See yon hoose with the number eight-two B that you just passed? Well, that will be mine.'

I hit the brakes and U-turn the car to stop in front of her house. She's out of the car in an instant. I follow her, but she ignores my offer of a hand and walks across the pavement to open her front door.

She turns to me. 'Just leave the bags on the street. I'll sort them.'

'Are you sure you don't need a hand in with them?' I say, getting out.

'Are you deaf?' is the reply.

I oblige, and as I drop the bags next to her door, she reaches into her purse to pay.

'Look, Mrs Lang, the ride is on me,' I say. 'But what were you going to say about Mum before you stopped talking?'

She blanks the question, avoiding my eyes by rooting for money. She forces coins into my palm.

'I pay my way, and you'll find that's right,' she says. 'But no tip.'

'Thanks,' I reply in a meek tone. 'About Mum . . .'

She wheels away, vanishes inside, leaving me with my mouth open.

Doddy's voice bursts from the radio. *'Blake, Blake?'* His tone is insistent.

As I wonder what Mrs Lang had been about to say, a rip of North Sea wind cuts down the street, followed by the shriek of a seagull. The cries of the birds around town never stop, forming a constant backbeat to life. This one's call, however, manages to stand out from the crowd. Maybe a little louder. Maybe a little higher in pitch. The noise bounces around the street. The bird is sitting on a nearby lamppost, looking down at me, a tiny splat of red shining on the end of its beak, as if it's just been ripping into some fresh and juicy fish. It holds its gaze on me for a few seconds. Tilting its head to one side. Sizing me up?

From behind me, a forty-footer's airbrakes hiss as the truck roars by. The bird takes fright and rises, catching the wind before flying over the chimney pot of Mrs Lang's house. I follow it out of sight.

'Son, don't let people catch you staring at the sky like that!' Mrs Lang says as she re-emerges from her house. 'Your mother had a good brain about her. Don't be letting people say she brought up an idiot.'

*'Blake, where the f' are ye?'* Doddy has only one volume setting – loud.

Mrs Lang shows me her back as she heaves the last two bags into the house. I reach into the car and yank the handset free. 'I'm here. Just helping Mrs Lang in with her bags.'

*'Don't shit me! She doesn't let anyone in her hoosie. F'ing haunted, they say.'*

'I heard that, Doddy Robertson.' I jolt. Mrs Lang is standing right behind me.

She must have turned around. She still has two shopping bags in her hands.

'He can't hear you unless I press the button,' I inform her.

'Aye, well, press it and tell him the only thing haunted around here is the spirits he throws down his neck!'

Doddy is screaming. *'Blake? Conn needs a hand.'*

I hit the button 'What's up?'

*'A flat tyre.'*

'She has a spare.' I look to see if Mrs Lang is still there, but she's vanished.

Doddy rattles on. *'F'ing Galahad, yer not,'* he says. *'Ah ken she has a spare, but changing it takes time and she has a car full o' kids that are supposed to be at Dalrymple Hall for their show. So, stop pissing aroon and go and get them. She's on the Strichen road just before the turn-off for Broomheed Farm.'*

I don't know the farm, but I know the road. There's no give with Doddy. From day one, he's been shooting directions at me like I never left the place.

*'And be quick!'* he adds. *'It's Wendy Lemby's kids. Her husband did time for serious assault a while back. He's been known to take out his rooze on tradesmen.'*

'Rooze?' I enquire.

'*Anger,*' he explains. Then adds, *'Ye halfwit.'*

'Brilliant, Doddy. I'm sure ex-policemen have a special place at the end of Mr Lemby's knuckles.'

*'Are you going?'*

I stare at Mrs Lang's door, weighing up if I should knock to ask more about my mother.

The radio crackles. *'Did ye hear what I said?'*

I swear with the button off.

'Yes,' with the button on.

I think of the sweetie jars lying on Mum's bed. I think about the questions in my head. What does Mrs Lang know about my mother's death? I got the impression she'd said too much and that's why she'd leapt out of the car. I take a last look at her door. I need to know what she knows, but as our other next-door neighbour had once said, *'Rhona Glover, you know the real problem with your laddie? He wants too many answers to too many questions, too quickly.'*

# TWO

## *'Blackmail'*

When I spot Conn's car, a Ford Sierra, a relic from the eighties, it's half on and half off the Strichen road. She's been trying for years to get Doddy to spring for a new vehicle. I thought the model she drives was long ago consigned to car hell. And I'd told them both so.

*'How many people do you know that are still driving Sierras?'*

Doddy, in his usual belligerent attempt to be right, had stuffed a piece of paper in my hand. Ripped from a car magazine, it predicted that, amongst others, the Ford Sierra would, one day, be seen as a minor classic. My repost, that 'one day' was also the alternative name of the Eagles comeback tour, had made Conn laugh and caused Doddy confusion. Only when Conn explained that the tour had actually been called 'The Hell Freezes Over Tour' did he reply.

*'Smart arse. But ken this, it'll be a classic one day.'*

There are four kids near to Conn's car. Two girls, two boys – designer labels on show to impress their peer group. They are running riot. Conn's convinced them to jump into the field next to her, probably scared that one of them would run out in front of a passing car.

Even as I pull up, I can see that their location doesn't bode well for the interior of my vehicle. The recent rain has turned the field into a mud bath. The kids are knee-deep in it.

'Blake, get the kids in your car!' she shouts as she stamps down on the wheel wrench.

Conn is Syd Little to Doddy's Eddie Large. Same height, different sack of potatoes on the weight scale. She's slim – a little too slim – athletic with it, and has short, blonde hair. Her killer feature are her eyes. They seem to lack colour, taking on the hue of her surroundings. On a sunny day, they sparkle with a blue tinge. On a day like today, they're melancholy dark pools that reflect her mood.

Her accent is neutral. Her dad is from Burton-on-Trent in Staffordshire, a brewer by trade. Her mum is from Peterhead, only a few miles down the road – but Peterhead is to Fraserburgh as cats are to dogs. The Blue Toon and the Broch do not get along.

Conn's dad had been made redundant from the brewery, and a friend had offered him a job working with a supply company to the oil industry in Peterhead. That's where he'd met Conn's mum. Conn turned up two years later.

'Can I help with the wheel?' I ask, as I size up the kids and the mess that's about to enter the car I'd spent the best part of an hour cleaning this morning.

'Yes, you can get that idiot of a partner of mine to cough up for a new vehicle,' she shouts back. 'That would help.'

'Conn,' I say. 'I can't get him to pay to fix my boot latch. Good luck with the new car thing.'

She smiles and waves at the kids. Time to fill my car with mud.

Once the kids are in, I can't help but think about what Mrs Lang had said to me. Or rather what she hadn't said. For the next twenty minutes, I blank out the noise the weans are making, and wonder on my next steps with her, getting nowhere.

I drop the brood at Dalrymple Hall, a spired edifice that hosts many of the town's local events.

When I was a kid, Dalrymple Hall was just up from my playground of choice, the abandoned train station. It closed to passengers in 1965, but ran freight until 1979, after which it was an ideal place for a kid looking for somewhere to explore. There was something addictive about playing there. It was a place for adventure – ironically, it would later be transformed into an adventure playground.

To me, it reflected a 'what might have been' era for the town. When they cut off the train from Aberdeen, it isolated the populace. Everything north and east of the town is water. In its own way, Fraserburgh can seem as cut off as an island, and I always looked back on the closing of the station akin to the cancelling of a vital ferry. Creating a barrier, another reason not to visit. A Beeching mistake, but while the freight trains ran, there was still a chance that paying punters would someday return. They never did. The last freight train ran on the 5th October 1979, and that was that.

Back then, I would stand on the platforms, staring at where the rails used to be, wondering who else had stood in the same spot, wondering where they had been going, wondering what life changes were about to happen to them. Soldiers leaving for the war, mothers shedding tears as they waved goodbye to their sons, maybe for the final time. Kids off to university. People heading for a new job. Or there were those others waiting on a train arriving. Waiting for people. A loved one returning. A new arrival for a new life.

Platforms across the world serve the same function. A point to depart and a point to arrive. A transient portal. And when I sat down, dangling my legs over the edge of the platform, I would close my eyes and hear the whoosh of steam or the howl of diesel as the trains approached or disappeared. The rails both veins and arteries. Taking and giving.

Just before I swing the car into the car park at Dalrymple Hall, I catch the distant smell of steam, and for a moment, I think I see a cloud floating above the building where the station stood. I listen for the whistle. There's nothing.

I don't want to dump the children in the car park. It's an industrial Tetris game of cars dropping off. With Doddy's warning of the father's predilection for violence on my mind, I think it's better if I see them safely inside.

'OK,' I say to the eldest. 'Where do we go?'

The boy seems more interested in the contents of his nose than the world outside, but he removes his finger long enough to point at the main hall entrance.

We all get out and are soon sliding down a dimly lit corridor. My mum told me the Beatles played here in the early sixties – traces of the décor still reflect this. You can almost smell Lennon's aftershave.

A young man is standing at a door. He's traffic coordinator to the wave of kids flowing towards him. He spots my four.

'John Lemby,' he shouts at the nosepicker. 'You're on in half an hour. Where have you been?'

Before John can answer, I step in. I want my version of the story to get an airing before the kids can warp it.

I hold out my hand. 'Hi. I'm Blake, the taxi driver.'

The traffic coordinator's young enough to still be wearing the scars of long-term acne. He shakes my hand. 'Hi.'

I step back to let my fares past. 'My colleague got a flat. I ran out as quick as I could to pick the kids up. Sorry we're a little late.'

The young man, eyes darting around, acknowledges my story. 'No matter, it's only the dress rehearsal. You know what they say – bad rehearsal, good show.'

I don't think that's what they say, but I'm happy if he's happy.

The young man ushers the four in, his eyes catching the dirt on their shoes.

'Sorry about the mud,' I say. 'My colleague had to put them into a field out of harm's way while they waited on me. Do they need to be picked up?'

'Kids,' is his reply.

He says the word with a well-used sigh. I've no experience with kids. Never married. No siblings. Friends' kids are a subject I'm happy to avoid. I have no dislike for kids. I just don't gel with them too well.

'No matter, they're getting changed into costumes anyway,' he adds. 'And no, they don't need to be picked up; they're getting a lift home.'

More children roll up, and I'm surplus to requirements. It's interesting how fast you vanish from people's lives when you drive cabs. All chatty and merry as the fare asks you the usual:

*'Are you busy?'*

*'When do you finish?'*

*'How long have you been driving taxis?'*

Then, once cash has been exchanged, you're a disposable asset that's served its purpose.

I fight my way upstream, against the advancing hordes, back to the main entrance. I'm exiting the building when a young lady walks up to me. 'Hi, are you Blake Glover?'

She's small, but with me at just over six feet four, most people are. She's keen on the colour black. Black T-shirt under a black bomber jacket lined with black fur. Skinny black jeans and black trainers finish off the theme.

'Yes, I'm Blake,' I reply.

'Could I have a word?' She points back into the hall.

'What about?' I ask.

'Can we talk inside?' Then she adds, 'Please.'

I'd guess she's in her early twenties. She might be pretty, but if she is, the heavy-duty make-up obscures her looks. Even so, there's something familiar about her eyes. I look to my car. Doddy will be having a fit by now. With Conn off the road, I'm it.

I try to step away. 'Look, could we talk later? I'm rather busy.'

She shakes her head, stepping in front of me.

'It will only take two minutes,' she says.

I give in and step back into the melee. The young woman turns away from the crowds to find a spot free of kids.

She leans on the wall. 'My name is Terry Lang.'

'Lang?'

'You met my gran earlier today.'

My breath catches a little. 'I dropped her off not forty minutes ago.'

'I saw you. I usually go up on Saturdays to visit her.'

Another wave of kids washes in through the door. Their noise rattles around the corridor, making talk all but impossible for a few minutes.

When it quietens, I ask the obvious question, 'How did you know I'd be here?'

'I phoned Doddy,' she says.

I don't bother asking how she knows Doddy. Everyone knows Doddy.

'What can I do for you?' I ask. 'I wasn't kidding when I said I'm busy.'

She gives a little shrug. A sort of apology. 'You used to be a policeman?'

'Yes.'

'Were you any good?'

'Good enough,' I answer.

'Gran said you worked in Glasgow.'

'Look, I'm not being rude, but could you cut to the chase.'

'Do you know Broch House?' she asks.

I nod. It's a large hotel-cum-spa out past the village of Rosehearty. Six or seven miles away along the coast road to the west. A five-star establishment buried behind a fortress wall and an ocean of trees. It's the retreat for the one percent that own the world.

'Well, I work there. I'm a waitress,' she says. 'I've been there for a year or so. Money's OK. Hours are OK, and they pay for the taxi out and back.'

Conn does the odd run out there.

'And?' I say.

I can almost hear Doddy yelling down the radio in frustration at my absence.

'I've a friend.' She pauses. 'One of the other workers. Kristina. She's Polish. She cleans the rooms.'

She pauses to let some more kids scream their way into the inner sanctum.

'Well,' she continues when they're gone, 'she was fired last week for stealing.'

'And what's this to do with me?'

'She wouldn't steal. Not Kristina. She's a churchgoer.'

I think of all the devout criminals I've lifted in my life. Religion doesn't make you immune to breaking the law. Although, for some, they thought it made them exempt from the repercussions. A mother weeping that her son was an innocent, God-fearing child, when I knew he'd just been caught cold, dealing heroin.

'What did she steal?' I ask.

'She didn't steal anything.'

I rephrase the question. 'What was she *accused* of stealing?'

'That's just it. Stupid stuff. I mean there are some very rich people at the house. But they said she was stealing really daft things.'

'Like what?'

'Brushes. Shoes. Perfume.'

'Knowing the people that stay there, those items could still be worth a lot of money,' I point out. 'Did they catch her with anything?'

'No.'

'Did she confess?'

'No.'

'Did the House call the police?'

'No.'

'How much stuff went missing?'

'Lots. Over a week, just about every guest had something taken. So they said.'

People steal the weirdest crap, but Broch House must be awash with jewellery and credit cards. If you're going to risk stealing, it would make more sense to steal big.

I probe a little more. 'And the police definitely weren't called?'

'No, the management just fired Kristina and left it at that.'

'And that was when?'

'Three days ago.'

'And the thefts stopped after that?'

She stops talking.

I ask again. 'Well, did they stop?'

'Yes,' she says in a whisper. 'But it wasn't Kristina that stole the stuff.'

'And she told you that?'

'Not as such.' She shuffles her back against the wall. 'I was off last week. I'm at college, and my mid-term exams were on. I only started back at the House yesterday and that's when I found out she'd been fired.'

'And what does she say about it all?'

'That's the odd bit. She's vanished. Her mobile just trips to voicemail. She shares a flat on Commerce Street with another waitress. I went up there. Her flatmate said Kristina just packed and left.'

'Did Kristina not tell her where she was going?'

'No, and I'm worried about her. You used to be a policeman. I was wondering if you would look into it?'

'Why not go to the non-retired police? It's what they are there for.'

'I can't . . .'

She looks down.

I get the gig. If she went to the police, she'd have to tell them about the thefts. That would go down like a bucket of sick with Broch House. Firing Kristina was their way of telling the patrons that the issue had been dealt with. The last thing they would want is my old boys in blue rolling up. Discretion is a matter of course at Broch House. Terry would be out of her job like a shot.

'I'm sorry,' I say. 'I really can't help. The only answer to this lies with Kristina or Broch House. If you don't know where Kristina is, then only the House will have answers, and they have no reason to talk to me. I know it would be hard, but if you're that worried, I'd highly recommend going to the police.'

She steps towards me. Easing herself off the wall. 'Mr Glover, I can't afford to lose this job right now. I really can't.' She flicks her eyes along the corridor. Looking to see if anyone is listening. 'I've been in trouble before. If I lose this job, I'll not get another that pays anything like as well.'

'I'm sorry,' I say. 'But the police are your best bet.'

'And' – she ignores what I've just said – 'I give money to my gran. She hasn't got much.'

Heartstring confessions. I know them all too well. Maybe one in ten is true.

Terry does a little handbrake moment on me. 'Gran says your mum was a good woman.'

I wait.

She touches my hand. 'Gran says your mum died when you were young. Says you're back looking for answers.'

I dislike blackmail.

Intensely.

'OK, you seem like a smart kid. Let's cut the crap. Your gran put you up to this. Didn't she? I get the story. I help you, and she talks to me. Is that it?'

'I'm only asking if you'll help me.'

'No. I told you: go to the police.' I raise my voice a little. 'The answer is no.'

She drops her gaze. 'I'm only passing on a message.'

'If your gran has something to say, let her say it to me direct. I don't like being played.'

'You're not being played.' She sounds indignant.

'Bloody sounds like it to me. Whatever your gran knows, she must think I'll jump through hoops for it. Well, that's not the way I work. I don't like threats, even veiled ones. I'm sorry about your friend, but if you feel that strongly, go see the police. You're asking me to stand on their toes, and I'm just fresh from the force myself. I know *exactly* how I'd react to some ex-cop getting his fingers in where they don't belong.'

And, at the moment, the last thing I want to do is reconnect with my old employers. I didn't leave on anything close to the best of terms.

Terry's early confidence is ebbing. 'I'm just worried about Kristina.'

I look to the main door, wanting this over, but I back down a little. 'Look, think on it. If Kristina isn't the guilty party, then the fact the House fired her means they think she was. Even if Kristina is innocent, you've little or no chance of changing things, but if you're that worried about her, then do the right thing and go to the police – just tell them that she's missing; don't mention the thefts. Now, if you don't mind, I've a taxi to drive.'

She shoves a piece of paper in my hand. 'My mobile number. Please think about it.'

As I leave the building, my head is spinning. Clearly, Mrs Lang has something to say to me about my mother, but I'm not going to dance to her tune.

# THREE

*'To the Horn and Back'*

Doddy is achieving a whole new level of apoplexy when I return to the car. He screams a fare at me. It's hard to figure out where I'm supposed to go because of the sheer number of swear words interspersed with the address.

I finally figure that the fare is down at the harbour. A pick-up from The Sailor's Rest. It's a little early for any of the pub's regulars to be bailing out. Most will be just getting into gear on the drinking front. I acknowledge Doddy's request. He fires off some more cryptic Doric swear words to send me on my way.

I think back on what Terry has asked me to do. Her gran knows I want to talk about my mum. She's using that to help her granddaughter. I don't like being messed about, but at the same time, if Mrs Lang does know something about my mum's death, I want to know what it is.

I'm aware that there are others in town who will have known my mother, but not many, and not as well as Mrs Lang. She was a fixture in my childhood. A trellis-hanging hotline to the underbelly of Fraserburgh. Most everyone else who knew Mum or Dad is dead or moved away, or were just casual acquaintances. I did a little checking before I moved back here.

I'm still not really sure why I'm back to my birthplace. Or if I'll stay. For the last few weeks, I've been breaking with type. Taking it easy. Edging my way back into the town. Not low profile. That's not possible in this town. But *lower* profile. Sometimes the best way to get answers is to sit back and let them come to you. Terry's proof positive of this approach.

I run the car along the harbour's edge. Swathes of grey concrete stretch to the water where far fewer boats than I remember being here, lie, tied up. I eye the revamped Seamen's Mission. Mum had a thing about the tea and cake in their café. I just liked the cake. We would sit, her nursing a cup of tea staring at the comings and goings on the harbour front. Me, pencil in hand, drawing. It's what I did back then. Boats, lighthouses, fish. I'd draw them all. My primary school teacher in my last year once showed off my work to the class. These things make an impression on the young. My work being held up as an example of excellence. I smile at the memory as I cruise towards The Sailor's Rest.

It sits not far from the mission. It's a new pub in a town where old pubs have been closing. Built on the site of the old lifeboat shed, it's unusual for a new bar – a drinking den not a cookie-cutter gastropub. The lifeboat that used to live on this spot now rides with the tide in the harbour.

I look down on it as I pull up at the pub. In the late 1800s, there were over 800 boats in the harbour, one for every ten people in the town. Even by the time I was a kid, the boats were still thick on the water, and the lifeboat commanded the respect of every sailor in town. Next time it might be coming for them. Fraserburgh has a hard history with the men of the Royal National Lifeboat Institute. Lifeboat disasters occurred in 1919, 1953 and 1970 – more than any other UK town. Thirteen brave lifeboat men died saving lives.

My childhood sidekick, Charlie Noble, owns The Sailor's Rest. As a kid, he'd watch, with me, as the lifeboat crashed into the water; now, he owns the building where the lifeboat once slept. Charlie owns a dozen pubs in the northeast. He also has a share in a range of other businesses. I've yet to bump into him since returning. He has a place in Spain and for the last two months has been taking in the sun. Doddy told me last week that Charlie was due back any day.

Charlie was a steel-wired whippet of energy when we were kids, with limbs as thin as dried twigs. You could have hung him out on a soaking wet day and the lightest breeze would have lifted him over the black dome of the Kinnaird Head Lighthouse. He had stamina to fry in. My energy was mental. In our worlds, two phrases were dominant.

*'Charlie, sit down.'*

*'Blake, shut up.'*

It's how we flew. Charlie's boundless vigour or my mouth getting us into trouble.

My rear was warmed on more than one occasion by the hand of my father on the back of some crazy Charlie-fuelled stunt. But in my father's head, it wasn't retribution. I think he viewed it as reinforcement of a lesson I needed to learn. A way to imprint into my head that being stupid wasn't going to enhance my life. I wasn't a great listener, and he saw his hand as far more effective than the harshest lecture.

Once, when we had moved to live in Glasgow, he broke down in my arms, drunk as a skunk, and cried over the times he had hit me. As a kid, I saw the slaps as nothing more than a parent's right to discipline his child. After all, most of the time the smacks were followed by ice cream or chocolate as his guilt overtook him. In my books, the pain faded with the first lick of a 99. That's just the way I thought all kids lived.

I pull up outside the pub, flipping on the radio to wait on the fare. Tune in and tune out. OMD lamenting the first atomic bomb being dropped. The mud from the kids' shoes had more than its fair share of cow shit mixed in it. Some people might like the country-fresh aroma, but not my passengers. I'll need to risk Doddy's wrath and detour to the garage at some point to clean the car.

As the radio DJ announces the next track, I look at the pub and wonder if I should go in. See if Charlie's home. Pretend I'm just hunting down my fare. Casual like. No big deal.

*'Charlie Noble, as I live and breathe. Long time no see.'*

I decide to leave it. Let things take their course. If he's back, he'll soon know I'm in town, if he doesn't know already. Let him make the first move. Play it like everything else to do with my past in this place. Play it cool.

There's a knock on the window. I hit the down button.

'Taxi?' says the stranger, beer breath streaming in behind the words. I suspect that The Sailor's Rest may have opened a little earlier than publicly advertised, or this guy has a vocation in breakfast boozing.

The man is wrapped in a heavyweight dark coat of indiscriminate material. A woollen bunnet is pulled down on his head. His nose is riddled with red veins, purple patches on his face outweighing healthy skin.

'The college campus on Henderson,' he says.

I wait until he's settled into the back seat, using the time to eye the pub door in case Charlie emerges.

We set off, squirrelling our way through town, the fare happy with silence. For a moment, we have to wait while a hearse pulls out from a funeral director's, the business name picked out in gold on the expansive window next to where the hearse is emerging, a single grey granite urn sitting on a black plinth as a display. The rest of the window is empty. Reminding you that, in a fishing town, death sits centre stage.

After a few minutes, we approach the college campus building. An impressive addition to the town. Then it dawns on my addled brain that it's Saturday.

'Is the college open on a Saturday?' I ask.

'How wid I ken?' comes the reply.

The palpable answer to that is to ask why he would be going if it wasn't.

'Here,' he says.

He leans over and looks at the meter. He shoves some money my way. 'You should drop in on Charlie Noble.'

I spin as he speaks, but he leaps from the car to avoid any questions. I unbuckle my seat belt and dive out.

'Did he tell you to tell me?' I'm shouting at him as he hobbles across the grass in front of the campus. There's a small clutch of homes not far away.

'Hey!' I cry out. He doesn't turn at my shout. Just keeps moving. He staggers a little under the influence of the drink. I consider giving chase, but as I do, Doddy's dulcet tones emanate from the car.

This is a day for the cryptic. First Mrs Lang's offer, through Terry, to tell me a bit more about my mother, and now a drunken messenger throwing me an invitation to catch up with my childhood friend.

I slide back into the driver's seat, ignoring Doddy.

My best memory of Charlie is that of his anaemic, drab-coloured, shorts-covered butt climbing up Mormond Hill. A mound lying to the south of the town with a summit that housed a USAAF monitoring station. The station was built on the site in 1960, the penultimate link in a chain of radio listening posts reaching from Yorkshire to Iceland, transmitting information to a complex in Cheyenne Mountain in the good old US of A. It closed in the early nineties.

We'd often climb the hill to find what Charlie called 'yon deer thing'. He claimed it was a million years old. Carved into the side of the hill by an ancient tribe. Charlie was full of crap. I discovered, from a book in the town library, that the hill figure of a stag had been constructed in 1870 by a local laird to celebrate a wedding. It was the size of a football park. A giant stag lying on its side, made of small white stones. You can see it from miles away.

Charlie had invented a game to play that summer. The great stone animal has two giant antlers. Charlie and I called them horns back then. One twisting out over the deer's nose, one curving back to its tail. Its four legs set out like a five-year-old's drawing beneath its belly – a neat row with no perspective built in. The game was simple. You had to start at the rearmost back foot and sprint up the hill. You ran along the body of the stag, looped up through the head, out on to the back horn, touched the far end of it and ran back.

Charlie owned a watch. Charlie owned a lot of watches. I didn't. I was just late for everything. The winner was the fastest to reach the horn and back. As I didn't trust Charlie's timekeeping, counting seconds was done out loud. Arguments raged over how fast we both counted.

I catch the distant echo of his laugh. The high-pitched sound of a donkey on helium followed by his shout. *'To the horn and back. To the horn and back!'*

My fare vanishes into one of the houses as two students exit from the main door of the campus building. The girl has a thick jacket on, but the boy, in a fit of bravado against the elements, has a light hoodie. The word 'Gdansk' is picked out on the back of the hoodie. A reference to Lech Walesa and the Solidarity movement? Or maybe that's his hometown. They are holding hands, and Carol Teach comes back to mind. I wonder what she's doing now.

The radio shouts at me. *'Blake, where the f' are ye?'*

# FOUR

## *'Expensive Tea'*

With Conn off the road, and Doddy showing no signs of extracting his carcass from his flat, I'm flying solo. As I drop and pick up, I chew over what the drunken fare said about Charlie, but I'm not ready to see my school-friend yet. I've other stuff to do. I need to talk to Mrs Lang, and I can either force that issue with her or run up to Broch House for Terry and do a bit of snooping.

At four o'clock, I buzz Doddy to say I'm taking a break.

*'Tak a break. Tak a break! Do ma customers tak a break?'*

It's always a compromise with Doddy, but it's a small price to pay. When I'd decided to come back to Fraserburgh, Doddy was a minor saviour. I didn't need the money, but I needed the job. Something to do. I'd thought about volunteering and had even visited a few charity shops, but I couldn't see myself there.

It took me a while to realize that there's an underlying friendliness to Doddy. Our back and forth seemed to grow naturally, moving from a Doddy monologue to something more confrontational.

We dicker over the break. I want four to seven. He wants five to six. We settle for four to six.

'Doddy, if I didn't know better, I'd place you as a slave driver.'

*'Son, who else would put up with yer crap? An ex-policeman with secrets isn't the most employable gadgie on the planet.'*

'Secrets, Doddy?'

The static from the speaker underlines his slip. Doddy backtracks. *'Doesn't everyone hiv secrets?'*

'That's not what you meant.'

*'What are ye? A mind reader? Now f' off an do yer jape.'*

The radio dies. I sit back. I wonder who Doddy's been talking to.

At five, I radio in, and Doddy tries to get me to take one more fare. I decline. He swears and I flip the radio to silent. I know

Conn is in the saddle. I'll be back on before the Saturday night shift heats up. I stop to pull the two magnetic 'Doddy's Taxis' signs off the door panels, throwing them into the boot.

I could do with a rest, a bite to eat. Saturday nights can be busy. Last week, I'd run from six to one in the morning without stopping, but I've decided that I'm going to take a turn up to Broch House. I can be up and back in an hour. Chances are no one will speak to me. Then I can tell Terry I tried and hope her grandmother has the good grace to talk to me about my mother.

I take a quick detour to the garage to scrub some of the mud from the back seat. I've not had time since I'd picked up the kids, and the smell is disgusting. I clean it as best I can, buy a packet of crisps, a can of IRN-BRU and a bar of Galaxy. I'm aware that I could do without the snack. Love handles are sprouting from my back. I'm beginning to resemble an overfed walrus. Being a cop on the streets kept some of my excess poundage in the freezer. Two months on my backside, ferrying the great and not-so-great of Fraserburgh, has added a stone to my weight, I suspect more. I'm now clinically intolerant of weighing machines.

I annoy the garage attendant by using my mobile. I need a quick chat with Terry. 'Terry, it's Blake Glover.'

There's a moment's confusion. As if she doesn't know who I am. Then, *'Hi.'*

'OK,' I start. 'I've given some thought to our conversation, and before I decide whether to help or not, I need a couple of answers to a few questions.'

*'Sure, shoot.'*

'Have you been to the police yet?'

*'No.'*

'Are you going?'

*'Are you going to help?'*

'Forget that. Are you going to the police?'

*'I'm not sure.'*

'Are you mixed up in the thefts in any way?'

*'No. Absolutely not.'*

I didn't expect her to confess, but I can spot a lie from a week away in deep fog. She's on the level.

'OK. What have you told your grandmother?'

*'About what?'* she asks.

'The thefts.'

She hesitates before replying. *'I told her all about it. Gran told me I should contact the police. I told her I wouldn't. That's when she said she might know someone else who could help. I went up to see her last Saturday at her request.'*

'You told me you usually go up Saturdays anyway?'

She takes a breath, holding it, thinking over the lie. Most people either rush to cover a lie or hesitate. She's a hesitater. *'Sundays. I usually go up on Sundays,'* she says. *'But I just thought telling you I was there for another reason was easier.'*

'And a lie,' I add.

The garage attendant is doing the finger and thumb thing with his hand. Telling me to get off the phone. I blank him.

'OK,' I say. 'I'll ask a couple of questions up at the House, but that's it. Then you go to the police.'

*'But . . .'*

'No buts. I'm not going to step on anyone's toes. I *will* ask a few friendly questions, but first you need to promise to go to the police.'

The silence from her and the whistle of wind in the background tell me she's contemplating lying again.

I jump in. 'If you don't go to them, I will.'

*'OK. Once you tell me what you find out, I'll go.'*

'And there's a couple of other conditions.'

*'What?'*

'You've to tell no one that I'm involved.'

*'What about my gran?'*

'Except your grandmother. But you've to get her to promise to keep it quiet. If I hear otherwise, I'm going to be unhappy as hell.'

*'OK.'*

'Next, when . . . and I mean *when* I say I'm done, I'm done. No negotiation.'

*'OK.'*

'And I want to talk to your grandmother about my mother in return.'

*'I'll need to chat with Gran on that.'*

'Phone her after this.'

*'Anything else?'* she adds.

'Yes. I need to know a bit more about who's who at Broch House.'

*'Do you want to meet up again?'*

I look at my phone. Time is already running away. 'No. Just give me the top line.'

The petrol attendant has given up the charades game. He's serving a customer but still has an eye on me.

Terry starts talking, *'My boss is a guy called Jose Martinez, the food and beverage manager. He's the big boss when it comes to the restaurant and events.'*

'Did Kristina report to him?'

*'No, she reported to Gail Till, the housekeeper.'*

'Are Jose and Gail nice people?'

*'Gail's a cow.'* She spits the words. *'Jose's OK, I suppose, but he's just a little too close to the general manager at times.'*

'Too close?' I can feel the police question routine building. My few friends in Glasgow gave me a right doing when I started it with them on a Friday night in the pub. I remind myself that Terry isn't a suspect in anything.

She keeps talking. *'Mr Melev is the GM. He has very high standards, but Jose doesn't challenge him on anything. He just does, if you know what I mean.'*

I did. I had an old sergeant who was the same. If the inspector shouted, he was there before spit hit the floor.

'So sometimes he drops you in the shit?' I venture.

*'How do you know that?'*

It's what my sergeant did to me.

'A guess.' I move on, conscious of time. 'Who fired Kristina?'

*'Gail.'*

'Do they go through a lot of cleaners up there?'

*'Yes. As I said, Gail's a cow. Bent out of shape. Kristina had done well. Been there over a year. Most cleaners leave inside three months. Kristina was popular as well. That didn't sit well with Gail. She likes to be the queen bee. As I said, a cow.'*

'Are most of the staff locals?'

*'Yes and no. It used to be mostly Eastern Europeans. But that's changing. Brexit, you know. Visas are thin on the ground now.'*

'And you said Broch House pays well.'

*'Better than anyone else in the area.'*

'Better than minimum wage.'

*'Better than living wage.'*

That sounds a little off. A lot of the less 'friendly' leisure establishments I know paid as little as they could get away with. Maybe Broch House wanted the best. After all, it's about as exclusive as it gets.

'OK, Terry, I'll be in touch. But remember, tell no one.'

*'Mr Glover?'*

'Yes.'

*'Can you be discreet?'*

'Of course.'

*'Thanks for doing this.'*

'Terry, I haven't done anything yet. I might get nowhere, and even if I do, you might not like what I find out. I'm only going to ask a couple of questions.'

*'Thanks anyway. I'll call Gran and text you.'*

I kill the call, wave to the attendant and breathe in. The smell of cow shit is still hanging around the car.

The road out to Broch House threads past Sandhaven and Pittulie. Places I used to visit when I was young. To my right, the North Sea is a blanket of dark grey, riddled with white horses. I spot a lone fishing trawler being tossed around like a bad salad.

My phone pings. I glance down. It's a text from Terry. *'Gran's cool. She'll talk to you about your mum after.'*

I drive.

Rosehearty appears. There used to be an outdoor swimming pool near the harbour, but it's long gone. Now, that was swimming for the brave. Cold wasn't the word. Try 'Screaming Baltic with Extra Ice'. That was closer.

I play with the ancient CD changer and pull up Mike Oldfield's *QE2*, sinking into the album.

Broch House lies a couple of miles outside Rosehearty. The original building was abandoned long ago – some local landowner lost his money in the gaming dens of Las Vegas and vanished. The new owners had moved in not long back and converted it into a hotel. Money no object, so I'd heard. I've not been before.

The place is not easy to find. This is not an establishment that plies for passing trade. I do a fly-by on the entrance twice before I spot the smallest of signs indicating where I need to turn right. The road is one-way, with passing places. About five hundred yards along, an even tinier sign – one that requires a magnifying glass for full effect – tells me to hang a left. I leave tarmac and hear the crunch of gravel and spitting stones as they ricochet off the underside of the car. Pine trees line the road. My clock shows four thirty. The daylight has almost gone. Beneath the trees, two lines of brilliant-white painted stones, like landing lights at an airport, show me the way.

A gate rises from the dark. Two concrete towers sit astride the road, massive snow-coloured blocks to complement the pathway stones. There's no further signage. The gates are open, but I've heard that they close them not long after dark. Then, only entry by the buzzer will be permitted.

I slip between the monoliths. Two massive wrought-iron gates, black as the night sky, hang from them. You can pick out the letter B on one and H on the other – but only if you look hard.

The sound under the tyres changes. Larger chunks of white pebbles rattle against each other as I pass. A deep, resonating growl. We're on the classy stuff now.

My headlights pick out the edge of two lawns, one on either side. They stretch for a couple of hundred yards to a line of trees. Both could be putting greens in next year's Open championship. The driveway finishes by circling a fountain that sits opposite the main door of the house. A car park sits to the right. It's small, lined for twelve cars. The lack of spaces is a bit of a hard one to fathom. I've been told they do weddings here.

Maybe there's parking for the proletariat somewhere else.

I haven't a plan, as such. I doubt I'll get to talk to Gail or Jose. Even if I do, there's little I could ask about Kristina that won't set off alarm bells. But there are other ways to extract information. Someone always knows something about something. You just have to be able to sift. Ignore the crap. Dig for the gold.

The marble-columned entrance door glows under a spray of illumination from multiple down-lighters. Not heavily lit. Subtle. The front door is a double glass affair that affords a view of the luxury inside. Black leaded letters, B and H, are picked out on the shining marble threshold to the building. Two tiny CCTV cameras, nestled high up in the corners of the porch, almost invisible unless you know what to look for, look down on me.

A man in his early sixties, weighed down by a heavy woollen coat, stands at the entrance, is watching me from under a peaked cap. I regret not changing into something a little less workman-like. I like to be comfortable when I'm driving. I'm not a slob, but my 'two for a tenner' shirt, lightweight trousers, functional shoes and half-length coat are all a bit tired. Broch House looks like it does Armani as standard, and I'm sporting Primark.

I crunch stones underfoot as I work my way to the door, walking with confidence. A policeman's gait. As though I'm back in uniform.

Upright stance. No slowing as I rise up the two steps that sit before the columns. I nod at the doorman. He says, 'Good evening, sir,' and pulls open the door to let me in. I thank him. If he thinks I'm wearing the wrong gear, he doesn't show it. But why would he? The rich dress down just as badly as the rest of us.

The entrance hall is a deep-pile-carpeted affair leading to a grandiose staircase at the rear. A shining oak-topped table lies in front of me, serving as a reception point. A young woman, dressed in a jade trouser suit, stands beside it. Behind her, the concierge's point is manned by a man in a similar coloured suit with an ivory tie. Jade and ivory are the key hues of this place.

The young woman steps forward. 'Can I help, sir?' Her accent is not local.

'I'm just after a cup of tea,' I say.

Her look says more than words.

I explain, 'I've not long moved here, and I've heard a lot about this place. I just wanted to have a look and take in the atmosphere.'

Her look is still one of slight disdain. 'The Saltoun Lounge serves drinks, or we have the Kinnaird Restaurant if you are looking for something more.'

I'm positive I can't afford to eat here. 'The lounge sounds just great.'

She points to a dark wood door. 'Through there, sir.'

Beyond the doorway is an oasis of calm. Large bi-fold windows dominate two sides, looking out on to a lawn that's vanishing in the dark. A well-stocked bar stretches along the far wall, and the entrance I've come through has bookshelves stretching either side of it. Small cream-topped tables are attended by jade-coloured, overstuffed, high-back armchairs studded with off-white buttons. There are ten tables in total. Apart from the barman and me, the place is deserted.

'Hi,' I say as I cross to the bar.

The barman is polishing glasses that need polishing in the same way Yul Brynner needed a regular haircut. He eyes me up as only high-end bar staff can, his eyes lifting from the glass, his head not moving. He's in his early twenties. His hair is a high fade with a hard parting and quiff. Deep blue eyes study me. I swear he's looking at my shoes.

'How can I help you, sir?' A non-UK brogue. Eastern European at a guess.

'Cup of tea, if that's OK?'

'Would you care to take a seat?'

I look at the empty room. 'If you don't mind, I think I'll sit at the bar.'

'As you wish, sir.' He picks up a phone. He orders up my tea and returns to polishing the glasses.

'Nice place,' I say.

'Yes, it is, sir.'

'Been working here long?' I drop myself on to a leather bar stool and lean on the bar.

'A year, sir.'

'You're not from around here?'

'No, sir.'

'Where do you call home?'

'I'm Polish, sir.'

He's not going to open up to me from the get-go. I'll need to prize him out of his shell.

'Who owns the place?' I ask.

'A company called AC Superiore.'

'Never heard of them.'

'They own a number of establishments around the world.'

'Tell me more.'

Despite himself, he's either going to lie that he knows nothing or give me something to use as a way I can access his haughty veneer.

'Why do you want to know, sir?'

I run my hand over the oak bar. 'Just curious. I'm new up this neck of the woods, and I've heard a lot about Broch House. I have a friend who is looking for a venue for his daughter's wedding. I said I'd check this place out for him.'

He can't help but look at my coat. I unbutton it, remove it and drop it on my lap.

'I can get the duty manager,' he offers. 'He would be far better placed than me to give you information.'

'No,' I reply. 'That won't be necessary. I'm sure he'll be busy. By the way, your English is superb.'

'I studied English at the University of Dublin.'

'Really?'

'One of the best universities in the world for teaching English.'

His shell is cracking.

'So I've heard.'

I've never heard that.

'Must have been tough studying there,' I say. 'English not being your first language and all.'

He puts the over-polished glass down, paying me some attention now. I think I've found a way in.

'Very hard,' he confesses. 'I had to hold down a few jobs at uni. My family don't have much money.'

'Work, study and learn a new language. Rather you than me. I struggle to drive and listen to the radio at the same time.'

He smiles.

We're definitely in.

'How did you get this job?' I enquire. 'Fraserburgh is a bit off the beaten track.'

'I had a friend working here. She recommended me.'

'What was your friend's name?'

His eyes narrow. Maybe a little too early with that question.

'Kristina,' he says. 'Why? Do you know her?'

I shake my head, smiling broadly. 'No chance. My circle is strictly the local pub and a dodgy Facebook group my friend created.' I change tack a little. 'Do you like it here?'

'It's good but, if I'm honest, a touch boring.'

'It does seem quiet. Is it always like this?'

He pulls out a stool from under the bar. He looks to the door before sitting on it. I suspect it's not allowed. The main door opens, and he jumps up. I turn as another jade-and-ivory-suited woman enters with my order spread on a silver tray. The bone china teapot is so fine you can see the tea inside. I indicate for her to put it on the bar. She looks at the barman. He nods. She lays the tray down with a polite, 'Enjoy, sir.'

I turn to the barman, 'Sorry, my name is Blake.'

He reaches over and shakes my hand, 'Tomas.'

'Nice to meet you, Tomas.'

There's a small slip of paper next to my teacup. The bill. I glance at it and choke. Fifteen quid, without tip. Bloody hell – no wonder they're quiet.

Tomas returns to his chair, ready to spring up should anyone else enter.

'You were saying,' I say, as I pour out a fiver's worth of tea. 'It's quiet?'

'Very. I can go a whole night without a customer.'

'What about weddings and the like?'

He reaches for a glass of water. 'What weddings?'

'I heard they do a lot of big events here. So my friend said. Am I wrong?'

'I've been here a year. I've never been asked to work at one and I'm on most days.'

'My friend must have heard wrong,' I say, sipping the liquid. I must admit the tea's good, but at fifteen quid it should be bloody fantastic. It makes me think that I should have negotiated some sort of expenses deal on this with Terry. My police pension is good, and the taxi tops it up, but I'm thinking of buying a house up here if things go well, and I need to husband my cash.

'Plenty of guests for the spa and hotel, though,' I venture.

'Spa guests stay clear of the bar. And the hotel's not busy. I fear for my job sometimes. I can't see the need for a full-time barman. And,' he adds, 'they pay well.'

He's being very honest.

'Where do you stay?' I ask.

'Fraserburgh.'

'Your own house?'

He shakes his head. 'No. The parent company of this place owns a block of flats on Commerce Street.'

That's the street where Kristina stayed.

Good wages, including accommodation, and no guests to be seen. Maybe Terry's right to be suspicious of this place.

The door opens again. A dishevelled man stands there. He's wearing a waterproof jacket and thick rubber boots. His head is buried under a flat woollen cap. He's unshaven and a faint smell of fish enters the room. Mrs Jade, from reception, appears and guides him out of the bar, closing the door behind her. She catches Tomas's eye. Her face is a soor ploom. She drops the look when she notices I'm watching and smiles at me. A fixed, no-humour smile.

I turn to Tomas, 'Do you know that man?'

'A guest.'

'Dressed like that? And here's me thinking I was going to get the bum's rush when I rolled up in my high street outfit.'

Tomas swigs at his water. 'Not someone I've seen before. He probably stays in the annexe.'

The door opens again and in walks Mrs Jade.

'The annexe?' I repeat. A little too loudly. Mrs Jade clearly hears me.

'Tomas.' Her voice is stern. 'Can you report to Mr Martinez. We need some help in the restaurant.' She looks at me, flashing a cold smile. 'I'm sorry, sir, but we need Tomas for a few moments. If you need anything, please just ask me. I'll be outside.'

'Sure,' I say.

Tomas leaves, and I'm left alone. I lift my teacup and pot, transferring them, with the sugar and milk, to one of the tables. If I'm going to drink a brew that could buy me half a night in the pub, I'm going to take my time and enjoy it.

As I sip, pinkie in the air, I look to the door.

I'd put a penny to a shilling that Mr Martinez has no staff issues at the restaurant.

I finish the tea, get up, cross the room and open the door. The restaurant sits directly opposite. It looks deserted.

Mrs Jade spots me. 'Do you require anything else?'

I put on my best polite-but-not-subservient smile. 'No, thanks. I've seen enough. Where do I pay?'

### *12th June 1995*

*'Are you going to Craig Chalmers' leaving do?'*

*Mary Colquhoun is licking her fingers after stuffing two sausage rolls down her throat in double-quick time. Mary and I are out on the beat together, and it's just past two in the morning. Mary's sausage rolls have come from the bakery on Clarendon Street. She understands the baker's routine well enough to know they had just fired the first batch. I'd grabbed a pie.*

*'Probably,' I reply. 'You?'*

*'Probably.'*

*We turn on to Maryhill Road and head towards town. The world around us is deep in slumber. Quiet. For June, we are having a chilly snap. But then again, Glasgow does chilly snaps in the same way that Oasis do hits. I scan the length and breadth of the street. There's no one about. The only sign of life is a dirt-brown Vauxhall Belmont, white smoke pouring from its exhaust as it lumbers towards us.*

*It grumbles past. Mary nods at it. 'That's one ugly car.'*

*Her radio buzzes, and I miss what is said as the Belmont growls and spits while sitting at a red light next to us. By the time it moves on, Mary is finished talking.*

*'What was that?' I ask.*

*'A domestic up the road.'*

*'Address?'*

*'Seven A, Seamore Street.'*

*She turns and marches off. I stay still, watching the Belmont grind gears. Mary realizes I'm not in tow and stops.*

*'What?'*

*'Seven A, Seamore Street?'*

*'Yes.'*

*'What flat number?'*

*'Third floor. The name's . . .'*

*'Campbell,' I add.*

*'You heard me on the radio?'*

*'No.'*

*'You know the flat?'*

*'Unfortunately, yes.'*

*'I take it they're not a friend?'*

*I cross the pavement and plank my backside on a wall. 'Used to be.'*

*'Care to share?'*

*'Not really. Anyway, he has lots of flats. Doesn't have to be him that's involved. It's probably just tenants trying to kill each other.'*

*Mary joins me on the wall. 'Who has lots of flats?'*

*'Mitch Campbell.'*

*'The drug dealer?'*

*'Yip.'*

*We sit. Mary waiting for me to talk. She gives it thirty seconds before she says, 'Look, we need to go. Can you talk and walk?'*

*I grunt. 'I'm male, I can't even piss and sing at the same time.'*

*'Yes, you can.'*

*'Really. How would you know?'*

*'The toilets at the station have walls as thin as bog paper. Come on, let's go.'*

*I move slowly. I'm bone-weary now. The years of patrolling suddenly deciding to weigh down on me.*

*Mary and I cross the road as a cold gust of wind travels down the centre white lines. I shiver.*

*'So, you know Campbell well?' Mary asks as we reach the far pavement.*

*'Used to. He was one of us for a short while.'*

*'I'd heard, but didn't he quit early on in his career?'*

*'You could say that.'*

*'He didn't quit?'*

*A late-night bus loaded up with clubbers rumbles past. The windows are opaque with condensation.*

*'No. He quit all right,' I say. 'But only because he was about to be pushed.'*

*'For what?'*

*'For just about everything.'*

*'Bent?'*

*'As a nine-bob note.'*

*'How well did you know him?'*

*'I was his best man at his wedding.'*

*Mary trudges up the road chewing on that one. The bus drops a couple at the stop ahead. They link arms around each other's waists and stagger away from us.*

*Mary turns to me, 'Best man?'*

*'Mitch joined the police at the same time as me. We met up at Tulliallan and became friends. We ended up in the city centre together and saw each other a lot off-duty. When he proposed to his girlfriend, June, he asked me to be his best man.'*

*'And you're still in touch with him?'*

*My hesitation probably says more than I want. 'No. Not really.'*

*'But he walked before he was pushed?' Mary asks.*

*The couple from the bus cross the road, narrowly missing an early-morning delivery van. Once they are safely on the other side, I reply, 'Mitch is the past master of being one step ahead of trouble, but back then he got cocky. The nail in his police coffin was his wedding?'*

*'In what way?'*

*'Mitch didn't join the police for the same reason most of us do. He realized that there was money to be had by turning his head the other way or supplying a little inside info to some of the street clientele we deal with. He was smart. He kept it all low-key at first, but the people he was dealing with have bugger all scruples. A bent copper is fair game to them. You know what they would do if they could?'*

*Mary nods. 'They'd turn an inch into twenty miles.'*

*'Mitch started to get in deep. Stories began to surface in the station, and even with his slippery skin, he was struggling to keep things under control. His card was well and truly marked.'*

*'What was he into?'*

*'Anything that made cash. Mitch loves his toys. And he likes them expensive.'*

*We turn the corner into Seamore Street. There's a convenience store on the corner and, two doors down from it, the entrance to Mitch's close. Sitting outside, as out of place as a live sex show in a monastery, is a bright crimson Ferrari.*

*I stop. 'Shit.'*

*Mary looks at the car. 'Campbell's?'*

*'Probably. Not many people around here can afford that sort of thing,' I say, pointing at the car.*

*I listen for any sign of noise from the flats, but all is quiet.*

*Mary also notices the silence. 'Maybe they've gone to bed?'*

*'Let's hope so.'*

*'You were telling me what Campbell was into?'*

*'It's probably easier to say what he wasn't into.'*

*'And how did his wedding sink him?'*

*'Mitch has a real ego,' I explain. 'That's why he adores the flashy gear. He wants to be seen. He wants to be noticed. He held the wedding up at Culcreuch Castle in Fintry. Not cheap. There was no expense spared. Coaches to get everyone there, accommodation for those that wanted it, seven-course meal, champagne and an open bar at night.'*

*'Sounds expensive.' Mary trails a hand along the sandstone wall of the tenement. 'Was it the money spent on the wedding that gave him away?'*

*'No. It was his guest list.'*

*'Why?'*

*We reach the close, and I study the Ferrari. Soft top down. Only Mitch would leave the soft top down around here. I touch the bonnet. Cold.*

*'The daytime guests were to be expected,' I went on. 'The usual. Close family, intimate friends and a few high heejuns that he knew from the station. But his ego got the better of him. When the night guests arrived, a few of them were a little too well known to me and some of the other polis.'*

*'Like who?'*

*'Chud Brechin. Sammy Traynor. Mad Len Calderwood.'*

*'Really?'*

*'Loyalty card holders at Her Majesty's finest establishment in the east end of Glasgow. Real Barlinnie fans. He tried to claim that they were old school friends, but that just made it worse.'*

*'Shit!'*

*'They'd hustled Mitch to be there. Wanted to strut in front of his police pals. He was in too deep to refuse them an invite. When he got back from honeymoon, I was on the beat with him and caught him dealing drugs. I gave him a chance to 'fess up. He never did, but after the wedding, and with me on his case, he knew his time was up and he quit the force.'*

*Mary is looking up at the flat windows. 'And no action was taken on our part?'*

*'Those that run our lives decided it was better to let sleeping dogs lie. He was off the force and it was no longer their problem.'*

*'And now he's a dealer.'*

*'Amongst other things.'*

*The door to the close is open. I turn to Mary. 'Look, let me handle this one. If it's Mitch, I can deal with him.'*

*We enter and rise up the stairs.*

*'It seems quiet,' Mary whispers as we arrive at the flat door. 'How did you recognize the flat number?'*

*'He has a bunch of places across the city.' I keep my voice low. 'He bought this one while still in the police. He had a few parties in here. He said he picked it up for a song. I was at a couple of the shindigs.'*

*The storm door to the flat is slightly ajar.*

*'Step up the stairs a little,' I say to Mary. 'I'll go in. If I need you, I'll shout.'*

*'Are you sure?'*

*'Positive.'*

*Reluctantly, she rises a few steps and places her back to the wall. I push the storm door in and am confronted with a solid metal sheet. That's new. I knock on the metal door.*

*A few seconds later, I hear a noise. Something sparks my radar and I look up. A brand-new, state-of-the-art CCTV camera is sitting above me. I smile and wave. Locks are thrown. The door is opened, and Mitch Campbell is standing before me.*

*'Hi, Blake.'*

*'Hi, Mitch.'*

*Mitch is a few inches shorter than me. He was a toned piece of work back in the day, but his lifestyle has thickened his waist. He sports designer stubble in the mistaken belief it makes him look a little like George Michael. I don't see it.*

*'Someone called about the noise, didn't they?' Mitch says.*

*'Yes.'*

*'And are you on your own?'*

*I shake my head as I swivel my eyes to the right.*

*Mitch flicks his eyes in that direction. 'Got it. Well, you'd better come in.'*

*I enter. Mitch stands back to let me past and closes the door. He throws a lock. Mary isn't going to be following me in anytime soon.*

*The hallway is in a desperate state. Bare floorboards and bare walls, both badly in need of some TLC. I'd lied about being here for a party. There were never any parties in this place. There is a strong smell of bleach. Not a good sign. Mitch pushes through a door at the far end of the hall, and I follow him in.*

*I freeze.*

*'For fuck's sake, Mitch.'*

*The room is as bare as the hall, save a single chair set near one wall. A man is strapped to the chair. Green clothes-line fixing him in place. He's naked. His head hangs limp and blood has pooled around his feet.*

*'Mitch,' I say. 'What the fuck?'*

*Mitch walks to the man. He grabs his head and lifts it, revealing his face.*

*'Recognize him?'*

*The man's face is a battered lump. Eyes swollen. Nose smashed. His tongue is lolling through bloodied lips. He has long, unwashed grey hair and is junkie-thin.*

*'Mitch, I can't fucking allow this.'*

*Mitch ignores my statement. 'I said, do you recognize him?'*

*I do. Even through all the damage. 'Freddy Spence.'*

*'Freddy Spence,' Mitch repeats.*

*Freddy is out cold, and given the damage, that's probably a good thing for him. 'Mitch, I'm calling this in.'*

*Again, he ignores me.*

*'Blake, do you know what they caught this bag of shite doing?'*

*'I don't care.'*

*'You should. I'm doing your lot a favour.'*

*'Mitch, I can't let this go.'*

*He drops Freddy's head. 'He was up at Joan Rawling's house. In the back garden. Fucking peeping Tom on Joan bathing her kiddies.'*

*'Mitch . . .'*

*'Her fucking kids. Six and four they are, and this shit was in the back garden taking videos.'*

*Freddy is not long out of the Barlinnie's E hall for a range of sex offences.*

*'You should have called us,' I point out.*

*'And then what?' Mitch backhands Freddy across the skull, and his head lolls to one side, but he doesn't wake up. 'To let him go back to three meals a day up at Bar-L and a meet with his fellow perverts? I'm just pointing out the error of his ways to him first. Making him see that there are worse consequences than a few months in prison.'*

*'He needs help.'*

*'Are you defending him?'*

*'No. Just pointing out that he's a sick bastard.'*

*'You've got that right, and if Joan's husband wasn't doing three years, Freddy here would be dead.'*

*I look at Freddy. Blood is still flowing from his mouth. 'And this will help?'*

*'What else would you have me do?'*

*I know Freddy is a real piece of work. He actively gets off on talking about his fantasies.*

*Mitch leans on the wall. 'Go on, tell me this is wrong. That it's OK for shite like this to do what they do.'*

*'Mitch, I can't condone this.'*

*'Who the fuck's asking you to? Just turn around and walk away. Tell your partner out there it's all sorted.'*

*Freddy moans. Mitch walks over to him and slaps him across the back of the head, hard.*

*'Blake, I didn't need to let you in here.'*

*But he had and I knew why. It was all about control with Mitch, and this was his way of exercising it over me.*

*'And when you kill him?' I ask.*

*Mitch returns to the wall. 'I've no intention of killing him. I want him alive for Joan's husband. He's due out in a month.'*

*'Jesus, Mitch, you can't tell me this shit. If Freddy dies, you've just given me a prime suspect.'*

*'Would you be sad if this piece of crap died? I wouldn't,' Mitch snaps. 'You've turned your head before, Blake Glover. And done well out of it. This is nothing. A few slaps and he'll be set free. I just need to send a message. Freddy has a couple of friends that also need a warning. This will get back to them.'*

*Mitch has played this game with me time and time again. Twisting his actions to reflect what he sees as street justice. I've flicked my eyes away a few times, probably more than I should have. Sometimes you know that people are going to walk, and Mitch shows them that there is no such thing as a free lunch or a free ride. Should I have looked away when I did? If I was the only one, then maybe not, but I wasn't.*

*'Mitch, you know this won't work. It never does.'*

*'All I know is that I'm putting this bastard on notice, and when Joan's man comes out, this piece of crap is going to have to run. And run far. That's what I know. Then he's someone else's problem.'*

*A string of blood slides from Freddy's lips. Spit mixed in with it. It swings to and fro as he moans. His head jerks and the drool arcs into the air. It splashes into the pool below. I scratch at my chin. Figuring out what to do.*

*'Mitch, I can't . . .'*

*Mitch lets out a gasp of exasperation. 'For fuck's sake, Blake, he's just scum. Fucking perverted scum, and you know fine well you can't report this.'*

*'Why not?'*

*'Why do you think?'*

*That's a threat. A way of saying to me that he'll let on to some of the stuff he knows about our past. He's pressurized me that way before.*

*There is nothing solid, not really, but he knows things that make times like this a stand-off.*

*'Mitch, you can't keep doing this to me. I can, and will report this. What you have on me is worth zip, and you know it.'*

*'Blake, all I'm doing is helping. Freddy here gets a few more slaps. He goes home. He spreads the word. But if you bring anyone in here, then there is a hell of a lot of shit going to go down, and I'm not falling alone if they take me for giving some perv a slapping, I'll tell you that. And how will it look when I*

*say to everyone that Blake Glover thought that all Freddy Spence needed was some therapy?'*

*My face crumples a little, 'You know that's not what I meant.'*

*'Look, I tell you what,' he says. 'I know where this shitbag is holing up. There's bound to be videos there. You leave now and I'll give you the address. You can go pick him up tomorrow.'*

*'And what about the husband?'*

*'He knows people inside. Even in E hall, Freddy won't get an easy ride. I'll drop Freddy off early tomorrow morning. You just tell your mates where to pick him up and Freddy is inside again. That way we are all winners. You can't say fairer than that.'*

*Mitch makes it sound like he's my best friend giving me tickets to an end-of-season Old Firm title decider.*

*I know I'm beaten. Mitch might be a criminal, but he's a man of his word. If he does what he says, I can walk out the door. I don't want to, but I can.*

*'Mitch, this has to be the last time!'*

*'Blake, I really am doing you a favour.'*

*Freddy tries to lift his head. It occurs to me that he's probably been listening to the last part of the conversation.*

*I shrug, turn, leave.*

*Outside, Mary is waiting. 'What happened? You locked the door. I was just about to call for back-up.'*

*I begin to walk down the stairs. Talking as I drop. Hiding my face from her.*

*'It was nothing,' I lie. 'Mitch and one of his mistresses having a tiff. She unloaded some of the ornaments and furniture on him. They were cuddling when I left. I told you I could handle it.'*

*Mary will sense something is off when I call in Freddy's whereabouts the next day; she will have questions I can't answer. Where did I get the info? Why was Freddy so badly beaten? She won't be slow in putting two and two together.*

*We walk back to the station in silence.*

*A month later, Freddy Spence was deep fried at the Linn Crematorium, having hanged himself in prison.*

*Mary never looked at me the same again.*

# FIVE

*'Fired'*

I cruise through the dark, heading back to Fraserburgh from Broch House. Traffic is light. I keep the taxi radio off and use the time to draw some conclusions. I flip on Ed Alleyene-Johnson's *Purple Electric Violin Concerto*. Music is the salt and pepper that helps my mind chew better. The moon breaks from cover and lights the neatly mown grass of a golf course. The sea almost washes the road here, extending a cold, inviting hand to a golfer's wayward shot.

I haven't really found out much about Kristina or the thefts. But I have that feeling. The one that sits in my bladder. A light buzzing. As if I need a pee but can't go. I call it my Fizz Buzz. My internal alarm.

*'Me? It wisnae me.'*

*'I was with ma mates in the pub then.'*

A light charge of electricity; my 'shit's not right here' detector.

There was nothing of real substance to set it off. Tomas hadn't said anything strange. The hotel was quiet. So what? At the prices they charge, they can afford to be quiet. Mrs Jade's offhand attitude when I walked in is easily explained. *No poor people welcome here.* Yet the way that Tomas was ordered out of the bar suggested Mrs Jade didn't want him to talk to me. The dead restaurant hadn't needed anything – other than to be used as an excuse to take Tomas away from me. And what was with the man in the stinking fishing gear?

I've half an hour before I'm due to bend to Doddy's wishes again. I need to grab some real food. I bypass the main road back to town and wind my way to Lochpots, a fish and chip shop that has received more than its fair share of my disposable income in the last two months. I wait in the queue, and then wait a bit longer as a new batch of fish is immolated in calorie-free batter. As I pay, I add in a can of IRN-BRU to my order. I'll start my diet tomorrow.

I check my phone for the time. I have ten minutes before I need to be back at the end of the radio. I sit in a small bus shelter that stands next to the fish and chip shop, the college campus behind me, and settle into my meal.

A few minutes later, a chill enters my bones. I'd love to eat in the car, but the smell of fried fish and chips can linger like cheap perfume in the sun. With the stink of cow shit still present, despite my attempt at cleaning, I'd rather not spend the rest of the night apologizing for an aroma that mixes fish and chips with crap. I munch down on the fish. It's good. Very good. If there was ever a place to eat fish and chips, it's in this town. At one time, it had the largest sea harbour in Europe.

I work out my next steps. I need to talk to Terry, but I've got nothing except a few suspicions to share. Such as why was Tomas really pulled away for talking to me? Or who was the tramp I had seen in the bar? Tomas said he didn't know him, but he was sure he was a guest. That suggests that other guests go for the distressed fisherman look. The man didn't look like he could afford the bus fare to Broch House, but Mrs Jade had been polite, careful, almost reverential, in her handling of him. His dress and stink had no effect on her. While I, on the other hand, offended her sensibilities.

I can't see me getting more answers from another trip to Broch House; it would just raise my suspicion rating a few notches if I rolled back in too soon. It won't take long for them to find out who I am. Chances are they know already. Social media has nothing on the gossip hotline around here. If you're not in the know, you're either dead or excommunicated.

Tomas had told me he was living on Commerce Street. If there are a number of the workers holed up there, then they must relax somewhere in town, and it won't be up at the hotel. Even if the pay is high, it probably wouldn't stand you a round in the Saltoun Lounge. Anyway, I doubt they encourage fraternization between the help and the residents. Maybe I could track Tomas down at the pub, when he can be a little more communicative? After all, he'd seemed keen enough to chat.

I know I could tell Terry I've done what she asked and talk to her gran about my mother, but something about Broch House is tickling my police gene. I feel a little more digging is in order. If I can find out where Tomas hangs his drinking boots, I've a few more questions in mind. I'll ask Terry; she'll know.

I wipe my hands of the fish and chip grease on the empty wrapping and sling it in the bin. As I walk to my car, I inhale the sea air, letting the bitter sting of the cold clear my throat. I grasp the door handle of the car, sliding my fingers around the chilled metal, and pause. Holding the breath. Warming it in the folds of my lungs. Enjoying a last moment of freedom. I exhale, a cloud of mist rising in front of me, and slide into the car. The faint reek of shit greets me. I unwrap an air freshener to stun the smell into submission, and switch on the radio.

*'Conn, hiv ye heard from yon Glaswegian halfwit?'*

*'No, Doddy. He's due on at six. It's just gone,'* replies Conn.

I join in the conversation. 'Halfwit to base. Halfwit to base. Can you hear me?'

*'Where have ye been?'* Doddy asks.

'Participating in a thing called my life. You know, that entity you don't think I have a right to.'

Doddy's already in shout mode. *'Ma phone is ringing off the hook wi fares, so cut the jokes an get to darg.'*

Darg means work. I hit back. 'Darg, Doddy. Are you sure that's the right word? I mean, what would you know about darg?'

*'It's what yer not doing,'* Doddy throws back. *'Now pick up Greg Maitland at The Ship Inn. Take him to Memsie, then get yer dowp back to the toon.'*

I salute. 'Yes, Hauptmann Robertson.'

I enter the Twilight Zone that is a weekend night on the cabs. I follow the inevitable track that runs from the early rush of the sober going out for the night, before it melts into the drunk returning to their nests. From light-hearted banter through to borderline abuse – all in one easy shift. Water and ducks to me. I've prowled most of the streets of Glasgow in my time. I've dealt with the bad, the worst and the insane. With no desire to rise through the ranks, I'd honed my street craft from beat cop to patrol car to local liaison officer and back to the beat. Taxis hold no fear for me. You don't need a uniform to command respect. You just need three decades wading through scum.

At ten o'clock, there's a lull. Everyone is where they want to be, for the moment. I pull into a parking space on Cross Street and kill my lights. I turn the radio down, not off. I call Terry on my phone. She answers with the thump of music in the background.

'Terry, it's Blake.' I'm shouting, which will make little difference at her end.

*'Hang on, Mr Glover, I need to go outside.'*

The music ramps up, presumably as she walks past speakers, then it dies, and she's back. *'Sorry, Mr Glover. I'm out with friends.'*

'Can anyone overhear you?' I ask.

*'No.'*

'OK, next time I phone, don't use my name. If you can't talk, just say "wrong number" and phone me back when you can.'

*'Sorry, I never thought.'*

'Forget it. I need a bit more information.'

*'Shoot!'*

'Do you know a guy called Tomas at the House, Polish guy, he knows Kristina?'

*'Yes,'* she replies. *'He works in the main bar.'*

'Would you know where he hangs out after work?'

The music slides up the racket scale. *'Hang on,'* she says. *'Someone is leaving.'*

The music wanes. *'OK,'* she continues. *'He hangs out here.'*

'Where's here?'

*'The Cauldron.'*

The Cauldron is one of the few nightclubs in the town. Strictly under twenty-fives. Floors to rival Velcro, tables that require complimentary stain removers, drinks that come in plastic glasses. Picking up from there is always an adventure in wonderland.

'Anywhere else?' I ask. I'd be as about anonymous as a clown at a wake if I turned up at The Cauldron.

*'Not that I know of. Anyway, he's here tonight. He says he saw you earlier.'*

'He did. He was on duty at teatime.'

*'He got fired. After you had been up.'*

That rocks my wheels on to a stone. Shit. 'Did he say why?'

*'They told him he was surplus to requirements.'*

Her tone is ice-chilled.

Well, if I wanted any proof that something was running off-kilter in billionaire land, I'd just been gifted it. Talking to the non-glitterati isn't career-enhancing.

'How is he?'

*'Blind drunk.'*

No chance of talking to him tonight, then.

*Annexe.*

The word leaps up in front of me. That was the word that Mrs Jade reacted to in the bar. 'Terry, what's the annexe?'

She takes a second to ingest what I've just asked her. *'It's a private area. A separate building away from the main place,'* she says. *'We're not allowed in. Strictly guests, and a very select team from the staff.'*

More music. She waits. I wait. I hear a buzz from my radio. Doddy is calling. This time the music drowning out Terry isn't fading.

*'Whoa,'* Terry says.

'What is it?'

*'Fight. I'll call you back.'*

The line dies.

I hope Terry's OK. I call back, but it flips to her voicemail. I don't leave a message. A few seconds later a text appears. *'I'm OK. No problem.'*

I text back. *'Can I still talk to your grandmother?'*

The reply takes a while. When it arrives, it's terse. *'One o'clock. Tomorrow. ASDA cafe?'*

I let my head spin free, slumping in my seat, eyes closed, trying to go for boneless. I block out Doddy's tinny voice. I wonder what Terry's grandmother might have to say about my mother. I also wonder what's going on up at Broch House.

With no answers, I reach for the taxi radio's volume control to let the late-night nonsense begin.

# SIX

## *'Blue Smarties'*

It was gone two thirty in the morning before I finished my shift. When I took this job, I knew that taxis wouldn't let me escape the curse of the shift, but I did think I'd have more control. Doddy has ensured that such control is illusionary.

In Glasgow, I was a long-term fan of the night shift. I enjoyed the relative peace and quiet of the wee hours. The drunks and skunks that interrupted the start of my shift, just as the pubs and clubs ejected the revellers, never bothered me. They were the entertainment before the calm set in. It's why driving a taxi is so easy for me. Drunks are the worst customers, but most drunks can be handled with the right words and tone of voice. On the beat, I always had the option of slapping on cuffs for those that needed more physical intervention, and I think restraint should be in the arsenal of the taxi driver. But, on the upside, unlike my police days, taxi driving has ejection as an option. I'd thrown a few out of my car and banned some, knowing that, in a small town, being barred from taxis is massively inconvenient. Sometimes, if someone is bad enough, when one bars, the other taxi firms follow. Unlike the anonymity provided by the big city for offenders, a ban is easily enforceable around here, and to some, in the outer-lying regions beyond walking distance, a ban is as good as a month in a cell.

I'd picked up at The Cauldron twice and learned that the fight Terry had witnessed was a handbags-at-dawn affair between two brothers chasing the same girl. On the second pick-up, I'd spotted Terry. She was trying to help another girl support a drunk Tomas. If ZZ Taxis hadn't rolled in to pick them all up, I was ready to step in. I don't think Terry saw me.

I spend Sunday morning catching up on domestic crap. My flat isn't large, and with most of my possessions still in storage, I've managed to reduce my chores to once a week. I flip on the radio to Five Live and listen to the world's woes.

I'm due back on the taxi at ten, but clothes for the week ahead need washing, and dishes that are a few days past their wash-by date, need to be cleaned. I coax the ancient Hoover into life – it's about as effective as cleaning George Square with a toothbrush. I worry some dust with a damp rag, change some sheets, rub the bog with Harpic, take a bath, clean, floss, spray, and I'm in my car by nine fifty-five.

There're a few regular runs this morning. I'm doing them all; Conn doesn't start till later. I haven't told Doddy that I'm having some me time with Mrs Lang at one o'clock. He'll just say no.

At twelve forty-five, I drive up to the ASDA, which lies out by the gutting factory. The smell the factory emitted still lives in my nose from forty years back.

*'Blake, where the f' are ye?'*

I stare at the CB before picking it up. 'Doddy,' I reply. 'You know you don't have to swear to get my attention. A polite "Base to Blake" would suffice.'

*'Ah'll fucking swear if I want tae fucking swear,'* he shouts. *'It's ma fucking radio.'*

'What can I do for you, lord and master?'

*'Conn can't pick up the women from the church club. Ae thirty. Yer it.'*

The church club he's referring to is five minutes from ASDA. Ae thirty is one thirty in Doric. That gives me twenty-five minutes with Terry's grandmother. Not long for a lifetime of questions.

'OK.' I kill the radio in case he finds something for me to do in between.

The ASDA car park is a patchwork quilt of cars. I zip into a space, checking the car clock, twelve fifty-five – I hope Mrs Lang is on time. I'll let her take point. She clearly had something to say last time, before she clammed up.

The supermarket's café is busy. I smile as I pass a few faces I recognize. I spot Mrs Lang sitting next to a window that looks out on to disabled parking spaces. She would have seen me park up from there. She's nursing a cup of tea. I approach, but before I can sit down, she gives me an order. 'Another cup of tea and a buttered fruit scone for me.'

I look at the queue. It snakes around the corner.

'Mrs Lang, I don't have long. The taxi's busy.'

She looks out the window. 'It's your mother. If you don't want to talk, that's fine with me.'

I'm not going to argue. I hit the queue and glare at the people in front of me with my Superman heat-ray eyes and realize my superpowers aren't working today.

I finally get back to Mrs Lang with tea and a scone in hand.

'Are you not wanting anything?' she asks, as I sit.

'No, thank you, Mrs Lang.'

She opens a couple of sachets of sugar and dumps them in the cup. Stirring the contents into her tea, slowly, she returns her gaze to the car park. Lifting the cup to her lips, she tests the liquid. I fear she might disapprove and send me back to get a fresh one. She sips; the tea passes muster.

She shifts her glasses off her nose. Heavyweight affairs with lenses to match.

'What do you remember about your mother?' she asks. Her voice is quiet.

'I was thirteen when she died,' I say. 'My memories aren't that great. She was kind. Always there for me. Her favourite perfume made her smell of flowers.'

I smile at that.

'You used to be in tight with Karen Noble's youngest?'

'Charlie.'

'Aye, Charlie. He's done well.'

I can't help but flick my eyes to the clock sitting above the café pay point. Quarter past already.

'They say a lot of things about Charlie Noble,' she adds.

I want to ask what things, but time isn't my friend.

'Do they?' Pause. 'What about Mum?'

'A good woman. You know she played the organ at the old parish church? Excellent player. She had real talent.'

'I used to sit at the back and listen as she practised.'

She sighs. 'Your dad never gave it any credence. Jock was more interested in the football and having his tea on the table when he got back from the Toolworks.'

The Toolworks was the colloquial term for the Consolidated Pneumatic Tool Company. Its sprawling factory complex, now a business park, sitting near the beach, had, at one point, employed thousands from Fraserburgh and its surrounds.

'Dad liked his football,' I agree.

'Aye. He did that. Did he take you to any games when you moved to Glasgow?'

'Not many,' I think back. 'A couple, but he died not long after we got there.'

'Your Aunt Rita brought you up. Jock's sister. Is she still with us?'

I shake my head. 'Passed on a few years back.'

Mrs Lang takes another drink. 'So, you're the last of the Glovers?'

'I am.'

'And you never married?'

It's the obvious question at my age. 'No. I guess it's just not for some people.'

My stock answer.

'Why not?'

'I never met the right person.'

'Are you gay?'

'What's that got to do with anything? Look, it's just never come up. I've had girlfriends. A few got serious, but something always got in the way.'

'Like what?'

'The police for a start. I worked shifts most of my life. That doesn't make for a great social life. I did a lot of overtime as well.'

A lot of overtime was an understatement. I was known to grab any extra work. An old timer once told me that, back in the sixties, he got paid eleven quid, half a week's wage, for every postmortem he attended. I didn't know if he was winding me up, but I'd have taken the money.

'So, no kids, then?' asks Mrs Lang.

'None.'

'Pity. Your mother would have loved to have been a granny. My Terry's a star granddaughter. Have you been able to help her?'

*Twenty past one.*

'I went up to Broch House.'

'Did you find out anything?'

'There's something not quite right up there, but I need a little more time. You know I made Terry promise to go to the police?'

'She said no to me when I told her to do that.'

Mrs Lang is back to car-park gazing. She gives the impression of someone who wants to say something important but can't find the way to open up the conversation. My clock has passed the witching hour.

'Mrs Lang,' I interrupt. 'I have a pick-up to do. It won't take long. Can you hang on?'

'I'll not be here for much longer, but we can meet up again another day.'

'I really won't be that long.'

She starts to slice the scone. 'Aye, but I'm going to see my sister in Aberdeen later today. I'll be away for a few days. We can meet when I get back.'

I really don't want to leave, but I can hear Doddy screaming in my head.

'I'll be twenty minutes tops, Mrs Lang.'

She pushes the teacup away. 'I need to pack. I'm getting the bus in an hour. When I come back from Agnes's will be time enough.'

The pent-up look is still on her face. A racehorse waiting to bolt the starting gate. When the starter pulls the lever, she'll talk like the wind. But she's decided this isn't the time or the place. There's no point in me pushing it.

'OK, Mrs Lang, when are you back?' I try to keep the note of disappointment out of my voice.

'I'm not sure,' she says. 'Later in the week. Maybe the weekend. Me and Agnes don't like to work out stuff too far in advance. At our age, it's better to enjoy what you enjoy while you can enjoy it.'

'How will I get in touch?'

'You've got Terry's mobile, and she's got yours. I'll let Terry know and she can call you.'

She bites into the scone, and I rise with the sort of reluctance I usually reserve for the last time I get off the sunbed at the end of a wonderful holiday. The dead weight of my torso fights the lift. 'Mrs Lang, thanks for seeing me.'

She speaks to the window. 'You do know that what you think you know about your mum might not be what's true.'

'In what way?'

'That's for later, Blake. For later.' More scone vanishes. She turns away and a lake of mist forms on the window as she exhales.

'I thought this was going to be easy, but it's not. I'm not quite ready.' She's talking to the world beyond the window. 'I never thought on what Rhona might have wanted me to say. I'm not sure she would have liked me talking about this. She was quite private, in her own way.'

I knew something had been holding her back.

'Look I can dizzy the next fare,' I offer. 'Talk now.'

'No, let's talk about it when I get back from Aberdeen. Let me think on it a little more. You had a great mother, Blake Glover. A great mother.'

The words set buried feelings free. I get up and rush through the supermarket. A few people say hi. I blank them. I want the exit. Air. Away. I hear the rattle of keys as a woman digs them from her handbag. They sound like the rattle of my mother's medicine bottles. The *sweetie* jars. All laid out on my mother's bed. I see my mother reaching for them. Opening each one. Eating them all. As I wandered to the shops for her money, she was chewing on those sweeties. Smarties – I think of them, mostly, as Smarties. Her favourites. I see her lift each packet. She doesn't eat them one sweet at a time. She tips the packets up, leans her head back and the contents tumble into her mouth. A cascade of sugar. Sweetness coating her tongue. Her tongue was blue when I was allowed up to see her. She must have eaten a lot of blue Smarties. Only, back then they didn't have blue Smarties. But her tongue was blue, so there must have been blue Smarties.

Special ones for Mum.

I lean on my car bonnet, my eyes filling with tears. I put my head down. Why am I back here? What do I want from this? I've been away for so long. Or too short? Another ten years and I'd be ready. Another decade to try to forget the unforgettable. To forget what I did.

*What I did?* It was what I did. I was the one who opened the drawer. I was the one who lifted out the pills. I was the one who put them on the bed. *So* close to her. To make it *easy* for her to reach them. The clickety-clack noise as I stood up was her bones rattling. A death rattle. I bought a comic at the shop. A comic to make me laugh. Laugh in the park while my mother chewed her way to her grave. Chewed on the pills I gave her. The pills that I laid out *so* close to her.

I sit on the car bonnet. I'm consumed by the moment. Buried under guilt. I hear someone ask if I'm OK. I haven't the energy to lift my head to reply. Black waves crash on my soul.

I helped my mother die. I was responsible for my mother's death. Me and me alone. I want to go back. To push that drawer shut. Tell Mum I'll get her sweeties later. Denying my mother's wishes. Say to her it will all be OK. Tell her that Dad says it will be OK – and put the sweeties out of reach.

Put the blue Smarties where she can't get them.

# SEVEN

*'Being a Dick'*

The rest of the Sunday shift is a cold blur. The afternoon streets are sprinkled with the hardy, clad against the North Sea chill, resolute in taking some air. Up here, you can't wait for the warm days to venture out. I pick up and drop off, and for all the chat I have, there may as well have been an automaton in the driver's seat. I might have been rude to some passengers. I can't remember if I said hello or goodbye to any of them. I can't remember taking fares or working out change. I don't remember Doddy's instructions. I must have carried them out. Maybe not.

Conn came back on at seven o'clock to relieve me. I don't remember if I said hi or bye.

My flat is dark. The curtains shut against the glare of the street-lamp that's fixed to the wall next to my front window. The second-hand sofa that I bought amongst a job lot of furniture is uncomfortable. I could easily afford new, but when I arrived, I wasn't ready to commit to my life in such an expensive way. The foam of the sofa has the arse shape of years of use by the previous owner. It's a well-worn groove that I'm trying to shape to my increasingly saggy rear.

The TV sits, waiting for me to turn it on, but it'll stay dead. I grew up with the TV running from morning to night. On cold nights, Mum would sit me in front of it and give me a fork and a slice of plain bread. Next to the telly was a three-bar electric fire. That's where I toasted the bread on the end of the fork, watching *Noggin the Nog* or *Captain Pugwash*. The smell of toast still sends me back there.

Police shift work killed my telly-watching habits. When I'd started in the force, I found the choice poor, so I took to books instead.

I look at the cheap IKEA bookcase on the far wall. It's crammed with paperbacks, some that I've read two or three times, some more. They are almost exclusively science fiction. Escapism written into every page for me. My first ever sci-fi book sits on a separate shelf, a Tom Swift book called *Tom Swift and His Cosmotron Express.*

I'm now over the worst of this afternoon. It's been a while since the guilt over my mum took me like that, but when it does, I sometimes think I could live in that dark place.

Until I was seventeen, I never even knew Mum took her own life. Dad told me Mum had just been too ill to get better. It was on the eve of me joining the police that my aunt told me another story. Sitting me in front of her stove, a cup of tea on the kitchen table, we had a casual conversation that sent me into a tailspin. The revelation about Mum's death blowing a hole in me so large that I nearly quit the police before I started. My aunt's timing amazed me. Only, in her eyes, it was a timetable driven by necessity. My aunt thinking that, as a policeman, I'd have easy access to the details of Mum's death. Fearing I would look it up the first chance I got, she had summoned up the courage to tell me.

I force myself to rise from my nest. Stretching, trying to blow the thoughts away, looking at the whisky bottle sitting on the mantelpiece. Sizing up how much I would need to blast the memories into shrapnel. Too much is the answer. I grab my coat.

I need to be out, to be doing something. Anything.

This could be a good time to talk to Tomas.

Commerce Street, where Tomas lives, is not that far from my flat. I dial Terry as I walk, and she picks up.

'Hi, it's Blake. Can you talk?'

'*Yes.*'

'Would you know where Tomas is just now?'

*'No.'*

'What flat does he live in?'

Silence.

'Terry.'

*'Tomas is gone.'*

There are tears around her words.

'Gone. Gone where?' I ask.

*'I don't know. I . . .'* I hear sobbing.

Tomas and Terry. An item. Fuck, I'm dumb.

'Terry, is Tomas your boyfriend?'

She speaks through tears, *'We're in love, but he's gone.'*

'How is he gone?' Not my best police question. I've adopted that annoying Glasgow habit of substituting the word how for why.

*'Just like Kristina.'* The words are a struggle for her. *'He packed up and left.'*

'Have you called him?'

*'His phone is dead. Not even voicemail.'*

Kristina missing, and now Tomas. 'And no one knows where he went?'

She sniffles hard. *'No. I've asked everyone.'*

'Why didn't you phone me?'

*'Because you'll make me go to the police.'*

'Bloody right. Terry, this is serious. Two people are missing. You haven't got any choice now.'

*'But my job!'*

The cold air forces me to flip the phone to my other ear. I plunge my freezing hand into my coat pocket for warmth. 'You just said you loved Tomas. What's more important? Him or your job?'

She can't reply for crying. Maybe that was a touch harsh. I soften my voice. 'You really should go to the police.'

*'I don't . . .'*

'Where are you?'

She recovers a little. *'At my flat.'*

'Give me your address. I'll come over.'

She feeds me the address between sobs, and I hang up.

The streets are quiet. A winter's Sunday night is one for telly and tea. The temperature is on the tumble. Frost is already biting at the car windows.

When I arrive at Terry's flat, she's standing outside her front door, waiting.

'The police, let's go,' I say.

She looks at me, 'OK, let's do it, let's get this over with.'

'Are you ready? I can tell you what I found out at Broch House first. Although it's not much,' I say.

'Let's just go.'

She marches off.

The police station is a ten-minute walk away. A relatively new build on the corner of Finlayson Street and Dennydruff Road. A minute from my front door. I've dropped and picked up there a lot. Doddy has an account with Police Scotland. Hell knows how he got *that* gig.

I catch up with Terry and we walk in silence. She's nervous. Me sanguine. I know the procedure in front of us. I'm also less than optimistic about the results. Tomas might not register as a MisPer yet. We're not even forty-eight hours out. Kristina's absence will be different, but given she packed, the police will assume she just moved on. I'm also wondering if maybe Kristina and Tomas were an item. Two lovers eloping? That could be an answer. But not one to suggest to Terry.

I'm conscious that I'm twisting Terry's arm on this. I could call on the police without her, but that would raise questions I couldn't answer.

*'Can you give me their full names?'*

*'A full description of both?'*

*'Do you have their home addresses?'*

*'Family contacts?'*

We turn a corner and the station heaves into view.

'Look,' I say, 'I know how this works. Let me do the talking at first. I'll explain the sensitivity of the situation with your job. They'll probably send someone up to Broch House, but I'll try and get them to keep you out of the picture.'

She still doesn't speak.

The entrance to the station sits on the corner of two streets. As the primary custody holding facility for the Sheriff court located in Peterhead, it's a sizeable building. I'm aware that calling 101 is the preferred way to report someone missing, but I have an ulterior motive. An ex-cop getting involved in a missing person case with a stranger smacks of a little private detective work. Not my former colleagues' favourite breed of people. I want to try to explain.

A sign informs us both that the front desk is open. It may be open but there's no one home when we enter. Over the years, a lot of the police stations in Scotland have closed their front desk. They call it efficiency in a changing landscape of communication options. Cost cutting by any other common-sense way of looking at it. A yellow-jacketed constable appears behind the protective window. Way too young. But I'm used to way too young. I was considered way too old for the last five years of my career.

I tell him what we want. He points out that we could have done this by phone. I tell him that I know and then play my trump card: inform him I used to be a police officer. If I expected an open-armed response, I get none. We go straight to form filling.

Terry throws out monosyllabic answers, not looking the police constable in the eye. He scribbles and never looks up. I learn a number of new facts.

Tomas's full name is Tomas Ren Kadlinski and he's from Warsaw. He's twenty-three and has been in the UK a little over a year. Terry met him through Kristina. Kristina's name is also Kadlinski. Tomas and Kristina are cousins. So not likely to be lovers. Kristina's a year older than Tomas. Terry shows the constable photos of Tomas and Kristina on her phone. She still doesn't look him in the eye and whips away the phone as soon as she can. Apart from the formal questions from the constable, and the terse answers from Terry, they say very little.

When all the details are down in black and white, Terry scuttles away at speed to stand at the door, wanting to be free. I ask the PC if I can talk to the inspector in charge. I'm told no. To anyone else? No. I ask Terry to sit down. She reluctantly crosses the room to sit on a bench seat. I lean over the reception desk, trying for discreet.

'Look,' I begin, 'I know the gig here.'

The young officer looks anxious to be somewhere else.

'The young woman is concerned for her job,' I say. 'I promised a bit of discretion. If you pass that sheet on to the investigating officer, can they keep her name out of this? I want to avoid that.'

'Sir,' the young officer plays with his radio, 'I understand your concern. But we'll handle it from here. We will follow up on each person, but the young man hasn't been gone long. Most people turn up within forty-eight hours.'

He's talking to me like I'm an idiot.

'I was in the police.'

'I know, sir. I'm just telling you as it is. And' – he looks at his notes – 'Kristina, she packed and could easily have just moved on. But again, we will check. It's the way we do things.'

I can feel anger rising. This lad is dismissing my thirty years as if it was fluff on his tunic. I try to push the point. 'I know how this works, but I just want to highlight the sensitivity.'

'Noted, sir,' he replies. 'Anything else?'

'Why are you being so off? I'm not asking for much.'

'You said yourself, sir. You *were* police.'

The word 'were' stings like a wasp.

'So,' he continues, 'you know that we are very busy, and although missing persons are important, we have to prioritize resources. But, rest assured, we will look into it, and if you or the young woman' – he emphasizes the word 'woman' – 'hear anything, please let us know. Now, is there anything else?'

'No.' I rotate away from the constable. 'Terry, let's go.'

She stands up and is out of the door, letting it swing closed, before I can catch up.

I find her standing at the bottom of the steps when I exit. Eyes fixed on mine. 'They'll mention me if they follow up. Won't they?'

'I told them not to.'

'And did Paul say they would keep my name out of it all?'

'Paul?'

'The policeman we just saw.'

I'd love to say yes, but I was at a loss as to why the young constable had been so offhand. 'Maybe.'

She thrusts her hands into her pockets. 'Gran said you were someone I could trust.'

'I am.'

'I told you she relies on my money. She hasn't got much. I need that job. What good did coming here do?' She's raising her voice. 'Well?'

'It needed to be done.'

'Why?' Her face is flushing. 'They'll see it as non-urgent. Tomas and Kristina packed. Both had been fired. Hardly a kidnapping in the making. Paul said as much. But if they go up there, they are *bound* to mention my name.'

'I asked them not to, and they won't just dismiss it that easily,' I say. 'They'll look into it. Coming here was the right thing to do.'

'Was it?' Her voice is loud. 'Did you learn anything up at Broch House? Because if you did, you've told me nothing. But you made me come here. So you must believe there's something wrong, or why do this?' She points to the police station.

'I didn't think you wanted to talk on the phone when I called you at the club. You were out for the night and I offered before we came here, but you blanked me. I'm just trying to do the right thing by you. And trying to keep things under wraps.'

She laughs. 'From who? My gran. My friends. My gran's friends. Doddy? Who? Do you think they don't all know Kristina went walkabout? And how long do you think it took them to find out about Tomas? My gran called me ten minutes after he left the flat. When did you find out he left, *Mr Detective*? I'll tell you when. When you called me. When I told you.' She stares at me before spitting, 'You got him fired.'

She's a ball of fire. Up on her toes. Spoiling for this.

'And who do you think knows you went up to Broch House?'

I decide not to answer that one.

She walks towards me. 'Let's see. There's Gail Till. She was told by Madeleine on reception who saw you with me at Dalrymple Hall when she was dropping off Claire Smithfield's kids, so she knew who you were as soon as you walked into reception at Broch House. She told Jose Martinez who told her to find out what you wanted.'

'Wanted. I went up for a cup of tea,' I say. 'Why would that raise suspicion?'

She opens her mouth to indicate amazement. 'Who goes up to Broch House for a cup of tea? I'll tell you. No one from around here. Fifteen quid for a cuppa keeps a lot of people away.'

'What did you expect me to do?' I fire back.

'A bit of bloody subtlety. You said you were a good policeman. Is that how you would have looked into the same situation when in uniform?'

In uniform, I would have gone up and done the formal bit. Talked to everyone, Till and Martinez included. Looked them in the eye as they replied. Made notes. Reported. Now, all I'd done was put any chat with them out of reach and advertised my interest in Kristina and Tomas.

Terry walks right up to me. 'You aren't a policeman anymore, Blake, and this isn't Glasgow. You fart up here and it's in the paper the next day.'

'You knew I was going up to Broch House. What did you think I was going to do? Use my psychic abilities to look over the place while sitting on the beach?'

'I thought you knew how to do these things.'

'I do, but you never mentioned you were in a relationship with Tomas.'

'It wasn't relevant.'

'He's Kristina's cousin and you are in love with him. How is that not relevant?'

'Because . . .' She stops.

'Look,' I say, 'this is something the police need to deal with. Not me. You blackmailed me into going to Broch House.'

'Blackmailed?'

'I scrub your Broch House itch; you scrub my mother itch.'

'Yeah, even so, you've made me do what you wanted,' she flares. 'Because if something has gone wrong, you're now in the clear. Done your duty. Told your friends.'

'It's not like that.'

'It's exactly like that.'

I'm not taking this. 'OK, if I'm that shit,' I say, 'why did you come with me to report it?'

She whistles. 'Really. Why do you think?'

I know. 'Because I'd have gone anyway.'

'Fucking bingo.' She almost laughs. 'I was screwed both ways. At least this way I know what was said. Look, talking to you was a mistake. My gran said you're fucked-up about your mother. And she's right.'

'What?' I shout. 'I'm not fucked-up.'

Instantly, I regret the outburst.

'Oh, so crying in ASDA car park is normal?'

Terry is right: you really can't take a dump around here without it being broadcast.

I defend myself. 'I was upset.'

'I'm sure you were. But this is over. I've no idea what happened to Tomas or Kristina. I—'

She stops. I can almost read the thought process. It's easy to push me away. After all, I've been an arsehole so far. But where does that leave her?

'You love Tomas,' I say.

'And he's gone – because you did the wrong thing,' she sobs. 'And now I'll lose my job, and if someone at work *does* know what happened to Tomas, and the police get involved, they'll all have been told to shut the fuck up by now.'

'OK, Terry. Who are *they*? The owners of Broch House? A secret Polish kidnap gang?'

I'm being a bit of a dick, and this isn't the place for this conversation. The young copper is standing just inside the door looking at us.

I raise both hands. 'Let's not do this here.'

She hisses back. 'We're not doing this anywhere. Do you know how bloody stupid you've been? I'm so angry.'

'Terry, I was trying to help.' I begin to walk, hoping she'll follow.

She stands still.

'I can help,' I say. 'This isn't over.'

She says nothing. The heat from her face could melt the rime in the gutter. I keep walking.

Thinking.

Thinking what a prick I've been.

# EIGHT

## *'Latchie'*

When I get back to my flat, my answer machine is flashing. Probably an invitation to change mobile phone company or an offer for someone to represent me due to my 'recent accident' or maybe a bargain, a once-in-a-lifetime deal on French doors for my third-floor dwelling. No one meaningful has my landline number. I never use it.

I stand looking at the bare walls. They reflect the emptiness that wraps my gut. I wander to the kitchen, open the small fridge, knowing it's empty. I flip open a cupboard. A single packet of spaghetti stares back at me. I wander back to the answering machine and press play to retrieve the message.

A voice from a hill forty years ago sounds out.

*'Race you to the horn and back. Hi, Blake! I'll be in The Sailor's Rest at twelve tomorrow. Twelve, OK? I hear you've taken up being a private dick.'*

He says the last word with gusto. Fuck, but this is a small town.

When Charlie says twelve o'clock tomorrow, he means *exactly* twelve. That's why he said it twice. Charlie was a nut for being on time as a kid. His bedroom wall was a shrine to clocks. The ticking in his room drove you daft, but Charlie loved it. If you arranged to meet him, he was never late. He might have mellowed with age, but somehow I doubt it.

I'm still mad at myself at how I dealt with Kristina and Tomas. I was so keen to learn what Mrs Lang had to say about my mum that I didn't think through what I was doing. Even going to the police station is now stacking up as a bad idea. It puts me right in the middle of things. If I had any intention of helping Terry further, I've done a great job in making myself the visible man.

I sit in the dark and consider phoning the police station to try to fix things. But it's gone midnight, and I'm fairly sure I'll just make it worse. I genuinely thought that the police would be friendly.

I can't fathom the cool, almost aggressive, way I was treated by Paul. Then again, how would I have felt if a copper from some other era had tried to tell me how to do my job? I should have called back to Glasgow. Someone there would know someone up here. Found the *friendly* way in. It's so obvious that I slam my hand down on the sofa arm, raising a tornado of dust.

My thinking is all in the washer.

Tomas fired. Tomas missing. The local polis pissed off. Go me.

I lie back.

Chill.

It's time for bed.

I sleep the sleep of the guilty. None. I spend the night going over and over my cack-handed approach to Terry's request. Diving in with both feet was something I thought I'd avoided. I'd convinced myself I was playing a slower game.

When the alarm rings, I can feel the lead weight that a sleepless night bestows on you. My next taxi shift starts at six this morning. I have to run through to two o'clock and then I'm back on at four. I can feel the heat of Doddy's breath if I quit at twelve to meet Charlie, and I'm also not sure I'm quite ready to meet up with Charlie just yet. I'll think on it.

I step into the shower, conscious that my expanding stomach is starting to block out the view of my undercarriage. A thing I swore I would never let happen. Breakfast is usually a roll and slice, chased with a pint of tea, at Candy's Café. Maybe even a double hit on the roll if I'm feeling hungry. Today is a day for a cup of tea and a breath of air.

In the shower, I scrub. Over-hard. I can feel tiredness around me. Pulling me down already. Driving tired is never a good shout, and if I meet Charlie during my break, there's not going to be any opportunity to grab a nap. I could switch to coffee. Go for the caffeine solution. But that's a short-term win. I'll keep it for emergencies. I'll fill a flask with the stuff. It holds four cups. I'll put in enough coffee granules for six. Do-it-yourself Red Bull.

The shower does little to lift my weariness. I flip the tap to full cold, forcing myself to stand in the stream.

When I'm finished, I make for the bedroom, open the wardrobe, consider what I should wear. I've got the fashion sense of a golfer. So many wrong colours in so many wrong places. I go for simple today. I select my best white shirt and a pair of black chinos.

My shoes need a polish, so I get down with the Cherry Blossom, imagining I'm due up for inspection. I skoosh up on antiperspirant and aftershave, overindulge on mouthwash, check the clock and settle down for ten minutes of breakfast TV.

I make five minutes before my eyes close.

My phone pulls me from sleep. I answer. It's Conn's number. 'Hi, Conn.'

*'Where are you?'*

'Just leaving to get into the car.'

*'You were supposed to be on at six?'*

I look at the clock. Seven forty. Shit.

'I overslept.'

*'Well, I've got another flat tyre. The spare I put on has a puncture. I've tried blowing it up, but it's a goner. I've two school runs this morning. Can you cover?'*

I yawn. 'Sure, what are the details?'

I'm slightly depressed to find one of the runs is to the Lemby house. The home of the nose-picking boy and his fellow thespians.

'OK, Conn. I'll do them. I'm guessing you'll need to wait till the garage is open.'

*'Two tyres. Doddy will have a cardiac.'*

'You haven't told him?'

*'Eh.'* She hesitates. *'No. He's still sleeping. I'll tell him later.'*

It sounds like The Macallan took another hammering last night in Doddy world, which also explains why Doddy hasn't phoned asking where I am.

'Do you want to flip the incoming calls to my phone?' I offer.

*'Blake, you're a darling.'* The relief is clear in her voice. *'Just till I get back on the road. Can you do that?'*

Mug central. It should be written on my head. 'Sure. But with you out of the picture, I'll mainly be doling out excuses.'

*'Better than not answering the phone.'*

Conn is the real reason the taxi company stays alive. She's wasted in the role. Conn could easily set up a far more successful business. If she puts her mind to something, it usually works out.

*'Look Blake, I need to go.'*

She hangs up.

I throw some more tea down my neck. I dig for my mobile, remembering I killed it last night. I switch it on and it's ringing before I've left my flat.

'Hi, Doddy's Taxis.'

*'Where's Doddy?'* says the caller.

'I'm taking calls this morning. Do you need a taxi?'

*'Do I fuck! Where's Doddy?'*

'Who is this?'

*'John Lemby.'*

The Serious Assault King. 'Hi, Mr Lemby. It's Blake Glover. Doddy's not here. Can I help?'

*'Glover! The fucker that picked up ma kids when the girl's car blew a tyre.'*

'That's me.'

*'They were all covered in coo shit when they got hame.'*

'Sorry, Mr Lemby.'

*'Ma hoosie stinks.'*

'Sorry.' Not much else I can say. 'Do you need your kids' taxi earlier. I'm doing the pick-up?'

*'Do I fuck! Conn is picking up the bairns.'*

*'Not today, she's at the garage.'*

*'Screw that. Just get yon wee bag of shite to phone me ASAP.'*

Another call is coming in. 'OK, Mr Lemby. I'll tell Doddy, and I'll be up for your children soon.'

I take the other call and tell them that, yes, I can take Mrs Craig to Aberdeen at eleven o'clock. I pull out the small notepad I keep in my pocket and note the booking.

The phone rings again as I plonk myself in my car seat. I toggle it to hands-free, a modern installation at my expense, and pick up a request for a run out to the college campus. I have to decline that one.

It's eight o'clock.

Sea fog has rolled in and is clinging to the land. It's thick enough that I need headlights. I ignite the engine as a young couple cross the road. She's whispering in his ear. He laughs. She kisses his cheek. Hands linked, they vanish into the mist.

For a moment, I think about my own love life. Or lack of it. I move off.

The Lembys live in a sprawling new build out towards Strichen. It has echoes of Broch House – gravel driveway, gated pillars, even a few trees. I don't know John Lemby, but the home says that either he or his wife has some cash to splash.

John Lemby is waiting at the front door with two of his kids by his side; his namesake, the Nose Picker, and one of the girls. I pull up at the front door.

John is about my height. The only difference is that he is twice as wide as me. He's dressed in a tight-fitting white T-shirt that shows his muscle but also his fat. His jeans are a shade too light in colour for comfort. Less Levi and more Lidl own label. A little off given the display of wealth around here. A pair of dog-eared trainers cling to his feet. Under his arm, he has a brown box.

I get out, and the kids make for the car's rear door. John walks over with them.

The wind from last night is still a razor across the land, but if John notices, he doesn't show it.

He thrusts the box at me as the kids climb in. 'Tak this tae fuckin' Doddy. Conn is supposed to be here, so no fucking around. I can't get the fat swine. He's nae answering his mobile.'

I look at the box with suspicion. 'What is it?'

He snarls, 'None of yer fucking business. Just tak it tae Doddy.'

'No.'

He does a classic double-take. He's obviously not used to people saying no to him.

'Do what yer fucking telt.'

I look up at him. 'I said no. And I don't take kindly to orders. Now, do you want me to get your children to school on time?'

He riles, shoulders back, head leaning in. I've seen it before. Getting ready to strike.

'Who do you think ye are?' he snarls.

'I'm a man who doesn't like being spoken to like that.'

'I could kick yer head in!'

I stand still. 'You could try, but I've fought bigger. How's your credibility with your children going to be if I hand you your arse?'

Blood boiling, he steps in. 'Yer fucking dead.'

There's no subtlety to a fight on the streets. No Bruce Lee fancy moves. You just want control. All the talk of kicking someone in the nuts or pulling off that once-in-a-lifetime Ali punch is for rubbish. You want them down, on the ground, you running the show.

I don't issue another warning. No last minute 'go ahead' or 'come on then'. I just step away from the car. I don't want to be pinned. John circles after me.

'What the hell are you doing, John Lemby?'

The voice comes from the direction of the house. A woman is standing in the doorway, looking at us both. She's dressed in a nightgown, hair an electric spray of black.

John turns. 'Fucker won't do what he's telt.'

The woman shakes her head. 'John, apologize to the man.'

'Will I fuck!'

She steps on to the gravel. 'Right now, John Lemby.'

John steps towards me, and I brace.

The woman takes one more step towards us, hands on hips. 'Now, John Lemby.'

'Fuck it. I'm away inside.' He spins on the spot, throwing the box at the woman as he passes. She catches it, and crosses over to me.

'I'm sorry,' she says. 'John's got a temper.'

'I'll say.'

She looks at the box. 'What did he want you to do with this?'

'To take it to Doddy Robertson.'

'And you said no?' She shakes it. 'I don't think it's a bomb.'

'Neither do I, but there's a polite way to ask.'

'Wendy.' She surprises me by holding out her hand. 'I'm Wendy Lemby. John's wife.'

'Blake Glover,' I reply, shaking her hand.

'Look,' she says. 'Can you take this to Doddy for me? I'll put an extra tip on the bill when we settle up. John'll calm down if it gets delivered.'

I relent. 'OK, but tell that man of yours that I don't like being talked to that way.'

'I will.'

She hands me the box and I push it into the passenger seat as the kids get in the rear.

I crunch gravel as I drive out, trying to calm my anger at the same time. I'm not sure I could have taken John in the fight. He looks well used to a brawl.

The children sit quietly in the back. They watched that all play out. Have probably seen it all before. The young girl's looking back as we exit, waving at her mum. The Nose Picker is mining already.

Out here, the fog is thinner, but thicker pockets sit in the fields. Alien clouds wandering around the landscape.

My phone rings. 'Doddy's Taxis.'

*'Blake, it's Conn.'*

'Did you get the tyre fixed?'

*'Forget that, Doddy's not well!'*

Neither would I be if I drank what he drank most nights. 'He'll sleep it off.'

Her voice comes back, scared. *'It's not the drink.'*

'What is it?'

*'I don't know. He's not right. He's slurring his words. Talking nonsense as well. He tried to leave the house, to start driving – but naked.'*

'Conn, hang up and call nine-nine-nine. Ask for an ambulance.'

*'Why, what is it?'*

'Just tell nine-nine-nine what you told me. I think Doddy's having a stroke.'

*'Blake?'*

'Call now, Conn, right now!' I'm shouting. I kill the call.

The Lemby kids are still quiet as I slam my foot down on the accelerator. I might be wrong, but from what Conn just told me, I think Doddy is in danger.

As I enter the town, I get stuck behind a forty-footer. One of the endless fish trucks that ply their trade from here to the south. I overtake on a blind corner and the Nose Picker swears at me.

After I drop the kids at school, I hit Conn's number, but it flips to voicemail. I don't leave a message. A few seconds later she rings back.

Her voice is trembling. *'The ambulance is here. You were right. They think he's had a stroke.'*

'How is he?'

*'They say they're stabilizing him. They're going to take him to the Royal in Aberdeen.'*

Fraserburgh has its own hospital, geared up for accidents, emergencies and day care. Aberdeen Royal Infirmary, in the Foresterhill area of the city, is the main hospital for the northeast. It's a better place to treat a stroke.

I try to reassure Conn. 'That means he must be fit enough to travel.'

*'Or he's so sick they need to operate?'*

So much for my reassurance. 'Are you going with him? I'll give you a lift if they can't take you.'

*'They say I can ride with them.'*

'I'll come down to Aberdeen anyway.'

*'No. You keep running the taxi.'*

I'm taken aback. 'Conn, I'm not leaving you to deal with this alone. The taxi service can wait.'

*'No! Have you dropped off Wendy's kids?'*

'Yes.'

*'Have you still to pick up Catriona Laidlaw's wee ones? She's confined to a wheelchair with MS. She can't get them to school.'*

'I'll call ZZ, get them to do it.' ZZ Taxis are one of the alternatives to Doddy.

*'No. And I mean no. I'll call when I get to the hospital. Doddy wouldn't want you to quit.'*

'Conn?'

*'Just do what I ask, Blake! I'll phone when I get to the hospital. There's nothing you can do here. I need you to do this for me. Can you?'*

She knows I'll say yes, so I say, 'Yes.'

*'Thanks. I'll be in touch as soon as I know something.'*

She hangs up.

I sit, engine running, watching the kids pile into the school. I haven't known Doddy that long, nor Conn, but it seems the wrong thing to do to go back to driving. Then again, what use would I be in Aberdeen? And if Doddy or Conn need anything from Fraserburgh, I'd just have to drive back up, and that's a two-hour round trip on a good day. There really is nothing to be gained from me driving to Aberdeen. I text Conn – *'Let me know as soon as you can what's going down.'*

I make my way to the Laidlaw house, a small, terraced affair out near Peathill. The kids are waiting for me. I glance at my phone. It tells me we'll be late for school. I need to remove the box Wendy Lemby gave me from the front seat, to get the four kids in. I put it in the boot.

The eldest, a boy with hair so greasy I'm sure he'll leave stains on my headrest, turns to me as we drive off. 'Where's Conn? Yer latchie. Why?'

Latchie means late. I ignore him. Before I tell anyone, especially a bunch of strange kids, what's going down, I want to be sure Doddy's OK. I'm surprised at my reaction to his stroke. Despite our differences, I've grown a genuine affection for the lump of lard.

I drop the Laidlaw kids at school with a farewell, from the greaseball, of 'Yer nae right in the heid'. I have the feeling that he might have more of a point than I'd like to admit. I still think I should be down with Conn in Aberdeen. I hit the text again, *'Conn, how's Doddy.'*

The phone rings a minute later. 'Doddy's Taxis,' I say. Then I spot that it's Terry Lang's number.

*'Blake, what happened to Doddy? Is he all right?'*

The jungle drums beat fast. 'He's on his way to Aberdeen Royal Infirmary. They think it's a stroke. Conn is with him. She said she'd phone as soon as she knows anything.'

*'And you're still doing the taxi?'* Incredulity.

'Conn insisted. There's nothing else I can do to help at the moment. Conn went with him in the ambulance. If they need anything from here, I can get it quicker.'

*'So, she's on her own. What if Doddy doesn't make it?'*

That hadn't crossed my mind. 'Conn was adamant I run the taxi.'

*'Fuck. Are you for real? She needs someone with her. I'll go. Can you give me a lift?'*

What else can I say but yes.

She sticks a knife in by adding, *'I'll pay.'*

# NINE

*'Talk of the Steamie'*

For the first ten miles of the journey to Aberdeen, Terry says nothing. I try repeating what Conn had said. Telling her that Doddy would have been mad if I'd quit. Terry just blanks me, and I wonder why I'm trying to defend myself to someone I hardly know. I turn down three fares on the way south.

The first stretch of road from Fraserburgh to Aberdeen has hardly changed since I was wee. A swirl of grey switch-backing, roller-coastering and blind-cornering that hasn't seen a decent upgrade since the seventies. OK, so there've been a couple of concessions for comfort to the road. The back-breaking humpback bridge at Mintlaw has been smoothed out, and when the Fraserburgh road meets the Peterhead road, things get a little smoother in patches, but that's about it in five decades.

'Did they fire you?' I ask Terry.

'Not yet.'

'Did you hear from Tomas or Kristina?'

'I haven't heard from either Tomas or Kristina. I called up to the House to say I wouldn't be in as I was going down to see Conn and Doddy. I got Gail.'

Terry continues, 'I asked if she'd heard from Tomas or Kristina. She said that Tomas's mother had phoned her. She said that she had told her that Tomas had called her to say all was OK.'

'That's got to be good news,' I say.

'You think?'

I can't get to grips with this woman. Different generation? Me? Her? I bite, 'Why do you say that?'

'Tomas's mother doesn't speak English.'

'Does Gail speak Polish?'

'Not a word. Arrogant bitch! There's been a dozen Poles up at Broch House and she can't even say hello or thank you in the language.'

'Maybe Tomas's mum got someone to help with the call.'

Terry looks at me. 'Why would anyone phone Broch House at all? If Tomas was in touch with his mum, he'd hardly ask her to call to say he was OK? Would he?'

That's a good point.

She's in the mood to talk now. 'I called Tomas's house in Poland, Tomas's sister Mara lives with her mother. She speaks English. She didn't know that Tomas had been fired. Neither did her mum. The last they heard from him was the day before he was let go. She said no one at their end had phoned Broch House. All I did was get them worried.'

'Did you tell them that you've reported it to the police?'

Her face sours. 'Yes. And Mara asked why I hadn't called her earlier. I should have.'

'You still did the right thing going to the police.'

'That's just you making yourself feel good about dragging me to the police station last night.'

'No, it's not. Did the sister say anything else?'

'Mara grilled me. I told her what I knew. She translated for her mum as we chatted. After a few moments, I could hear crying in the background. This is a mess. I should have never asked you to go up there.'

A truck rides ahead of me. Another forty feet of fresh fish fleeing to London. Conscious of time, I pick my spot and overtake. I misjudge slightly and need to nip in sharp to avoid an oncoming car. The truck lays down a horn that screams outrage.

'Are Tomas's family coming over here?' I ask.

She gives it a little thought. 'I'm not sure. I'm assuming they will, if Tomas doesn't turn up soon.'

While she's in the talking mood, I ask her something that's been bugging me. 'Terry, do you know any more about this annexe that Tomas mentioned?'

She plays with her hair, looking for a way to buy time. I've seen it so often. The fidgets, the tics, the nervous gestures. People with something to say but unsure of the consequences. The innocent fearing that they might incriminate themselves, or the guilty backed into a corner, considering turning on their friends. If you patrol the lanes and darker corners, these signs are an unspoken language. A signal that, with a little more skill, you can extract the hidden.

We fly through New Leeds, a village that is gone almost before you enter it. Farmland, dormant in the winter sun, surrounds the car, waiting for warmer days. A muted brown blanket that extends to the four points.

Terry needs a little prod 'Do you think the annexe has something to do with Tomas and Kristina vanishing?' I ask.

'I don't know.'

'Tomas was asked to leave the bar when the receptionist heard me talking to him about what happened there.'

'We're told not to talk about it.'

'When I was talking to Tomas, I saw a guest. At least Tomas told me he was a guest. But he was dressed as if he'd just got off a fishing boat. Would he be connected to the annexe?'

'I've seen some right states. But those in the annexe rarely come into the main building.'

'Have you been to the annexe?'

'No.'

'What do the annexe staff tell you when you talk to them?'

'I've never met any of the annexe staff. They keep away from the main building. They never mix with the staff at the house.'

'Not at all?'

'Never.'

'They must go into town now and again.'

'If they do, I've never seen them.'

'How big is this annexe?'

'Not that big.' Her phone buzzes. She pulls it out, checking for a message. When she's satisfied no one needs her attention, she speaks. 'It's the size of a bungalow. I looked it up on Google Maps once. There are a lot of trees around it; I assume the staff quarters are hidden in there somewhere. It's off-limits. You can't get to the annexe without passing through a security fence.'

'Security fence?'

'Razor wire and all.'

'Razor wire? For a hotel?'

'Yes, and CCTV.'

'And no one thinks that's odd?'

'We all do, but they tell us the guests in the annexe pay for privacy. That's why they have the fencing.'

'Privacy? Sounds like a prison.'

'A few have tried to take a peek, now and again. But you can't see anything, save the bungalow.'

Broch House is a more and more interesting place.

'Putting razor wire fencing around it must make it the talk of the steamie up here?' I say.

She stops playing with her hair. 'Talk of the what?'

'Steamie. A Glasgow phrase. Talk of the town.'

'I suppose.'

'The annexe staff must get some time off.'

'Now and again a coach turns up. Black windows. Posh job.'

'For the staff?'

'Or the customers. No one knows. Mary-Anne, one of the other cleaners, heard that the bus comes up from Aberdeen. That the staff live down there.'

'So, they ship in the staff from down south and none of them ever go out locally? That's not normal.'

'They say there are guards with guns.'

I shake my head. 'You'd need licences for that stuff. The local police would need to be notified.'

'The police have been up. Were invited in to have a look around.'

'So someone has seen inside?'

She nods. 'Ask Kyle or Paul at the police station. They were up there a while back. But they said it's just a house. A couple of bedrooms and a main living room. No one else was there when they went in. No guns. No aliens.'

'Aliens?'

'A stupid rumour that went around the town for a while.'

I make a mental note to question the local police. *If* they'll talk to me.

'Just talking about the annexe can get you in trouble,' she says. 'They don't like it. If they heard Tomas talking to you, that would probably be enough to get him fired.'

I think about the reaction to me asking about the annexe over my cup of tea. To the fact that Tomas was let go right away.

We reach the outskirts of Aberdeen. A finger of industrial buildings funnels us towards the city. The dual carriageway is filling up. I slot into the outside lane and reach for my phone to Google the hospital's location.

Terry stops me. 'I'll tell you how to get to the Royal. Do you want to get done for using your mobile while driving?'

She directs me, and, as we near the hospital, she says, 'I'm going in; what are you going to do?'

'I've a pick-up at eleven back in Fraserburgh. It's a run back here. I'll be back in a little over two hours.'

'But you're coming in just now to see Conn and Doddy? Aren't you?'

I hadn't planned to, but I say, 'Of course.'

I park. The hospital is a sprawling campus of the old and new. It's the largest hospital in the region and it takes us fifteen minutes to find Conn. She's sitting in a small waiting area under a poster that advertises counselling for the bereaved. She spots me and stands up. Her eyes are red circles on white skin. 'I told you not to come.'

I step back to reveal Terry. Terry wraps her arms around Conn. 'I'm so sorry, Conn. How is he?'

Conn seems glad to see Terry. 'Better than he should be, the fat, lazy bastard. The doctor says things don't look too bad.'

When I'd been living in Glasgow with my Aunt Rita, after my dad died, her best friend had had a series of mini-strokes. She had looked fine when Rita took me up to the hospital to see her. But a few weeks after the friend was discharged, she came up to visit. Her left arm, not working, was strapped across her chest. Her face had collapsed on one side, giving her a permanent lop-sided smile that reminded me of the Joker from Batman.

Conn checks the time, 'Did you get a call to take Laura Craig to Aberdeen University at eleven?' she asks me.

'Yes.'

'Well, she'll be mad if you're late.'

'Conn, do you need anything? Can I see Doddy?'

'No, I don't need anything, and they won't even let me see him at the moment. I'll call once I know what's what.'

I turn to Terry. 'I can pick you back up later.'

'Let me see how things are first,' she says.

I say my goodbyes and unwind the maze that seems to be the design plan of every hospital I've ever been in. My phone rings.

'Doddy's Taxis.'

*'How's Doddy?'*

'Sorry, but who is this?'

*'Laura Craig.'*

'He just got to hospital. They're checking him. Hard to tell, but the doctor seems hopeful. I'm on my way to get you. I might be a little late.'

*'I thought you'd be helping Conn, given what's happened? I've phoned ZZ. They're going to take me.'*

'It's OK, Mrs Craig,' I say as I pass through the hospital entrance and out on to the car park. 'Conn insists I keep going. You know what Doddy's like with money.'

My attempt at humour backfires. She goes on the offensive, *'What's money got to do with anything at a time like this? If money's that important, tell Conn I'll pay for the cancellation.'*

I backtrack. 'No, Mrs Craig, there's no need for that. I was just saying—'

She jumps in. *'You were just saying that Doddy Robertson would rather you were running the taxi than worrying about him.'*

I'd put a pound to a penny on that being true if I asked Doddy. In Doddy's world, money comes a close first to Conn. But I'll be slaughtered if I agree with Mrs Craig on that.

'No, Mrs Craig,' I say. 'That's not what I'm saying. I'm in Aberdeen now. I've just been to the hospital, but there's nothing I can do.'

*'I'll phone Conn later. Don't bother coming for me, and mind and tell Conn I was asking after them both.'*

I sigh.

*You can't do right for doing wrong, Blake Glover.*

The lessons are hard for me back here. One word out of place and I'm doused with a flamethrower. I'm learning the hard way what it's like to be back in a smaller community.

With no pick-up at eleven, I turn to go back into the hospital, but the devil hates the lazy and the phone rings.

'Doddy's Taxis.'

*'I need a taxi to Peterhead in half an hour, going to Fraserburgh.'*

I decide to take the run. I can still be back if Conn needs something.

'It might be nearer forty-five minutes if that's all right?'

*'Fine.'*

The caller gives me an address. I jump in the car and leave Aberdeen. I stop halfway to Peterhead to text both Conn and Terry for an update. Neither reply.

I turn my mind back to the conversation with Terry. Why would Gail at Broch House lie about Tomas's mother calling? I suspect she has slipped up. Telling Terry that Tomas's mum had phoned was a mistake. There was no need to lie if they had fired him. Just say nothing.

Where the hell is he?

I make a call I probably shouldn't make.

The mobile, on hands-free, bursts into life as the call is answered. *'BG, for fuck's sake! How's the fish?'*

I smile. 'Hi Kam, how's my after-sun applier?'

*'Best in town,'* comes the reply. *'How's your luck in having sex with your distant relations?'*

'You know,' I reply. 'It has its ups and downs.'

Kam Ali is my oldest friend from Glasgow. We met on a training course twenty years back. Kam's grandfather was born in India and moved to Kenya. In the fifties, he had emigrated to Britain and made his money selling shoes door to door on the south side of Glasgow, before buying a cash-and-carry business, which Kam's dad had then turned into a bit of a powerhouse. Kam had been fated to be generation three in the cash-and-carry world. He hadn't wanted that. Instead, he became dead set on the police. He's a detective chief inspector, and despite my decision to avoid any form of promotion and him a rising star, we've developed a friendship that transcends our jobs.

The tan joke goes back to when we took a holiday in Ibiza, and I sunburned my back so badly on the first day that I was hospitalized. I screwed up his holiday that year. For three days, he came to visit me. For the rest of the holiday, I dressed like Nanook of the North and ventured out only at night, and he rubbed after-sun lotion into my scorched back every time I asked.

*'To what do I owe the pleasure?'* Kam asks.

It's been a while since I talked to Kam. And for that I feel guilty. I last chatted with him just after I left the force. And it wasn't the sweetest of partings, given the circumstances.

'Kam, I've been doing the good-boy thing. New leaf. Taxi. Early nights. Quiet life.'

*'Quiet? Yeah, right,'* he snorts. *'BG, you couldn't be quiet if they cut your tongue out.'*

'Yeah, well, people change.'

*'Sorry, BG, but what do you want? I've a briefing in ten minutes.'*

'I need a contact,' I say and run him quickly through what I know about Broch House, Terry, Kristina and Tomas.

'Do you know anyone up here that might talk to me?' I ask.

He's dismissive. *'Why are you getting involved? Leave it to the locals.'*

'Kam, it might get me some more information on my mum.'

He sighs.

'Your mum, Blake. Why are you going back there?'

We've had this conversation a lot over the years. Me laying my guilt on Kam's shoulders. Him doing the good-friend thing, listening.

'I need to do this, Kam.'

He doesn't reply immediately. 'Kam,' I say, 'are you still there?'

*'I know one of the DI's up there, BG. A guy called Kyle Anderson, but, Blake, I'm not sure it's a good idea to talk to him.'*

I wonder if that's the Kyle that Terry told me had visited the annexe with the constable.

'I just want a few words, Kam. One of the others at the station cold-shouldered me big time.'

*'Blake, can I be honest with you?'*

'Always.'

*'You fucked up, you know that. Really fucked up when you were down here.'*

'Depends how you look on it?'

*'Really, Blake? Two days before you retire you try to fit up a drug dealer. Do you know how much that took to fix?'*

'He had it coming, Kam.'

*'Mitch Campbell, Blake.'*

'I know who it was I tried to fit up.'

*'You were his best man.'*

I'd seen an opportunity. A good one. A way to close the book on a man that had never seen the inside of a prison, when he should have spent a lifetime there. Only, it all went sour. Mitch knew that I'd planted some shit in his office. When the bust was made, he made it clear what I had done. He had video evidence of me.

*'And that was worth throwing away thirty years of goodwill for?'*

This is a well-worn conversation. Kam's right: I really did fuck up. 'Kam, it's in the past.'

*'For you, Blake, but not for me. You got lucky. The assistant chief constable wanted your arse on a plate. You could have lost your pension.'*

'The ACC didn't want the bad publicity that would come with exposing me, and Mitch wasn't going to take it any further. You know it. I know it. I'm not stupid. That's why I waited until the end before I did it. He deserved to be behind bars. It nearly worked. He should have been put away an age ago.'

*'People still think you're friends. Even now.'*

'Do friends fit each other up?'

*'In Mitch's world, everyone is out for number one.'*

'And what I did made me look like one of them. Is that what you are saying?'

*'You said that, not me.'*

'You know better than that.'

*'Blake, you were dumb; there was never a right time to do what you did.'*

That's the second time I've been called stupid in twenty-four hours. Terry, now Kam.

'I knew what I was doing, Kam.'

*'That's just it, Blake. You didn't know what you were doing. How many people do you think know about what you did?'*

'Not many. They kept it quiet.'

Kam laughs, a shrill sound that sounds false.

*'Are you kidding? You almost made the front page of* 1919.*'*

*1919* is the digital magazine that covers justice and social affairs issues in Scotland. It's funded by the Scottish Police Federation.

'Kam, are you going to help me or not?'

*'I should say no. But I assume you'll go and talk to someone anyway?'*

I let the rhetorical question hang.

He caves in. *'I've only met Kyle Anderson a few times. Smart as anything. I'll WhatsApp him. If he's any sense, he'll tell you to piss off.'*

As I enter Peterhead, Kam has one last word of wisdom before he cuts the call. *'Blake, please don't fuck up again.'*

He hangs up before I can reply.

My fare is up near the Peterhead football ground. A fisherman heading for his boat up in the Broch. I don't know him, and he isn't a talker.

I drop him not far from The Sailor's Rest. My mobile has been quiet. With me on point for the taxi calls, I would have expected it to ring a lot more. It's coming up to midday, and the cup of tea from this morning needs some more solid company in my stomach.

Charlie will be waiting for me at his pub but I'm not ready to see him yet.

Doddy's stroke has knocked me a little.

I'll see Charlie later, maybe.

I text Conn and Terry again. This time, Terry replies telling me no news is good news, and they'll call if they need me.

My phone buzzes. It's a text from Kam. He says Kyle can meet me tonight at six o'clock. I've to pop up to the station in Fraserburgh.

I park at the harbour and walk up to the town centre, and on to Broad Street. Little has changed in forty-odd years, it seems. A few shops have gone. No more Woolworth's. Maitland's toy shop, a wonderland for children, is missing. If I could really remember the line-up of stores, there's probably more gone than I would believe. But something about the setting is timeless. The street is true to its name. Before it concludes at one end, it broadens out. Mum's church sits on the right.

I opt for the café near the church, ordering up a couple of rolls and sausage while saying hi to the waitress who surprises me by calling me by my first name; I don't know her. I splash tomato sauce across the dead meat when it arrives and overfill the mug of tea with sugar. A copy of the *Fraserburgh Siren* is sitting on the counter and I ask if I can have a read.

The newspaper is a new venture. Paper in a world where digital is the norm. It's become a lightning rod for local gossip. I flick through, stopping when a picture catches my eye. Balder, fatter, but the eyes and the crooked smile are a giveaway. It's a picture of Charlie Noble. He's wearing a suit, no tie. I'm not a doyen of sartorial excellence, but despite the weight he's put on, the cut of the suit hangs well on him. I check the date on the paper. It's a week old. I thought Doddy had said that Charlie was in Spain last week? Maybe it's an old photo or a delayed press release. I read the byline:

> Charlie Noble, Fraserburgh's pub king, is to open his twentieth pub. Called The Classroom, it's built on what was once the site of Hillside Primary School, in Dundee. The Classroom is phase 1 of a plan that will eventually include a hotel and health club. Charlie Noble said, 'My first love is pubs. I love the traditional pub and think its days are far from numbered. Good pubs with a good atmosphere, that aren't swamped by the overpowering smell of food, are still in demand. The Classroom is the eighth in our "Make it Your Local" chain. We have plans for ten more over the coming years and I'm delighted that Dundee is the site of the latest addition and of our twentieth pub. I look forward to the opening of the hotel and health spa next year.'

> Charlie Noble also owns a number of local properties and is the son of Keith Noble, who many of our readers will remember as one of the most respected GPs in the town.

A vision of Mum's bed appears in front of me. Charlie's dad is bending down to kiss my mother. I'm at the door. Watching.

I put the newspaper down. Trying to shut out the vision. The waitress bundles some cups and saucers onto a tray as she clears a nearby table. They rattle together. I look up, expecting to see her carrying a stack of pill boxes. I scratch at my chin. I missed a bit when shaving this morning. Rubbing the stubble with my finger, I try to push the rising thoughts of Mum from my head. I fold the newspaper and pick up one of the rolls and sausage. But my hunger is gone. I nibble a little, swirl it down with a thimbleful of tea, give up the ghost, pay and leave.

When I'm clear of the café, I cross the road, passing Mum's church. I haven't been in it since her funeral. Rain-blackened streaks of dirt flow from the window ledges. The spire is reaching for a sky that wants to rain. This is one of half a dozen churches in the town. Fishermen are inherently religious. It pays to believe in a God when the sea is trying to kill you.

I don't have much recall of the day of Mum's funeral. Dank, dark, people in black – the same people who had told me how big I had grown when they came to visit Mum when she was sick, now telling me that I have to help Dad, to be a man.

The faded red church door is open. I can see the dark wood of the narthex, shielding the nave of the church. A scraping sound indicates someone is moving something to somewhere. I consider walking in. Will it be the way I remember? But all I recall is that people and weather dominated the day. The church little more than an ancient blur of singing, high vaulted ceilings and rain battering the roof. My mother's grave lies out at the cemetery near the golf course. I haven't been back there either.

Not yet.

I walk past the church. If I can't eat in a café for the memories, I'd be a wasteland in the church. I skirt it and wander down to the harbour, away from my car, away from The Sailor's Rest, towards the North Pier.

Oversized fishing boats rest in rows. Most have bright blue or red hulls, topped off in white. These are industrial brutes, designed to max out the quotas given to their owners as efficiently as possible.

I've been down here quite a few times over the weeks. Eating up the sights, dipping back into the past. Searching for happier memories. As I step on to the pier, I let my head run free.

*'Yon's a bloody big boat.'* Charlie had said that, back when he and I had been in school, days from breaking for the summer. He had been referring to a crippled Russian trawler that was the centre of attention down in the harbour. Back then, the word 'bloody' was unacceptable. Back then, the Russian trawler was a Cold War spy ship. Charlie had been belted by our teacher, who had given me four of the same for repeating part of Charlie's phrase.

*'BLOODY big boat,'* I'd shouted.

The Russian trawler, stranded, waiting on spare parts from the motherland, was the latest in a long line of short-lived fascinations and provided most of the town's gossip for a brief time that summer. It had been placed out of bounds, docked at the far end of the North Pier because the KGB, so Mrs Lang said, had sealed it off.

*'They dinnae want those Ruskie laddies to see what the West has to offer.'*

If Fraserburgh's North Pier was the ship crew's first view of the West, then I pitied them. If I'd been one of the sailors, I'd have gone home extolling the virtues of the USSR. I'd imagine, as I stared at the rusting hulk, thirty or so of us huddled near the temporary barrier erected to keep us at bay, the Russian captain returning home. *'Comrade, we have seen the miracle that the Westerners call home, and all I can say is, let them keep the fucking place.'*

I let the memory drift as I climb up on to the top of the pier wall, looking out on the North Sea. The wind slices through me as the shelter of the harbour is stripped away. I pull my coat tight and mentally give myself ten minutes before hypothermia says hello.

The sea is a maelstrom of white breakers and waves. Even high up on the wall, spray is raining down on me. There are no boats in sight. That doesn't mean that they are all safely tucked up behind me in the harbour. They're just somewhere out beyond the horizon. Fishing is for the hardy. This probably doesn't even rate as a storm warning on the shipping forecast.

The summer of the Russian trawler was in 1976. It would be hot that summer. A summer never to be bettered. Only we didn't know that then. We just moaned about the heat and the lack of things to do.

When Charlie and I had been stalking the Russian trawler, the serious heatwave was still a month away – but everyone knew it was coming. A freight train in the distance on a still day. You could feel it. Sense it. The temperature in the ground was building from within. As if the earth was off the back of an exercise class. Heat pouring from its pores.

Then the trawler left, and things got hotter and duller.

A large wave crashes at my feet, snapping me back to the present. Atomized saline solution gushes into the air. I duck but still come up dripping. I stumble back down to the road, shaking off the water, tasting the salt on my lips, beginning to lose feeling in my fingers.

I turn my back on the pier, dipping between the harbour buildings to find shelter. I need to be back in the car. Doing something. Anything. Driving people who don't need to be where they are going or from where they should never have been in the first place. Inane chatter.

*Football.*

*Rugby.*

*Love Island.*

*'Did you see what they found on* Antiques Roadshow*?'*

*'Do you think* Doctor Who *is better than the old days?'*

The café, the church, the memories. I can't let this build.

I unlock the car and dive in, firing it up, turning the heater to full, revving the engine to banish the silence.

I've never been so grateful for a phone call when it comes.

'Doddy's Taxis'

*'It's Terry.'*

Doddy had slipped from my mind. 'How's Doddy?'

*'Nice of you to ask.'*

'I texted.'

Defensive.

*'We're waiting on the doctor, but Conn was in such a hurry to get down here, she left Doddy's stuff. She packed it all in a case and then, in the rush, ran out without it.'*

I'm relieved I can help. 'I can get it. How do I get into their flat?'

*'Conn says Mr Lachlan over the landing has a key. She's going to call him. He's been phoning about Doddy anyway.'*

'On my way.'

I take delight in doing something. I pass The Sailor's Rest, wondering if Charlie's in there, waiting on me. I'll bet you a gold dollar he was – bang on twelve.

Doddy's flat, on Mid Street, is a first-floor, two-bedroom affair with décor from the late sixties. I find a parking space outside the barber's I occasionally use. I swipe at my hair; it needs a cut. It needed a cut a couple of weeks ago. Another stickie for my brain.

The door to the bingo hall, next door to the barber's, swings open. A young lad, grimace on his face, has a brush in his hand. He begins sweeping the entrance, working his way round the two Ionic columns that guard the doors. Fraserburgh can seem a sparse, soulless town, but if you take out your magnifying glass, there is architecture to be found.

I buzz Mr Lachlan's flat number. I've met him a few times, usually when I'm up seeing Doddy. He's ten years older than me and didn't know Mum or Dad – I'd asked Conn to ask him. He's an author by trade, writing history books. He's written over forty, mostly to a brief. Publishers who spot a market, order up a book and pay a flat rate for the effort. I'd read one of them, *Fraserburgh, The Broch through the Ages*. My expectations had been low. I'd been surprised, both at the content and the sweep the town had cut through time, and also at Mr Lachlan's writing skill – functional but informative with an unexpected thread of humour.

I hear the buzzer flick the electric lock of the main door and I'm in. I climb the stairs to the smell of chips being fried. My stomach isn't in the mood.

Mr Lachlan is waiting at his door. I'd like to call him George, but he'd told me on our few meetings, 'Blake, Mr Lachlan is fine by me.'

He isn't as fat as Doddy but he's on his way. He's wearing elasticated jogging trousers and a voluminous T-shirt carrying a huge 'MY OTHER T-SHIRT IS A CIRCUS TENT' print.

I told you, humour.

'Hi, Blake, how's Doddy?' No hint of Doric here. Mr Lachlan is Edinburgh born and bred, posh with it. I update him on what I know.

He rubs at his stomach, 'Do you know what?'

I don't.

'I could be going the same way. Stroke. Maybe even my heart.'

The smell of chips is emanating from his flat.

He keeps rubbing at his belly, 'Do you think they could suck some of this out? Do they have fat Hoovers?'

'I hear they might,' I answer.

'It would have to be an industrial one for me,' he adds. 'I wonder what they would do with the fat? Maybe recycle it. Could be a business in there. Suck the fat from the people and sell it to the restaurants to cook the food that puts the fat there in the first place. You know, like *Soylent Green*.'

Mr Lachlan is like this. I think it's because he spends all day trying to make dry facts interesting that he likes to wander through a wild story now and then.

I look at Doddy's door. I'm not in the mood for this chat, but Mr Lachlan is a nice man, and cutting him off is something he dislikes.

'Sounds like an idea to me,' I offer.

'Doddy and I could keep the chippie going for a year if they sucked us dry.'

'I'm not doing so well myself.' I join him in the antediluvian man art of *rubbing of the lard*. I find I'm quite pleased I dodged the two rolls and sausage earlier. Maybe today's the day to start that diet.

'Blake,' Mr Lachlan points to my gut as he speaks, 'you've a long way to go. You're tall. You can carry it off.'

I've heard that line for a lifetime. Looks are deceptive. Tall and fat is not the way to go.

'Smells like you're frying up some more calories, Mr Lachlan?'

Tapping the door frame with a chubby finger, he rolls his eyes. 'But chips don't contain calories if,' he stage whispers, 'you air fry them.' He throws me a wink. 'It's a gastronomic rule that's little known to the general public and a secret that you can only pass on to one person at a time.'

'Thanks for the heads up?'

He flashes a car crash of teeth. 'I'm thinking of writing a book called "The Calorie-Free All You Can Eat Cook Book." What do you think?'

'Cool, now do you have the keys to Doddy's flat?' I enquire.

He reaches into his pocket. 'Can you make sure you give them back to me? It's the last set I have.'

'Last set. Do you usually have more?'

'Blake, I usually have three or four.'

I can't help but bow to my curiosity bug. 'Why do you need so many keys, if you don't mind me asking?'

'Has Doddy never told you? I'm his official keeper of the keys. Earl Derr Biggers' closing act.'

'Who?'

'Earl Derr Biggers. He wrote the Charlie Chan books. Six in all. The last one was *Keeper of the Keys*. He died in a car crash before he could write any more.'

I'm always amazed at Mr Lachlan's brain.

'I'm still a little lost as to why you need so many keys?' I say.

His chubby finger is tracing a line in the wood of the door frame. 'Doddy keeps some odd hours and, occasionally, I'm the gatekeeper that lets his friends in if he's not around. This' – he raises the chubby finger to point at me – 'being a fine case in point. And take last night. Two o'clock in the morning, I get a call.'

'Doddy was out at two in the morning?' I'm surprised.

'Sure,' he says. 'I told you he keeps odd hours. But what do you expect if you run a taxi business? I'm not shocked he's in hospital. He's too old to be doing all that running around.'

As far as I knew, Doddy was as close to housebound as makes no difference. Conn told me she does all the shopping.

Mr Lachlan has that look that used to be part of my life. The one that says, *Am I saying too much?*

'Do you and Doddy not talk?' he asks me.

'Mr Lachlan, you know Doddy. If he thinks you don't need to know, then that's the end of it.'

'Well, tell him I need more keys cut. I didn't get paid for the last lot. Tell him to get that big swine to do it. Too mouthy for my liking. Likes to give orders, that one.'

'Who?'

'John Lemby. He was the one that I had to let in last night. All drink and noise.'

'John Lemby was here last night?'

'Lemby's always here. What they do is beyond me. Drink. And lose keys.'

I had no notion that Doddy and Lemby were friends. The first I'd heard of the man was when I was asked to pick up his kids. That reminds me, Wendy Lemby asked me to take John's package to Doddy. It's still in my boot.

'Here you go.' Mr Lachlan pushes the keys into my hand. They're moist and hot.

'Thanks, Mr Lachlan. I'll drop them in when I leave. I'll only be a minute.'

'Sure.'

He closes the door.

*John Lemby and Doddy?*

*Doddy out and about?*

I let myself into Conn and Doddy's flat. The place smells of whisky and fast food. The hallway is dominated by a night-time picture of New York. Doddy found it at a jumble sale and, despite Conn's objections, had installed it on a wall that's far too small to take the print.

I find the bag Conn has packed for Doddy in their bedroom, sitting in the middle of the huge king-size. The room is a bit of a mess. Had Doddy been looking for something when the stroke hit? Or was it Conn packing up Doddy's stuff at speed? Conn likes to keep things neat. I could tidy up a little, but Conn would view it as poking around where I've no right.

I spot a diary lying on the dresser. I read the open page. *'Pick up, Calder Glen. 2.'* There's nothing else written on the page. I flick back to yesterday, conscious that I'm overstepping the mark. *'Pick up, Milly's Pride. 2, Lemby at house.'* I open a few more pages and see the odd similar message at intervals. I leave it open where I found it and decide it's time to leave.

Instead of knocking on Mr Lachlan's door, I push the keys through his letterbox. Much as I'd like to know a little more about Doddy's nocturnal dealings, I promised Terry I'd be quick.

Before I head south, I pull in at the petrol station to fill up, and add a diet Mars Bar to the bill, then make it two. My hunger pangs are returning.

I dial up a little ambient music and slot the car back into the Fraserburgh-to-Aberdeen Scalextric track.

I wonder what Doddy was doing late last night with John Lemby. Mr Lachlan suggested Lemby was there a lot. Lemby was an arse to me at his home, but *I've* been friends with arseholes, so why can't Doddy have such friends?

Mr Lachlan had talked about Doddy doing 'all that running around'. It's so at odds with what I thought I knew about Doddy. Not that it's any of my bee's wax, but it makes me think. Lemby as a friend sounds toxic. I'm sure he's just short of psychotic, and Doddy is often an inch from needing serious anger management. The pair can't be a good partnership. And if Lemby drinks anything like the way Doddy does, then the brew isn't just toxic – it's lethal.

I dwell on the diary I saw in Doddy's bedroom and what the entries might mean. If the number two in the diary referred to the time last night, then Doddy, or Lemby, was picking something, or someone, up with another pick-up due tonight. *Calder Glen. Milly's Pride.* My trainspotting days down at the harbour ring a small bell. As well as the fishing boat registration code, every fishing boat has a name. *Calder Glen. Milly's Pride.* They could be boats. But what or who would Doddy or Lemby be picking up from fishing boats at two in the morning?

I enter Aberdeen for the second time that day.

# TEN

*'People Smuggling'*

Conn is sitting with Terry in a different waiting room in the hospital when I arrive.

'Hi, here's the bag,' I say as I enter. 'How's Doddy?'

The room has a couple of bookshelves filled with paperbacks, mostly that well-known legal entity of Patterson, King, Child, McDermid, Rankin and Binchy.

Conn moves along the bench seat to let me sit down. 'Not a lot more to tell. He's sleeping. We've still to see the doctor. A nurse told us that he's doing well.'

'I'd have thought the doctor would have been in to see you by now?' I say.

'This place is a mad house,' Terry tells me. 'A tourist coach overturned on the road to Kemnay.'

'That sounds bad.' I shuffle a little; the seat is plastic and hard on the butt.

'I don't think anyone died, but there were a lot of injuries,' says Terry. 'We were put in here, out of the way.'

'Well,' I reassure them, 'this is the best place for Doddy. I'm sure they're doing all they can. How are you both?'

Conn decides to offload. 'I've been on at Doddy for ages to lose weight. He won't listen. He just eats crap and drinks like a fish.'

'Has he always been like that?' I ask.

Conn stands up, loosening off her muscles. 'I thought he was getting better. Six months ago, he was the worst I've ever seen him. God, I was worried. Drivers left, days after starting. He was doing a bottle of whisky a day. Yelling at the slightest thing.'

'More than now?'

'Much worse. But he'd calmed down a bit – still, I'm amazed you've put up with it.'

'He's not that bad,' I admit. 'When I first started driving, his directness threw me. It took me a little while to realize that giving as much as you take is the way to handle him.'

'It's his way.'

'What changed in the last six months?' I ask.

Conn doesn't reply.

'John Lemby?' I venture.

Conn whirls round. 'What about John Lemby?'

'Is he the reason things changed?'

'Why would you say that?'

Honesty is the best way forward here. 'Mr Lachlan told me that Doddy and Lemby had been seeing a lot of each other.'

Terry is playing tennis with our conversation. 'I didn't know Doddy knew John Lemby well,' she says to Conn.

'He tells me all the time that Lemby is bad news. But he still sees him,' says Conn.

'So' – I rise to join her at the window – 'if Lemby's bad news, why's Doddy hanging around with him and how has Lemby made things better? Do you know?'

She looks at the floor. I think Conn sees Doddy's weaknesses as a challenge. She's highly perceptive. She loves Doddy for what he is, not what he might be. She knows that changing him is a gargantuan task, maybe a mission too far. Underlying it all, it seems to me that Conn is bonded to Doddy as a soul mate.

'Look, it's hard,' she says. 'Doddy had money problems. Or still has. I don't know the full details, but he owed or owes money to some people, and he won't tell me who or how much.'

She pauses. That last sentence sounds like a lie to me, but I let it go.

'Doddy gambles,' she continues. 'Although he thinks I don't know.'

'And his gambling is bad?' I ask.

'Oh, yes. Before you arrived, we used to have a good taxi business. Six cars on the road and a limo. Then Doddy started to piss off the drivers. He didn't care what they wanted. He just wanted them on the road earning. Soon they were all gone. Blake, you've no idea what a Godsend you've been to him.'

'Me?' I'm surprised. 'Seriously. How much do I add? How much can Doddy be making with just two of us on the road?'

Conn circles the room. 'Not much, but it's better than nothing. No one would work for us. Our reputation with drivers was shot. But the good news is that lately the conversation about money has eased off. He's still drinking and eating too much, but the money conversation seems to have gone.'

In my experience, that isn't always good news. But I say nothing.

'I was hoping that this meant he might ease off on booze and grub.'

'But he hasn't?'

'Not a bit.'

I think about this. 'And where does Lemby come in? He doesn't seem a likely knight in shining armour for Doddy's money woes.'

'He's no knight – but I'm scared he's the one that might have sorted Doddy's money troubles.'

'How so?'

'Six months ago, Lemby gets out of jail,' she states.

'Doddy mentioned something about serious assault,' I say.

'Lemby got into a fight with a driver up near Rosehearty. He was drunk. When the police arrived, he was beating the other driver up. He was sentenced to six months. Lemby's not a stranger to prison.'

'And he got in touch with Doddy when he got out,' I venture.

'Lemby came up to see him one night, a few days after he was released. We'd had the mother of all fallouts over cash the night before Lemby appeared. Doddy told me to leave when Lemby arrived, to let them talk.'

'What did Lemby want?'

'Doddy wouldn't say. It all went quiet until a while later when Doddy tells me that we have a late-night booking, down at the harbour at two in the morning, and would I do it? He says that he's coming with me. Doddy's never come with me on a fare.'

She stops pacing and sits down next to Terry. 'So,' she carries on, 'I agree to do the run and then he throws in something else. We have to go out and pick up John Lemby first. Now I really kick off. I put my foot down. Doddy tells me it is what it is, and I give in. Lemby was reeking of drink when we picked him up to take him to our place. The bastard even tried to touch my leg when he reached over to turn the radio up. I don't like him at all.'

Lemby sounds more and more like the sort of person that could do with a much longer stretch inside.

'And you picked someone up from one of the fishing boats?' I ask.

'Yes. How did you know?'

'A guess,' I lie.

'Doddy and Lemby hit the whisky bottle at midnight. By the time we all got in the car, they were both rat-arsed. It takes a lot to get Doddy out of the house, and, even though he's dealing with Lemby, it's clear he doesn't trust him. I was told to park up by the fish market,' she says, talking more quickly now. 'Doddy and Lemby got out. Fifteen minutes later, they came back, only now there's three of them. The new man is dressed in wet-weather gear and stinks of fish. He doesn't speak. We drove. Doddy tells me to go to our place. I don't want to take the stranger into my home, but he insists. And once we are in, Doddy spends the whole time looking out of the flat window to the road below. Next, we are back in the car, Lemby and Doddy drunk as skunks and the new man saying nothing.'

'So, the man definitely came off a boat?' I enquire.

'Yes.'

'What did he look like?' Terry asks, joining in.

'It was hard to see. He never took his bunnet off. Kept his head well down, even in the flat. I think he was foreign. Maybe in his late twenties. He seemed very nervous. He didn't say a word the whole time. Anyway, we drove to Broch House. We had to wait till they opened the gates. I parked up near the house and Doddy told me to sit tight.'

'Did they all go into the house?' I ask.

'No, they went off to that annexe place. They were gone for half an hour. When Doddy and Lemby came back, they were both grinning like cats. The other man wasn't with them.'

'And have you picked up from the harbour since?' Terry asks.

Conn gives it a little thought. 'Yes, but it varies. Sometimes it can be a couple of weeks between runs, or, like this week, we've had two already and another tonight.'

'And Doddy and Lemby go every time?'

'Doddy won't let me go alone, and Lemby insists on being there.'

'So, it's always the three of you?'

'A couple of times Doddy and Lemby have done it without me, but Doddy struggles without me there. He's not up to driving anymore. Once when Doddy was down with the flu, I said I'd do it with Lemby. Doddy fought me on it. Lemby refused to go with just me; he dragged Doddy out of his bed. He always wants Doddy there.'

It's my turn to stand up. Stretch. 'And Doddy won't say what's going on?'

Conn rolls her head back on her neck. 'No. But I'm not dumb. People smuggling is my guess.'

I shake my head. 'No. I disagree. People smuggling is a numbers game,' I say. 'Thirty in a truck and hide them in some shithole. Broch House doesn't fit the mould. It makes no sense as people smuggling.'

'Blake, none of this makes sense,' Conn says. 'But I know one thing: there's a lot of cash in it. As I said, Doddy's eased off big time on money since the runs started.'

'But he's still stressed,' I point out.

'Twenty-four seven,' says Conn. 'He won't leave the house for anything other than the runs. Paranoid about anyone visiting, and when Lemby comes, you should hear them go at each other.'

'What about?'

'They think I'm deaf. Money. Or rather how the money they are getting should be split. Who does what? Who arranges what?'

The waiting-room door opens, and a nurse looks in. She doesn't say anything. She closes the door.

'Conn, did Doddy or Lemby mention how much money was involved?'

She rolls her eyes, almost comically. 'I heard a number once, when they thought I wasn't listening,' she admits.

'How much?'

'A hundred thousand pounds – there and back. That's the number I heard.'

I whistle, 'A hundred K for a taxi ride? No wonder they were arguing. Hell's teeth, that's a lot of cash.' I stop, thinking on what Conn had just said. 'Hang on, you said there and *back*. What do you mean there and *back*?'

'That's the deal. We take them there and then we take them back.'

'Back to where?'

'The harbour.'

'And they drop the person on a boat.'

'It's Doddy and Lemby's job to arrange the fishing boat as well. The hundred thousand is for the whole thing. Boat, taxi and God knows what else. Doddy won't talk, but I think it's him who arranges the boats. Lemby isn't well liked by any of the fishermen. It's another reason he attaches himself at the hip to Doddy on the runs.'

'When do they go back to the harbour? The same night?'

'Usually the next day. But sometimes not at all. At least not with us.' She slumps a little in the chair. 'I'm good with faces, and over the months, three haven't come back, or if they have, I didn't take them.'

'And you always drive?'

'Lemby got banned from driving, and the police know his car well. A white Range Rover. Wendy doesn't drive. If Lemby drove his car, he knows he could be spotted, and Doddy avoids driving like the plague. I'm it.'

She turns to Terry. 'You work at the House. Have you heard about any of this before now?'

'I haven't,' Terry says. 'But,' she adds, 'that doesn't mean that Kristina and Tomas didn't see or hear anything. Maybe that's why they were fired. We do chat a lot about the annexe, and I've asked about it a few times, but it's always the same line. "Exclusive. For the patrons. Now stop asking!"'

'Conn, I saw a guy in fishing gear up at the house the evening before last,' I say. 'It wasn't late. He stank of fish. Looked confused. Did you drop anyone off on Saturday when I was on my break?'

'No,' Conn replies. 'We did do one run in the early hours of Saturday morning. Only that was a little different.'

'In what way?'

'Doddy and Lemby had been on a mega-happy trip for a start. Three drops in four days. That's a lot of cash. They were both full to the gills all the time, and then some. Doddy was so hungover the next day that he made me take the CB unit to the toilet. He runs the business from there most mornings. He had a couple of extra-long leads made that let him do that.'

Unbelievable.

She returns to the night trip. 'So, early Saturday morning, we get to Broch House as usual. Those two are slammed again, singing like Pavarotti and Mick Jagger. The passenger looking like he was about to shit himself. I pull up, and they all vanish towards the annexe. Then, ten minutes later, they return, walking towards the House with the stranger, and Gail appears. She takes the stranger by the hand before pointing to our car. As Doddy and Lemby stagger towards me, she takes the man inside the main house.'

'Maybe that's who I saw? Maybe the annexe was full?'

Conn doesn't reply.

The nurse that appeared earlier returns. 'Sorry,' she says. 'Would we be able to use this room? We've a lot of relations worried about the coach crash.'

The nurse holds the door wide.

'The café is open,' she informs us. 'I'll tell the doctor you're down there. Mr Robertson's asleep. There won't be an update until he wakes and the doctor can see him.'

My phone rings.

I answer, 'Doddy's Taxis.' I listen.

I put my hand over the phone. 'Wendy Lemby needs the kids picked up from school. Do you need me?'

Conn shakes her head, as does Terry. 'OK, Mrs Lemby, I can do it.'

I consider telling Conn and Terry about my meeting later with Kyle Anderson at the police station, then I decide against it. First I need to know what's what.

I escort them both to the café and leave them nursing tea and buns, with a promise to phone me as soon as they hear anything.

When I arrive at the school in Fraserburgh, the first kid in the car is the Nose Picker. He's his father's son. 'Why are ye always so bloody latchie?'

I want to tell him I'll not be latchie in letting him feel the back of my hand.

Wendy Lemby is waiting at the end of the gravel driveway when I pull in. There's no sign of her husband.

'Any news on Doddy?' she asks when I get out.

'Nothing. But I think that's good news.'

The kids vacate my car. The Nose Picker grates another of my nerves. 'Yer car stinks o' coo shit.'

I look at him. 'Well, you shouldn't have stood in it.'

'Yer girlfriend pit us in the field,' he throws at me.

I shrug my shoulders at Wendy. She points out the obvious. 'His father's loon. Tell Conn I'm asking after her.'

'Where's your husband?'

'He went out a while ago. Used your rival's company. Why?'

'I know he and Doddy are friends. I thought he might want an update.'

'I'll tell him what you told me.'

She doesn't sound like she thinks her husband being friends with Doddy is a good idea either.

It's quarter past five by the time I get back to the town and, to put a phrase of my aunt's to the test, I'm Hank Marvin. Lochpots takes some more of my hard-earned for a fish supper, two cans of IRN-BRU and two Mars Bars.

The sun is long gone. On the way to the fish and chip shop, I'd passed a clutch of kids huddled next to a vacant shop. I think they were playing pitch'n'toss. I used to lose my pocket money playing that game in school. I'd smiled as one of the kids had fist-pumped a win. It's nice to know that the Gods of PlayStation, Xbox and Switch are not all-powerful.

It's too cold to eat outdoors. The customers will just have to like it or lump the smell in the car if I need to pick anyone up before I see Kyle. I give thought to what I'm going to talk to him about as I eat. I need to be careful. There's no way I can tell him what Conn has said about Doddy and Lemby. If he's as smart as Kam says, then I'll need to tread with glass slippers on this. Any mention of the people being smuggled up to Broch House, and I'll drop Doddy and Conn right in the mincer.

Ten minutes later, I bin the fish supper detritus and let a few burps out.

# ELEVEN

## *'Saying Too Much'*

I arrive at the police station with five minutes to spare. I'd expected to feel a little sense of something lost when I entered a police station for the first time since leaving the force, but I had realized, on the recent visit with Terry, that I was laid back about being on the lawless side of the reception desk. I even felt a minuscule air of relief. For a hard world left behind.

Déjà vu washes over me as I push into the reception area. Paul, the officer who acted so cold when I brought Terry to give her statement, is at the desk.

He looks up. 'Hello, Mr Glover, Detective Inspector Anderson asked me to tell you he's running ten minutes late and to take a seat. Do you want a cup of tea?'

The offer is on a par with *Would you like a punch in the face?* I decline.

Around me, the usual assortment of public information posters are on display. A couple of MisPers are up, but not Tomas or Kristina – not yet. The whole space has a functional depression that wears away the soul. The stink of fear, anger, resentment and resignation mixes with lemon-scented bleach. I've always wondered if anyone actually likes being in a police station reception. Certainly, none of my colleagues did – unless it was to see the back of it on the way home. The general public are only ever here to report bad news or to be questioned or when they've been arrested.

I know of one exception. When I was working in Glasgow, we used to have a guy who appeared on a regular basis. We called him Joker Wullie. Two or three times a day, or night, he'd come into the station, lean round the door and tell a joke. Nothing offensive. Pre-watershed stuff. He was actually quite good. He did it regardless of who was in the reception area. One Saturday, after a Celtic versus Rangers cup final, we'd had our fill of the drunk and violent from the game. Joker Wullie arrived, leapt on to a chair and shouted out:

*'A Celtic supporter and a Rangers supporter both feel sick and go to their doctor to find out what's wrong with them.'*

I'd immediately screamed at him to be quiet. But he ignored me; we were full to the gunnels and Wullie liked a crowd. He went on . . .

*'"Your problem is you're both too fat," says the doctor.*

*"I'd like a second opinion," says the Rangers fan.*

*"So would I," says the Celtic fan.*

*The doctor looks them up and down and says, "OK, you're both ugly, too."'*

He actually got a laugh. I asked him once why he did it. He told me that the world needed to laugh now and then, and never more so than when you were dealing with the police. You can't disagree with that.

Kyle Anderson appears. He's about six feet tall, thin, clipped hair with a look on his face that most detectives are cursed with – suspicious.

'Blake?' He puts out his hand and I take it.

'Kyle,' I bat back. 'Thanks for seeing me.'

'Sorry I'm late.' No explanation. 'What can I do for you?' To the point.

'Could we find somewhere to talk?'

'Sure, but I'm busy. DCI Ali told me it wouldn't take long.'

'It won't.'

He signals to the constable. 'Paul, are any of the rooms free?'

'You can use number one.'

Paul buzzes us into the inner sanctum. I follow Kyle and we step into one of the interview rooms. The interior has the same design as most stations. A place to try to separate facts from lies. Spartan. Unwelcoming. Overused. Always in need of a coat of paint and a dust. Chairs that have been designed by the devil's brother to get comfortable in. I'm not under suspicion of anything, so Kyle does me the favour of pulling the chairs out to sit next to each other, rather than face to face. He drops on to one and signals for me to join him.

'OK,' he starts. 'What's this about?'

'Do you know Terry Lang?'

'Yes.'

'Well, a couple of friends of hers went missing.'

'So I believe. You reported it to Paul.'

'I did, but I think I fucked up a little.'

'And?'

'I was trying to help out Terry.'

Kyle puts up a hand.

'Blake. Cut the crap! I haven't got the time. Let's see if I can make this succinct. You've stirred up the people at Broch House. Implied we didn't know what we were doing. Pissed off Paul out there. Used the old boy's network to see me, which will go down like a bucket of cold fish guts with my boss when he finds out. Did I miss anything?'

This is stone cold. No allowance for my thirty years in the police here.

'OK,' I say. 'Look, I was trying to help out. Terry's grandmother knew my mother back in the day. She promised me some time to talk about her if I helped Terry. I didn't know that going up to Broch House would cause a fuss. I was just asking a few questions.'

'Questions we should have been asking.'

'Like I said, I was trying to help.'

'I'm sorry but I don't care. You should have passed it to us and left it at that.'

'Terry wouldn't come here. She was scared she'd lose her job.'

Kyle closes his eyes for a second. When he opens them, he says, 'Is that what she told you?'

'Yes.'

'Not that she didn't want to come here because of Paul?'

'What?'

'How long were you in the force?'

'Thirty years.'

'Kam said you were a good copper.'

There's no reply to that.

'Look, I need to go, but here's a heads-up,' he says. 'Terry didn't want to come here because she only just dumped Paul for the Polish guy that's gone missing.'

I chew on that for a minute. 'She told me she'd been going out with Tomas for over a year.'

'I think you need to get to know Terry Lang a little better. She stopped going out with Paul less than a week ago. Paul and Terry have been an item since school. Paul's devastated.'

And there I was telling Paul how to do his job while his ex-girlfriend listened on. No wonder he had been so cold, and Terry so keen to leave.

'Even so, she could still lose her job,' I point out.

Kyle stands up, ready to leave.

'Why? Because she was talking about two fired employees? So what? I'm sorry, but this conversation is over, and, if I were you, I'd back out of this altogether. Now, goodbye.'

I sit. Showing no signs of moving. I rub my tongue over the back of my teeth, trying to move a stubborn piece of fish from a gap.

Kyle is in a hurry. 'Can you leave?'

I've no intention of leaving. OK, so I might not have played this as well as I should have, and maybe Terry is a little heavy on the white-lie side of the coin, but I know when something is off-kilter. My Fizz Buzz is gurgling.

'Kyle, sit down,' I say.

Kyle ignores my request. 'This is over.'

I don't move. Kyle reaches for the door handle. I lean back, hands behind my neck. Using my body language to make a point. I'm comfortable. In control.

'Just let me say my piece and I'll be out of here.'

Kyle relents, 'You have two minutes.'

I work my fingers around the back of my neck. Settling them into each other. 'Let's skip over the love action in this story between Terry and your man out there. Let's look at the simple facts. Two people are missing.'

I see him ready to speak. I stop him. 'Kristina was accused of stealing, but denied it to Terry. What's interesting is that Broch House didn't call in the police. Now, if Terry is to be believed, there was a whole string of thefts. Yet when I went up, the place was dead. So, who the hell was Kristina stealing from? There's no one there. And if there was, and I know what the rich are like, at least one of them would have been on the phone to the police in seconds. Firing a staff member wouldn't have been enough. There's discretion and there's stupidity. Discreet or not, if there is a spate of thefts, you call in the police and show you've got it under control. That's how you keep your reputation. Firing the suspect wouldn't make me happy if they had broken into my room and stolen something personal. So, the real reason they didn't call the police is because there were no thefts. It was just an excuse to get rid of Kristina.'

Kyle keeps his peace.

'And' – I'm motoring – 'let's take Tomas. Maybe Terry poured it on a bit thick with the "losing her job" thing, hoping I'd back down from coming here. But when I go up to Broch House, who gets canned? The very person I'm talking to. This time, the House doesn't need a reason. Tomas is suddenly surplus to requirements. Where does that leave us? At a minimum, neither Kristina nor Tomas can be traced. Both have vanished. And then Terry tells me that Broch House claimed to have talked to Tomas's mum and that she told them Tomas was OK. Which, given she doesn't speak English and the woman at Broch House doesn't speak Polish, is a miracle.'

Kyle hasn't moved an inch.

I stand up. 'So, let's get this bloody straight. I've been in. I've reported, *twice*, my suspicions. Once on paper to your boy out there and now again. I know how this works. If two bodies turn up at some point, and fuck all has been done about my reports, I know who is going to get shit-canned next.'

I'm building to a volcano here. 'Forget what I should have or shouldn't have done. Forget my little attempt at some private investigation. Let's be clear. I spent thirty years on the streets of one of the hardest cities on the planet and I know when something's fucking wrong. And this is fucking wrong. It smells bad. So, you can be a fucking arse about it. Worry about what your boss will say. I expected a little colleague-on-colleague support here. I see that's not going to happen. Fine. I fucked up. If that's the way it is, then that's the way it is. But I know what you should be doing, and so do you.'

A thought sprints to the front of my raging head. Shit, I'm an idiot. I get up. I walk to the door. 'I'd like to leave before I say anything else that I might regret.'

*Shit.*

My outburst puts Kyle on the back foot. But only a little – I won't have been the first man to shout at him in this place.

Kyle opens the door and stands back to let me out. My head is reeling. I want to take some – *all* – of that outburst back, but, instead, in silence, we re-enter the reception area where I'm allowed to exit without a word being spoken.

As soon as I step outside, I want to shout. Tell the people of this town that I'm a fucking idiot. I ignore my car. I walk. What the hell was I thinking? I have an anger issue if pushed too far. I've learned to keep it suppressed, but, when it surfaces, I roar into a red mist only to emerge on the other side in a cold swathe of regret.

And now, regret is washing over me like a drunk man pissing on a fire.

Right at the end of my outburst, I'd realized what I was doing. Hell, yes, they'll investigate now. I've given them no choice. More or less threatened to report them. I even had to stop myself saying I'd go to the local rag. But what will they find out when they get up there? Conn's just told me she's involved in the people-smuggling thing, and I've just sent in the cavalry. If Tomas's and Kristina's disappearances are linked to the annexe and the people smuggling, how long will it be before Conn, Doddy and Lemby are implicated?

I kick the pavement.

I don't give a flying monkey's about Lemby, but I might just have sentenced Conn and Doddy to a long wait in a dark cell.

What the hell was I thinking?

# TWELVE

## *'Old Friends'*

I walk around town for an hour. I can't let go of how angry I was in the police station. So angry at being dismissed that I lost the plot. *Treated like a civilian.* And I've involved Kam in it as well. When this all comes out – and it will – I'll be in the firing line.

*'Well, Mr Glover, when did you find out about the suspected people smuggling from the defendant?'*

I can hear Kam. *'BG, why the hell didn't you tell the locals what you knew? Why the hell didn't you tell me the whole story?'*

I couldn't. I owe Conn and Doddy. And I always pay my debts. It's a rule. Up there on my list of things you always do, along with never pass a bathroom or turn down a pint. Doddy might shout and scream at me on the radio every day, but he's been good to me. He's certainly flawed, but he hasn't asked many questions about my past. Neither has Conn. And around here that's hard for them to do. Employing an ex-Glasgow policeman with a local mother who killed herself must have raised some questions, but they've stood by me, and, now, I might just have put their future into a liquidizer.

My phone rings. It's Conn. 'Hi, Conn. How's Doddy?'

*'Awake and better than the fat sod has any right to be. Still confused as hell. He doesn't remember much. They've got him on a shedload of drugs, and he's under constant observation. I saw him for about five minutes. I'm being allowed back later, if he's up to it.'*

'That's good news.'

She lets me hang in the wind for a minute.

*'Blake, we have another problem.'*

Let's just keep piling them up.

'What kind of problem?' I ask.

*'John Lemby phoned.'*

'Asking after Doddy?'

*'Did he, hell! He was in a right state. Wanted to know if tonight's run is still on.'*

'Doddy's had a stroke, and he's worried about *that*?'

*'You should have heard him. Massively drunk. Telling me that we needed to do this run. Me and him.'*

'I hope you told him where to go.'

*'I told him to do it himself, that we're out. The stress of it is killing Doddy. I told him that. Told him straight. But he didn't listen. He told me you don't just shut up shop on these guys. That he's already been paid for all three deliveries. I told him to hand the money back.'*

'But he's spent it?'

*'I think he has serious money problems. You should have heard him. Desperate isn't the word. He was screaming at me.'*

'Just get him to call ZZ.'

*'Blake, I can't drop ZZ in on this. That's not on. Zach Zane's a nice guy. Anyway, Lemby won't buy it. He's scared enough of the number of people who know already. I asked him if there was anyone else he could use. And do you know what he did – he laughed. Laughed. Told me that there was, but if he had to go back to him, then he'd really fuck over Doddy.'*

'Back to who?'

*'Charlie Noble.'*

'Charlie Noble's involved in this?'

*'Charlie was Lemby's partner before us. But they fell out.'*

'Charlie used to run the people to the annexe?'

*'Yes.'*

'Why in the hell would Charlie do it? He can't need the money – he's loaded.'

*'He did a run or two before Lemby went to jail. I'm amazed that Lemby is chasing Charlie.'*

'Why?'

*'They had a massive fallout. Charlie's the reason Lemby went to jail. Charlie was the driver Lemby beat up.'*

'Charlie! Bloody hell. Look, Conn, just blank Lemby. Focus on Doddy. Let Lemby sort out his own mess.'

*'I tried, but Lemby went on and on at me. In the end, when I wouldn't back down, he said that he'd make it clear to whoever's paying that I refused to help. He also said if this gets out, he'll make sure Doddy and I are front and centre with the guys behind this.'*

'Look, Conn, I hate to say this, but Lemby would probably have turned you in anyway, if it went south. But if these people off the boats are that important, the staff up at the House will find a way to pick them up. They'll just send down one of their own.'

*'And they'll want their money back. Money that I don't think Lemby has. Who will they come after for it next? We don't have enough to cover Lemby's share. I'm not even sure how much we have. Doddy has never told me. Blake, I'm scared.'*

I think on this. 'Conn, I need to talk to Lemby. Figure a way of squaring it.'

*'Blake, please hear me out.'* A car horn sounds in the background. *'There is a way to square this.'*

'How?'

*'You do the run tonight.'*

I stop walking, checking that no one is in earshot. 'Me?'

*'It makes sense.'*

'I can't. Conn, I can't.'

*'Why not? It's easy. Lemby will do the pick-up from the boat and the drop-off at the House. All you need to do is drive. It's the answer. I trust you. You get the person to the House. Lemby doesn't have to pay anything back. Then we deal with what comes next. Tell them that we are out.'*

'They won't want a stranger involved.'

*'They'll never know. You don't have to get out of the car.'*

'And when Lemby comes back for more? And he will. I know the sort.'

*'Doddy will need to rest after this. I'm planning to take him away for a while. Lemby will have to make other arrangements and deal with the fallout. Let him go back to Charlie Noble if need be. If you can do this one thing, then I can try and distance us from it all.'*

As I walk and talk, the sound of a stereo pumping some late-sixties classics drifts from across the street. Shadows behind a window are moving, dancing. A party, gearing up. That would be nice. Slip across the road. Ask if they wouldn't mind an interloper. I'd be happy to nip out and get some booze as my ticket to the do. Cut some moves on the carpet. Forget about this night.

The neat row of leaden homes, bearing that Broch styling of mottled building blocks of varying dark hues, looks welcoming to me right at this moment – even the lifeless ones with curtains closed and lights out.

*'Blake, are you still there?'*

'Conn, I need to think this over. I'll call you back.'

She tries one more plea. *'Blake, do this for me, and I promise I'll sort everything else.'*

'I'll call you back.'

As I put the phone back in my pocket, the party's sound system is playing the Beatles' 'Hard Day's Night'.

I keep walking.

An hour later, and I've a two-step plan.

First, I need to stop Lemby doing something stupid. I have his landline number from the taxi call this morning. I don't want to talk to him, I just need to put him on hold while I move to the second part of my plan.

I ring the number, praying Wendy answers. She does. 'Hi, Mrs Lemby, it's Blake Glover.'

*'Hi. How's Doddy?'*

'That's why I'm phoning. He's not doing too bad. Conn's seen him, and they seem to think he's as good as can be expected. I don't know much about these things, but I know the first few hours are the most dangerous and he's through that.'

*'That's nice to know.'*

'Can you tell your husband the news?'

*'Sure.'*

'Conn also asked me to pass on a message for John.'

*'John's here.'*

'I don't need to talk to him. Just say that Conn says tonight will be fine.'

*'What does that mean?'*

'I don't know, Mrs Lemby; Conn is a bit all over the place.'

*'OK.'*

'Thanks. I need to go.' I hang up.

Now for part two.

I look up the number for The Sailor's Rest on the internet and phone it. It's answered on the fourth ring.

*'Hello, The Sailor's Rest.'* A woman's voice.

'Hi, can you tell me if Charlie Noble is in the bar tonight.'

*'Who's calling?'*

'An old friend. I've been trying to track him down.'

*'I'll see if he can come to the phone.'*

'No.' A little too sharp. 'I'm in the area. I'll pop in. Surprise him.'

*'Eh, OK.'* The woman doesn't sound very sure of herself. Probably worrying if she should have said Charlie was in the pub at all.

As I walk to my car, my phone rings. I recognize the number. The Lembys. I let it trip to voicemail. It rings twice more before I arrive at The Sailor's Rest. It has to be John Lemby.

I park up in the shadow of the pub. There are a few cars around, but winter Mondays are a graveyard for most bars. I notice a Porsche 911 squatting beneath a streetlight, parked over two spaces. I circle around to look at the number plate 'B13 CJN'. It has to be Charlie's. CJN. Charles James Noble. I'm not sure what the B13 means.

I climb the steps to the pub. Taking my time. My phone rings once more. Lemby again. He must be climbing the wall by now wondering what's going on. I let it ring out, pushing through the pub door, letting the age-old smell of liquor and cleaning fluid assault my nose.

The pub's quiet. A bar across the back wall faces away from me. The sides of the pub are slotted with rows of small booths. The centre is carpeted in dark red, littered with low tables and cushioned chairs. The far wall is dominated by a floor-to-ceiling window that looks out over the harbour. The ceiling is lower than I would have expected. It's stripped with down-lighters. The colour scheme is quiet, the décor muted. There's a nod to the sea theme, but no tacky ships' wheels or netting or buoys. A framed print on the wall of the three lifeboats involved in the disasters over the years hangs near the entrance. A plaque beneath it says a percentage of the pub's profits go directly to the Royal National Lifeboat Institution.

A couple of men are standing at the bar. A young couple are sitting in one of the booths, and that's the sum total of tonight's crowd. Charlie is nowhere in sight. I walk up to the bar, a shrine to all things whisky. The bartender is maybe in her fifties, dressed in colours to match the pub. Probably the woman that answered the phone.

'Hi,' I say.

'What can I get you?'

'I'm looking for Charlie Noble. Is he around? I phoned earlier.'

She looks me up and down. I wait for her to announce that she knows me, that her sister told her that a cousin had seen me in the chip shop, that my mother was her mother's best friend and *Blake, don't you remember me? Susan. We were friends in primary school.*

None of this happens.

'Who shall I say is looking for him?' is her question.

'Can you just say an old friend?' I have a mini brainwave. 'Tell him I'm here to touch the horn and back.'

She has no clue what to say to that. She walks to the far end of the bar before pushing through a door.

Ten seconds later, a whirlwind enters the room in the form of one Charlie Noble. Fatter, balder, but still with energy to burn. He flings his arms around me. 'Blake fucking Glover. How long? How many years?'

'Hi, Charlie.' I feel a little lost for words.

Charlie grins. 'Man, but I never thought I'd see you again. It's been a while.'

'It's been an age, Charlie.'

He indicates to one of the booths. 'Let's grab a seat. What do you want to drink?'

'I'll have an IRN-BRU.'

'You driving?'

I'm praying that, later tonight, the answer to that one will be no. 'Taxi.'

'I heard. How's Doddy?'

'Did you hear about his stroke?'

'In this town? Be serious. Of course, I did.'

'Conn's seen him. He's as well as can be expected.' There really should be another way of saying that. It's such a cop-out. 'Sorry I didn't get in at twelve today.'

'I was here, waiting. I tried to call the taxi number to see where you were, but it flipped to Conn's voicemail. I then tried Conn's number. It also tripped. I'll get the drinks.'

It should be a surprise that Charlie has Conn's mobile number, but it's not. I watch him place the drinks order. He returns with my IRN-BRU, a glass of something clear for himself.

'So, are you still a time lord?' I ask.

'I just like people to be on time. Not much to ask, is it?'

He squeezes in opposite me. 'So, how the hell have you been?'

'Good. You?'

He grins. 'I'm doing fine, but what I want to know is, why are you back? It's more than forty years since we were loons up at school.'

'I retired from the police and wanted a change.'

If he expected a longer answer, he doesn't show it. 'Aye, I ken. Heard you were a policeman.'

'And you've done well. Pubs, property. And when we were wee, I thought you were going to be an athlete.'

Charlie smiles. 'I was. Well, for a while. Made the Scotland youth team for the eight hundred metres. But you know what it's like. All that training. Same routine, day after day. It wisnae for me.'

'Are you married?'

'Aye. And I have a boy, Taylor, fantastic lad. You?'

'Young, single and free, only not so young now. How did you get into this game?' I wave my arm around.

'My dad.'

I'm surprised. 'Is he doing well?'

'Not so good.' Charlie lifts his glass to his lips. I can't tell if it's just lemonade or has something stronger in it. 'But still doling out medical advice when it's needed. You know he went on to specialize in cancer?'

'No, I didn't.'

'He only retired a few years back. But he hasn't really retired, if you know what I mean.'

I do.

I sip my drink. 'So how did he get you into pubs?'

'By accident. I was back from uni for the summer. Third year. I got my dad's back up by fucking around rather than getting a job. He knew a guy called Roddy Glen who worked at the bar at the golf course. Roddy was short on bar staff. Dad arranged for me to do some shifts. I didn't want to do that. No way. But Dad is a force when he gets going.'

'You got that,' I say. 'My memory of your dad was of a giant man, red beard flowing around his face like a lion's mane. He seemed to dominate a room when he walked in. I remember that he owned a lurid green cardigan that smelled of compost; he was always in the back garden pottering in his shed. The cardigan was three or four sizes too big, and flowed behind him like a kite in a storm.'

'He still has it.'

'And the golf course job?'

'So,' Charlie says, 'I was forced to serve the Fraserburgh elite. I thought I'd hate it. You know, having to suffer all that "the seventh was a bit tricky today" stuff. Only I didn't. I loved it. The chat, the buzz when it was busy. The whole thing. By the end of the summer, Roddy damn near let me run the place. When I went back to uni, I got a job in the students' union. I was running the bar by the end of the second term. Loved that, too. So, when I finished my exams, I bought a pub.'

'Just like that?'

He laughs. He might have grown older and gained weight, but that high-pitched kid's giggle is still in there. 'Not far off. There was an old boozer on King Street in Aberdeen that had just gone bust. Not far from the uni halls of residence. I thought that the students would like a bit of live music, and I was right. I borrowed the money from the old man and paid him back inside two years. I now work with a couple of people who partner me on the pubs.'

'Like who?'

'Like the Tom—' He doesn't finish the word. 'It doesn't matter, you wouldn't know them. Anyway, it's been my life since.'

'Why stay in Fraserburgh?'

'It's my home. I know most kids move on from here, but when I finished uni, I wanted to come back. I like this town, and I like these people. I like the simple stuff that this place offers. Chatting to punters on Mid Street on a Saturday morning. Watching the football when Fraserburgh play down at Bellslea Park. There's, what, twelve thousand people in the town, and I still feel like I know most of them. That can't be true, but this is a close-knit community.'

'A bit too close-knit?'

'What's wrong with that? The town's a wee outpost on the fringes of Scotland. You visit Fraserburgh for a reason. Few pass through. Why would you? Passing from where to where? They always say that John O'Groats is the furthest-flung corner of the mainland. It's not. This is. People go to John O'Groats because it's famous for being remote. But how remote is a place that's swamped by tourists. You know Fraserburgh. You know what it's like. This can be as remote as you want it to be.'

'Charlie, I used to know the town. I've not been back in forty years. I was a kid last time I was here.'

'And that begs the question. Why have you never been back?'

'Are you aware that not long after my dad took me to Glasgow, he died?'

'I heard. Sorry.'

'That's why I didn't come back. I was a kid. An orphan. I had no choice. I was brought up by Aunt Rita. She had no reason to come here.'

'You could have come back later?'

'I always meant to,' I say, taking a sip of my drink. 'But, one day, I woke up, fancied joining the police and I signed up. I got lost in the force and, over the years, there was always a reason not to come here.'

'Blake, we're the same age. And you did, what, thirty years in the force?'

'Yip.'

'So, you joined when, in your early thirties?'

'Again, correct.'

'And you left here when you were what, fourteen?'

'Yip.'

'What about the years between leaving here and the police?'

'School, then not a lot.'

Charlie senses something's amiss. 'So, you just fancied the police?'

'Yes.'

'Come on, Blake, there has to be more. Did you have a uniform fetish, or had you been watching too many cop shows?'

'OK, so maybe there's a bit more to it.'

'Like what?'

The men at the bar are ordering some more drinks; the couple in the booth are lost in each other. 'Why do you want to know?'

'Just catching up. You left not long after your mum died. We never really got to say goodbye.'

Charlie loses himself in his drink for a second, spinning the ice with his finger, dipping a shining, studded gold ring in the liquid.

'Cancer?' he says.

'What?'

'She died of cancer. Your mum.'

'No.'

There's something off-kilter with Charlie. He must know what happened to Mum.

'She took her own life.'

The words are out before I can stop them. The first time I've said them out loud in years.

Charlie looks at me, spinning more ice. His pause is just long enough to throw doubt on what he says next. 'I think I did hear something.'

I sniff a lie.

'Mum overdosed. I think she just wanted the pain to stop. She had so many drugs back then' – I almost say sweeties – 'that she could choose her own timing to leave. I've seen more than a fair share of what drugs do to people. I grew to hate the stuff, hate the dealers and pity the junkies. They weren't the same as Mum, but something about drugs stayed with me. I think that was part of why I joined the police. Early on in the police, I thought about applying for the drugs squad, but I couldn't. Every time I lifted a dealer, it just brought Mum to mind. It took all I had not to beat the bastards into a pulp.'

'And the drugs squad would have been too much.'

'I'd have probably ended up killing someone. But I wanted to do good. Does that sound odd?'

'Not really.'

'So, after a few years, I settled down to a life as a constable. Not a bad life in the end.'

'You never got promoted.'

'Never had the desire.'

Charlie rubs his hands together, a little nervous gesture, reflecting his awkwardness at my confession. 'Aye, well, anyway, maybe I should hiv been in touch by now. I never tried.'

The odd 'hiv', 'wis' and 'wisnae' slip out now and again, betraying his background.

'How did your dad die?' he asks.

'He passed a year and one day after my mother. Her death was his death. He couldn't stand to be here, in Fraserburgh. That's why we left so quickly. It reminded him of Mum. But it turns out he couldn't stand to be anywhere. Dad drank a lot after Mum died. Too much. On the anniversary of the day she died, he went on a bender so extreme that he stole a car. He ploughed the centre lane of Kingsway in Dundee at over a hundred miles an hour, side-swiping a bus before ramming a bridge. I think he was driving to Fraserburgh to visit Mum's grave, something he hadn't done since the funeral. He lasted fifteen hours in intensive care – then I was an orphan and my Aunt Rita's responsibility.'

'I'm sorry.'

'So, where do you live?' I ask, trying to lighten the mood.

He laughs. 'Fucking Dallas. Can you credit it? Me in Dallas.'

Dallas was the name for some of the big houses out at the back of Boothby Road.

He keeps laughing. 'I dinnae credit it. Me and a big hoosie. Where are you?'

'I'm renting. Thinking of buying.'

'Are you staying in town for good?'

'I've not worked that out yet. And while I remember, why did you tell the fare I picked up here to ask me to call you?'

'I saw you draw up in the car through my office window. Thought I'd extend an invite, give you a nudge. Wanted to see if you were avoiding me.'

The bartender comes over. 'Mr Noble, there's a John Lemby on the phone for you?'

Charlie scratches at an eyebrow. 'Tell him I'll call later.'

She doesn't move. 'He says it's urgent.'

'Linn, just tell him, thanks.'

I wait for Charlie to say something. When he doesn't, I do. 'Do you know John Lemby well?'

'More than I want to,' he replies. 'He's bad news. Do you ken him?'

'I only met him for the first time the other day. I was picking his kids up.'

'What do you think?'

'Got a hell of a temper on him.'

'Don't I know it.'

'He beat you up at the car crash on the Rosehearty road?'

Charlie puts down his drink. 'How the hell would you know that? The papers?'

'No. I heard from Conn.'

'I wouldn't say I was beaten up. He caught me from behind with a metal bar.'

'A metal bar? Shit. Conn did say he was drunk.'

Some music rolls in. Background. Gentle. Charlie's smile has gone. 'He's always drunk. He's barred from all my pubs.'

'But you still talk to him?'

*Blake Glover. You want too many answers to too many questions, too quickly.*

Charlie's suspicious. 'Blake, why are you really here?'

'What, back in Fraserburgh?'

'No. Here. Now.'

'You asked me to pop in. Remember, you used the man I picked up the other day to pass on your wishes, and you also left me a phone message. By the way, Doddy said you were only due back from Spain a few days ago, but I saw your picture in the paper with a new pub in Dundee. That was last week.'

'Aye, well.' His mood darkens. 'Doddy Robertson might know a lot of what goes on in this town, but he doesn't know everything. I had to come home early for the pub launch.'

I'm thinking that if John Lemby's been on the phone to Charlie tonight, it could only be for one reason.

'Can I ask you something?' I say.

'To the horn and back, Blake.'

I take a deep breath. 'OK, answer me this. Does John Lemby want you to drive someone to Broch House tonight?'

Charlie doesn't answer. The background music shifts to Ronan Keating killing a Burt Bacharach song. Charlie's thinking about what to say next. He slides out of the booth. 'Not here.'

He urges me to follow him behind the bar. We slip into a small office that accommodates a couple of chairs and a computer-laden desk. A filing cabinet fills one corner. The room has a small window that must look out over the harbour road, but the curtains are shut. I know I've broken Conn's confidence on this, but with Lemby on the rampage and Charlie clearly part of it, now or then, I'm certain that Charlie knows what's what. And if he does, he knows Conn and Doddy are involved.

I drop into one of the seats, placing my glass on the desk.

Charlie doesn't sit. 'Blake, I've thought a lot about meeting you again. I knew you were working for Doddy, and I know what he's up to. It was only a matter of time before you found out. I told Conn that having an ex-policeman wasn't the brightest move Doddy ever made. But she said Doddy liked you, and I vouched for you.'

'Nice to know.'

'I asked a few of my pub pals about you before I did. After all, I haven't seen you in an eon. You were rated as a good policeman. No ambition and a little mouthy at times, but a good one. Only, you have a few skeletons.'

'You had me checked out?' I stifle my surprise.

'Sure. Forty years and then yer back. Why? Before you took up with Doddy I just made a few calls for him. You know what the pub trade's like for getting info.'

'So? You got some feedback on me?' I ask.

'Aye. As I said, you were rated.'

'And?'

'You fucked up.'

'Fucked up?'

I wonder if someone has set up a Wiki page with those words on it. *Blake Glover, an ex-policeman who fucked up*. Charlie moves his weight from one foot to the other.

'Blake, this town isn't a place for secrets.'

'What do you know?'

'You tried to fit up a drug dealer.'

'I tried,' I correct him, 'to put a piece of scum away.'

'I'm not passing judgement on you.'

'Are you sure? Sounds like it to me.'

He decides to sit down. 'Look, what have Conn and Doddy told you?'

'More than I want to know.'

He's struggling to know where to go with this. So would I. Forty years on, and we're at the serious end of a conversation without even doing the reminiscing thing.

'Blake, I knew you when we were kids, and if there's one thing this isn't, it's kid's stuff.'

'Charlie, I'm worried about Conn and Doddy. Lemby seems off the scale.'

'He is. Been trying to get hold of me all night. I haven't seen him since the court case after the car crash. I take it Doddy and Lemby are still running people to the House?'

It's an admission I didn't expect him to make. Lemby has him spooked. 'Yes,' I say. 'One is due tonight?'

'And Conn and Doddy are off-line.'

He gives that a little thought.

'Ah, I get it.' He nods. 'The big question that you're asking yourself is, are you going to help out, if I don't?'

Charlie always was smart.

'Charlie, I don't really know what's going on. What would I be helping out with? I feel like I'm being cornered.'

'I hear you've been snooping around up at Broch House.'

'I should have told the *Press and Journal*; it would have been less public.'

'The place is quiet. Isn't it?'

'As a closed cemetery.'

'What time's the pick-up tonight?'

'Two o'clock. Charlie, tell me – why is Lemby so keen to talk to you?'

Charlie perches on the edge of the desk. 'Blake, don't treat me as dumb! You know why he wants to talk to me.' Then he adds, 'Because I know the score and he's shit scared of Broch House. He can't drive himself and needs someone he can trust.'

'Conn wants me to do the run.'

'With Lemby?'

'Yes.'

'And Lemby is OK with that?'

'I've no idea. Why in hell did you get involved with whatever is going on up there?'

Charlie takes his time. No doubt working over where we are in all this. Me. Him. Friends back then. But now, for all he knows, I'm freelancing for my old work colleagues, and for all I know, Charlie's as crooked as a broken walking stick and running a prostitute ring for pensioners.

He decides to open up. 'I was dumb really. I didn't need the agro. Ye ken. The pub business was doing well. I just wanted it to do better, quicker.'

*'Charlie, sit down.'*

*'Blake, shut up.'*

*It's how we flew. Back then.*

Charlie hasn't changed.

'Whatever it is they've been doing up there, it's been going on for a while,' he says. 'I made the mistake of telling Conn about how I wanted to speed things up on the pub front. She told Wendy, and Lemby was at my door in a shot. He said that he had a way to earn serious cash. Easy money. He needed my connections with the fishing guys. He's persona non grata with them.'

'A hundred thousand a pop,' I say.

Charlie's face creases. 'Doddy and Conn *have* been talking.'

'A lot of cash.'

'Lemby was right when he said easy money. I built my next pub on the back of a year of runs. And built two more six months later.'

'Who are the people that are being transported?'

Charlie slugs some liquid. 'Screwed if I know.'

'You must know?'

'Not a clue. The whole game is played very close to the chest. Money in a bag, left at the annexe for us. Staff won't, or can't, talk. We picked up and dropped off. We arranged the boat, paid off the crew. If I queried it, Lemby would say the words "gift horse" and we'd do another run.'

I'm not buying it all, but I press on. 'How long did you ship people in and out for?'

'A while. Someone on the continent brought them out to sea from the Netherlands, sometimes Belgium, and we arranged for them to be met halfway across. Then we'd do the same in reverse to send them back.'

'And the boats you used, will no one talk – *has* no one talked – about picking up people in the middle of the sea?'

'Given what we pay, no way. Plus the guys up at the house are scary as hell.'

'A hundred K a pop.'

'That's why I do know one thing about the people we have shipped: they must have been seriously wealthy. Most didn't speak or wouldn't speak or had been told not to speak. They all dressed like tramps, but some had watches that cost more than my hoosie.'

He stops. Then says, 'Look, I'll deny all of this if you say a word.'

I lean back. 'Charlie, I don't give a shit. I just need to help Conn and Doddy.'

'Then my advice is simple. Get the hell to Aberdeen for the night and let Lemby sort it oot.'

I might have broken Conn's confidence, but I wasn't going to pull all her washing out for Charlie in order to tell him why leaving was not possible. I make it simple. 'I can't. Flat can't.'

'Why not? The way I see it is that, at the moment, you could walk away. If you pick up tonight, then you're in it, swimming in it!'

'Why are you telling me this, Charlie? You could have just said nothing.'

'Really? With what you know already, what would I have said? No comment? I'm talking because these guys are serious guys. I'm talking because we were once friends. I'm giving you a warning: these guys play for keeps.'

'I'm surprised Lemby's not here by now, Charlie?'

Charlie plays my sentence through his skull. 'Fuck. I should have told Linn to say I wasn't here, shouldn't I? Of course, he could be on his way.'

# THIRTEEN

*'Fate'*

'I'd say he might be flying down here as we speak,' I say.

Charlie groans. 'OK, my old school friend. We need to exit stage right. Find some space. Give this a wee bit more thought.'

He's up and at the door with the sort of agility that I used to admire.

As he enters the bar, he shouts to Linn. 'We're shutting early. Make it quick. I want the lights oot and everyone away as soon as possible.'

He turns to the two men and the couple that make up his clientele. 'Mikey, Jimmy, Rachel, Steve – I need to close the place early. The Dumb Duck is still open. Yir on free drinks up there if you leave right now. Family emergency.'

They all look at him. Then stand up and are soon on the move. No questions.

Two minutes later, the lights are out, Linn is locking the front door, having switched on the alarm. Charlie chats on the mobile and warns The Dumb Duck, one of his other pubs, about the free drinkers that are on their way.

'We'll take my car,' he says to me as he walks down the pub stairs. 'We can pick yours up later.'

'Scared he'll key your paintwork when he finds out you're not here?'

'He's capable of a lot worse. I'd also whip off the taxi signs if I were you.'

I jog over, bundle them up, throwing them in the boot. I notice the box that Wendy Lemby gave me for Doddy is still there. I ignore it.

Once I've used my yoga skills to climb into the passenger seat of Charlie's Porsche, he asks Stuttgart's finest engineering for a little help. We zip along the harbour and follow the road to the beach.

We strobe beneath some of the alien-designed white streetlights that are spread across the town.

I consult my ageing mobile phone. It's ten minutes past ten. We've a little under four hours before the pick-up is due.

Charlie turns off on to the road that runs past the cemetery and out by the golf course. There's a stonemason on the corner, just after the cemetery's main gates. I think my mum's gravestone was carved by them. Charlie pulls in front of the business, his headlights lighting up the sample gravestones that are lined up behind a small white fence.

I turn to look at the cemetery. The main gate is locked tight. I'm so aware that I should have visited by now, but I just don't feel ready.

Charlie kills the engine and the lights. We sit in darkness.

'People will talk,' I say. 'This car's a bit conspicuous for late-night smooching.'

'Blake, you were never my type.'

'I'm hurt.' Then I get serious. 'Do you think Lemby will try your other pubs?' I ask, knowing the answer but just looking for a way into the conversation again.

'Probably,' Charlie replies.

His phone buzzes. Charlie blanks it.

'Does Lemby have your mobile number?' I ask.

'No. Not this one. I've got four phones. This one is for the select few.'

A few seconds later his voicemail bleeps. He listens to the message. He puts the phone on speaker and replays the message so I can hear it.

Lemby's voice enters the car. *'Charlie, answer yer fucking phone or call me back. We need to blether right fucking now.'*

Lemby sounds out of his head. So much for Charlie's private phone.

'You know him. What do you think he'll do if we blank him?' I say.

'Knowing Lemby, something incredibly fucking stupid. He's nae a man to put too much thought into things. He'll try to do the pick-up himself. Maybe give Zach Zane a call. Whoever Zach sends will tell that story more than once. That'll fry Zach's arse. The guys behind this won't be happy if Lemby introduces a stranger.'

'I'm a stranger.'

'Fuck sake, Blake. What makes you think that?'

'I've not been involved so far.'

Charlie rubs the dashboard. 'You work for Doddy and Conn, you ken me – do you think they don't know you exist?'

'I'm ex-polis.'

'Ex-polis that fucked up. Why do you think Doddy employed you? You're not averse to breaking the law.'

'I'm not a criminal.'

'Fitting up a dealer – that doesn't qualify? Anyway, I wouldn't be surprised if Doddy didn't have to get the OK from Broch House on hiring you.'

That stops me in my tracks.

'Maybe.' I ask something that's been bugging me. 'Doddy takes the passengers to his home. Why doesn't he take them straight to Broch House from the harbour?'

'How do you know he does that? Did Conn tell you?'

'Mr Lachlan across the landing said there had been lots of visitors. That doesn't tie with Doddy's isolation.'

'Your years in the police weren't wasted. Why do you think he takes them there first?'

I take a stab at an answer. 'To make sure he's not followed?'

'To make sure the *passenger* isn't being followed. That's why he has to sit it out. To be sure no one is on their tail. If he takes a tail to Broch House, he'd be mince. It was my idea; when I did it. We used a flat I own. Checked outside until we were blue and then took them up to the House. Doddy does the same at his place. Do you know that Lemby's convinced that we might be killed one day? That the passengers have people after them. I laughed at that . . . at first.'

'Now it's not so funny. You said it yourself. A hundred grand is not kid's stuff. I've known people killed over a tenner.'

Charlie ducks a little as a car runs by us. 'I know that. That's why I got out. There's only so long that sort of shit can go on before something comes crashing down. That's why you should just piss off.'

I ignore the advice. 'Is that why Lemby gave you the beating?'

'Stop calling it that. But yes. I pissed off on the night of a run. I wanted oot. Lemby made the delivery so drunk he could hardly stand up. After that, he came looking for me at my hoosie. I saw him pull up and got the hell away. I thought I'd lost him, but when I was trying to get back home, he rammed me. Hid in a farm track and rammed me with that stupid white-on-white Range

Rover of his. He jumped out, hit me over the head. It was his way of saying you don't quit.'

'And the police just happened to be there?'

'He'd been spotted earlier by someone who phoned in because he was driving like an idiot. They were out looking for him and came across us. Thank God. He wis too drunk to know when to stop.'

'And with him in prison, the people up at Broch House came after you to keep the deliveries going?'

'You can see why they rated you as a policeman.' His face is lit up by another passing car. 'Of course, they did.'

'And you declined?'

'That's when I found oot you dinnae say no to them. They set fire to my shed, killed my Alsatian and poisoned the fish in my pond – all in one night. Kane, my dog, was sleeping in my bedroom when they slit his throat. Me and the wife were two feet away. *Two feet* and we didn't hear a thing. I've an alarm system recommended by an ex-MI6 security expert, and it was worth shit. So, I kept right on delivering until Lemby got oot.'

'And when he got out of jail, he wanted back in.'

'He also wanted a split of the money I'd made while he was inside. I told him to fuck off and that I was done.'

'And he just let you go?'

'I know a few guys that hire out their muscle. He still threatened and threatened, but then he suddenly just shut up. I knew he had found someone else. I just didn't know, and really didn't care, who.'

'When did you find out Doddy and Conn were running people with Lemby?'

He pauses. 'A little later.'

A lie?

Two cars appear, headlights dancing in front of them. Both are moving as if they are being hunted by a cheetah, reflecting the love that some of the locals have for speed. Late nights, quiet roads, a lack of alternative leisure and teenage blood burning with post-pubescent testosterone will do that. This isn't the subtlest of parking spots. Charlie's Porsche might not be a rarity around here, but it'll be spotted by someone.

'And whoever it is that's running this whole show just let you walk away?' I ask.

Charlie eyes the cars outside. 'Apart from having all my fish poisoned again.'

'Why?'

'A warning. Keep your mouth shut.'

'And now you're talking to me?'

He shakes his head. 'Come on, Blake, you're supposed to be a good piggy.'

It hits me. 'Shit. They think I know about it all already. That's it.'

'As good as. Since Doddy took on the transportation with Lemby, he's lost a fistful of drivers, save you.'

'I heard. I assumed they just couldn't put up with his attitude.'

'There's that. But whoever "they" are, they assumed Doddy's drivers might be in the know, that Doddy had talked to them. Anonymous threats of a very vicious nature were doled out, telling them to keep quiet. The drivers quit to get away from it all.'

'You know this for a fact?'

'Not directly. I'm making an educated assumption. I asked one a very innocent question about why he left Doddy, and he looked like he wis going to cack himself there and then. Look, Blake, I'm scared of these guys. Kane. *Two fucking feet* from my bed.'

So, it wasn't Doddy that drove the other drivers away. And then I'd gone up and talked to Tomas about the annexe. Putting myself right in the firing line.

'So why haven't I been threatened?'

'No idea, Blake. Did you miss the message?'

'If they kill dogs in the owner's bedroom, they're not about being subtle. I think I'd know if I'd been threatened.'

'As I said, maybe they checked you out and think you're OK.'

My phone rings. I check it. Lemby.

'OK, Charlie, so what's the plan?'

I wait for Charlie to come up with the obvious answer. And the answer sits there, nestled between us, looking up, begging to be set free. 'Charlie, why open up to me?'

'I already telt you.'

'I don't buy that. This conversation has the sniff of planned written across the back of your hand. What about Mormond Hill or stealing old man Chiltern's bike or setting fire to Morag Brown's washing? What about the time you nearly died on the wheelbarrow down at Broadsea? Isn't that how old friends, who haven't seen each other since school, start the conversation? At the very least, you could have admitted to kissing Carol Teach.'

'Never happened!' he snaps back.

'It so did. In my mum and dad's bathroom of all places.'

'Never.'

We actually laugh. Just a little.

'Blake, think on it,' he says. 'All of this was carved in stone as soon as you started to work for Doddy. We're here because there's no other place this was going to go.'

'If it was that obvious, why not warn me?'

'Because there was still a chance you'd quit. Head home.'

'And when I didn't?'

'Fate.'

'In other words, I was always going to help when it came down to it.'

'You work for Doddy, you know me. You decided to hang around. It was only a matter of time, Blake, only a matter of time.'

It's now quarter to eleven and Charlie's phone rings once more. Then mine. Then Charlie's. Then mine. Every call is Lemby.

He's more than desperate.

I let a large breath drift over my tongue. 'Charlie, I think one of us is going to have to make a delivery tonight.'

'To the horn and back, Blake.'

'To the horn and back, Charlie.'

# FOURTEEN

*'Pulling a Fast One'*

'OK, so who phones Lemby?' I ask as another headlight sweeps over us.

'Who do you think? I do and you get to take an early night.'

'What?' I speak too loud for the confined space. 'Do I hell. I go with him and *you* get the early night.'

'And how does that make sense? Whit are you thinking aboot? *You* can still walk away. I can't. Lemby and I do the deed, then we work out what comes next.'

'Charlie Noble, I thought you a touch smarter than that. I'm already on the hook. OK, so they haven't threatened me, but as you say, they will assume I know. Whoever they are. Whether I go tonight or not makes no difference. I'm screwed. Let me take the pain. Why would you want to get back in? I'm not going to let you ride with that nutter on your own. He's as likely to push you in the harbour as anything else. He's just spent six months in prison, and he'll blame you for that. With me there, he'll need to behave.'

'And what if he doesn't want you there?'

'Why do you think he's ringing me? Look, I got a lad fired, maybe worse. I've screwed up with Terry Lang, and both Doddy and Conn are counting on me, so I'm in.'

'Not without me.'

'Fine. Deal done. We both go.'

Charlie picks up his phone. 'I want to make the bastard sweat for this, though. Claim neither of us are doing it, and he'll need to find another way. Then just when he begs, I'll agree, on the basis that we're well and truly finished after this one. How does that sound?'

'I can see why you're a good businessman. Do you want to make the call on your own?'

'I don't care. Are you sure this is what you want?'

'If you don't phone him, I'll make the call.'

When he phones, he does it on speaker. 'John.'

*'Where the fuck are ye?'*

'In the house. Why? Where should I be?'

*'I've been trying to get a hold of ye for fucking ages. Why don't you answer yer phone?'*

Charlie snorts. 'Because I was watching a movie. Now, what do you want?'

*'Ye ken fucking fine what I want?'*

'Do I? Enlighten me.'

Lemby splutters. *'Stop screwing with me. I know Doddy's out of action, he's spue.'*

'I know Doddy's sick, but I hear he's going to be OK. Why? Are you wanting to go down and see him? A bit late tonight. Is that why you are calling, for a lift?'

*'I don't want to see Doddy. Stop pissing me aroon. Wendy got a message from that ex-pig saying tonight was fixed, but how? Conn is in Aberdeen.'*

'Conn?' Charlie's enjoying this. 'What has she to do with anything?'

*'Ye fucking ken what I want,'* Lemby says. *'There's a pick-up to do.'*

'A pick-up. John, I think you've got things a little confused. Doddy runs the taxi company, not me.'

More spluttering. *'Fur fuck's sake, what are ye talking aboot? Just come and get me and we'll get this done.'*

'Do what?'

Lemby flies into a rage. *'Do. Do. I'll fucking do ye. Fucking come ben and pick me up or . . .'*

'Or what, John?'

*'I'll . . . I'll . . . I'll fucking firebomb yer hoosie,'* he screams.

Even in his fucked-up state, Lemby realizes that he's gone too far. He tries to rescue it. *'Charlie, I fucking didn't mean that.'*

'OK, John. Calm it doon,' Charlie says. 'Let's get this perfectly straight. You need to do this run tonight, and you need me. They know who I am. I know the score. I run with you and they stay sweet. You ring the changes, bring in a stranger, and they could fuck you right up.'

*'Tell me something I dinnae ken.'*

'And I'm assuming you've already spent the money, so I get nothing for this.'

*'I'll see ye right.'*

'Sure you will. With whit?'

*'I've more buckie coming in.'*

'More money? From where, John? From future runs? And who'll do them with you?'

*'Doddy's wifie.'*

'You think Doddy will let that happen.'

*'What's he going to do? He's fucked.'*

'He might be fucked, but I've got a mouth on me, and I ken your Wendy must be suspicious as hell.'

*'Keep her oot of it.'*

'I will, John. I will. But only if you agree to something.'

*'What?'*

'After this, you're on your own. No Doddy. No Conn. No me. You go fix this shit.'

*'Is that it?'*

'I mean it. Or I speed-dial Wendy.'

*'Fucking deal!'* No hesitation. No consideration. The relief in his voice is palpable.

Charlie closes off with, 'Which boat is it?'

*'Calder Glen.'*

'OK. I'll call.'

Charlie hangs up.

'Charlie,' I say, 'you might be about to make the worst mistake of your life, but the bit about Wendy is genius.'

'I'm not that clever. I'm sure she knows. But Lemby doesn't think she does and that's all that counts.'

'What's with the no money bit?'

'We get paid up front. If Lemby doesn't deliver, they'll come looking for his sorry backside and cash back. That's why he's in a panic. He's spent the money. He's between a rock and another dirtier rock that's got his balls in its sights.'

That gels with what Conn told me. I stare through the windscreen. Behind the stonemason's shop lie the sand dunes that guard the beach. The play area of all play areas for kids. The largest dune is silhouetted by a half-moon. At least we're not in looney tunes, full-lunar territory. Except, maybe we are. Once I step into this, I'm way beyond the pale. Meting out justice on the streets of Glasgow from the moral high ground is easier than from the amoral swamp that comes when you've walked on both sides of the criminal fence.

I spent my life trying to avoid indiscretions. I failed a lot but justified my slips in the name of securing a conviction. But then, somehow, bit by bit, I'd found myself walking on the wrong side of the thin blue line more than I would have liked. But what I'm about to do is to go full rogue. Not just because people smuggling is illegal, but because what I know should have been passed on when I visited the police station. If Kyle Anderson gets a sniff of all of this, he won't be slow in playing back my indignation, pointing out my double standards and banging me up for a long stretch.

Beyond this, there is a whole new land called *I don't know*. If Lemby's paymasters are in the habit of slicing dogs' throats or dropping weed killer into your fishpond, you can take it to the bank that there's far more to this than skipping a few smelly individuals past the UK border guards. This is not about people taking a quick break in Scotland, no matter how hard Visit Scotland would like to believe the country has that sort of pull. Those that don't return from the annexe, the three that Conn knew of, are even more of a worry. Where are they? If they didn't leave, what happened to them? And are Kristina and Tomas two more on the list of the 'non-returned'?

'You never mentioned me on the call to Lemby,' I point out as Charlie guns the car, pointing us back to town.

Charlie has his eyes fixed ahead. 'I need you up my sleeve.'

'Charlie, don't think of doing this without me. That isn't happening.'

'I'm not.' He downshifts to turn. 'If I'd mentioned you, he would have lost the rag. He might have wanted you earlier, but he'll take me over you any day for the run. These guys don't like strangers.'

'And he won't lose it when he sees me later?'

Charlie flicks the Porsche on to Seaforth Street. 'It'll be too late by then. Right now, I'll drop you at your flat and pick you up later.'

A few minutes later, we pull up at my place. A woman, entombed in a jet-black overcoat, is dragging a small terrier behind her. The dog stops to pee on a lamppost. As soon as it's finished, the woman rips the dog along the pavement, wanting home. Wanting out of the cold.

'What are you going to do now?' I ask Charlie before getting out.

His tone is weary. 'Close my eyes for a bit. This could be a long night. I'll pick you up about half past one-ish. We'll then get Lemby.'

'Give me your mobile number,' I say.

'Why?'

'So I can sell it to a marketing firm to noise you up. Why do you think?'

He reads it out and I dial it into my phone. I call him and he puts my number in his machine.

The world is a quiet place as I begin to extract myself from the car.

'Blake.' Charlie puts out a hand to touch me as he speaks. 'You really don't need to come. This isn't a thing you drop lightly once you've picked it up. We're not loons and this isn't playtime, ye ken?'

'I tell you what, if you confess you kissed Carol Teach, I'll think about staying home.'

'Fuck off. I could tell you she was my first blowjob, and you'd say thanks for the info and still come along for the ride.'

'You can't blame a guy for trying. See you later.'

I watch the Porsche growl away, and I'm aware I still have a get-out-of-jail-free card. Just go for a very long walk and let Charlie deal with Lemby and the run. It's a thought I know will be bouncing around right up until the moment I get back into the Porsche. The two of them could easily do this without me. It would solve Conn's problem and keep me out of it.

I let myself into the main entrance of my flat. I climb the stairs. Charlie's idea of a rest has appeal. Then I remember my car is down at the harbour. I'll need it in the morning. Some air might not be a bad idea. I turn around, walk back into the night.

As I leave, I put my hands in my pocket, feeling my phone. Strange that it's stopped ringing. The local populace might have sympathy for Doddy, but they can't *all* have heard he's in hospital. Then I remember that Charlie said he tried to call the taxi number earlier and got flipped to Conn's voicemail. She must have diverted it.

My phone rings.

It's Conn.

'Hi, Conn, any update?'

*'Doddy's out for the count. They gave him something. The doctor says he should sleep through.'*

'Do you need me to come and pick you up?'

*'Terry's phoned a friend. Her friend is going to put us both up. I want to be here in the morning when Doddy wakes up.'*

The real reason she phoned is evident in her next question. *'Blake, are you going to pick up . . .?'*

'It's sorted'

*'So that's a yes?'*

'It's sorted.'

*'What does that mean?'*

'You worry about Doddy, and I'll worry about the pick-up. All you need to know is that it's sorted. And did you take the taxi number divert off me?'

*'Yes. I wanted to give you some space to think. I've recorded a message that tells people we'll be back the day after tomorrow.'*

'Why so long?'

*'If you are up all night tonight, you'll need some sleep time. Or does this "sorted" thing not involve you?'*

She's way ahead of me. She had it figured out from the get-go that I'd help out. Conn has a way of drawing you in. She's not manipulative in a bad way. She just knows how to get you on side, letting you think it was your decision all along. It was a matter of when, not if. 'When' was the only way forward. And when the 'when' becomes 'now', this could be a shitstorm.

'Conn,' I say, 'it's being taken care of. Go back with Terry, open a bottle of wine, then get your head down. I'll call when it's all over.'

*'Blake, you need to take care. I'm grateful for your help, but this is asking a lot.'*

'Conn, just take care of yourself and Doddy. I need to go.'

*'Before you do, please promise you'll not do anything dumb.'*

'Conn, this whole thing is dumb!'

*'I need you to do this for Doddy, but not at any cost.'*

'I'm doing this for you as well.'

*'I know, and that's the bit that worries me. I'm Doddy's girl first and foremost.'*

'What does that mean?'

*'You know.'*

She kills the call, leaving me with a sense of numbness in my gut. Each conversation I have, each decision I make is a shovel to soft soil at the moment. I'm digging so fast I've not stepped back to admire my handiwork, or to reproach my efforts. And what does 'Doddy's girl' mean?

My car is where I left it. I had a notion that Lemby might have recognized it, if he'd come to the pub, and played smash and trash. I do a look round, just in case the halfwit has decided to stake it out.

I recall the box Wendy Lemby gave me is still in the boot and remind myself to take it out when I get back to the flat.

When I get back home, I grab the box, take it up the stairs, dropping it in the corner of the living room.

I'm too awake for sleep. I mix up a couple of extra-strength coffees just to kick any potential sleep bunny right in the nuts. With the fridge empty, I suffer the bitterness of both drinks black. I flick on the telly, but I haven't the concentration for it. I open the laptop but even the wonders of the internet hold no fascination for me. A few unread novels lie next to the TV, but they'll lie there a while yet.

There's a crack in the corner of one of the windows. It's been snaking across the pane for days. I mentally add it to the growing list of defects that I need to contact the letting agent about.

I check the time. I've still over an hour and a half to kill until Charlie rides in for the main event.

As I wear the foam on the sofa a little more into my shape, I sip at the coffee. I press play on my ancient iPod, and John Grant tells me why he's the Queen of Denmark.

Charlie seemed reluctant to say how long he'd been in the people-smuggling business. Or how many he had helped transport, but if he could buy three pubs in a year on half the earnings, it indicates a fair traffic. Of course, it would all depend on how he cut up the money with Lemby.

A hundred K a run sounds lucrative, but there was paying for the boat, paying for the boat's crew and paying for their silence – although slit dog throats might negate the need for that last payment. All would come at a cost. Then there was the Lemby/partner split. So where would that take them? Twenty-five thousand each. Fifty for the boat. Is that too much to recruit a fishing boat and crew? Not likely. Fishermen are not a stupid breed. They'd know the risks and the downside for people smuggling is prison time. Screwing with the UK Border Force is not a recommended hobby.

With an hour left until Charlie's arrival, I head for a pee. I'm standing, waiting on what is becoming less easy to decant as birthdays fly by, looking at the small, frosted window that provides ventilation and light to the toilet.

I finish by dipping my hands under the tap to wash them.

A car revs its engine. I wonder if Charlie has turned up early. But the note is all wrong. Higher, a screamer, maybe a motorbike, not a car.

Charlie's words come back to me.
*About half past one-ish. About? Ish?*
I grab my car keys and sprint down the stairs.
Charlie Noble's pulling a fast one on me.

# FIFTEEN

## *'Cost'*

A*bout half past one-ish.* Not at half past one. About. Charlie wouldn't say 'about' anything. He would have been specific. It's his way. There's no 'ish' in his world; at least there wasn't when he was a kid. The pick-up from the boat is set for two. *About half past one-ish* means he's going to do this on his own, hoping I'll stay in my flat until it's too late.

I don't bother trying his mobile. If he hasn't left yet, I want to catch him by surprise. I coax my car to life. I don't know exactly where he lives, but I know it's Dallas. That's not far from my flat.

Fog is rolling in again. I've travelled less than two hundred yards when I slam on my brakes. Squeals echo off the houses around me. I do a fast three-point turn and head away from Dallas. It occurs to me that if Charlie's been able to contact the boat, pulling the pick-up forward, then I don't have the time to hunt his house down. I need to be at the harbour.

I zip into town, taking it easy as I pass the police station, when all I want to do is plant my right foot to the floor.

On reflection, the conversation between us in the pub and in Charlie's car had been him sussing out what I knew, rather than the reminiscing of two old friends reuniting. Charlie had no intention of letting me ride shotgun on this. No wonder we jumped from reminiscing to the serious stuff so quickly. If I'm right and he's pulled the pick-up forward, then he *could* be trying to protect me. Or there's another side to this story that I haven't figured out yet.

The fish market – that's where Conn said they picked up last time – sits at the beach end of the harbour on Harbour Road. I loop round Dalrymple Hall – thinking that blanking Terry when she collared me in there would have been rude but sensible; thinking that some of this would have still come home to roost anyway; that fate was sending me this way all the time.

I park up a street back from the fish market. Just across from the rear of the hall.

A man is walking away, his gait suggesting a night in the pub behind him. I wait until he's a little further away before getting out. I lock the car manually, not wanting flashing lights and the beep-beep of the key fob.

I spot a few boats bobbing in the water in the marina. That space was once wall-to-wall with fishing boats. No longer. There are a few leisure craft, but they are thin on the briny at this time of year. To be fair, pleasure boats are lacking at most times of the year here. The eastern shore of Scotland hasn't the same attraction as its western sister. The wilds of the Hebrides and the shelter of the Clyde Firth outpunch anything on offer around this shore. A shame. The coast along here can be stunning.

I turn the corner that leads to the fish market, trying to keep it casual. No slinking around. No head down. Not doing furtive. Those are the best ways to draw attention.

A small car park lies between me and the marina. It's empty.

As I approach the fish market, I slow down. Listening for voices.

Nothing.

The market comes into view. It's about a hundred yards long and fifteen feet or so high. Red bricks make up the bottom of the building, before brown cladding rises to the roof. Seven large red doors, which, during the day, are guarded by plastic slats to keep the cold in, serve to allow the crates of fish to be loaded into the waiting trucks. The whole place is air-conditioned. I can see the A/C units sitting on top of the building.

There's no reason for anyone to be down here at this time of night. It's a pure industrial play – the only nod to leisure is Angela's Tea Room, and it shut its doors hours ago.

I reach the corner of the street, checking once more for voices. Hearing nothing, I walk out.

I see a Porsche.

*Charlie Noble, you're a bastard.*

The car is sitting, exhaust leaking into the night, in front of the last door of the fish market. There's the outline of a single person sitting in the passenger seat. The figure looks too big for the Porsche, and I only know one person of that scale who would be in Charlie's car. I cross the road, stroll to the vehicle, keeping an eye out for Charlie. Fog swirls around me as I knock on the car window.

I have to wait while Lemby figures out how the window mechanism works. He gets it to zip down and squints up at me. Even in the half light of the streetlights, his eyes are a shocking wire diagram of red veins.

'What the fuck?' he slurs. He's coated in sweat.

'Hi, John.'

He still hasn't recognized me. 'What?'

'How's Charlie?'

A lightbulb pops. 'The fucking pig!'

'Ex-pig to you.'

I'm sure if I could open his head, it would be fizzing and short-circuiting.

'What are ye doing here? Piss aff!'

I bend down. 'John, I'm here offering my aid for free, and this is how you greet me.'

He fumbles at the door handle. I'm thinking he'd like a swing at me. He begins to open the door, and I slam my arse into it. He yells as it catches him on the hand.

'Ye fucker!'

The sweet smell of recent vomit hangs on his lips.

'John,' I say, 'just sit tight. We'll wait for Charlie. It'll be easier on you.'

'I'll kick yer head in!'

'John, we've had this conversation once already. Do I need to call Wendy and have her slap your wrist again?'

He pushes on the door and I put my full weight into shoving back. I feel the car metal bend a little. I may have put a dent in Charlie's classy car.

'Yer fucking dead!'

'John, I'm here to help.' He gives another shove. He has some strength. I can't hold out for long. Maybe this was a mistake. Should have waited for Charlie.

'I'll show ye help, arsehole,' he shouts.

He rams his shoulder into the door. I'm thrown back. I trip on a loose paving stone. I swear. My anger bunny pops up and I kick at the door handle, slamming it shut. There's no doubt there will be a dent this time.

'John,' I say as I lean on the door. 'Calm down.'

'Don't tell me tae fucking keep my ginger doon.'

To my relief, Charlie appears, walking quickly around the corner of the fish market. He has a small man beside him. He sees me and stops. He lifts both hands in the air, then slams them to his side. He reaches the car and, before I can talk, pushes the new man through the driver's door, into the back seat. He slams the door shut.

Lemby's still pushing and shouting, 'What's he doing here? We need tae go. I'm begging for it here. Wendy dumped my stash, Noble, she dumped it. Found it in the garage and dumped it. Whit was she thinking aboot? I've none, none!'

Charlie shoves me out of the way and leans down. 'John, shut the fuck up. I'll deal with this. You know the game. Say nowt while in transit.'

John is fit to burst, but he keeps quiet. Charlie gives me a thump in the chest. 'Over there.' He walks to the fish-market door. 'And what the fuck do you think you're doing here?'

'What I said I was going to do all along. Only you thought you'd piss off and do it without me.'

'Are you dumb? I'm trying to keep you out of this.'

'I don't want to be kept out.'

'How the fuck did you know I'd do it alone?'

'About half past one-ish.'

'What?'

I repeat. 'You said *about* half past one-*ish*. Since when do you do about or ish?'

Then he gets it. 'Oh, very fucking clever. Amazing you never made detective.'

He sighs, stands back.

'I've no idea what they'll do when four of us arrive,' he says.

'What can they do? I'm in the frame anyway. Don't you just hand the goods over to the staff and leave?'

'Yes, but they watch us.'

I can't help but look around. I see nothing out of the ordinary. 'So, they are probably watching us right now?'

'Probably.'

'Then let's go. It'll look far worse if I don't go with you. That'll raise more questions than me coming along. Ex-copper. Where might I be going? Off to my friends for a chat in the police station?'

I know I've placed him in a bind. He grunts, 'OK, get in. And shut up. I know that's hard for you, but please shut up. It's one of the rules. Nae talking to, or in front of, the cargo. Full stop!'

'Cargo?'

'Aye, cargo.'

'I'll be as quiet as a sleeping baby.'

'We need to go straight there this time. No hanging around. Lemby won't last if we hole up as usual. I hope the hell they're chilled about this. If we're followed—'

'Lemby won't last – what does that mean?' I ask.

'Nothing, just leave it.'

'Charlie, if they are hanging around at this time of night watching us, why don't they just pick the people up?'

'What and go down like a lead submarine if the Border guys have latched on to things? They can deny everything up at the House. If someone asks, they just say they booked in a guest. Get caught down here and . . .'

I understand.

'We need to move,' he adds. 'Lemby was in The Dumb Duck earlier. Shouting his mouth off. He's in a bad way. Hell knows who heard, who's talked. Let's get this over with.'

'Charlie?'

'What?'

'What's going on up at Broch House? What's with Lemby and Wendy dumping his stash? What stash?'

'You don't need to know right now. Just leave it at that. *Please*.'

'It has to be bad.'

'Leave it, please, Blake. *Just leave it*.'

I don't leave it. 'I mean, these guys could just fly in from wherever. Why all the cloak and dagger?'

'Honestly, Blake, if we get rid of this guy, we can say goodbye to it all. Just let it fucking lie for the moment.'

He opens the driver's door, allowing me to climb in next to the passenger. The rear seats are more suitable if you're a kid or missing your legs. I'm rammed up against the passenger. The whiff of fish from him is strong. Lemby turns to me. Charlie hisses, putting his finger to his mouth before Lemby can speak. Lemby gives me a look that can be translated as *Fuck off and die*. His skin appears yellow in the interior light.

The passenger observes me. He looks tired, a little lost, but a pair of well-manicured hands tell me he's used to the good life. This is no working fisherman. This must all be a bit of a culture shock.

As Charlie opens up the throttle, I think about talking to the passenger. His eyes are bright, smart. This is no dumb idiot trying to run to a better life. This is someone with intelligence, who, for some reason, seems happy to dress as a hardline piscatorial fan. Whatever pot lies at the end of this rainbow must be a cracker – something worth putting your life in the hands of strangers who don't talk to you, who treat you like cattle and, in the case of Lemby, howl of vomit. I try to imagine under what circumstances someone would subject themselves to all of this. Swapped out between boats in the middle of the North Sea at night, little more than a parcel being delivered. Although the man seems a relaxed, willing parcel.

We leave Fraserburgh behind. The occasional oncoming car headlight and the glow from the dash provide illumination. I keep watching the passenger. Noting detail when he comes into view. He's in his late twenties, maybe younger. Heavy lips, thick nose and well-cared-for skin that has a soft glow.

He raises his arm to adjust himself. Gold flashes. The watch on his wrist is a chunky item. Expensive-looking. Manicured hands, well-toned skin, gold watch and I know we are transporting expensive flesh.

I still wonder why the hell you would subject yourself to this if you are that well-heeled. Private jets are ten a penny in wealthy-land.

Occasionally, Lemby looks over his shoulder. His face awash with sweat. The veins in his eyes seem to be spreading to his face.

Charlie nearly misses the side road leading to Broch House. We're all thrown forward as he brakes. When we reach the gates, Charlie gets out. He fiddles with the squawk box. The gates swing open as he climbs back into the car, and I slide down, low.

A few minutes later, all our heels are cooling in the small car park next to the main house. It only has one other car in it. A black Audi.

Lemby begins to haul himself out. Charlie has to give him a hand. The passenger watches with an amused grin. Charlie heaves John into the night air, then pulls back the seat to let the passenger out.

Charlie leans in. 'Blake, stay the fuck down, out of sight; they may not see you. Do not get out, Blake. *Do not get out!*'

He closes the door.

The three walk away towards a small path leading to some trees. I'm on my Jack Jones.

After twenty minutes, my nerves, already strung-out, are tight enough for Nigel Kennedy to play an entire concert on. From where

I'm sitting, I can see the entrance to Broch House. Dark, no sign of life. The moon is playing tag with the clouds. Leaves and branches rustle. A high wind was predicted. It sounds like it's here.

The back of the car is cramped. I'm still trying to keep my head low, but I need to stretch and can't do so without sitting up. I massage my legs, one at a time, kneading the muscle of my calves with my knuckles to loosen them, to give me a little relief.

There's a crack, as somewhere a branch snaps. The gusts of wind are building. The weather can change with the click of your fingers in these climes. The noise of the wind carving between the trees and the splendour of the Porsche engineers' soundproofing will cover the sound of anyone approaching.

I raise my head a little. The path the three took is now invisible. The swaying branches robbing the ground of light.

Five more minutes and I can't take it any longer. I'm not the best at waiting. I'd been co-opted on a few stakeouts back in Glasgow and found I didn't have the temperament for it. I was told I talked too much. I push the driver's seat forward, reaching for the door handle. I crack the lock. The night sounds whistle in. The wind catches the door, pulling it from my hand. The interior light flashes on.

*Shit!*

I quickly slide a foot across the sill. My backside follows. I drop my foot down on to the gravel. The wind covers the sound of the crunch. I slip from the car, bum to the ground, head below the driver's window. I roll free of the sill, grab the door handle and push the door shut. With my ear next to the bodywork, I hear the soft clunk as the catch engages.

I sit on the gravel, hidden from the house by the car. I know there are cameras around the house, but I don't remember seeing any in the car park. If they are there, I'm guessing they could be infrared. Nothing but the best for Broch House.

Sensing no motion around me, I push myself on to my knees, feeling the stones bite into my kneecaps. I wince. I have Osgood–Schlatter. Have had since I was a kid. Any pressure on my knee when I kneel results in a shooting pain that hurts like hell. Experience has taught me to keep my weight forward.

I raise myself, peeking above the bonnet, looking out for Charlie or Lemby or anybody.

Nothing.

Keeping to a crouch, I work my way to the path they took. The sound of the wind all but covers my footsteps, but they still sound too loud to me. When I reach the path, I stand up, not all the way but enough to allow me to walk a little more easily. The track is covered in bark, lined on both sides with small logs. In a brief flash of moonlight, I can see that it falls down an incline, veering away from the main house.

I start down, playing tic-tac-toe as it's now so dark I can barely see the ground. I take it slowly as the path begins to wind to my right. The bark under foot is soft, and a few times I slide, once knocking one of the logs out of place. The route turns back on itself, still dropping. It's now pitch-black. I'm forced to use the logs as guides, dragging my foot along their edges to make sure I'm still on the path. Charlie must have used a phone light, or if he didn't, maybe that explains why he's taking so long. I consider using my own phone. It might let me see a few feet, but it'll be visible from a mile away to anyone else, so I decide against it.

The path levels out as a light appears through the trees. I can see the ground now and speed up. The trees stop as the path exits on to a wide expanse of grass. A large metal gate lies open ten yards away. Either side of it is the security fence that Conn talked about. Razor wire loops along the top. I stop. The light I saw is coming from a small lamp sitting above the door of a building. Conn was right: it looks like a bungalow. Nothing fancy. A concrete path extends up to the front door. I stay in the shadows.

Charlie will have an issue if he finds me here. I wait another five minutes. I'm just beginning to think I should take a closer look when the door smashes open. Lemby staggers into the night, the light from the house casting his giant shadow across the lawn. He tumbles to the ground, moaning.

He looks up. Sees me.

'Did ye give yon box tae Doddy?' he shouts.

I've no idea why he wants to know about that now.

Lemby tries to stand. He gets off his knees, doubles up, vomiting on to the grass. I step forward. 'John, what's wrong?'

He wipes the sick from his mouth. 'Did ye give the fucking box tae Doddy or not?' Charlie appears behind him. He spots me. 'What the fuck?'

Lemby grabs at Charlie's legs. 'Ye need to go back and make them give you more stuff. Mine's all gone. Wendy found it. She trashed it.' Lemby throws up again. 'It's all gone,' he croaks. 'I need mair. It's starting to hurt. Really hurt. Charlie, you know what it does.'

Charlie starts to walk away. 'I can't fucking help you, John. I don't have any. And I'm not going back in there.' He nods his head towards the building.

Lemby points to me. 'I gave him some for Doddy. They found out I took it. Told me I'd to get it back to them. I'd no choice; they'd have killed me. Doddy was to drop it. I kept some, for me, but Wendy found it. Flushed it all away. I need and need bad.'

'What are you on about?' I ask Lemby.

'The box. Did you give Doddy the box or do you still have it?' he gasps.

'What's in it?'

Lemby coughs up phlegm. 'Cost.'

'What?'

'Drugs,' says Charlie. 'Cost is a drug.'

'This is all about drugs?'

Obvious when I think about it. Especially given Lemby's state now and earlier.

Charlie looks around. 'That mad bastard stole from them.' He points at Lemby. 'We need to get the hell away, and now.'

'Stole what? From whom?' I ask. 'What the fuck did he mean – Cost?' Charlie blanks my questions.

'Fucking mess, this is a fucking mess,' says Charlie. 'The prick'll die if he doesn't get more soon.'

'Die?'

'Twenty-four hours and he'll be dead.'

I try to process the information. 'Charlie, what the hell are you talking about?'

'Fuck, Blake, we need to get away from here. This is for later. They'll call in the heavy mob. We got lucky – there's only one guy in there at the moment. But they'll come. Lemby was begging for more. Said he'd call the police if they didn't give him more of it. The guy was straight on his phone as soon as Lemby said that. You can't threaten these guys. Lemby's dropped us right in it. They'll come after us now. I didn't know he'd nicked some stuff. I just found out. Lemby is an idiot.'

'What's wrong with Lemby. Has he overdosed?'

'For fuck's sake, this isn't the time or the place.'

I close in on him. 'What do you mean, he'll be dead in twenty-four hours?'

Lemby is trying to throw up again. He's nothing left.

Charlie watches. 'Shit, John.' He swings towards me. 'Did John give you something for Doddy?'

'What do you mean, he'll die, Charlie?'

Charlie looks panicked, almost wild. 'What a fucking mess. Tell me, do you have a package for Doddy?'

'Wendy Lemby gave me a box from John, to give to Doddy, but I never got the chance,' I admit.

Lemby is now crawling towards us. 'There's stuff in yon box. A lot of stuff. I need some stuff. *We need tae get yon box*.'

'What stuff?' I ask Charlie. 'This Cost drug? Is that what is in the box?'

Charlie blanks me again. 'John, can you walk?' he asks. Lemby's answer is to try to vomit again.

Charlie moves. 'We need to get him away from here. Help me!'

I grab Lemby by the coat. Charlie does likewise. He's a dead weight, and with John that's a lot of baggage.

'Fuck, John,' I say. 'You need to help.'

The trip back to the car is slow and painful. Every few steps, Lemby stops to try to throw up. Halfway up the hill, I catch the whiff of shit. Charlie does too. He looks at Lemby. 'John, have you cacked yourself?'

Lemby croaks, 'I'm fucking spue. Right spue. I'm needin', needin'.'

We pull his sorry backside up to the car. The smell of excrement is strong. In Charlie's car, it'll be far worse than the bovine version I've been carrying around in my taxi for the last few days.

We bundle Lemby into the back seat. Charlie stands away, heaving with the effort. I'm hands on knees grabbing for air as well.

I begin to recover. 'What is he on? No street names. Give me the proper designation.'

'It's called Cost. I don't know if it has a proper name. Bad shit. Real bad shit. But can we talk about this later?'

I hear a shout in the distance, almost lost on the wind.

'Is that them?' I ask.

Charlie doesn't answer; he just runs around the car and leaps in. I'm about to do the same when a figure bursts from the trees. Charlie hits the start button and his headlights flick on, illuminating the running figure. I recognize her from Terry's phone photo at the police station. It's Kristina. She's dressed in a skirt that's no more than a belt, has a bra on, and that's all. I rush forward and catch her as she starts to fall. Compared to Lemby, she's a feather. I see lights bobbing through the trees. I open the passenger door and push Kristina into the back with Lemby. She doesn't resist. I throw my coat over her.

Charlie stares but says nothing.

I scream at him. 'Drive!'

Lights appear, dancing just beyond the edge of the car park. Charlie sprays gravel as we accelerate. Something cracks off the door next to me. Gunfire?

Charlie fishtails on to the main drive, the car fighting him. He keeps his foot to the floor. We clip the edge of the lawn, a shower of grass and dirt rising into the moonlight, before he cuts a swathe through the pared grass. He flips the full beam on, and we dive into the avenue of trees. I turn to see if we are being followed. There's nothing behind us.

The Porsche hurtles down the driveway, Charlie barely in control. We arrive at the gates – they're closed.

'Shit,' shouts Charlie, as we slide to a halt.

I open the door. 'Give me a second.'

I sprint to the gates and push at them. They shift a little. Closed but not locked. But they are too heavy for me to move. I run back to the car. 'Charlie, try and push them with the car.'

'Are you kidding? This thing's not a bulldozer.'

'What else do you suggest?'

He doesn't even need to think about that one. He rolls the car until it touches the gate and then gently accelerates. The gates creak and the nose of his Porsche takes a caning, but the gates open with a squeal. I wince as both sides of the car scrape along the gates. That'll take more than T-Cut to fix.

I follow the car, avoid the closing gates and jump back in.

We eat more gravel before gaining tarmac. I keep my eyes on the rear of the car, expecting to see headlights. Lemby is dry retching; his smell is bad. Kristina doesn't seem to notice. Her eyes are wide. It's too dark to see much more, but she looks spaced-out. Charlie just keeps muttering 'fucking mess' under his breath. When we've settled on the main road, I open my window to let some of Lemby's stink out.

'Where are we going?' I ask.

'Do you have the box Lemby was on about?' Charlie asks.

'It's at my flat.'

Charlie doesn't look at me, eyes on the road, 'Your flat first, then. Get the box and who knows where after that. Who's the girl?'

'Kristina, a friend of Terry Lang's.'

'The one that went missing?'

'You know about that?'

'Fraserburgh.' It's all he has to say. 'She doesn't look good.'

'No, she doesn't.' I check her. She just stares at the ceiling. 'OK, Charlie, what's this with drugs?'

'That's why I wanted you out of it.'

'Drugs?'

'Shit. If I'd known that Lemby had become hooked on the stuff, I'd never have come tonight.'

I do another look round to see if we are being followed. We are still clear. 'What is it, Charlie? Heroin?'

'Nothing you would know.'

'Charlie, I know a lot.'

'Not this stuff, you don't. Some real fancy designer shit. Unbelievably strong. Almost instantly addictive. Three or four hits and it's almost impossible to wean someone off it. It's supposed to give a high like no other. I hear that they charge a million pounds a trip to this place.'

'A million quid for what?'

'To get high.'

'You're kidding? A million quid?'

'A million.'

'Who the hell pays a million quid for a hit?'

'I looked it up on the internet.' His eyes keep glancing at the rear-view mirror. 'I found a lot of rumours. A drug called Cost.'

Lemby is dribbling and muttering incoherently.

'What else do you know?' I ask Charlie.

'It's rumours and conjecture.'

Charlie's eyes flick to the rear-view mirror, checking for pursuers. We're sweeping back along the coast. Rocks reflect the headlights creating a ragged, disco light show.

'And?' I ask.

'OK, so the story goes that one of the big pharma companies was approached by the military for a new painkiller. Something different. High-impact stuff.'

'What, like morphine?'

'Except morphine takes you out of the game. Makes you woozy – useless as a soldier. The military wanted something that wiped out pain, period, but left you clear-headed.'

'Doesn't that already exist? Stuff like Vicodin.'

Charlie slows for the next corner. Lemby's muttering has subsided a little. Kristina is still staring at the night as if she's in a trance.

'This wasn't the search for a painkiller for a headache or a sore joint, Blake. This was stuff to help with the pain of a bullet wound or losing a limb. They were looking for shit that would numb the worst of traumas. The brief to the pharma company was to allow the soldier to still function regardless of the injury.'

I think on this. 'I was once stabbed by a junkie off his nuts,' I say. 'I still have a scar on my shoulder. I didn't feel it at first. I called for back-up, and once the guy was under arrest, I remember sitting down. Fuck, but then it started to hurt. The paramedic wanted to give me diamorphine. I thought I could cope without it, but I was wrong. I fought the pain all the way to the hospital before I gave in, and they injected me. You could get *too* used to that crap.'

'And how were you after they gave you the diamorphine? Were you any use to man or beast?'

'No. I didn't much care about anything.'

'Not much use if you're a soldier in the field, then. The military wants fully functioning combatants.'

I remember the sensation when they injected the diamorphine. The way the pain had vanished, to be replaced by a world bathed in a gorgeous, comforting hue. I had spent my life, up to that point, hating drugs. I don't even take paracetamol. What worried me was how much I'd enjoyed the sensation. As that feeling of euphoria spread, I could see the attraction of narcotics.

I hated that memory.

'Keep talking,' I say.

'The pharma company delivered a compound that worked. They skipped the niceties of the regulatory agency and went straight to battlefield trials in Afghanistan back in 2001.'

'And it worked?'

'Very well.'

'So, some soldier gets injured by an improvised explosive device, pops the magic pill and the pain vanishes – isn't that good?'

'You'd think.'

We wheel through a small smattering of houses: dark, people asleep. Charlie checks the mirror again. 'Blake, have you ever heard of congenital analgesia?'

'No.'

'It's the inability to feel pain. People who have it, for some reason, don't experience pain. Those guys need to be careful. Pain's there to warn you that you're hurting your body. Take it away and you can injure yourself and never know.'

'But in the middle of a war, what's the downside?'

'Well, for a start, soldiers carried on. Feeling little pain, they didn't treat the wound the way they should have. Most died of their injuries.'

'And?'

'Think about it. Soldiers on their own, no one to help them. Instead of treating the wound, they pop the pill and think they're back to normal. A generation of young soldiers, weaned on Call of Duty, who could now regenerate for real. But it was a lie. No matter how they felt, they would be bleeding out or worse. They were dying but still fighting.'

Charlie carries on. 'The first batch of the drug wore off too quickly, but the army liked what they had seen. So they just ordered up a stronger version. One that would last. Soldiers are trained to deal with wounds. The army believed that all they needed to do was train them better. To look after the wounds better. But, importantly, still function as close to normal as possible. The pharma company was sailing in illegal waters; they'd short-circuited all the usual tests, but the rewards for getting this right were astronomic.'

'And?'

'Stronger didn't work, but during the process they stumbled on other variants.'

'Let me guess, these variants had some interesting side effects.'

Charlie nods. 'They tried multiple new variants, always seeking the perfect painkiller. And then, one day, they shut the programme down. There are stories that one of the trials got out of hand. Stories of soldiers who tripped on unbelievable highs and then, deprived of the trial drug, killed themselves.'

'Because it was so addictive?'

'Unbelievably addictive. Whatever they stumbled on wasn't just a painkiller but, up there with the Satan of narcotics.'

'What kind of high is worth getting hooked on a drug you can never come off.'

'Cost. That's what it's called. And it's why these guys come here.'

'That good?'

'Supposed to be.'

'And the guys at Broch House have this shit and are shipping in people to try a drug that, what, kills if you stop taking it?'

'Withdrawal will kill you slowly or you can take the quick way and kill yourself. It's that bad to come off. Real bad.'

'Who in the hell would pay for that?'

'Who pays?' Charlie says. 'I'll tell you who pays. The filthy rich, that's who. Bored sons and daughters of billionaires looking for the ultimate high and not caring about the price.'

'But you said it kills.'

'If you take too much. A single dose and you can stop. Even a couple. Three or four and you're screwed. Pay the big bucks but don't get hooked. That's for shit. The high is supposed to be so good they all want more. All of them think they can beat the downside. Quit when they want. But they can't. No one can. At least no one that I've heard of.'

'And the people at Broch House know this?'

'And don't care. It's all about the money.'

'That's insane.'

'Tell me about it.'

'You told me you didn't know who you were transporting?'

He doesn't answer.

'Charlie, you couldn't keep something like this a secret at Broch House. People must know. People would talk.'

'Have you heard anything?'

'No.'

He waits until we round the next corner before answering. 'They have ways of keeping things quiet at the house.'

'What ways?'

'Ways.'

'And you say you can die from the withdrawal.'

'And that's the money shot for these guys. A drug you can't live without. That's a junkie who'll pay you forever. There could be hundreds of the poor bastards out there that can never get off the stuff. And they'll pay through the nose for it. This business could be worth hundreds of millions. Once the billionaire junkies leave here, I'm sure they are all kept on a very short and very expensive leash.'

'Why bring them here? Why not just send the drug to them?'

'To keep complete control. They don't want this stuff on the street, or out there to be analysed. They want a monopoly on it. Plus, charging a million quid for a pill wouldn't fly. They've built a real mystique around all of this. Select invites only. You need to be one of the elite to be invited. Guarantee of total anonymity. It is the club to belong to. The most exclusive on the planet. The whole people-smuggling thing just makes the rich want in. They could fly them in, but they've turned the whole thing into a circus. The must-have experience of the decade. It's all a thrill. Broch House knows it has a shelf life, so they are milking it. At some point, no doubt, they'll put Cost on the street, but, for the moment, they are selling the "million-quid hit" and the super-rich love it.'

'But if these customers get hooked, then they must be shipping the drug to them once they leave Broch House. Or, if you are right, they would die. So it must be on the street already.'

'They keep the users on a short leash, so I guess. Just enough to keep them going, no spare. The customers stay alive; they stay high and are compliant as hell. For they can never come off it. Talk about customers for life. And if the user gives them any nonsense, threaten to out the guys at Broch House, Broch House just withdraws supply of the drug – twenty-four hours later, the problem junkie is dead.'

I sit back. I'd seen junkies hooked on the cheapest of crap. I'd watched some go cold turkey. It was a horror show. Seen a few dead from overdosing. I'd also seen many go clean. Get off the stuff. But what if you just couldn't get off a drug? And what if you really would *die* if you didn't get a fix – then what? What in hell would you do to keep it coming?

'And Lemby is a user?' I ask.

'I didn't know. Arsehole. He must have lifted the stuff on a run. He's a dick.'

'But you knew all the time that this was about drugs?'

'I had a suspicion. Some of the guys we picked up for the return trip seemed out of their skull. But I thought it was cocaine or something. Then Lemby told me about Cost.'

'And you kept going?'

Charlie looks at me. 'Don't fucking lecture me. You've not got the full picture.'

'Enlighten me.'

'I didn't know it was this Cost they were taking at first.'

'You still shipped drug takers to build your pub empire.'

'Yeah, well, at the time I thought it was a few cocaine heads, and that didn't worry me.'

'Really? A hundred K a pop for shipping in some punters to snort some coke. That's bollocks you're talking. Just bollocks. Charlie, I don't know you at all.'

'No shit, Blake. You know nothing. We knew each other at school – that's it. And when I say you know nothing, I mean you *really* know nothing.'

I shake my head.

He doesn't say anything more.

'Doddy's in hospital,' I add. 'If he's on this stuff, then what?'

'It won't be the stroke that will kill him.'

'He seemed to be OK when Conn last saw him. But now you're saying he could be on a drug that kills him.'

I dealt with people on drugs in Glasgow almost daily. People will take anything if they think it'll help ease the pain of life, and there was always a new drug around the corner. The next big thing. Someone in a room, somewhere, mixing chemicals to find a cheap way to mass-produce an intoxicant.

In my experience, the young were at the biggest risk. Convinced by their peer group that the pill in their hand was safe. That there's now some new high-end designer crap that rich kids were into is no surprise. Bored, loaded with cash, able to buy anything they want. Spreading gold flakes on their coffee at a hundred pounds a cup, a bottle of champagne for ten grand, a servant to do nothing but clean your shoes. A drug at a million pounds a pop isn't that out there. But what kind of high do you get for a million? By the look of Lemby, it had better be good if this was the downside.

Kristina laughs. I look at her. Her eyes are shining. She's not acting like any junkie I've ever seen. She seems so serene, happy. She has the look of someone deeply in love. And there's something else. She's radiating confidence. As if she's in control of all this. She has the sort of face I used to see on criminals who thought themselves bullet-proof, when I knew they'd committed a crime, but I had no evidence. The look that says *I'm king around here. Now piss off.* Is this what you look like with a million-quid hit?

Lemby stops dribbling long enough to mumble, 'Yon box.'

'We need to get the box for Lemby,' says Charlie.

'Charlie, if this stuff is as expensive as you say, they will be looking for us. You say Lemby admitted stealing the stuff. He wanted me to give that box to Doddy. Why? I'm guessing that Doddy was supposed to return it to Broch House. Lemby told us the guys at Broch House told him to return it. They'll go to Doddy's place. And they'll also want Kristina. I don't know what she's seen or done, but what I do know is that Broch House is built on discretion. Rich guys who are shipped in and out are one thing. Having the staff wander the countryside, maybe talking, won't go down well with them. We need somewhere around here we can hole up for a while. Then I can go get the box from my flat.'

'Box,' cries Lemby.

'One of my pubs?' Charlie offers.

'No,' I say. 'Too obvious.'

He thinks. 'I've got a thought. What about one of the boats at the harbour?'

'A fishing boat?'

'Yes.'

'The one that brought in the man?'

'No. I wouldn't put them at more risk. I've the keys to a smaller craft. I use it from time to time for a little recreational fishing. It should be out of the water this time of year, but I've never got around to it.'

I rub the dashboard, feeling the ripples of the material. 'If they see this car down at the harbour, they'll put two and two together.'

'Shit, Blake, I'm not fucking Superman!' I can feel the stress of the situation from him. 'If we park at The Sailor's Rest, they'd have to be psychic to know we were on a boat.'

I don't add *unless they are following us right now.*

I need space to sort this out. To figure what to do next.

My gut is to hand it all over to my ex-colleagues. But until I know what the hell is what, that could be the worst of decisions. After all, I'm right in the centre of this now.

'On to the water it is,' I say.

# SIXTEEN

## *'Theft'*

When I'd stood at the start of the North Pier earlier, catching the waves, I'd seen the spot Charlie and I used to fish from. I loved fishing with Charlie on the weekend when I lived here. We would buy a roll of fishing line from the chandlers. Ten pence bought enough line to stretch around the harbour. We would raid the fallen fish from the off-loading boats, setting up camp at the rocks just below Kinnaird Lighthouse. We'd bait the hooks and try to catch poddies. I've still no idea what a poddy is. It's just what we called the grey fish we pulled out.

I'd tried taking up fishing later in life. It was another hobby I was destined to fail at. I wanted to recapture those times with Charlie. The carefree hours. All I discovered is that I get bored real easy sitting with a pole in my hand.

Fraserburgh is an old town. It was chartered back in 1546. A guy called Alexander Fraser built the first pier here some thirty years later. That's where the place gets its name – the burgh of Fraser. It was the family home, and after being educated in Edinburgh, he returned to build the port. He spent so much money on the town that he had to sell a fair bit of his estate to pay his debts. He clearly loved the place.

So had I. But now? Well, now I'm just not sure I am still in love.

As we park up in the lee of Charlie's pub, I have a mad notion to tell him that a little bit of late-night fishing would be just the ticket. Lemby retches and brings me back to the moment.

Charlie and I get out of the Porsche. I fold the seat back to let Lemby escape. He doesn't want to move. 'Box.' It's the only word he says. Over and over again. We end up dragging him out. Charlie's back seat is a mess.

I screw up my nose. 'Charlie, I don't think you'll need a valet. I think you'll need a new seat.'

'You think? Now help me get this idiot upright.'

I get him on to Charlie's shoulder, and go back to the car for Kristina.

'Kristina,' I say as I hold the door open. 'I'm a friend of Terry Lang. She sent me to help you. How are you?'

'Don't know you.' Each syllable is spoken as if it's an effort. The drug is losing its grip. She's lost the confident look, appears scared.

'I know you don't know me, but you do know Terry?'

'Terr . . . rry.'

'That's it. Terry. I need you to come with me. Are you OK with that?'

'Men touch me.'

That makes my mind up. She needs hospital treatment. If she's been abused, she should go straight there.

'Kristina, do you want to go to hospital?'

She tries to get out and says, 'Yes.'

I return to Charlie who's limping away with Lemby. 'Charlie, Kristina needs to go to hospital. She might have been abused.'

Charlie's hauling air in large gulps. I take some of Lemby's weight and he whispers 'Box' into my ear.

'I'll get the box, John,' I say. 'Just help us by walking a little.'

This seems to give him a boost. I feel some of his weight lift.

'Charlie, I'll help you with him into the boat, then I'll take Kristina to the hospital.'

We swing Lemby between our shoulders and walk. A corrugated iron building, functional and lacking in any aesthetic quality, looms out of the night. A cat scrambles from a rust-ridden skip, scared by our passing. Charlie points at a small row of boats bobbing ten feet below, dwarfed by the giant fishing fleet. Each has a front cabin with a tiny porthole just above the waterline, near the bow.

Charlie gasps, 'That one. Yon blue one.'

Charlie drops Lemby on to me and climbs down the metal stairs. In the dark, he nearly misses his footing but manages to jump safely on to the boat.

I pull Lemby's head towards me. 'John, listen. I need you to climb down. Climb down into the boat. I'm going to get the box.'

'Box,' he mumbles.

'Yes, John. The box. Down the stairs and I'll get the box.'

'Box.'

He tries to step on to the ladder, but his hand is slick with sweat. It slips from mine. He tumbles back. Released of his weight, I fall on my backside. I hear a thump and a grunt. I stand up to look over. It might not be the recommended way to board a boat, but Lemby's on. Charlie's already trying to get him into the cabin.

I call down to Charlie. 'I'll be back as soon as I can. I need your car keys.'

He drops Lemby, fumbles in his pocket and throws them to me. I catch them.

Kristina is still in the car when I get back. 'OK, Kristina, we're going to the hospital.'

'Terry.'

'I'll call Terry to tell her you're OK.'

'Tomas,' she says.

I start up the engine before spending a few seconds figuring where things are in the unfamiliar car. 'What about Tomas?'

'Tomas sick.'

'Is he back at the house?'

'Tomas sick.'

I get us moving, window down to keep Lemby's smell at bay. 'Is Tomas at the house?'

'Sick.'

She won't say anything else.

The hospital lies up near Fraserburgh Academy. It was built a couple of years after I was born on the site of the old Infectious Diseases Hospital. I'd contributed a childhood's stint of breaks and cuts to its history. The low-level, two-storey building is an unwelcoming edifice with a scattering of outbuildings circling it. Dentists, GP practices, maternity services, emergency services, care – the full gambit for the body is on show. Most buildings are clad in Fraserburgh grey.

I give some thought to the story that I might spin when I drop Kristina off. I need to be as honest as possible. Tell them that she might be on drugs and that she talked about being abused. To do otherwise could put her in danger. And I'll need to make it clear that I'm not sure what she's on. I can tell them I used to be in the police, that I've never seen the like. Hopefully, that way they don't fly to any wrong assumptions.

I reach the hospital, parking up in a nearby street. I don't want the cameras to see me arrive in Charlie's car. I encourage Kristina out of the vehicle, careful to keep my coat wrapped around her. She's shivering. We enter to find the A&E quiet. I place Kristina in a seat, cross the floor to get to help.

A voice rings out from behind me. 'Blake Glover?'

I turn to see Detective Inspector Kyle Anderson standing at the door.

*Shit!*

'Hi, Detective,' I say.

'And what are you doing here?'

'Give me two minutes to get Kristina sorted and I'll talk.'

After I give the receptionist details, a nurse and doctor appear. They sit with Kristina, and I tell them what I know. Kyle listens in.

Then Kristina keels over. She makes no attempt to break the fall, her arms flapping out, her head slamming into the floor. The doctor drops to the floor with the nurse and shouts for help. A dolly rolls in with two more nurses in tow. The doctor turns to me. 'What did she take?'

'I don't know. But I've never, ever seen the like, and I used to be a policeman. That's all I know.'

Kyle stares at me as the medical help flows around Kristina. She's lifted on to the dolly and rushed out of sight, leaving Kyle and me standing, as if watching a receding riptide.

In the silence that follows, I take in the reception area. I spent the last hours of Dad's life in such a place, in Dundee. When they brought him in, after the road accident, Aunt Rita tried to get me to go home, but I wasn't having it. With Mum gone, I wouldn't leave my last parent alone. I'd slept in the waiting room. It's where Aunt Rita woke me up to tell me that Dad had died.

Over the intervening years, I've been in enough hospitals in Glasgow to fill a lifetime. I hate the places. I always feel so helpless. The feeling is crawling across me now.

I drop to a seat. Kyle sits next to me. His suit is crushed. There are stains on the lapels. He looks at me. 'You look pale. Are you OK?'

'I don't like hospitals.'

'Who does?'

He turns towards me. 'OK, Blake. Is that the same Kristina that Terry Lang said went missing?'

My mind is clouded, but I know enough to delay this conversation. 'Can we do this over a coffee? There's a machine there, and I've had a hell of a night.'

I slowly rise and muck around at the coffee machine for as long as I can before we both sit down in the far corner of the waiting area.

'What are you doing here?' I ask, playing for time.

'Caught a housebreaker. Twat fell out of a window when we called out. Landed on me. I only bought this suit a week ago. Look at it.' He brushes at the stains. 'The idiot is in seeing the doctor now. I've got one of the constables making sure he doesn't run.'

'A housebreaker? That's no DI's job.'

'Maybe not in Glasgow, but up here we all muck in. So, what are *you* doing here?'

'Your job.'

Offence is the best form of defence.

Kyle's face flashes annoyance. 'What does that mean?'

'Well, have you been up to Broch House yet?'

He's straight back at me. 'For your information, I have. I questioned the manager and the two heads of department. Kristina was fired for theft, but no one wants to prosecute. Tomas wasn't needed any more. He was let go. We talked to their flatmates. Kristina and Tomas packed and left. We've talked to their families. They haven't heard anything. So, the answer is, yes, I've been doing my job.'

I'm not backing down. 'Well, you didn't look very hard. I found Kristina wandering up near Broch House.'

'Tonight. At this time of night? Why were you up there at this time of night?'

'Doing what I promised Terry I would.'

'At' – he looks at his watch – 'three thirty in the morning.'

'Tomas told me he'd seen some funny goings-on late at night when I saw him up at the House.' He hadn't said anything of the sort, but Kyle can't check. 'Conn has me off the road. She's shut down the taxis for a bit because Doddy's sick. I couldn't sleep, so I drove up to see what I could see.'

Kyle can smell the bullshit, so he goes looking for it, 'Let me get this straight. You drove up to Broch House at three thirty in the morning and found Kristina just wandering around.'

'She's out of her head on something. I couldn't get any sense from her. She told me that some men hurt her, so I brought her straight here.'

'Really?'

'Yes.'

'What took you up to Broch House?'

'I just told you.'

'And?'

'And what?'

'That's it?'

He's getting under my skin just when I need to be calm. 'OK, Kyle, I admit it. I've really been holding Kristina in my flat and then she overdosed. I got cold feet and whisked her down here. Is that better?'

The door of the A&E opens. A doctor enters and then vanishes into the guts of the hospital.

'Sounds plausible.' Kyle is watching me like a hawk waiting for its breakfast to make a run for it.

I fish in my pocket. 'Here's my flat keys. Go have the boys in Tyvek have a look and see what they can find.'

'Funny. So where *exactly* did you find her?'

'Up near the main gate to the House.'

'And tell me again why you were there?'

'I've told you, Tomas talked about some strange stuff going on at night.'

'Like what?'

'He said comings and goings. That was all.'

'Comings and goings?'

'We were cut off by the receptionist before I could get anything else from him. Given it was so quiet when I was first up there, I thought maybe I'd see something later on.'

My story is as thin as wet bog paper and as likely to stand up to a bit of prodding.

It's clear Kyle doesn't believe me. He doesn't let his eyes wander from mine. 'Let's say you're up checking out the *comings and goings*. Where did you see Kristina?'

'I told you, right next to the main gate.'

'Just standing there?'

'More like staggering there.'

'And what did you do?'

'I got out of the car and asked her if she was OK. She could barely respond. She only had a bra and a short skirt on, so I gave her my coat and put her in the car.'

'And you brought her straight here?'

I'm so used to being on the other side of this conversation. 'No. We went for a drive and a Burger King.'

He ignores the jibes. 'And that's it?'

'What do you want me to say? Look, I found Kristina, and Tomas might still be up there.'

'Where? Broch House?'

How much do I hate being on the other end of this? But I need to tread lightly. It would be too easy to supply more information than I could know. It doesn't take much to give yourself away. Sometimes just the desire to fill in silence can drop you in it. 'Probably. I don't know. Ask Kristina?'

'I will. Can you stay here? I want to talk to the doctor.'

I'm thinking that Charlie will have to deal with Lemby on his own for a bit longer. I can only get the box from my flat once Kyle is happy. My story might just hold up in the short term. I did find Kristina wandering up near Broch House. I doubt she'll know if it was inside or outside the boundary.

Kyle comes back ten minutes later.

'Well?' I ask.

'They're still assessing her. She's taken something. But they don't know what. Did she say anything in the car?'

'She said that men touched her.'

'She hasn't got any bruising, but that doesn't mean anything. They'll need to do a more thorough examination. Is there anything else you can tell me?'

'Like what?'

'Were you the one that touched her?'

'Did I hell!'

'Nice-looking girl, single man. You take her for a run and things get out of hand. It wouldn't be the first time.'

'You think?'

'Maybe a few pills to ease things, then a bit of remorse after the event. Is that why she's here?'

'Do you really believe that?'

'We'll test for rape. Your details will be on the system as ex-police.'

I stare at him. My mind is churning.

Kyle keeps pressing. 'Where were you before you went up to Broch House?'

'In my flat.'

I think of all the driving around I've done in both my car and Charlie's Porsche. CCTV will pick that up at some point. I'm praying none of the footage shows me getting in or out of the Porsche, or the little episode while we got Lemby on to the boat.

'Look,' I say. 'You need to get your backside up to the House. Tomas could be there.'

Kyle crosses his legs. 'What makes you think that?'

'Are you going to make me repeat everything? You do know I've sat where you are. I know what the hell you're up to. I'm not lying. I didn't touch her. I rescued her. Come on, Kyle, stop with the fucking detective bit. You know that if Kristina was there, then Tomas could be there as well.'

'Maybe.'

I stand up. 'I'm going to go back to Broch House. If you don't, I will.'

'I wouldn't advise that. Leave this to us. I'll call it in.'

'When?'

'When I'm ready. Are you saying I won't do my job?'

'No.' I surprise myself by yawning. I'm beginning to fall off the back of the rush. 'Look, do I have to stay? As long as Kristina is OK and you're on the case with Tomas, can I leave? I didn't sleep last night and I'm the walking dead.'

'I'll need a full statement.'

'Are you going to take me in?'

He sits back. 'No.'

'I'm not going anywhere. Can I do it tomorrow? Maybe Kristina can throw some light on it all. Maybe Tomas, if you find him. That's more use than me. I've told you everything I know.'

A doctor appears, 'Detective Anderson, your housebreaker's X-rays show nothing. Your constable wants to know what he should do.'

Kyle nods at the doctor. 'I'll be through in a moment. Thanks for letting me know.'

When the doctor leaves, Kyle turns back to me. His whole demeanour shifts. 'OK,' he says. 'I need to book this idiot. And then I'll sort out your mess.'

My mess. I wish it was only my mess. It's everyone else's mess as well. I'm just the patsy at the front taking it on the chin. 'Am I free to go?'

Kyle stands up. 'Be at the station for twelve tomorrow. Give me your mobile number and keep it switched on.'

I give him my number. He puts it into his phone.

'Blake, I hope you're being straight with me. If there's more to all this, you need to tell me. Do you understand?'

I nod, and as he leaves, I make for the toilet. If he sees me get into Charlie's car, I'll be down at the police station for the night answering questions.

I string out the toilet visit until my thighs hurt from sitting on the pan too long. When I get back to reception, I ask the receptionist if Kyle's still around. She tells me he's left.

The smell in Charlie's car is a little better for leaving the window open while I was inside the hospital, but not much. I'm not sure where to leave the Porsche. I sure as hell can't park up near my flat. Forget the 'men in black' from Broch House; even this late, someone will see it and might wonder what Charlie was doing in the area. If I knew his house number, I could drop it there. The only sensible place is back at The Sailor's Rest. My car is there.

The Porsche purrs through the streets. This is the quietest of the quietest times in town. In Glasgow, there are always people around: night workers, late-night drunks, the homeless. Here, I'm slipping through a ghost town. I take the back way, away from prying cameras.

I park up at the pub, giving some thought about whether I should see how Charlie and Lemby are doing on the boat before I fetch the box, but I just want this over with. I'll go get the drugs, drop them and sleep for Scotland – even if I have to kip next to Lemby.

I jump in my car and make my way up the small rise that leads away from the harbour. It's only a short drive to my flat, but weariness is turning my bones to worn rubber. The drama of the night and lack of sleep last night has taken its toll. I spot the inset door of a newsagent, enveloped in brown wooden panels and glass; in my state, it would provide an inviting place for a quick kip.

I cross Broad Street to drive along Frithside Street, cutting on to School Street and past Terry's flat on to Commerce Street. That makes me think that I should call Terry about Kristina, but it's too late. I'll do it in the morning. I circle Fraserburgh West Parish Church, looking up at the library. Benches for better days cower in front of the building. Deep-carved letters spelling out the words 'Public Library' float above the entrance, ensuring visitors are in no doubt of where they are. I read every one of the Hardy Boys books in there.

As I close in on Queen Street, I shake myself. If anyone's waiting for me, it will be here. I could park near the church, climb up over the back of the library and get into my flat that way, but I figure it's less effort to check if anyone is watching first.

The wind has died a death, and a chill has dropped in.

I deliberately drive away from my flat to check for strangers, eyeing the cars. All the windows I can see are grey with frost. The cold tonight is hard. Scrapers will be needed in the morning. No one is out on the street. I see no clouds of breath from doorways. I double back, and with a last look-see, I park and let myself into the entrance of my building. I stop as the outside door closes behind me, listening for unusual sounds.

Comfortable that there's nothing out of place, I rise up the stairs. I unlock my door and wait: just in case a mad axeman is about to leap. When there's no splinter of wood, I walk in. The central heating hits me. It's a sand-filled sap to my head.

I drop into my chair, then push upright again. If I sit down, I'll not get back up. I walk over to fetch the box from the corner of the room.

There's no box.

I look around. I'm positive I put it in the corner, next to the small table that serves as my dining spot. I look again, checking under the table. I examine the rest of the living room, then my bedroom, the kitchen and, finally, the bathroom. Nothing. No sign of it. I'm certain I put the box in the corner. I'm sure of it. My Bose SoundLink sits on the table and my Mac is stowed where it should be. If I'd been burgled, they would have been taken.

I do another circle of the flat, racking my head in case I'd put the box away in a safe place – but I'm certain I dropped it in the corner of the living room, and it's too big not to be seen. Someone has to have taken it. I track back to the hall and check the lock on the front door. No obvious signs of forced entry. You would require a key or need to know what you were doing to get in without leaving any evidence.

I check my stash of cash that's hidden in my wardrobe. A dumb place to hide it when I know what I know about break-ins, but there's nowhere else in the flat that's any safer. I like cash at hand, and while I've looked online for a floor safe, I've never got round to ordering one.

The money is still there.

I close my eyes. Could I be mistaken? Maybe the box is still in the boot of my car? But I'm sure I removed it.

One more circuit of the flat and I'm sure it's gone.

So, who took it? And why just the box? They had to know what was in it. A housebreaker would have taken the electronic stuff, not just the box.

Who knew I had it? Wendy Lemby. John Lemby. Charlie. That's the sum total. Did I tell Conn? I don't think so. I know I didn't tell Doddy. I sit down. Who took it? John was crying out for the box. Why would he do that if he had the box? Wendy? Why would she have asked me to take it to Doddy when Lemby lost the plot, if she wanted it? It makes no sense. Charlie? He only found out about it at Broch House, and I've been with him most of the time since then.

So who?

The people at Broch House?

I drop into the sofa, go back over the timeline, draw the same conclusion again and again. At some point, earlier tonight, someone broke into my flat and took the box. Between me leaving to help Charlie and returning. A four-hour window – max.

So, again, who?

I sit turning it over in my head. The central heating wraps warmth around my skin. I begin to doze.

My phone lifts me from sleep. It trips to voicemail before I can get to it.

I dial voicemail. *'Blake, are you there? Where the fuck are you? I've . . .'* The message cuts out. Charlie Noble.

How long have I been out? I check the clock. An hour. Hell. I try to call back, but it flips to Charlie's voicemail. I don't leave a message.

I feel worse for the sleep than I did before. I'm disorientated. Heavy-headed. I take a minute to visit the bathroom. I throw some water on my face. I leave the flat, ensuring I lock it.

Did I lock it last time?

Charlie sounded desperate. I call again and again as I drive to the boat.

When I arrive at the harbour, there's some activity around me, as the early-morning workers appear. All the fishing boats have to report in by seven thirty, at latest, for the market. Some will start arriving soon. A few souls are beginning to gear up for the first arrivals.

Charlie is standing on the harbour side. He runs up to me. 'Where in the fuck have you been?'

'Up at the hospital with Kristina.'

'How is she?'

'I'm not sure, but she didn't look good. She collapsed on the floor. I also ran into Kyle Anderson.'

'The police lifted you?' His voice quivers.

'No. But he questioned me.'

'What did you say?'

'Enough to get Kyle to leave, but he's as suspicious as hell about the whole thing. Where's Lemby?'

Charlie throws his hands out. 'No idea. He wouldn't sit still in the boat. Half an hour ago, he went berserk. Started thrashing around. Smashed the cabin to bits. He ran up the ladder like a madman. I chased after him, but it was like trying to catch a fucking gazelle.'

'Where did he go?'

'I've no idea. He ran towards the lighthouse, and I lost him.'

The fuzz in my brain is clouding my thinking. Lemby on the loose can't be good. 'We need to find him.'

'Tell me something I don't know.'

'Let's take my car,' I say.

Fraserburgh is about a mile and a half by a mile and a half square. Nearly fifteen hundred acres. Not large, but large enough to hide if you want to. I start by driving to the lighthouse. Both of us scanning for Lemby.

An hour later, I pull over. We've criss-crossed and cross-crissed every bloody road in the town. There's no sign of him.

'Charlie, I've no idea where he is,' I say as I stare into the dark. We're parked up near the leisure centre, looking down on the bay.

Charlie has an idea. 'Maybe he's trying to get home?'

So obvious when you think about it. I take us out to Lemby's house. Eyes open for him on the way. We don't see him, and when we arrive, his home lies in darkness.

We sit outside. The night a cloak. Nothing to see. But I know that even in the daylight the land around here is featureless. Ironed flat by nature.

'Charlie,' I say. 'Someone broke into my flat tonight and stole the box Lemby wanted.'

'Who in the hell would do that?'

'Good question. How much of the drug was in it? Do you know?'

'No,' he replies. 'Only Lemby would know.'

'It had a bit of weight to it.'

The headlight beam from a passing car brushes our faces, throwing Charlie's worried expression into sharp relief.

'When Lemby phoned Conn,' I say, 'he said he needed to get up to Broch House soon. He must have been hurting by then. You say twenty-four hours and you're dead.'

Charlie rubs the back of his wrist. 'If you are well hooked, it's about that.'

'Up at the annexe, Lemby said that Wendy had trashed his stash at some point. Lemby phoned Conn about eight o'clock last night to tell her she needed to do the run. That's a little over ten hours ago, Charlie.'

*Is that all it is? It feels like an eternity.*

'But,' I continue, 'Wendy could have trashed the drugs much earlier in the day. Maybe she discovered them, destroyed them, and he only found out when he went for a fix. Charlie, tell me more about the drug.'

He rubs his wrist. 'I don't know much more,' he says. 'I told you it's all supposition and rumours. Whatever Cost is, it gives a high like no other. People describe it as the closest thing to true ecstasy.'

'What people?'

He hesitates.

'What people, Charlie?'

'Just people.'

'I don't believe you. You keep talking as if you've had experience. Are you on it?'

'Hell, no!'

'But you know people that have tried it?'

He looks down at the glovebox and his voice changes. A lower note. A tinge of sadness deep within. 'I'd been running people for a while. Me and Lemby picking up and dropping off. I didn't ask too many questions. Dumb, I know. Even when I did ask about it, Lemby blanked me. I should have backed out, but I needed the money. One night, we were waiting for a pick-up down at the harbour. Lemby was pickled. Proper, in the gutter, smashed. He mentioned an old friend of mine. A guy that was now on the local council.'

'Who?'

'Do you remember a boy at school called Frank Barbour?'

'Vaguely?'

Charlie sits back. Staring at Lemby's house. I study his face. The boy within is well hidden, but every so often his eyes betray him. The childhood friend looking back at me.

'Well, I got back in touch after a few years,' he continues, 'back when I first started the business. When Frank stepped on to the council, he was more than a little useful for some of my planning and licence applications, if you know what I mean.' Charlie plays with the glovebox, and once more I can see the kid he used to be reappearing. 'Lemby was mostly incoherent that night, but he lets slip that he saw Frank coming out of the annexe up at Broch House. He wouldn't say any more. Two weeks later, I hear that Frank was in hospital. Serious stuff. I go to see him, and he's a mess. They've maxed him out on painkillers and he's still in agony, not screaming but actually *howling*. He eventually calms down for a bit, long enough to ask me if I could take him to Broch House. Or if I couldn't, could I go up and say he was sorry and that he needed a fix.'

'Of this Cost?'

'Yes. He starts jabbering about what this Cost did to him. That I couldn't imagine how good it made you feel. Invincible – that was the word he used over and over again. Then he started writhing and bellowing so hard his vocal chords packed in. They gave him a massive sedative, and I promised to myself that I'd come back to see him the next day. Except that night he woke up, walked out to Broadsea and threw himself in the sea.'

'Why did he jump?'

'I'm guessing the pain of withdrawal. That's what Lemby said when I asked him. That's also when Lemby told me the background to the stuff.'

'But isn't the drug for the rich? How could Frank afford a million quid?'

Charlie raises his gaze to the dashboard, shaking his head slowly. 'He couldn't. Lemby has a theory. He reckons that the people up at Broch House have targeted key individuals in the area. Got them hooked on Cost and threatened to cut off supply unless they do what they say. It's their way of keeping a lid on things. In the main, to keep any heat away from the house. Frank being a senior person on the council made him useful to them.'

'Say that again.'

'They are hooking high heejuns on the stuff. You asked earlier why no one is asking questions. My best guess is that they have hooked a slew of people that they think will help keep the whole thing quiet. Their message is simple to these people: talk and we cut off the supply.'

'Bloody hell. That's what you meant when you said the House

had ways to keep it all quiet? But surely if Frank Barbour blabbed to you, he must have told others, if he was that desperate.'

'He did. Kyle Anderson has been up. He went to visit the place, because of Frank's rantings.'

'Terry said he'd been up. But she said they found nothing in the annexe?'

'They were always going to find nothing. Broch House is too smart to leave that shit just lying around or to leave any record of what is going on.'

'Charlie, how in the hell did the people at Broch House get this stuff in the first place?'

'Who knows? A scientist working on the programme was bribed? It was stolen? The formula leaked on the internet? The military might have stopped the trials, but perhaps someone thought it would make a hell of a recreational drug? I've no real idea. All I ken is it's real.'

Recreational doesn't sound like the right word for this shit. I'd nicked a man once. A cokehead. He still had powder on his moustache when we caught him. We also found a baby dead in a cot. White crap on the wee fella's face. The arsehole had given the baby some cocaine to stop him crying.

*'He wouldn't stop. Wailing and wailing. I gave him a wee sniff. Only a wee sniff. A harmless sniff. It's recreational stuff, you know.'*

*Recreational my arse.*

'And why is this crap called Cost?' I ask.

'Take your pick. Because it costs so much? Because of the cost to the user when they come off it?'

'I'm still struggling with the idea that someone would get involved with this shit if they knew it had such a fatal outcome, Charlie. Whoever is behind Broch House sets up a drug den in this annexe, ships in the rich and lets them indulge themselves.' I picture Kristina in her bra and skirt. 'They also lay on some "entertainment" and charge a million quid a go. And you thought getting involved in all this was OK?'

'Don't get on your high horse with me!' His voice is hard. 'If a bunch of rich kids want to ram piss into their body, who am I to stop it? Do you think that they just woke up one day and thought, *I'll smuggle myself to an out-of-the-way hotel in Scotland and jack up on some new gear*? Get real. Most were probably junkies anyway.'

'And that makes it OK?'

'Blake, I don't care about making it OK. I never knew about Cost for most of the time.'

I dig in at him. 'Yeah, but when you suspected, you didn't stop.'

'I never suspected.'

'Sure. A hundred K to pick up a person, and you thought they might be on coke? Get real, Charlie. And when did Lemby tell you all about the military link?'

'After Frank Barbour died.'

'And when was that?'

'A while back.'

'You told me earlier you only found out not that long ago.'

'Aye, well, I lied.'

'You were happy to be a taxi service to a drug den. But because you didn't touch the drugs, your conscience is clear. Is that it? Do you know how often I've heard that story?'

He balls up both fists. 'Don't start. You're not so fucking clean yourself.'

I sit back. 'What in the hell does that mean?'

'You didn't just screw up once, did you? Down in Glasgow. There were other times.'

If we sit here much longer, Wendy might spot us, but I need to ask, 'What other times?'

Charlie points to the road. 'Fuck this, you know fine well.'

'What are you talking about?'

'Mitch Campbell?'

'Who?'

'Blake, you're a shite liar. You know fine well who the hell Mitch Campbell is. And what about Freddy Spence?'

'Who?'

'Fuck this. I'm not playing silly buggers.' His voice is low. 'Just take me home. Lemby will turn up at some point.'

'I've no idea what you're talking about,' I say.

'I'm not doing this,' he says. 'You can lie all you want to yourself, but I know better. Let's not fall out on the first day together in four decades, OK? Lemby will surface.'

'Or he'll turn up dead.'

Charlie taps the dashboard, 'And who would miss him?'

'What?'

'Just drive.'

I slam the car into gear and drive.

I glance at Charlie. 'I'll take you to your house.' I'm angry and sulking in equal measure.

Home is the right call. It could be a disaster of a day ahead, and there's nothing left we can do right now. We could look for Lemby for hours, but I'm dead on my feet.

There's a laundry basket full of what ifs in my world today. What if Doddy is on Cost? He could be going through hell right now. What if Lemby has been lifted by the police? Even in his current state, he could drop us in it from such a height that it would put Charlie and me in jail. Ex-policemen don't have much fun in such places. What if he's lying somewhere dying or has taken Frank Barbour's way out? What if my box of drugs gets on to the street? If Charlie is right and it's that lethal when you come off it, Fraserburgh could be looking at a stack of dead bodies in the near future . . .

What ifs are a bastard.

*Campbell and Spence.*

Charlie knows about Campbell and Spence.

How? How does he know? You can't do thirty years on the streets and not cross the line now and then. In my case, I've crossed the line again with this shit – but I also crossed it much more back then than I'd like to admit.

But Campbell and Spence.

Shit!

# SEVENTEEN

## *'An Affair'*

The text comes in at eleven o'clock in the morning. My eyes opened only a few seconds earlier. The message is from Conn. It's a weblink. Sitting up in bed, I click it. It opens up a page on the *Fraserburgh Siren* site.

'Body Found in Harbour,' reads the headline.

Underneath there's a generic picture of the harbour. The copy below is brief, but informative.

> A body was found off the Balaclava Pier this morning. Police haven't confirmed the identity of the man, but it's believed to be that of John Lemby. Sebastian Taylor, of High Street, phoned the police when he saw a large man tumble over the edge of the pier early this morning. Sebastian said, 'John was screaming and shouting. Staggering around the pier. He came up to me asking if I knew where a box was. I recognized him from our local pub. Then he just jumped into the harbour. I threw him a lifebelt, but he ignored it and started to swim away. That's when I phoned the police.'
>
> The body was recovered near the fish market. Formal identification will take place this morning.

I close the browser. So Lemby's dead. I've no right to feel relieved at the news, but I am. Why? A man's dead, a family back at home, a wife and kids without their dad, and I'm relieved. Charlie will probably be questioned by the police if Wendy saw him pick Lemby up last night. They'll want to know where they were going so late. That might lead to me. I need to talk to Charlie.

Before I get in touch with him, I text Conn. *'How's Doddy?'*

It pings back. *'Doing well. He's sitting up. Still confused but he wanted some breakfast. How did it go last night?'*

'About as well as you could expect.'

If Charlie is correct on the timeline of Cost, then Doddy can't be on the drug. It's been more than twenty-four hours since he went into hospital and he's showing no signs of withdrawal. Whatever way this stacks, someone knew what was in the box in my flat and stole it. Wanted it and nothing else. The question of *who* surfaces again.

Kyle Anderson told me in the hospital last night that I'd have to attend the police station at twelve.

I need to check on Kristina first. I should say something to Terry about her, but that will raise too many questions at the moment. I stay in bed. I'm well short of the sort of sleep needed to put me back on my feet properly, and just as I begin to slip back to the land of nod, my mobile pings. Charlie has texted a weblink. I click on it. It's a news article from a website called www.allthenewsand-more.com. It's headed up *The Cost of Broch House*. It outlines what I already know. The background to the drug. The rich kids. The drug's fatal downside. It was only posted this morning at eight o'clock and has already had several thousand views. Naming the venue will put a nail in the coffin of the House's activities. Who'd risk going there now?

When I leave the flat, the day is clear and fresh. A bright breeze is blowing from the east. I detour via Candy's Café. The interior is a fug of breath and sweat. Coats hang from the backs of chairs. Patrons are getting down on hot liquid and warm food. I order up a couple of coffees, using them to wash down a roll and square. It helps clear my head a little.

I exit the café, collar up as the cold strikes me. I decide that I'll check in on Kristina after going to the police station.

I enter the police station at one minute to twelve.

Paul is on reception. He points to the seats. No offer of tea.

Kyle is twenty minutes late. He ushers me through into an office. No interview room for me today.

'Blake, take a seat.'

He looks tired. Probably no sleep.

'How's your housebreaker?' I ask him.

'The least of my problems.'

'And Kristina?'

'She's not good, but she backs up your story. Says you picked her up at Broch House.'

'Have you been up to the annexe?'

'You haven't heard then?'

'Heard what?'

'The annexe is gone.'

'Gone?'

'Burnt to the ground. The fire started early this morning. Looks deliberate. It was gutted. By the time the fire brigade got there, there was not a lot they could do.'

'Was anyone hurt?'

'Not that we know of. There were no guests last night according to the general manager. He called in the fire when he arrived this morning.'

'And no one saw anything.'

'The annexe is well hidden. It was just a burnt shell by the time the fire brigade got there.'

'There was no night porter on?'

'None.'

'That's odd.'

He agrees with me. 'It stinks, and if I think it stinks at this stage, then they are screwed if they expect the insurance to pay out.'

'You think someone at the House did it?'

'What in the hell was going on there?'

I blank that question as I feel a rod of cold slide down my back. If the annexe had a secret area, there could have been people in there. Tomas? Others? We dropped a man there last night.

I need to tell him. 'Tomas said the annexe was bigger than it looked. Was it empty?'

'Did he? Tomas said a lot for such a short conversation.' Kyle sizes me up. 'They found a maze of rooms under the annexe. All burnt out. But no bodies. There's no record of planning permission for the rooms. It might explain the "comings and goings" that Tomas talked to you about. I get the impression that whoever was in the annexe skipped out last night. We've nothing to go on. We're interviewing everyone we can, but no one knows anything about that annexe, save putting the odd guest up in the main building. No one was allowed in. So, I ask again, what was going on there?'

'I've no idea. And there is nothing left?'

'The annexe was eviscerated. Whoever set the fire knew what they were doing. The forensic team will have their work cut out on this one.'

'Do you still need a statement from me?'

He twirls the pen in his right hand. Holding it out. I reach out, thinking he means me to take it. He grabs it back. 'Yes, but not now. Unless you saw something else when you were up last night that might help with the investigation into the fire?'

'Nothing. I've told you what I saw.'

'And you were on your own?'

I nod.

I'm stacking lie on lie here.

He considers this. 'OK. You can go.'

We walk back through the station, and he stops me as we reach the main door. A woman and a young kid are standing at reception. The kid has blood on his face. They both look at us as Kyle asks me, 'One more question?'

'Sure.'

'Do you know a guy called John Lemby?'

It takes all my police nous to hide my surprise. I'm not sure I succeed. 'I've met him. I picked up his kids the other morning for school. Why?'

'We fished him out of the harbour this morning.'

'What happened?'

Kyle walks out the station's front door and I follow him. Behind me, the woman looks disappointed at not hearing the conclusion to our conversation. The boy is smearing his blood on the reception desk.

Kyle stops at the top of the small flight of stairs in front of the station. 'It looks like Lemby killed himself. Off his head on something according to a witness.'

'Why are you asking me about him?'

'His wife mentioned you'd seen him when you picked up the children.'

'I'm a taxi driver. I see a lot of people.'

'So you do, Blake. Funny, though. Broch House, Kristina, Tomas, Lemby – and the one connection I have at the moment is you.'

The air loses a few degrees of warmth around my shoulders. 'You think I'm to blame for all this?'

'What do you think?'

'I think if I have any thoughts on it all, I'll make sure to phone you.'

I walk away, head down, feet slightly shuffling – a kid that's nearly been caught with his hand in the till – waiting to be called back by the shopkeeper.

I text Conn. She replies to tell me there's no change with Doddy's condition. That makes me think that he definitely can't be using Cost. Conn's text ends with a kiss.

I follow up by ringing Terry. 'Hi, Terry. Are you with Conn?'

*'No. I'm meeting her up at the hospital later. I hear you rescued Kristina,'* she says.

Man, are people telepathic around here? 'Who told you?'

*'Paul.'*

'Is that the Paul that you were two-timing with Tomas?'

*'It wasn't like that.'*

'It sounds like it was to me.'

*'Why didn't you tell me about Kristina yourself?'* Her tone is sharp.

'Because,' I say, 'it happened at three thirty in the morning. I didn't think you'd appreciate a call at that time. I took her to the hospital and then went to bed. I'm not long up. Kyle says she's woozy and not making much sense.'

*'You still should have called. Paul says you found her up at Broch House. That you were up there at that time in the morning.'*

'Couldn't sleep,' is all I say. 'Did you hear about the fire at the House?'

*'Yes.'*

'Well, Tomas wasn't there.'

*'How do you know?'*

'Kyle Anderson told me. Said the place was a right mess. The fire might even have been started deliberately. But no one was hurt.'

I hear a little gasp. *'Deliberately?'*

'You didn't hear that from me.' The last thing I need is Kyle on my case for spreading rumours. 'Has Tomas been in touch?'

*'No, but his sister phoned me after they heard Kristina had been found. No one's heard from Tomas. She wanted to know if I knew anything.'*

'Well, we found Kristina, so don't give up on Tomas.'

She changes the subject. *'Conn's checked into a hotel. She bought stuff to be going on with. I'll come back up, pack her some more and bring it down to her later. I think she's intending to stay there for a while. Can you come down to Aberdeen and get me?'*

I could do with the run. Clear my head and pop in to see Doddy at the same time. 'I'll leave shortly,' I say.

*'OK. I'll be at the hospital with Conn. Can you also give my gran a lift back as well?'*

'I thought she was seeing her sister all week.'

*'They fell out with each other.'*

'Oh.'

*'Don't worry,'* she reassures me. *'They fall out all the time. We can pick her up after you get me.'*

I consider calling Charlie, but he knows where I am if he wants me. With Lemby dead and the annexe firebombed, the urgency of last night has receded a little – if you don't count a box of ex-military drugs that might be on the street.

I drive to the newsagent to pick up a few snacks for the road.

There is a chill set into the landscape. My phone tells me that will be the way for a few days to come. I make a mental stickie that my coat is still with Kristina at the hospital. The one I'm wearing is great for the rain, but a net curtain against wind.

As I drive back to Aberdeen, I ram some rock into the CD player to clear my head. After half an hour, I switch up the beat and put on some good old-fashioned nineties Trance Dance. But even with Paul Van Dyk kicking it clean out of the park, I can't get the stolen box out of my head. Somewhere out there, someone is sitting on a time bomb. It's clear that the people behind Broch House have now shut up shop. Once the story broke on the internet, and Kristina escaped, there was no way that the fundamentally wealthy were going to be beating a path to their door anymore. The scorched earth policy signals that the business has moved on. No doubt to open in some other corner of the planet. The stuff might be deadly, but there are addicts in need of servicing and money to be made.

It occurs to me, as I skirt the edge of Aberdeen, that the people behind Broch House might have been the ones in my flat. I wonder about Lemby handing back what he stole, but if these guys were that scary, then he'd know what would happen if he didn't return it. Why didn't they go get it? Then again why expose yourself when you can get the thief to give your stuff back? Conn should have picked it up from Lemby. Except Conn didn't go to Lemby's – I did. Only all of that is now irrelevant. If the people at Broch House have bailed, then they won't be back for the drug. Why risk it? Just make more. And if they took the box, then we have an issue. Charlie said there are others in Fraserburgh that are on the drug. If the box is gone, and the people at Broch House are gone, then what happens to the people on Cost? If Charlie is right, they'll die. Whatever way you look at this, even with Broch House out of the equation, this is still a hell of a mess.

It takes me a while to find a parking space at the hospital. I kill the engine and sit. For a few moments, I eye up the hustle and bustle of the hospital entrance. Then I close my eyes. I blank my head. Pulling up nothing. Chilling. My urge is to be up and into the hospital. I fight it. I know it's the policeman in me. Wanting to get things done. Solve the puzzle. Find the guilty. Because that's what I did for most of my adult life. I may not have a uniform now, but you don't hang up the blue that easily. After a while, I text Terry and ask where she is. She replies, telling me that she and Conn are in the hospital café. I sit a few more minutes before pushing the car door open.

I negotiate the hospital, find Terry and Conn, and order up some tea for myself. 'Do you ladies want anything?'

They both decline.

'Any more news?' I ask as I collapse into a seat.

Conn answers, 'Doddy's out for the count. He got a little bit agitated.'

My heart leaps. 'Agitated?'

*Cost withdrawal?*

'They *say* it's normal,' she says. 'So they gave him something to calm him down.'

I relax.

'I wanted to say "hi" to him.'

'Maybe later,' says Conn. 'But not now.'

'He'll think I don't care.'

Conn reaches over and rests her hand on my wrist. 'I know you care.'

Terry looks a little askance at the show of affection. 'Eh,' she says, 'is there something I should know about you two?'

Conn pulls her hand away. 'Terry Lang,' she laughs. 'Your mind!'

I find myself a bit blindsided by Conn. There was real tenderness in her touch. I bluster my way out. 'Aye, Terry. Doddy would have me strung up from the floodlights at Bellslea Park for even thinking about his girl.'

Except I *was* thinking about Conn. And it isn't the first time. Maybe the 'Doddy's girl' statement she said the other day was a warning. *Stay away.* I'm attracted to Conn. I've been on the celibacy train so long that I might be close to getting a lifetime pass, and Conn's a gorgeous, warm woman. Have I been giving out signals that have her worried? I push the thoughts away and drain my tea as quickly as I can. 'Come on, Terry, let's go pick up your grandmother.'

*Thinking about Conn a lot.*

Conn smiles at me. 'Thanks, Blake.'

'For what?'

'Being a friend to Doddy and me.'

Whatever way you look at this, I'm now part of this inner sanctum. The good news is, with the Broch House brigade on their horses and fleeing, it cuts Conn and Doddy free. I only hope that Doddy's money issues are behind them. There's no more hundred-K fares for Doddy's Taxis in the future.

A few minutes later, I'm driving Terry through the early-afternoon streets of Aberdeen.

Terry tells me her great-aunt lives just off King Street.

We pass Charlie's first pub. Terry points it out as we go. 'Didn't you go to school with Charlie Noble?' she asks me.

'I did.'

'Gran says his dad knew your mum?'

'He was her doctor.'

'Just her doctor?'

Something in her tone catches me. 'Sure. Why? What did your grandmother tell you?'

'Nothing. I thought he was a friend of the family as well.'

'I remember seeing him a lot when I was young. Charlie and I lived in each other's pocket. I was in his house as much as he was in mine.'

And Charlie's dad was in ours a lot, wasn't he? His kiss with Mum the day she died looms up. I can feel that dark wave coming at me. I can't do this in front of Terry. I bite down, winding the window to let in a stream of fresh icy air.

*Charlie's dad was around a lot.*

*Thinking about Conn a lot.*

'Over there,' says Terry, breaking into my thoughts. She points at a small row of terraced houses. 'I'll get Gran. I need to say hi to Agnes and see if I can't build a tiny bridge to let them start talking again. Last time, they spent a month not communicating.'

She jumps out. I leave the engine running, the window down. Heat at my feet, cool on my face. I can see Charlie's pub from here.

It's adding to Aberdeen's early-afternoon ambience with a little disco beat.

It's been a while since I was out for an evening. In the last two months, I've worked all but four days. Through choice. Preferring to throw myself under the wheels of Doddy's bus rather than sit at home.

I turn back to last night, thinking of all the ways it can bite me on the posterior. Other than the Lemby/Charlie link, I'm coming up empty, except if Kristina changes her story – then Kyle would have all the reasons he needs to question my soul to hell and back if he found I was in the grounds of the House with Charlie and Lemby.

The world spins on its axis for twenty minutes before the door to Terry's great-aunt's house opens and Mrs Lang emerges. There's no sign of Terry. Mrs Lang gets in the front seat.

I wait on Terry.

'OK,' says Mrs Lang. 'Let's get going before that idiot sister of mine appears.'

'What about Terry?'

'She's talking to Agnes.'

'Terry's not coming?'

'I see you've got no smarter in the last couple of days.'

A man walking a small poodle crosses in front of us. The poodle looks as miserable as sin. Dragging at its lead. When I see the man enter the pub, I have sympathy with the dog. Unless, of course, the dog likes a pint. Maybe that'll cheer it up.

'How's Terry going to get home?' I ask.

'She tells me you can pick her up later.'

It's nice to be consulted on my services.

'Straight back home for you, then?' I ask.

'How else would you suggest? Via Glasgow?'

I slip the clutch and stall. Mrs Lang says nothing. She doesn't have to. The tutting under her breath is enough to tell me what she thinks.

Mrs Lang does not deign to speak to me until we pass the break in the road for Peterhead.

She fractures the silence. 'I've been giving some thought to what your mother would have wanted. Rhona was her own woman. Knew her own mind . . . Except when it came to men. Don't get me wrong, your dad worked hard, but he wasn't the man of her dreams.'

'Sorry?'

'Do you want me to write this down for you? Or should I get an interpreter in?'

I blank the digs. 'Dad said they met at a dance.'

'Did they? Rhona never mentioned that. She never really talked about your father. At least, not enough that I can remember. Talked about you a lot. Doted on you. Loved you to bits. She had all the time in the world for you. Not so much your dad; he was a drinker.'

'I knew he drank in Glasgow, but not so much that I noticed in Fraserburgh.'

'Oh, he drank up here, all right.'

A house catches her eye as we fly by. A small white bungalow, sitting on its own surrounded by barren fields. 'That's Rene Thompson's old house,' she says. 'She was a piano player like your mum.'

A small dirt-white farmhouse whizzes by. It looks nothing special, just another of the myriad cookie-cutter brown-roofed bungalows that pepper the area, but it holds Mrs Lang's attention. 'And that's Sonny Michael's old place. Now, he could play the fiddle.'

Mrs Lang seems hardwired into the people around here.

'Your mum played with him once or twice, I think. At the church hall of a Saturday afternoon, before she got sick. I think she would have liked to play more, but your dad was never keen on it. Always thought him the jealous type. Keeping Rhona on a short leash most of the time.'

'Really?'

'You never noticed?

'I was a kid.'

'Kids notice more than you think. But maybe you don't have to be bright to be a policeman.'

She likes her barbed comments. But this conversation feels light, so far. A dip in the pool's shallow end rather than a dive into the deep end.

'Mrs Lang, what was stopping you talking to me at ASDA?'

She studies another house, a large two-floor detached barn of a place. 'Willy and Mabel Reynolds' old home. I hear that a commune tried to move in.'

'Mrs Lang, my mum?'

'Your mum had a private streak, Blake. Kept things in. Her mother taught her that. I never heard a blind word of gossip from Elizabeth, your grandmother. You never knew her, did you?'

'No, she died before I was born; so did all my other grandparents.'

'Now that's a shame. Look at Terry and me. It can be special between grandmothers and granddaughters. Terry sees me right. She works hard.'

'Mamie Ross's old place.' Mrs Lang points to another house by the side of the road as if showing off her local knowledge is important. 'I wonder what your mother would have done if she'd not met Jock. She was a fine-looking girl. No end of suitors. I used to be jealous. They'd hang around the door of your grandmother's house, hoping to catch Rhona coming out. No one did that for me, and yet she chose Jock.'

She definitely has something to say but she's still skirting around it. 'Mrs Lang, is there something specific you want to tell me?' I ask.

'Can you stop the car?'

I signal and pull us across the road to stop in a farm track.

Mrs Lang rotates her whole body to face me. 'OK, Blake Glover, I've given this some thought. You know your mother was a good woman?' she says.

I nod.

'She had a hard time with Jock. Drinking wasn't his only vice. He liked to bet as well. That made money in the house tight.' She continues, 'Anyway, I'm only telling you this because you'll meet up with Charlie Noble, if you haven't done so already.'

She looks at me for confirmation.

'And?' I try to make it sound like I might or might not have met him.

She grabs at her coat lapel with one hand. A little personal security moment. 'You know Charlie's dad, Keith, still lives in the same house as he did when you were a kid. Charlie's mum, Karen, died a while back, but she'd left Keith a long time before that. She died in a car crash in France with her boyfriend about ten years ago. She and Keith split up not long after your mother passed. Karen brought the kids up while he went through every available woman in the area – from A to Z. Disgraceful. He screwed his way through every one of his female patients that would play ball. Karen struggled to bring up Charlie and his brothers. Keith played silly buggers with the divorce, kept her short on money.'

A truck rocks us in its wash as it flashes by.

'Mrs Lang, can we keep it to my mum?'

'Son, I *am* keeping it about your mum.' She keeps talking.

'Anyway, your mum's death was tragic. A bad way to die. Slow. Painful. I might be struck from above for saying this, but she did the right thing taking those pills. There was no cure. Pancreatic cancer. It's a hard cancer today. Forty years back, it was almost a stone-cold killer every time. I saw her a couple of days before she died. She was so out of it on painkillers she could hardly speak.'

*'Just take them all out. Lay them on the bed. I need to sort them anyway. I'll find it.'*

Mrs Lang sighs. 'Your dad took Rhona's death hard. Very hard. He might have been a poor husband, but he loved her.'

'That's why he took me away. He couldn't face being there without her.'

She snorts. 'Not really. Sure, he was heartbroken, but it was the funeral that laid the truth bare for him. He didn't leave Fraserburgh because she was gone.'

'Why did he leave?'

'Do you remember much about the funeral?'

'Not a lot.'

'A lovely affair until later. Everyone had been up at the old Alexandra Hotel after the burial. Then your dad and Keith Noble went back to Keith's house.' She draws breath. 'You need to know this.'

She stops, as if the words in her throat have jammed. She looks to the car roof. Searching for permission to talk?

'Know what?' I ask.

'That was the day that your dad found out about your mum and Keith.'

'Mum and Charlie's dad,' I splutter. 'What about them?'

'There was a fight that night at Keith's house. I don't know if your dad threw the first punch or if it was Keith. Keith and Rhona's affair had been going on for years. Off and on. Towards the end, more on than off. Keith Noble and your mum were very close.'

My stomach churns.

*He bends down and kisses Mum. I think this is a little odd but maybe it's what doctors do.*

'And Dad never knew?' I whisper.

*Blake, your mum is very brave.*

'No,' Mrs Lang says. 'And that takes some doing in this town. I suppose a GP is good cover. House visits were the norm. I don't think Rhona loved Keith. I think she just needed someone to show her affection. To make her feel like a woman. I think Keith *did* love your mum. Karen Noble, Keith's wife, knew about it. It's not true that the wife is the last to know. That's why she left him.'

'And the fight in Keith's house was over my mum?'

'Your dad gave Keith a real battering. And I mean a real doing. Left him near dead.'

'Mrs Lang?' My head is spinning.

'Yes?'

'Is that the thing you wanted to tell me?'

'You never knew?'

I shake my head. 'God, no!'

'You needed to know. Should have known before now if you'd bothered to visit your mother's grave.'

I've nothing to say to that.

'I've not much else to add,' she says. 'I know this must hurt. I'm sorry I had to be the one to tell you, but you would have found out sooner or later. Charlie Noble probably knows all about it. I didn't want him to be the one that told you. You deserve better. Your mother deserved better.'

She stops talking. I'm struggling. Needing time to process this. Mrs Lang talks some more, but it's little more than waffle. I pull the car back on to the road.

For the rest of the drive, I think on what Mrs Lang has said. Every so often, I ask her a question, but she adds nothing of note.

It was so long ago. Does the revelation change anything? Questions are stacking up like a major motorway car crash. Keith Noble is still around. He must know I'm back. He must know I'll find out about him and Mum. He might even think that's *why* I'm back. That I've always known. That I've been biding my time before I track him down.

Confront him.

# EIGHTEEN

## *'Drop It'*

I drop Mrs Lang off at her house. Before she gets out, she has one last thing to say. 'Blake, don't go seeking Keith on this too quickly. I'm not saying that you shouldn't talk to him at some point. But not now. Your dad hurt Keith's pride that night. Badly. Keith always saw himself as a bit of a man's man. I think it's why Keith slept with so many women afterwards. I heard he was rough with them.'

She pauses.

'Rough,' she repeats. 'Keith's one of those people. Violent. He knows you are back. Expects you to visit. Probably surprised you haven't done so yet. Just don't rush in. It takes two to make the two-backed beast – your mum isn't any less guilty just because Jock was a bit of a bastard. She knew what she was doing. Remember that.'

'Why would I go to see him?'

'If I found out something like this, I'd want to know more, much more.'

'I don't know what I'm going to do, Mrs Lang. Thanks for telling me what you know.'

'Blake, I'm not sure I'd be thanking me in your position.'

I'm not sure I mean it either.

'Blake,' she continues, 'you're back here to find out more about your mum. Keith Noble probably knows more about her than anyone else alive. I don't know what answers you're looking for. There may be none. But you're angry. Wait till you calm down before you see him. Your face says it all. You're also Jock's boy. A direct connection to Jock and that night. If you go now, you'll regret it. You asked me earlier why I didn't feel I could talk to you up at ASDA. I'd already decided you should know about your mum and Keith, but I was scared he might get physical if confronted. I wanted to have time to calm you down.'

'Calm me down, Mrs Lang? It was forty years ago.'

'How angry are you right now, Blake Glover?'

I'm more upset than angry, but the anger will come. It's never far away.

'Think on it,' she says. 'It'll make no difference to you that it was forty years ago when you meet him. It'll make no difference to Keith Noble either. If you storm in, he'll be back to the night he took a beating from your dad. Keith will want to lash out if you give him a chance. You aren't your dad, but you're the next best thing. That night has burned in him for four decades. All I'm saying is to be careful.'

She gets out of the car, and I'm left to my thoughts. My mobile rings. Terry. I answer.

'Hi Terry, do you need a lift?'

*'No. I'm going back up to the hospital.'*

'Is something up?'

*'Doddy had a turn. The doctors say it happens. He's OK, but I want to see Conn, and then I'll spend the night with Aunt Agnes. She's spitting mad at Gran for something and won't tell me what. Are you free tomorrow morning?'*

'As long as Conn keeps the taxi service on ice, I can get you anytime.'

*'Did Gran talk to you?'*

'Yes.'

*'I'm sorry, Blake. Did you know about Keith and your mum?'*

'No.'

*'Do you want to talk about it?'*

'Maybe tomorrow. I'll pick you up at your aunt's at ten.'

*'OK. Sorry again.'*

With nothing else to do, I drive back to my flat to think about Mum. Mrs Lang's words play in my skull.

*. . . she did the right thing taking those pills.*

Dad kept telling me she'd get better. Lying to me. Or was he lying to himself, unable or unwilling to face the truth?

Mrs Lang's words act as a barrier to the usual debilitating descent into guilt. Shoring up the other way of looking at what happened. A guilt-free way. That, regardless of my role, Mum would have taken the pills anyway. Found a way to get to them. Making me no more than an aid to something she was going to do with or without me. An inevitable act. Something that she had to do. To relieve the misery. Her cancer *a stone-cold killer . . .*

By five o'clock, I need to go for a walk. Maybe even a drink. Something to help take the edge off my thinking.

I find myself wandering towards the harbour and The Sailor's Rest. I walk down Commerce Street and stop under a Blue Plaque pinned to the wall. I can recite the few short words by rote.

Thomas Blake Glover, 1838–1911.
Born and spent early years here in Commerce Street.

The plaque sits above a breeze-block-filled garage entrance. My namesake. I reach up and stroke it.

There's been no word from Charlie. I need to see him – and now, more importantly, his dad.

The Sailor's Rest is a little busier than the first time I visited it. In the corner, a man is setting up two keyboards. A notice on the door says that 'Flicked Out' are playing tonight at seven. I ask the bartender what kind of music they play. She tells me it's covers of eighties songs.

There's no sign of Charlie. The bartender hasn't seen him since she closed up early. I order up a pint of Tennent's lager and a packet of cheese and onion crisps. Then make it two packets. I skipped on lunch.

I watch as a woman dressed in a 'Frankie Says' T-shirt comes in, dragging a speaker with her. She dumps it next to one of the keyboards. A few more people arrive, and she waves at them.

There's an hour or so before the band is due to play. Seven o'clock sounds early to me, but on ordering my second pint, I'm told they play twice tonight. Seven to eight thirty, and then again at ten. The norm for a Wednesday.

I indulge in a few whiskies. I'm informed that there will also be free crisps, dips and other snacks for both performances. I think I might have my food for this evening sorted.

As I order up my third pint, I know I'm drinking too fast. Chasing the shadows away. Driving taxis has made me almost alcohol-free for the last few months. If I'm driving the next morning, I don't imbibe the night before. With less than half a dozen free mornings in two months, I've taken to tea and IRN-BRU of an evening. Only tickling the occasional whisky when I have a late start.

By eight, I'm well on the way to a hangover tomorrow. The pub is busy and the band is in full swing. I can see their appeal.

The keyboard players look like brother and sister. They are way too young to have been around when the songs they are playing got their first spin, but with the aid of a Mac, they're doing a fine job of putting their own colour on each song. The audience is a mix of my age and a little younger. A few are wearing eighties retro T-shirts.

As the band finishes their first set, the pub door bursts open. A man dressed in a sharp-cut suit runs in. He stumbles towards the small stage and grabs a microphone. Before any of the band can react, the man starts shouting into the mic, 'I can help you all. Be anything you want to be. I can help.'

The woman in the duo kills the mic, but the man keeps shouting. The bartender walks over and, with a little encouragement, she manages to steer him to the front door. All the way out, the man tells her he can help her. His eyes have the same confident gaze I saw on Kristina.

He's out of his head.

When the bartender comes back, I stand up, unsteady. 'Who was that?'

'Laurie Makewith.'

'Who?'

'Nice guy. He knows Charlie well. One of his drinking buddies. He owns a lot of property. That's the third time in the last few weeks I've seen him in such a state, and him such a respectable man. He's on the school board, you know, and he's up for some government job. I can't see him getting it if he keeps this up.'

Drunk as I am, I'm scared I can smell Cost on Laurie. Charlie told me there was no one else he knew on it. I thought he'd been lying when he said that, and Laurie looks like proof to me tonight.

I decide, since I'm now standing, I should stagger home. When I get into my flat, I collapse on the sofa.

I fall asleep almost instantly.

My dreams are muddled. Mum and Dad flying above me. Me trying to reach up to their outstretched hands and failing. Then it's me in the air and they're shouting at me to come down.

Kam's favourite, and overused, phrase sums up my entry into Wednesday morning as I awaken. *'A bear came into my house in the middle of the night and shat in my mouth.'*

In my case, the bear had a bad diet.

It's not yet eight o'clock. I try to count back my drinks. Working out if I'm safe to drive. I'm a bit woozy on the final score. I reach over and text Terry.

*'Would twelve be OK, rather than ten?'*

A text pings back saying yes and to pick her up at Agnes's. I send another, 'Any update on Doddy?'

*'A lot better last night. See you later.'*

With an extra two hours in the bag, I roll over to nap.

Just after eleven, I'm still feeling the after-effects of my impromptu night out as I make yet another run to Aberdeen. Traffic is light, and I've not even reached the Peterhead turn-off when my phone rings. I answer it.

*'Blake, where are you?'*

It's Charlie.

'Hi, Charlie. On my way to pick up Terry Lang in Aberdeen.'

*'Can you turn around? We need to talk.'*

'What over?'

*'What do you think?'*

'Can it wait? Terry is expecting me.'

He thinks about it. *'How long will you be?'*

'A couple of hours. Maybe longer. I was going in to see Doddy.'

He thinks about it again. *'Can you be at The Sailor's Rest for two thirty?'*

'Only if I skip on seeing Doddy. Is it that urgent?'

*'Yes.'*

'Why can't you tell me over the phone?'

*'It's complicated. Can you make it?'*

I agree to the time. If Terry needs to pick up Conn's stuff from her flat, she'll need a lift back to Aberdeen later. I can see Doddy then.

Terry is waiting outside her aunt's house when I arrive. She jumps in. 'Are you going up to see Doddy?'

'Later. Does Conn still need her stuff?'

'She does. I've to get it.'

'I'll go and see Doddy when we drop his stuff off. I've something I need to do in between.'

'What?'

'Just a bit of private business.'

When we are under way, she jumps to my conversation with her grandmother. 'Are you going to see Charlie Noble's dad?'

I'd played with that notion on the drive down. 'I've not decided.'

'Gran thought that he might get violent.'

'I doubt it. It's a long time ago.'

'Blake,' she says, 'can I tell you something and can you *promise* not to tell anyone?'

'That depends.'

'On what?'

'What you tell me.'

'It's nothing that will get you or me into trouble. It's just something you need to know.'

We pass the spot where Mrs Lang and I parked up. Where she changed my life with the revelation about my mum's affair with Charlie's dad.

'OK,' I answer.

'Promise?'

'I promise.'

'Gran told you all about Keith Noble, the fight, your mum, and all the other women he slept with.'

'She didn't name any of the women. She just said Keith slept around a lot.'

She takes a breath. 'Did she tell you that Keith hit some of the women?'

'She said he was rough with them.'

'Well,' she says, 'I think Gran was one of those women.'

That stops me. 'Are you sure?' I say.

'Fairly.'

That would explain Mrs Lang's knowledge of Keith's violence.

'What do you know?' I ask.

'You promise not to say anything?'

'I told you, I promise.'

'OK, last Sunday, I was going up to Gran's as usual. She likes humbugs so I called into Bicocchis. There was a queue, and I was standing near the front window. You can see Gran's house from there. I was looking out when I saw her door open. Keith Noble came out. Now, Gran hardly lets anyone into the house.'

I think back to being told to leave the shopping outside and Doddy's quip about the house being haunted. 'What was Keith doing there?'

'I nipped out just in time to hear him shout that Gran was to "say fuck all to Glover".'

'Are you sure?'

'Crystal. He was loud. Then he staggered off. I asked Gran about him when I got in. She tried to blank me at first and then opened up. Came right out with it. She and Keith had slept together.'

'Really?'

She rearranges a loose hair before speaking. 'Long ago, before I was born, I heard that Gran spent a few nights in hospital when she fell down some stairs. Grandpa said he came home from work one day and found her lying in the hall. Mum also told me that story. Except once, after a few drinks, Mum told me that Keith Noble was in the house that day.'

'You think Keith pushed your gran down the stairs? Is that what he meant by telling her to say nothing to me?'

'I'm not sure. Mum never said. Gran blanked me when I asked.'

'Can you ask your mother?'

'No. She passed away ten years ago. Dad and her drowned in Greece. A ferry . . .'

She leaves it there.

'I'm so sorry. I didn't know. So, it's just been you and your gran since then?'

'Yes. My other gran and grandpa are dead.'

'Do you have any brothers or sisters?'

'None.'

'So that's why you help your gran out with money.'

'There's only me, her and Aunt Agnes. That's why I don't like it when they fall out with each other. It's hard enough without them fighting.'

If Keith Noble did push Mrs Lang down the stairs, then her warning to me about his violence wasn't based on conjecture. It was rooted in first-hand experience.

'Why do you think Keith Noble chose to talk to her now?' I ask. 'I've been back in town for weeks.'

She falls quiet.

'Terry?'

'It might have been something to do with me. I was out with Taylor Noble, and I told Taylor I was going to talk to you about Kristina. It's not much of a leap to think that you might chat to Gran.'

'Taylor? Charlie Noble's son?'

'Yes. He told his dad, and I assume Charlie told Keith.'

'So are you and Taylor an item?'

'No. Just friends.'

It occurs to me that I never asked who Charlie was married to. 'Who is Taylor's mum?'

'Carol. You know her, I think?'

'I do?'

'Her maiden name was Teach.'

*At the minimum, you could have admitted to kissing Carol Teach.*

'For fuck's sake. Of course, it is. Who else would Charlie marry? My ex-girlfriend.' I actually laugh.

'What's so funny?' she asks.

'Carol was my first girlfriend. I was certain Charlie had kissed her when we were young, when I was supposed to be her boyfriend. I asked and asked, but he denied it. He even denied it the other night in his pub. Back then, it felt like the biggest betrayal ever, and now I find they're married. Did Keith see you when you saw him shouting at your grandmother?'

'I don't think so.'

'I want you to promise me that you'll not say anything to anyone else.'

'OK, but why?'

'I need to talk to Keith Noble. Your grandmother said to wait, but I'm not going to. I'm only telling you because you were good enough to tell me about her and Keith.'

I flip the subject again. 'Any news on Tomas?'

'Nothing, but I'm going to see Kristina. Her mum and sister are coming over from Poland today. They are staying with me.'

'Where are they flying into.'

'Glasgow. It was the quickest flight. They are on the train north now.'

'Do they need a lift from the station at Aberdeen?'

'I don't know. I left it to them.'

'Well, if they do, shout.'

When we arrive back in Fraserburgh, Terry promises to let me know how Kristina is doing and says she will phone when she has Conn's stuff together or if Kristina's mum and sister need a lift.

I can still feel the hangover floating in my system and put in a pit stop at the garage to grab a few Mars Bars and a couple of cans of IRN-BRU. I drink and eat it all on the way to meet Charlie. Trying to stun the hangover to death.

When I pull up at The Sailor's Rest, I text Conn to ask after Doddy and tell her I'll be down later with her stuff. She replies that he's doing OK.

Charlie must have seen me pull up. When I look up from the text, he's walking down the stairs of the pub.

I get out of my car. 'OK, so what's up?'

He points along the harbour, towards the North Pier. 'Let's walk and talk.'

I belch as the fizz and chocolate pays me back for being so greedy.

As we turn on to the pier, I say to Charlie. 'So, you didn't just kiss Carol Teach. You married her.'

'Who told you?'

'Terry Lang. And I think you owe me an apology!' I point out.

'For what?'

'Nicking my girlfriend.'

'I didn't nick her,' he says indignantly. 'She came on to me. It was my first kiss. She cornered me. She just fancied me more than you.'

I shake my head. 'Does she remember me?'

'Of course. I told her that once I caught up with you, I'd invite you to the house.'

We reach the gate near the end of the pier. When I was a kid, you could walk all the way to the small lighthouse that sits at the end, but it's sealed off now.

I stare out at the harbour, scanning the buildings in the distance. I pick out the crenelated tower of Dalrymple Hall and count the spires across the town. I look down. The tide is low and the pillars that support the piers are fully exposed, dripping with sickly green seaweed.

'OK, Charlie,' I say. 'What did you need to see me about? Did the police call? Did Wendy?'

'No, I thought Wendy would call the police if she saw me pick Lemby up that morning, but she either didn't see me or hasn't got around to telling the police yet.'

The latter seems unlikely to me. If your husband takes his own life, you'd remember what his last movements were. I'm guessing Lemby never told her where he was going or with whom.

A clutch of seagulls eye us up as Charlie talks. 'I'll need to go up to Wendy's house today and pay my respects. Lemby might have been an arsehole, but Wendy still loved him.'

'Why did you want to see me so urgently?'

'You were in The Sailor's Rest last night?'

'Yeah, and I'm suffering the consequences.'

'You were putting it away like a good one, I hear.'

'What's that to do with anything?'

'Not much. Just saying.'

I wait. Whatever he has to say, he'll do it in his own time.

'Look, Blake,' he starts. 'I think we should just leave all this alone. Let it settle for a bit. See where it all goes.'

A lone fishing boat is motoring out of the harbour. I watch it leave.

'Charlie, we can't just forget it. The box. The drugs. They are out there. And you've told me how bad they are.'

'I didn't say forget it. I just said we should leave well enough alone.'

'A man came into the pub last night. A guy called Laurie Makewith. He was off his head on something. Cost?'

'I heard. I've no idea what he is on.'

'The barperson said he was a drinking buddy of yours. Had been acting that way for weeks. You must know what he's on.'

'I don't. Now let's just leave this.'

'We can't,' I say. 'We have to act. We can't let things run their course and do nothing. As I see it, we have a couple of options.'

Charlie doesn't even look as though he's listening. I plough on regardless. 'We could drop an anonymous call to the police about our suspicions. Let them deal with it. If this stuff is hitting the street, they'll know about it soon enough.'

'And the other option?' His voice is listless.

'We track down the thief.'

Charlie keeps quiet.

'If the people behind Broch House have done a runner,' I say, 'then we have to look at how many know about the drug. There's you, me and whoever worked in the annexe that had access to the drugs, or saw them being used. Social media will be full of stuff after that fire. Speculation. If whoever stole the box wants to make a quick buck, they'll look to shift it fast. It'll be on the streets and screwing people up at a rate of knots. Cut-rate price to offload it. A quick, quick buck.'

'Or,' points out Charlie, 'the people behind Broch House lifted it from your flat.'

'Maybe, but how did they know I had it?'

'Lemby.'

'I doubt it. You were with him in the annexe. Did he talk to anyone about where the box was?'

'No, but he'd admitted to taking it – and you were there. They could have easily put two and two together.'

'Whoever is behind this didn't even follow us, never mind sending someone to raid my house. They were expecting the box to be returned through Doddy. They may even have expected it to be with us when we went up. After all, it should have been Conn driving – that's how Doddy would have got it back to them. No, I think someone else took it. Someone else knew about it. I'm guessing a staff member. Someone up there saw Lemby lift the box, knew what it was and . . .'

'And what?'

'And lifted it from my house. Or maybe they knew someone that was into housebreaking.'

'So what are you trying to say?'

'I've already said it. We need to catch the thief.'

'OK, Blake, so we become Noble and Glover, the crime-busting duo.' He turns his back to the wind.

'Glover and Noble. It sounds better.' I join him with my back to the gusts of ice. We must look like two kids lighting up a fag at the back of the school shed. 'There must be someone in the know on dealers around here. Any thief is going to need a dealer to shift this stuff. Someone out there will have heard word if there's new shit on the street. The drug trade is all about word of mouth.'

'Is it?'

His disinterest is hacking me off. 'Is the drug in the form of a pill?'

'Yes. About the size of an aspirin.'

'The box was heavy. There could be thousands of the things in there. A hundred quid a pill and you're away.'

'A hundred quid?'

'Easily. As I said, quick buck. If it's good enough for the rich to pay a million, a hundred quid is nothing.' Another blast of wind tears at our backs. 'You're in the pub trade. You must know someone that knows someone.'

'Fuck, Blake, not everyone in the pub trade is a criminal. Some of us are clean. I don't know anyone. No one. I've got licences and a reputation to think on around these parts. This isn't our job.'

'It so is, Charlie.'

'Blake, back off. You're not police anymore. I'm not going on some fucking hunting expedition for any drug dealer. I'm betting big time that Broch House took the box. Doddy was to get it from Lemby. As you say, they figure Conn will deliver it. But Doddy had the stroke and Conn heads for Aberdeen. So you get handed it. Not a great leap to figure Lemby gave it to you, and bingo, they lift it. Was there any sign of a break-in?'

'No. Nothing.'

'That takes a pro. Anyone else around here would just smash your door. It's hardly the vault door of the Bank of England.'

'I'm not buying that.'

'Your choice.' He walks towards the edge of the pier. 'I'm out. You do what you need to.'

'OK, if you won't help, I might know someone who will.'

'Who?'

'I'd prefer not to say.'

'Blake. Just fucking drop it!'

'I'm not dropping it.'

Charlie storms off.

# NINETEEN

## *'Singing on the Fountain'*

As I watch Charlie wheel away, I slump on a yellow bollard, dangling my legs over the water. A film of oil is spread on the surface, the rainbow colours a contrast to both the murk around it and the darkness in my heart. I dial Kam on my mobile.

*'BG,'* he answers. *'I do you one little favour and it bites me so hard on the backside that the teeth marks show through my jeans.'*

'Hi, Kam,' I say. 'What are you on about?'

*'Well, let me see! You phone and ask me for a small favour. I shouldn't have done it, but I did. You told me it was a MisPer. A little "in" with the locals. Next thing, I'm being raked over hot coals by Carnie.'*

Carnie is Sandy Carnagan. Kam's boss. An evil cockroach who pisses acid and sweats bile. He joined the police at the same time as me and has never failed to point out how well he's done. In return, I pointed out that Jim Dale is the ACC, and he joined at the same time as both of us. It makes me feel better, and worse, to tell him that.

'What did he want?'

*'Oh, he has a lovely relationship with Kyle Anderson's commanding officer, and Kyle told his boss all about your visit. I got a lecture on protocol.'* He stops. *'No, let me rephrase that: I got a rectal on protocol and a warning to stay out of other people's business and to leave "flawed" ex-police officers out of any loop – except a hangman's loop – in which case I've to insert you in it and pull – tight.'*

Flawed ex-police officer – that hurts.

'Kam, I take it me phoning for another favour isn't something that our fragile friendship will stand.'

*'Do you know what the penance is for my indiscretion?'*

'A promotion?'

*'Close. A one-week stint lecturing at "strategic schools" in the Glasgow area about the perils of antisocial behaviour.'*

Despite my mood, I can't help but laugh. 'You're giving *the* talk to school kids?'

*'Funny, isn't it?'*

When I'd done a little time helping out a community officer, I'd had to do the same. The audience had listened to my dire warnings of what would happen to them if they transcended the law. Meanwhile, their mates had stripped my car.

*'OK, BG. What is it you want?'*

'Right, let's make this hypothetical.'

*'My least favourite type of 'thetical.'*

'Say that we needed to get a list of the known drug dealers on the streets of a town. Say a town like . . . Well, say a town like Fraserburgh.'

*'Go on.'*

'Not the low-level scum but the ones behind the ones behind the low-level scum. Where, hypothetically speaking, would one obtain such a list?'

*'Why are you asking me? You know better than I do.'*

'Humour me.'

*'Well,'* he says with a sardonic twang. *'Would this list include dealers who also retail to the general public or is it a pure business-to-business play?'*

'Both, and they would need to be in touch with the gentrified end of the narcotic trade. We are talking many pounds sterling per transaction.'

*'Anything else?'*

'Probably known for their discretion and may not even have a record.'

*'Well, my friend!'* He sticks on a posh accent. *'One's list would be very short. And very well known to our cousins at the SCD.'*

The Specialist Crime Division had been created when Police Scotland was formed in 2013 to target a range of crimes, including drug dealing.

'And, dear friend,' I say. 'Hypothetically speaking, would you know anyone that can help with such a list?'

*'OK, Blake, cut the daft chat.'* He gets serious. *'I could, but if I wanted to put money on the best place to go for info, you've already had a run in with him.'*

'Kyle?'

*'Local knowledge on this will trump national. You know better*

*than anyone how this plays out. Who would you have talked to in Glasgow?'*

I wouldn't have talked to anyone. I knew every drug-dealing arsehole on my patch and beyond. I was just hoping there was a shortcut. That Kam might have made a phone call for me that I can't.

Kam changes the conversation. *'Blake, why the hell are you really back in Fraserburgh?'*

'It's my old home.'

I contemplate the bleak skyline laid out before me. *It's also my new home, I think.*

*'And it's nothing to do with screwing up down here?'* says Kam. *'And now, for fun, you're investigating the local drug trade?'*

I blank that. 'Kam, when are you taking a break? I have a sofa bed that's very comfortable.'

*'And I have very delicate bones. But we do need to catch up. I'm getting withdrawal symptoms.'*

The phrase catches me, and I give a small cough. 'Let me know when you're free, and we'll work something out. See you, Kam.'

*'Blake, whatever it is you are into – get the hell out. OK?'*

'I hear you.'

*'That's not the same as agreeing with me.'*

'See you, Kam.'

I kill the call.

Kam has me figured. My fuck-up at the end of my career was part of the reason I had wound up back here. I had burnt a few bridges with some of my colleagues, and friends had become thin on the ground. Fraserburgh seemed like an opportunity to move on. Only now it was feeling like a move backwards.

I walk to The Sailor's Rest. My feet dragging. One of a row of brown shuttered garage doors I'm passing is being pulled open by a man in a duffle coat. He squeezes inside the tight gap and fires up an ancient diesel pick-up. A cloud of smoke belches from the garage providing him with a *Stars in Your Eyes* entrance as he exits. The engine noise echoes off the pebble-dashed walls as he fully opens the garage door.

I continue on, eventually mounting the steps to Charlie's place. Inside is quiet. I find Charlie at the bar, sipping a coffee.

'Truce?' I say.

He nods.

No one is close enough to hear us talk, but, even so, Charlie moves us to a booth. 'Right, let's just leave this alone.' He studies me through the steam from his coffee.

I have a flash of inspiration. 'Hang on. I'll be back.'

I move outside. I dial on my mobile.

'Hi, Conn, how's Doddy?'

*'Belligerent bastard. Thinks he's all well. Wants to come home.'*

'Really?'

*'Got up and got dressed. Made it to the end of the ward and fell over.'*

'That can't be Doddy. Sounds like too much exercise.'

*'He's an idiot.'*

'I can't disagree with you on that,' I say. 'Conn, I need a favour.'

*'Name it.'*

'When you and Doddy were shipping people up to Broch House, did you hear anything about drugs?'

The lack of immediate response is all that I need to hear to know. 'OK, Conn. I don't care about what you knew. What I do care about is that someone could be selling that shit on the streets as we speak.'

She gasps.

'OK, Conn, I'm going to ask you something that you'll not like.'

*'What?'*

In that moment, I feel a warmth towards her beyond that of a growing friendship. It leaks from the phone. A small swirl of fire that curls round my body, touching me, a fire that I'm about to pour cold, iced water on. I'm not sure that's what I want to do, but it's what's needed. The policeman in me rising to the fore again.

'Conn, please believe me when I say it's better that *I* ask this question than anyone else.'

*'Ask then.'* Exasperated.

'How long has Doddy been dealing drugs?'

The answer is swift. Curt. *'I can't do this over the phone.'*

'Can we chat when I bring your stuff down?'

*'OK.'*

I hang up and go back inside.

'Charlie, I need to go back to Aberdeen.'

'What for?'

I tell him about my conversation.

'And you think Doddy stole the box? But he's in hospital. Has been there for the last few days. Out of it.'

'I don't think he stole the drugs. But Lemby wanted to send them to him. If Doddy is into dealing drugs, then he gets them from somewhere. And whoever that is might have got wind of the box.'

'How do you know Doddy is dealing drugs?'

'I asked Conn and there was no denial. I'm not saying he's a kingpin, but taxis are a ready-made cover for selling and distributing drugs. Wash the cash through the business and transport the merchandise in the boot of the fleet. It's been on the go since Hansom first hired out one of his cabs back in old New York. I just took a punt and, as I said, Conn didn't deny it.'

Charlie reaches out. 'Blake, Conn's not a player in this.'

'I know.'

'She just loves Doddy.'

'I know. Where are you going with this?'

'I don't want to see her hurt.'

And neither do I. Not in any shape. 'Charlie, I understand.'

'Not sure you do.'

'Go on!'

'If Doddy is dealing drugs, Conn will know all about it. They were up to their eyes in debt. I know that Doddy only got involved with Lemby out of desperation.'

'He made his own bed. He can lie in it.'

Charlie drops a big sigh. 'Not really.'

'Charlie, if you have something to say, then say it.'

It feels like I'm peeling layer after layer with him.

'When Lemby got back out of prison,' he says, 'I didn't stop the runs straight away.'

'You said you hadn't seen him since the court case.'

'Yeah, well, maybe I lied a little.' His head is down. Not looking me in the eyes. 'Lemby was never going to just let me go that easy. It wasn't his call.'

'The people at Broch House didn't want you to go?'

'I had to do a little recruiting first. To hire my replacement.'

'You put Doddy in the frame?'

'Conn told me how bad things were, financially. A hundred K a run. Doddy gets twenty-five per cent after costs. He could clear his debt in a year, but he didn't trust Lemby.'

'So you acted as a guarantor? Doddy trusts you.'

Charlie's head is still down. 'Doddy doesn't trust me, but when he heard what could be possible, he was all in.'

'And Doddy dragged Conn into it.'

'He had to; he doesn't drive and Lemby is banned.'

'You must have known that Conn would be involved?'

'Doddy said he'd get back in a car.'

'And you believed him.'

'Yes and no.'

'You knew what was being done and you put Doddy and Conn right in the middle.'

'Conn approached me. Told me that she feared losing everything. The flat, the business, even Doddy, if they couldn't find some more cash. I had to help. Had to.'

'You have money. Why not help that way.'

'I couldn't.'

'Why not?'

'There's a lot you don't know.'

'Like what?'

'Like . . . stuff.'

'So if you can't help with cash, why drop them in it with the drugs?'

'I needed to help Conn. And I knew that Doddy had been dealing weed – so it was no big leap.'

'A drug that kills against some weed? Really?'

'As I said, I needed to help Conn.'

'Conn, not Doddy?'

I put on my mental handbrake. Blake Glover! One day, you'll add up the dumb days and they'll outnumber the sensible ones.

'You and Conn?' I gasp. 'Is that why you handed them the bloody poisoned chalice?'

He won't look at me.

'Charlie? You and Conn?'

He sighs. 'A long time back. Things were bad with me and Carol. I was out too often, driving the business, while she wanted me at home with Taylor. We fought. I knew Conn through Carol. They used to be in a book club together. Taking it in turns to meet up at each other's house to discuss the book of the month. One night, I went to pick Carol up from Conn's and I was late. Very late. We'd had a break-in at one of the pubs. I could have let the pub manager deal with it, but I was twenty-four/seven Harry by then. When I got to Conn's, Carol and I had a stand-up blazing row in the street about me and my pubs. She stormed off, and Conn asked me to come in and cool down, and . . .'

He stops.

'Was this before she knew Doddy.'

'No. Doddy was driving his taxi that night. He was out a lot when he started the firm.'

'And?'

'You know the "and".'

'And was there only one "and"?'

'No. Quite a few.'

I have to ask. 'The last "and" was when?'

'A year ago. Conn said it wasn't working for her. She wanted Doddy and not me.'

Only a year ago.

'A year?'

I feel a pang of jealousy. Possessive anger.

'OK, Charlie.' I try to keep the anger out of my voice. 'I'm still going to talk to Conn. She might know something.'

'Fuck it, Blake! Leave it alone. What do you want from this? It's one box of that shit. Even if Broch House didn't take it, it'll run out soon enough. Then it'll be over.'

'Over? You know what it does. It kills. This will only be over when the users are all dead. How many? How many will die?'

I stand up and briefly consider just getting the hell out of here. Leave it all to whoever fancies cleaning up this shit. Let someone else take on the weight. I exit, and as I get into the car, I notice the ancient diesel pick-up is back. I text Terry and wait for a reply, watching as the owner of the pick-up shifts a stack of plastic fish boxes into the garage.

I wonder if he's stolen them.

My phone pings, and Terry tells me she has been to Conn's and packed stuff, left it in the hall of Doddy and Conn's flat. Mr Lachlan knows I'm coming.

I reach Doddy's flat and trudge up the stairs. Mr Lachlan answers the door as if he had been standing on the other side waiting. Which he probably was.

'Hi, Mr Lachlan. It's me.'

'No,' he replies. 'Is it? And there's me thinking it was you.'

I'm in no mood for his humour, and he can tell.

'How's Doddy?' he asks.

'As well as can be expected.' God, I so hate that phrase.

'Tell him I'm asking after him.'

'I will do. Mr Lachlan,' I say as he hands me the house keys, 'do you mind if I ask you a question?'

'As long as it's not about my sex life, fire away!'

'OK. Last time I was here, you said you let a lot of people into Doddy's house?'

'I did.'

'How often and who?'

Mr Lachlan blows out a breath through his nose. A crude whistle. 'A fair few, to be honest. People who knew where Doddy lived would come up and ask for a taxi, and he would let them wait inside until he could get them one.'

'Was this going on recently?'

'Right up till he went into hospital. Even after. I've had to tell a few people over the last few days that he's not in. It's amazing how disappointed they were that they couldn't get a taxi.'

I've never picked up at Doddy's flat in the entire time I've been driving for him. I've never heard Conn talk about doing it either. It has to be punters looking for dope.

'Thanks,' I say.

I take the keys from him. He closes the door. I'm guessing his peephole is full of eye as I open Doddy's door.

As Terry said, the bag is lying in the hall. I'm tempted to search Doddy's house. If he has been dealing drugs, I might get lucky and find the box that was lifted from my flat. But I can't be too long, or Mr Lachlan will remember. Conn will have told him what I was there for. I still risk a quick look-see. I tread through the house feeling like an intruder. I dig around as much as I dare but see nothing. I leave feeling like the New York print on the wall is watching me.

Back in the car, I text Conn to tell her that I'm on my way to the hospital in Aberdeen. She replies that Doddy is looking forward to shouting at me.

It seems his funny bone survived the stroke.

As I drive, I'm thinking that Conn has to be wrapped up with Doddy on drugs. As I'd pointed out to Charlie, we wouldn't be the first taxi company to be filling our boots with drugs and peddling them to the masses. I'd been part of a raid on a taxi firm in Glasgow when we had recovered three hundred grand worth of assorted narcotics. Most of it was stored in the roof joists of the taxi company's office. The owner, one Mitch Campbell, had claimed, at first, that it must have been left there by the previous owners. Then his defence at the trial made a good job of pinning it on Mitch's employees. Mitch walked, but his manager and sidekick in the taxi business both got sent down. Neither grassed on Mitch, even when they got five years each.

At first, the trip to Aberdeen passes in a mild haze as my head drifts over the events of the last few days. A few speed nutters race by and snap me back to the moment.

Mormond Hill rises on my right, a low dark hump, a whale breaching the surface, and I drift away again, thinking of Charlie and his reaction to our conversations.

Once I've parked at the hospital car park, I nip into the hospital shop for chocolate bars, Doddy's third poison of choice, after The Macallan and fish suppers.

Conn texted me the ward number.

I find the man himself sitting up. Conn's sitting on a chair next to his bed. Doddy's in a ward with another eleven patients. All stroke victims.

'Hi, Doddy? Have you lost weight?' I say.

'With the meat they give you in here, I'm dyin' of starvation.' He has a slight slur.

Conn throws a smile my way. I find myself thinking about her, again.

'Here.' I hand over the clothes bag to Conn. 'Do you need anything else?'

'No,' she replies. 'I'm good. The doctor is due round soon, so we only have a few minutes. They're going to run a few tests on Doddy.'

Doddy speaks up. 'I'm here. I can clype him myself.'

'Sorry, Doddy,' she says.

'So, how are you?' I ask him.

'Been better. Keep forgetting words.' He points to the door. 'What's yon called?'

'What? The door?'

'Aye, the door. How can you forget whit a door's called? And when I need tae go for a piss, I can't remember the name of the fucking placie you piss in.'

'The toilet?' I suggest.

'Nah.'

'The watterie?' Conn says.

'That's it, the *watterie*. For fuck's sake.'

'What's the prognosis, Doddy?'

'I'm still bein' assessed. They've gotten me on drugs and a speech . . .' He struggles to find the word.

'Therapist?' I volunteer.

'Aye, one of them.'

The nurse appears. 'Mr Robertson, time for a few tests. You can see your visitors in a wee while.'

'They think I'm soft in the heid,' he says to me.

The nurse admonishes him. 'Mr Robertson, we don't talk like that in here.'

'OK. Keep your heid on. I'm just saying.'

We say our farewells, and as we leave, I hear Doddy say, 'Can I have a dram tonight if I'm a braw loon?'

The answer from the nurse is a firm no.

Conn and I walk down to the café in silence. Conn orders up two teas when we get there.

We sit down in a quiet corner, and it's clear that Conn doesn't want to start any conversation. So I do.

'Conn,' I say, 'Doddy's dealing drugs.'

She rolls her backside around the chair, trying to find comfort where there's none to be had. 'It's not like it seems,' she starts. 'You've got to understand how much Doddy owes.'

'To whom? You told me that you didn't know much about it all.'

She says nothing. I seem to be fair game for lies this weather.

'I told you before, he gambles,' she explains. 'And not at William Hill. He's in for a small fortune with some guy in Glasgow.'

I wonder if I know the bookie. 'You told me that Doddy had backed down on the money front a little lately.'

'He has, but he still owes a lot.'

'What's a lot?'

'He'll kill me if I tell.'

'Then don't. But dealing drugs is a hell of a way to raise cash.'

'The drugs are small time. Cannabis and nothing else.'

'That's it? Just cannabis? Nothing to do with Broch House?'

I'm surprised, but it explains the frequent comings and goings at their flat.

'The runs to Broch House came well after we'd started dealing weed. Doddy was desperate for money. He knew someone who had asked on a few occasions if he didn't fancy dealing some cannabis as a sideline.'

'Knew someone. Who did he know? Someone in Fraserburgh?'

She drops her voice to a level that's barely audible. 'No. He's not that stupid. A guy in Glasgow. The same guy he owes most of the money to.'

An old story. Rack up the debt with some poor bastard and then use them as a drug mule or dealer to help them out of the debt.

'And Doddy deals out of the flat?' More silence, so I take a guess. 'And offers a delivery service via Doddy's Taxis?' It was a well-used method during my time in the force.

'Sometimes half my runs are for that.'

'For crying out loud, Conn, how long do you think before the police find out? You've got bright yellow panels that say Doddy's Taxis on the side of the car. When did it start?'

'A year ago, maybe a little less. Personal-use cannabis is no big deal. So Doddy says.'

'Conn, personal use isn't a big deal – but you're selling the stuff.'

'I know that. I'm not stupid.' Her face flushes red. 'I've been nursing Doddy and his habits for a long time, Blake Glover. We get by. Sometimes it's a struggle, but when you love someone, you don't give up on them. Doddy needed cash. I helped him get cash. It's that simple.'

'Did he ever tell you who it was that supplied him?'

'It's the one bloody thing I couldn't get out of him. And I tried. I did think about asking you. You know Glasgow well. I thought you might be able to help.'

'And what stopped you?'

'Blake, I don't need you as a complication in my life. Asking you for favours on the taxi is one thing. Asking you to do the run was desperation, but anything further and I'm too beholden to you. I told you, I'm Doddy's girl.'

'I'd have helped,' I say.

'I know. That's why I didn't ask. I'm not blind to the way you look at me, Blake Glover.'

I'm left with no reply.

'Anyway, I thought Doddy and I were getting on top of it with the money from the Broch House runs, but I was wrong.'

'And you knew it was drugs up at Broch House?' I ask.

'We've never touched them.'

Raised voices distract Conn. A man and a young girl are having a debate over whether the child should get an apple or a Snickers bar.

The Snickers bar is winning. Conn rests her hand on my wrist and I get a disproportionate lift. 'Blake, he still owes thousands.'

'That stuff at Broch House kills,' I say. 'And surely the pay cheque from those runs must have paid off what Doddy owed.'

'He owed a lot.'

'And you kept the cannabis dealing going as well?'

'The man in Glasgow has Doddy by the balls. I don't think he'll let Doddy stop, even when he's paid off the debt.'

'It's the way it works. It's what happens when you play with the wrong people.' I sigh. 'Cannabis – OK, I get that. Don't like it, but get it. But this other shit – Charlie paints it as the worst drug on the planet.'

She tries to shift the blame. 'We don't touch it. We just ferry the people going to Broch House.'

'That's what your friend Charlie said.'

'My friend?' She sighs. 'I take it Charlie told you about him and me? Didn't he?'

'No,' I lie. 'What about you and Charlie?'

'Don't fib. I know he did.'

Charlie must have phoned Conn while I was driving to Aberdeen. Maybe it's not over between them, after all. Or, if it is, does that mean Conn is looking for someone else? There's no reason for that to be true, but my head is tumbling. I'm into unreasonable thought territory here for me. If Conn was willing to risk losing Doddy over Charlie, would she do the same for me?

I push that thought away.

'Before you criticize me,' she says, 'Doddy knew.'

'About you and Charlie?'

'A while back. He found out and it stopped, but . . .'

She lets it trail. I drop my hand on her forearm.

'It started again,' I say, wanting to pull my hand away but finding myself unable, or maybe unwilling, to remove it. 'All I'm really worried about is a box that I was supposed to deliver to Doddy.'

'What box?'

'John Lemby wanted me to get it to Doddy, when I went to get the Lemby kids. You were supposed to do the pick up.'

'What was in the box?'

'The drug from Broch House – lots of it.'

'Why would he have that stuff?'

I explain.

'Look, Blake,' she says when I'm finished, 'maybe you should tell the police. Just tell them, Blake. This is so out of control.'

I let her think on that one. 'Really, Conn? In what way will that help? How do I explain I know about the drug in the first place? Why would I have had the box? And if this starts to unwind, where do you think it will leave us all? Cannabis, people smuggling, vanishing people, Lemby's death. Do you think the police will miss on any of this?'

'Charlie told me about the night up at Broch House when you rescued Kristina. You saved her.'

'It was nothing, Conn. Now the key question is do you know who might have stolen the box from me? Would Doddy know? After all, Lemby wanted to get the box to him.'

Conn is watching the young girl chewing down on her prize of a Snickers – the father's resigned look suggests he loses more than he wins.

'I don't know anything about any box,' Conn says. 'And that's straight up. Doddy's only ever dealt cannabis. I can't see him selling that other stuff. If Broch House expected him to deliver the box, then he'd have asked me to take it. And he said nothing about any box. Transporting the men was dangerous enough without getting on the wrong side of the people at Broch.'

'I think it's on the street already.'

'What makes you say that?'

I tell her about Laurie and his love fest in The Sailor's Rest.

'Laurie Makewith. He's on the school board. How do you know he was on the drug?' she asks.

'He had the same look on his face that Kristina did when I picked her up. Have you any idea at all about who might be dealing? We need to find them.'

She shakes her head. 'No one. Why not talk to Laurie? Face him up. He might talk.'

'That's not a bad idea. Do you know him well enough to talk to?'

'I know his wife, June; she's in my book group. But I can't ask her about Laurie and drugs.'

'Why not? Do you think she won't have noticed that her husband is wandering around town high as the proverbial?' I place my other hand on her wrist. 'Conn, we don't have much time. I think we should ask Doddy.'

'I don't want to stress him out.'

'He had a stroke not a heart attack,' I point out. 'But you're right. We'd need to be careful. Look, I need to go back to Fraserburgh. Whatever's going down is going to go down up there. When Doddy gets back, tell him everything I've said. He has a right to know. Then see if he has a thought on who might have stolen the box.'

As I stand to leave, she grabs my hand. 'Blake, whatever happens, be careful. If someone really is selling this stuff, then they don't care it kills. Whoever is dealing this stuff doesn't care about people.'

'I know. I'll call.'

The journey back to Fraserburgh is full of thoughts about Conn. I'm almost back when my phone rings. Conn again.

'Hi, Conn. Missing me already?'

*'You wish.'*

'What is it?'

*'You know you told me about Laurie Makewith?'*

'Yes.'

*'Well, I just got off the phone to a friend, and she says that he's not the only one that has lost the plot in town. There's a couple more.'*

'Who else?'

*'She says that Amy Milton is sitting on top of the old fountain on Saltoun Place, right this minute, singing. She's been there for two hours.'*

'On top of the fountain?'

*'Singing her heart out. Won't come down.'*

'What does Amy do for a living?'

*'A big-time lawyer working out of Aberdeen.'*

'And the other person?'

*'Mohamed Laghari. He took a boat out to the bay and won't come back in. Says he wants to be a pirate. Is racing around the harbour like a loon, with a megaphone, shouting pirate shit.'*

'And Mohamed does what?'

'Employs half the town one way or the other.'

'Charlie had suggested that the people at Broch House were targeting senior, influential people, hooking them on the drug, using them to keep things quiet.'

*'What?'*

'Sounds mad, but you have Laurie, Mohamed and Amy all acting like they are sucking space dust. And all are big players in town. My thought is that even with the Broch people gone, they sound like they are still getting the drug. Unless they had some extra. Or they are new users, and the dealer is targeting people with money. Something is wrong with all of that, but it still sounds like the drug is on the streets.'

*'I managed to talk to Doddy about the box. He admits he was told, in no uncertain terms, to get it to Broch House, but he knows no more as he never received the box from Lemby.'*

'Did he say anything else?'

*'I did get something, although I'm not sure how it fits.'*

'Fire away.'

*'I asked him about Keith Noble.'*

'Charlie's dad? What has he to do with this?'

*'In the last few months, I've had to take Keith Noble up to Broch House a few times.'*

'Why?'

*'He has, or had, a contract with them as a private GP. He's had it since they opened. If someone got sick, they wanted discretion, so they retained Keith.'*

'Charlie said he's retired.'

*'I think they pay well.'*

The Broch House people don't believe in the minimum wage. 'Go on.'

*'Most times I dropped him at the main house, but – and it was Doddy that sparked this in my head – I saw him head for the annexe on a couple of occasions.'*

I fly through the gears on this one. If the annexe was only used for the drug users, then the only people Keith could be seeing were the addicts. And that puts him right inside the whole shebang.

'And Doddy knew about this?'

*'He told me to leave it all alone when I mentioned Keith.'*

'Anything else?'

*'No.'*

'Are you sure?'

*'Yes.'*

What in the hell has Charlie's dad got to do with this? After I hang up, I call Terry.

'Terry, a quick question. Did you ever see Keith Noble up at Broch House?'

*'Sure. He was on call as a private GP.'*

'Why didn't you mention it?'

*'It slipped my mind. Why?'*

'Just curious.'

*'Did you get the bag to Conn?'*

'Yes. Was Keith Noble up at the House a lot?'

*'A few times that I can remember. Why?'*

'Nothing. Do Kristina's mum and sister need a lift at all?'

*'No. They made their own way here. We're all going up to see Kristina now.'*

'Let me know how she is?'

*'Will do.'*

If Terry remembers seeing Keith a few times, that could mean he was a regular. And that leads to a bad thought. If you're dealing a new drug, what happens when it goes wrong? Overdose, allergic reaction. You can't call 999 or the local NHS doctor. It would raise too many questions. Billionaires would want that like a hole in the throat. So you hire a private GP. My opinion of Charlie's dad is bad enough after Mrs Lang's revelation of his involvement with my mum. It's getting worse.

The key question now is could Keith Noble be the dealer? He's certainly a prime suspect. He has to know a lot about the drug. He couldn't be up at Broch House for any other reason. Did he know about the box?

How in the hell do I deal with Charlie on this?

*Hey, Charlie, your dad might be a drug dealer, and I hear he might have abused women and screwed my mum.*

The only way this works is to front up Keith myself.

# TWENTY

*'I Did That Thing'*

Another quick call to Terry.

'You said Keith is still in Charlie's old house?'

*'Yes, but, Blake, be careful with him,'* she says. *'He's an old man now. And don't talk about Gran. I promised to keep her out of this.'*

I agree and set off for Keith Noble's house.

Saltoun Place is a row of old-money homes near the football ground. Keith lives in one of the granite mansions. As a kid, I'd thought it a palace compared to the place we lived in. I pass what used to be the old doctor's surgery. Its rear wall backs on to Bellslea Park. A stray ball can bounce off it and back on to the pitch. The grimy patchwork stonework of the building is brightened by a small multicoloured painted fence and windows displaying bright images. It's now a nursery school.

The fountain that Terry mentioned is across from Keith's house. There's a police car parked next to it. I slow down, wind down my window. There is a woman on top. Singing. The singer must be Amy Milton. She's in full voice. Her stage is a silver-painted affair about fifteen feet high topped by a bird that Amy is clinging to while she sings. Victorian scrollwork dominates the top with coloured circles dotting the edges. Eight pillars stand it clear of the ground, and the drinking fountain lies beneath her. A single constable is shivering while looking up at Amy. She's dressed in a pair of pyjamas and must be freezing, but she seems happy to be singing 'Radio Ga Ga' by Queen. Her face radiates the same confidence that I saw in Kristina and Laurie Makewith. I park around the corner from Keith's house. As I walk towards the house, I stumble on Kyle Anderson sheltering across the road from the fountain.

'Blake Glover, what are you doing here?'

'Hi, Kyle. I'm out for a walk.'

'You wouldn't know anything about this?' He points at Amy Milton.

'What's she doing?'

Kyle picks at a small scab on his chin. 'My head in. That's what she's doing. We can't even get her to talk to us. She won't stop singing. Three hours. Three hours she's been up there. She has to have hypothermia by now. We've tried to get her down. We even brought in the fire engine, but she screamed blue murder. We had to give in for the moment.'

'Why are you here?' I ask. 'This situation hardly needs a detective.'

'Moral support for Graham there. I'm hoping she'll give in and come down herself. We just need to wait her out.'

'Good luck with that.'

I walk away, eyeing Keith Noble's house as I pass. Keith's standing in the front room, watching Amy give her solo performance. His beard has lost the fire-red I remember, and he looks much thinner with less hair. He's wearing a grubby cardigan. I think it's the same lurid green creation from back in the day. He sees me. I know he recognizes me as he ducks out of sight. I look back; Kyle is watching. I keep going.

Amy launches into 'Carrie' by Cliff Richard, and Kyle crosses the road. I double back, sprinting up Keith's path while Kyle is looking at Amy. There are two storm doors guarding Keith's home, and both are open. I nip into the porch, closing one of the doors behind me, hiding me from Kyle. Unless Kyle walks right up the path, I'm out of sight.

I hit the doorbell and wait, peeking out to see if Kyle has seen me. He's chatting to the constable.

Keith ignores the bell. I hit it again. Still nothing.

I bend down to his letterbox.

'Keith, it's Blake Glover. I'd open up if I were you. I'm happy to tell the police here about your visits to Broch House.'

This gets his attention. I see his shadow move down the hallway. The door opens.

'Fit do you want?'

'To talk.'

He looks ill, emaciated. The cardigan was always too big, but now it's hanging from his frame like a shroud. His face is drawn, cheeks sunk so far that they could be touching each other inside his mouth. He's a fraction of the man I remember. If Mrs Lang thinks this man could be a threat to me now, she's living off an old memory. He's struggling to stand up. He looks so weak that I wonder how he got up to Mrs Lang's place.

'Talk about what?' he asks.

'Broch House for a start.'

'Fuck off!' He tries to be authoritative, but whatever sickness he's suffering from has stolen his ability to shout. It comes out as a dry whisper.

*Didn't Terry say he shouted at Mrs Lang?*

He tries to shut the front door in my face. I step in, blocking.

'Cost,' I say.

The door freezes in his hand. 'The fuck does that mean?'

'A word I heard.'

He steps back. 'Get in before that daft prick out there sees you.'

Close up, Keith looks even worse. Heavy bags under his eyes, pale, almost translucent skin, and as I enter, he drops to a stoop that threatens to fail and force him to the ground.

I'm admitted to a world of old-school decoration. Dark brown the norm, layered with dust. A monumental coat stand dominates the hall, behind which an equally monumental wooden staircase rises. The floorboards are heavily varnished, and the grandfather clock's tick echoes around me just as it did forty years ago. I'd swear nothing has changed since I was a kid. Keith points to a back room and I follow him. As I enter, I'm confronted with the massive dining table that Charlie and I used to play Risk on, sitting against one wall.

Keith leans against it for support. 'Say fit you have to say, and then fuck off.'

I'm not sure where to start. So, I take the police route. Direct. What's the worst that can happen?

'Are you dealing drugs, Keith?'

The laugh sends him into a coughing fit. When he recovers, he tries to stare me down. 'Are you fucking serious? Where in the fuck do you get off accusing me of that?' His voice quivers. Warbles. He's trying to force out bravado, but everything about him signals feebleness.

'You let me in when I mentioned Broch House,' I point out.

'I let you in because if that daft bastard of a policeman sees you here, he'll ask questions I don't need. So, go out the back door and leave well enough alone.'

He had been Lemby's equal in his day, but old age and illness have pickpocketed him of that power.

I don't move.

'I'm not going anywhere. I know you're up to your neck in this Broch House stuff, Keith.'

'You know nothing son, nothing. What the hell has Broch House to do with anything? Look, piss off! I shouldn't have let you in.'

I blank the instruction. 'You're the doctor up there. At the annexe.'

'I told you to fuck off!' He walks, slowly, out of the room.

I'm not sure how I'd expected this to go, but this isn't it. I'm left standing in the room on my own. I hear the clink of dishes, then the hiss of water hitting the boil. It sounds like he's making a cup of tea or coffee.

I've no choice but to go find him.

He's in the kitchen, a large farmhouse affair that looks on to the back garden. Apart from a new fridge and cooker, it has sat in the same time-warp as the rest of the house. The rear door is open. Keith is standing next to the kettle, pointing at the exit.

'Fuck off!'

When I was young, Keith had been a man I looked up to. A respected doctor, living in a large house that was alive with people coming and going. He didn't treat me like a kid, more like a young adult, giving me the time of day when I had questions.

But this is a different man. He's ice-cold with me. I stand my ground and we both wait as the kettle boils. He pours the water into a cup and mixes up a brew. I watch as he dumps the used tea bag in the bin and crosses to the fridge to fetch milk.

'I like mine milky,' I say.

'Fuck off!'

'What? Do you think I'm just going to let this drop? Walk away. Really?'

'If you know what's good for you, yes.'

'I'm sorry you're not the man I remember.'

He stirs the milk into his tea. 'And you're a fucking Glover!'

I hate the way my name comes out of his mouth. He smiles with it, and if this is the way he talked to Dad, I understand why Dad beat the shit out of him.

'Does that make you feel good?' I say. 'That little smile? Did you forget to add in the knowing wink?'

I'm losing it. I don't mean to. It's just too much shit that's landing at my door. As a policeman, I've dealt with worse, but it's easier when it's other people's crap. I came back to this town for closure. And now I feel like closing this bastard's face.

'Did my father leave you any of your own teeth or did he knock them all out?'

His eyes flare. 'The fuck you know. He caught me unaware. If I'd been ready . . .'

'Aye,' I exclaim. 'How long have you been telling yourself that? Forty years, more? He caned your sorry arse all over the room and you couldn't do a single thing about it.'

He steps. Just one step. Then stops. 'Bastard hit me from behind.'

I laugh. A hard, deliberate laugh. 'Sure. The way I heard it from *a guy in the pub* was that you were beat stupid. Got wiped across the floor by a man ten times you.'

He snaps. Rushing at me. It's easy to step out of the way. He clips my shoulder as he tries to swing a fist, and I duck. His momentum carries him into the door. He goes down. Hits the floor. I swing round, waiting for him to get up. He doesn't move. He just lies there. Then I hear a sound I didn't expect. Sobbing.

My fury is lanced. All I can see is an old man on the floor. Crying. I stand, unsure what to do.

'You've no idea. Have you?' he whispers. 'No idea, Blake Glover.'

'No idea about what?'

'Anything.'

'What does that mean? All I know is that you tried to take my mother from my father. What else do I need to know?'

'You know nothing.'

'So, tell me what it is I should know.'

'What in the hell dragged you back here? You should have stayed in Glasgow.'

'This town is my home.'

He pushes himself upright. '*Was* your home. There's no one for you here now. If that fat alcoholic Doddy is the best friend you can make around here, I'd piss off south again.'

I let his words settle.

'Jesus, son,' he says. A more conciliatory tone creeping in. 'For fuck's sake, sit down. I can't get up easily. Sit down and I'll enlighten you.'

I don't want to sit. I want to stand on his head.

He sees the rage. 'Cool it, son. I'm an old man, and this isn't doing either of us any good. Pass me my tea. If you fancy one for yourself, then feel free. But if you want to know some facts amongst the shit you have in your head, then sit down.'

I keep standing, not passing him his drink, a minor protest from me to him. I can still feel the heat in my system.

'I don't care what you think you know about me and your mum, or your dad. I'll tell you the truth and then please piss off.'

'Why should I believe you?'

'You don't have to. Listen and make your own mind up.'

'Talk.'

'Could you get my tea? Please. And sit down.'

I relent and give him the tea before sliding to the floor. He sips at it. 'You've been talking to Jill Lang?'

I say nothing.

'No need to deny it. I knew she was itching to talk to you. She's been dying to talk to you since you got back. To put you straight. I told her not to, but that's like trying to stuff a roar back into a lion.

'What did she tell you?' he asks. 'That I stole your mother away?' He sees my eyes blaze. 'Oh, calm down, son. I stole your mother just as much as your father drove her away. Your mum and I go back a long time – long before your dad. I asked her to marry me once. And she said no. Probably quite rightly. I was young, a hothead, and I thought getting accepted into medical school made me the biggest catch in the town. She thought me an arse. We weren't even going out when I asked her. I was that cocky. She laughed and walked away. I deserved it.'

He stops to drink more tea.

His own rage at me seems to have drained like water from a sink. I'm still on the boil inside. He lays his cup on the tiled floor.

'Your dad wasn't the most attentive man. But then again, we were both from a different generation,' he went on. 'The men worked, the women did the housework, brought up the kids. It's what our parents taught us. It's how we lived. When I left university in Aberdeen, I got a job in Fraserburgh. I didn't want to come back, but this town sort of draws you in. At least, it did for me. You were born not long after I got back. Your mum had a bad time with the pregnancy.'

For the first time, he's said something that's of interest, and despite my still simmering anger I am curious.

'In what way?' I ask.

'You were a breech birth. They tried to turn you the right way. It didn't work and the C-section was messy. It was botched. You made it out OK, but it all but ended your mum's chances of another kid. If it had happened today, your parents would have sued the hospital. Both your mum and dad wanted more kids, but that was out, and adoption wasn't something they wanted to look at.

'Your mum talked a lot about you,' he continues. 'You were her *it* because of that. Her one and only. I was just starting out as a GP, and Rhona was one of my patients. I saw a lot of her just after you were born. Then, as you got older, things kind of happened.'

'Kind of happened?'

'Don't get all het up. It wasn't one-sided, OK? It was mutual. No one knew about it. We were very careful.' He sees me about to berate him and puts his hand up. 'I told you, don't get het up. I'm telling you it the way it was. Don't believe me if you don't want to, but at least let me finish.'

He drinks more tea. 'Your mother wouldn't have ever left your dad, and I never asked her to.'

'How long did it go on for?'

'Until she died. I was still seeing her right up to the end. I was just grateful she wanted me. Karen, my wife, and I had issues. She was seeing someone else too, but I didn't care. When Karen asked me about Rhona, after the fight with your dad that night, she left.' His eyes wander, the memory probably running in his head. He adds, 'Karen would have left anyway.'

His story has plausibility. But if this is a man who hits women, then he could easily make up a good tale. That's how abusers fly. Credible. Nice people who couldn't *possibly* have done *that.* I have met a truckload of them in my time.

'What do you want me to say?' I ask.

'Say? Son, I don't want you to say anything. You've heard my side of the story. If Jill Lang told you anything different, I'd like to hear it.'

In truth, nothing that Mrs Lang had said contradicts his story. Even his attempt to attack me backs up her view that he has a violent streak.

'So, you fought Dad over Mum?'

'I told you, I'm a hothead. We were both drunk. Way too drunk. Both of us grieving over your mother, and both believing the other had no place in that grief. The funeral was a raw affair. He hit me right in this bloody room. And do you know what I did?'

'What?'

'Fuck all! I wasn't kidding when I said he hit me from behind. Put me on the floor. I could have got up, but I didn't, and he started laying into me. Right here.' He points to the spot where he's sitting. 'Ironic, isn't it? I'm back on the same fucking floor. Put there by another Glover. I didn't resist him. I deserved it, in a way. I just took it. A bit too much, but I took it. Karen knew why. That's why she left. I think the kids maybe knew why. And Jock knew. But no one else. Not back then.'

'Is that the best you can do after all this time?'

'I said you can believe what you want. But that's what happened.'

The last of my rage parks itself.

'Mum saw a lot of you before she died,' I say.

'I know. Her cancer was eating her alive. In the end, she didn't know day from night half the time. Your dad tried to drink the problem away, and I came around to your house so often that I got a warning from the practice for not attending to my other duties. There was nothing to be done. She wouldn't go into a hospice, and all she could see was the pain that would keep coming until she died.'

'She swallowed all those pills,' I whisper. 'Opened all those containers and swallowed them all down dry.'

'When you're in that much pain, you find a way to ease it.' He doesn't look at me when he says this.

*Could you get one of my sweetie jars out for me?*

He slumps.

My heart fails. Misses a beat. 'You were there. That day. Your car was still outside when I left to get the money. I always wondered why the hell Mum needed money right then? I always thought that was a bit crazy. But I was a kid. Did what Mum said. Anything to make her happy.'

Keith places his head in his hands.

The Fizz Buzz in my stomach ignites. 'Oh my God. You went back in. After I left. You went back to her bedroom.'

He doesn't deny it, and that's as good as admitting it in my world.

'You did. You were there when . . .' My stomach flips and I want to throw up. 'She couldn't have opened those containers on her own. Could she? She couldn't even squeeze my hand that day.'

*Thank you for getting my sweeties. I can manage from here.*

'No, Mum could barely close her hand. Why the hell am I only seeing that now?'

Keith isn't moving. I can't stand up. I've no energy. I want to lash out. I scream at him, 'You gave her the pills! You gave her the pills!'

He whispers, 'She was in so much pain, son, so much pain.'

'You did! You did! The pills! You gave her the pills!'

*The sweeties.*

'She asked me to do it every day for weeks,' he mutters. 'There were no painkillers left that would work for her. I only helped her do what she wanted to do. *Needed* to do. She was pleading to end it. I'd run out of ways to help. Risked everything to make her better. Spent a fortune on alternative treatment, but it was for nothing.'

I stand up. 'All these years, I thought it was my fault. That I was to blame.'

I need out of here.

He keeps talking, 'The other treatments failed, and, in the end, she begged me to help her. She asked your dad, but he just vanished into a bottle. He couldn't deal with it. Someone had to help her. She was in so, so much pain.'

My vision clouds. I step back, but he keeps speaking, 'Your dad didn't beat me up because I'd had an affair with his wife. He beat me up because I helped your mother die. May God forgive me, but I did that thing.'

I want him to shut up. I want to stop him. But he wants to tell me more.

'She was so peaceful at the end. At rest. No more pain. No more suffering. And I so know her pain. Believe me, I now do.'

I stumble out of the door, onto the garden.

He's still talking. 'She said she loved you, Blake. Just before she . . .'

I climb into the next garden, losing the last words, pushing through bushes, and on to the garden after, and on, scraping myself on fences, falling on to slabs. Then I fall out on to the road. I stagger to my feet. I begin to walk. Away from the town. Away from Fraserburgh.

Just away.

# TWENTY-ONE

## *'Death'*

Hours later, I'm sitting on the top of the largest dune on the beach, looking back at the town. I'm buried in sand to keep the cold at bay – a wounded beast in its lair. It's dark. My phone has rung itself out of battery.

In the daytime, you can see most of Fraserburgh from up here. A few steps to my left, and I could look down on the cemetery where my mother is buried.

As kids, this was the king-of-the-castle spot. The perch to be knocked off.

When I'd staggered away from Keith's house, I'd convinced myself I should go to the police to report him to them. In his state, he might have admitted to what he had done. I don't care about the drugs, or Charlie, or Doddy, or Conn, or Terry, or Mrs Lang – I'm only focused on Keith Noble.

The man who killed my mother.

But what do I gain from reporting him? A trial? Mum's infidelity brought into the open? Dad's drinking? All to be dug up. Some of Mum's life used as defence and some for prosecution. What else would come out? Who else might come forward? What else might Keith know that he could reveal? What else don't I know? And if Mum really did want to end it – if it was that bad – then did Keith do the best thing for her?

My head spins.

I'm the last of the Glovers. After me, there are no more. The only thing left on this earth is my family legacy, and putting an old man on trial will just take that and trash it. My own guilt rises. Irrationality rises. I would be cross-examined. *Why did you get the pills out for her? Why didn't you stay? You sat in the park and read a comic?*

I fight my desire to act. I don't need to do anything right now. Or do I? Is Keith more likely to admit to what he did when things are so raw? Confessions often come on the back of the intense. He deserves to be exposed, but, again, what if he denies it? Where's the evidence? What proof is there? I know better than most what a lack of evidence means. And if he does deny it, my time back here would be at an end. Accusing the most respected of GPs of the ultimate crime for a doctor. I'd be hounded out.

I need to be more measured, but he still needs to pay.

I dig into my police training. Rule number one. Gather more evidence and then strike.

I bury myself a little deeper in the sand, noodling my head into a gorse bush, trying to banish the internal chill. My mind picks up the original reason I was visiting Keith, and I remember that somewhere, out there, is a dealer, handing out death. And given Keith's health, I can't see it being him doling out the pills.

Unable to take the cold any longer, I extract myself from the sand and start the walk back to town.

I cut along the promenade on to the Links, tracking across the grass towards the leisure centre. It's not the direct way back to my car. It's just the way I'd have gone as a kid. When I reach the football ground, I stop. A large sign advertises the Jim Adam stand. I feel I should know who he is, but I don't. A ubiquitous church sits close by.

Two religious structures in close proximity.

I pass the fountain. Amy is gone. My car is where I left it. I sit for half an hour both charging my phone and letting the heater warm my bones. Keith Noble's lights were not on as I walked by. If he's in, he's hiding in the dark. He must be wondering what I'll do or say, now I know what he did.

When I access the voicemail on my phone, I have a slew of calls. Conn, Terry and Charlie. Conn and Terry are trying to get me to do some pick-ups and drop-offs tomorrow. Charlie has left three messages, all urgent.

Does he know about his dad, about what he did? Does he know I went today? Keith said the kids might have known about his and Mum's affair, but what about the sweeties? Does anyone else know about them?

I call Charlie.

He answers on the first ring. *'Where have you been?'*

'Thinking.'

*'And?'*

'I can't see that we have any choice but to go to the police.'

*'That's not a good idea. There's no way we can keep ourselves out of this. Have you talked to Terry? She saw Kristina today.'*

I'd forgotten about Kristina. 'I've not heard from Terry in a while.'

*'Kristina can still place us all at Broch House.'*

'Charlie, she can place you. I'm already in the frame.'

*'What does that mean?'*

'Nothing. I'm too tired to do anything else tonight. I'm calling it quits. I'll see where my head is in the morning. Maybe the dealer has seen sense and stopped. Or maybe I'll go to the police myself. Just fess all this up.'

*'That's not wise.'*

'Charlie, none of this is wise.'

I hang up and call Terry.

*'Hi, Blake.'*

'Hi. How's Kristina?'

*'She's in a bad way. The doctors are worried. She's not responding to any of the treatments. Charlie Noble phoned to ask how she was.'*

'Did he?'

*'It was nice of him. I think Taylor put him up to it.'*

'Does Kristina remember anything else about that night up at Broch House.'

*'No, she can't talk. She's barely conscious. The doctor's having her transferred to Aberdeen. He's really worried.'*

'How's her mother and sister?'

*'Holding up. And before you ask, there's still no news on Tomas.'*

'I saw Doddy.'

*'How is he?'*

'He was trying to convince the nurse to let him have a dram.'

Despite the situation with Kristina, she giggles. *'Sounds like he's not ready to call it quits on this planet just yet.'*

'Doddy will outlive us all, and most of the town. Do you need anything?'

*'Maybe a lift tomorrow. I need to know when they are going to move Kristina, and then I need to get her mum and sister down to somewhere near the hospital in Aberdeen.'*

'OK. Call me.'

I hang up and drive back to my flat.

At one in the morning, sleep is a far, far-away thing. The events of the last few days play in and out amongst the midnight weeds. Keith and Mum. The drugs. The deaths. The dealer. But, under all this, something is grinding at the back of my head – and a small Fizz Buzz joins it in my stomach.

On the drug front, Charlie is dead against doing anything. But knowing what Cost can do, I don't understand why. But if there are no more cases, then maybe I'm rushing at a door that doesn't need to be opened yet. I'm also not surprised that Charlie phoned Terry about Kristina, but I doubt it had anything to do with his concern for her. Kristina can put him inside the grounds of Broch House with both Lemby and me on the night of the fire. Charlie wants to know if that's going to happen.

So do I.

I eventually drift off. When I wake up the next morning, my stomach is telling me that IRN-BRU and Mars Bars do not make a good diet. I hit my favourite café and do the roll-and-sausage thing with added tea.

Mum and Keith are never far from my thoughts. Every time I think about it, I feel lead in my stomach. All these years believing I was responsible for her death. And maybe I still was. What if I'd refused to go to the shop? What if I'd stayed?

I shake my head. I'm going nowhere with this.

Around me, the café is quieter than usual. A couple of college students are playing with laptops. An older woman who reminds me of Mrs Lang is watching her iPad. She has the volume too loud. She's on catch-up with *Coronation Street*.

I call up the *Fraserburgh Siren* website on my phone. The fire at Broch House has been given the full treatment.

The pictures back up Kyle's word: *eviscerated*. Fire-raising is the main lead, but there is no mention of the drug link. I find Charlie's text and click the link on www.allthenewsandmore.com to find the webpage is gone. I try putting 'Cost' and 'drug' into my search engine, but it's way too general and leads nowhere. I wonder who got that story pulled down.

Who else but the people behind Broch House? That's worrying.

I decide to go up to the library. More to think than anything else. Mum took me up there almost daily when I was wee. Then, one day, I just started taking myself. And from that day on, I could lose myself in the printed page for hours. I exit the café, but when I reach the main door of the library, I can't bring myself to go in.

I'm still thinking about Keith Noble and the past – I don't want to go back to such places at the moment. And the library will take me there.

My phone drags me into the present. Terry.

*'Blake. Oh my God. Blake!'*

'What is it, Terry?'

*'She's gone!'*

'Who's gone?'

*'Kristina.'*

'What do you mean "gone"?'

*'She's dead.'*

'Dead. How?'

*'Overdose.'*

'In hospital? An overdose of what?'

*'They don't know, but they found a bunch of pills by her bed.'*

I repeat myself. 'In hospital?'

*'Her mum and sister are a wreck. The police are here. What will I do?'*

'Stay with her mum and sister. I'll come up. We can take it from there.'

I walk to my car, drive to the hospital. The first person I see, standing in the car park, is DI Kyle Anderson.

'Are you just a bad penny?' he asks.

'Terry phoned. She doesn't know what to do. What happened?'

'It's an ongoing investigation; I can't comment.'

'Terry said an overdose.'

'Blake, leave it.'

I don't. 'How in the hell do you overdose in a hospital without anyone intervening?'

'Blake, I need to go.' He walks away saying, 'Let us do our job.'

I call after him, 'Where's Terry?'

'In the main waiting area. She's been interviewed, but we'll need to talk to her again.'

'Surely you can't suspect her?'

Kyle turns and walks back towards me. 'Would you be saying that about a friend of someone who had just OD'd, if you were one of the policemen on the scene? Would you?'

'OK. I just don't see her being involved.'

'I need to go.'

'Before you do, what happened with the woman up at the fountain?' I ask.

'She's in hospital. Whatever she was on isn't good. She isn't responding to treatment. She can't tell them what it was she took.'

I wait until he walks off before I enter the A&E area. It's hardly any time since I was sitting here with Kristina. It feels far longer. The area is all but deserted. I spot Terry, arms around the shoulder of a smartly dressed older woman, a young woman next to her. Terry spots me and signals for me to stay where I am. She says something to the young woman, who whispers to the older woman. She gets up, pointing me towards the main entrance.

I join her just outside. Her eyes are raw, rubbed red. She's been crying.

In the distance, there's a roar. It gives me an excuse to look away as she dries her eyes. I look up as a small silver dart streaks across the sky, its contrail sharp white on blue. Probably one of the military jets out of Lossiemouth. I hear they use Fraserburgh for bombing run training.

'Sorry,' says Terry.

I turn from the sky. Terry is putting a hankie away.

'What are you sorry for?' I ask.

'Kristina's mum doesn't want to meet anyone. She's distraught.'

'I understand. When did they find Kristina?'

'First thing. They tried to call me, but my phone was off. We only found out when we came up here at nine.'

'Do they know what happened?'

She rubs her eyes. 'She took pills. They interviewed me and Kristina's mother and sister. They asked if we brought anything in with us last night.'

'They have to do that.'

'Like we would have brought in pills.'

'You said she was getting worse last night.'

'Much worse. Kristina's mum didn't want to leave, but they had given Kristina a heavy sedative and convinced us to go. We shouldn't have gone.'

I touch her shoulder. 'Why? What would you have done?'

'Maybe we would have seen who gave her the pills. Kyle said there were lots of them. She must have just chewed and chewed and . . .'

She breaks down. I let her lean on me.

'Was she ranting last night?' I ask.

'Yes. Kyle said that she woke up most of the ward in the middle of the night, trying to get out.'

I think of Charlie, telling me how Lemby was screaming on the boat before he ran off. Of how it was death if you were hooked on Cost. Of Kristina being in the annexe. Seeing what was going on with the drugs. Taking them. Or being forced to. And all the time knowing how it would end.

'Was Kristina on any other drugs before this?'

Terry nods. 'I think so. I didn't want to say to her mum, but Kristina could be high as a kite sometimes. But it was only dope. I'm sure.'

I think on what Charlie told me about the drug. How it could be fatally addictive after three or four doses. That the super-rich would risk a dose for the high, but knew what would happen if they kept taking it. If Kristina was part of the 'entertainment' for the visitors, had she been force-fed the drug? If so, she'd have gone through what Lemby went through, and Lemby drowned himself rather than endure the suffering. Threw himself into the sea to end it all. Kristina ate pills. Is that it?

*Sweeties.*

'Terry, this is important,' I say. 'Kristina must have been given the pills by someone. Did anyone visit her?'

'I don't know. Can't they check?'

'They can.' I think back to when I dropped her off. 'She couldn't have had them when she came in. She wasn't carrying anything when I picked her up. Did she ask you to bring anything for her?'

'I brought some chocolate and grapes. That's it.'

'What about her mum?'

'More chocolate.'

'Her sister.'

'A few magazines.'

'This will take a while to sort out. A suspicious death. Will her mum and sister stay with you?'

'Yes. Kristina's brother is coming out to join them.'

An ambulance pulls up. A man is wheeled past us on a dolly. His leg is bent at an impossible angle.

'I can give you a lift home,' I say.

'Not yet. I can't get her mum to move.' Terry looks back into the waiting area. 'I need to go. I can't leave her on her own. Kristina's sister is all but useless.'

'Call when you need me.'

'OK.'

She starts to cry as she walks away. I want to run after her and give some comfort. I admire her for looking after Kristina's family when she's hurting herself.

I call Charlie.

'Did you hear about Kristina?'

*'No. What about her?'*

Maybe the jungle drums aren't as all-pervasive as I thought. 'She's dead.'

*'Is she?'*

'I'm up at the hospital. I've just left Terry with Kristina's mum. Where are you?'

*'At home. Carol asks if you want to come up and have a bite to eat tonight.'*

I'm a little taken aback. 'Charlie, I'm not really in the entertaining mood. We still have a box of that crap out there and a girl has just died.'

*'Sure, but what can we do?'*

'There are people out there behaving like they just injected sunshine in their veins.'

*'It doesn't mean they are on Cost.'*

'What else could it be?'

*'I told you before, I don't know that much about it all.'*

I can almost read his thoughts. 'Charlie, just because Kristina is dead, it doesn't put this all behind us.'

*'Doesn't it?'*

'No. Two people are dead, maybe more if Tomas and the other sunshine brigade die. And what about the strangers that never made the return trip from Broch House – where are they? A box of the worst drug ever is on the loose and—'

*'And what?'* he cuts in. *'What is it you want me to do?'*

'Do? We need to find the dealer.'

*'OK. How?'*

'I don't know but we can't let it lie.'

*'Really?'*

'Yes, really. You can't possibly think that a box of that stuff will just vanish. If the dealer knows what they have, they will punt it like crazy, and there will be chaos and a lot of dead bodies.'

*'Brilliant, Sherlock!'*

'Why in the hell are you being like this, Charlie? We need to do something.'

*'OK, you think on it and give me a call when you've got it figured. I promised Taylor that I would drop him off at Ellon. I need to go.'*

He cuts the connection.

I stand in the hospital car park watching two constables chatting. Waiting to be told what to do next. One is Paul, the other Graham. Either used to be me.

I consider giving Conn a call, but I'd only be doing that to hear her voice. I could call Kam, but I've nothing to say to him.

As I twist my phone in my hand, it dawns on me that I'm more on my own now than I can ever remember. Conn and Doddy are there for each other at this moment, regardless of what I might think about Conn and me. Terry is a stranger and from a different timeline, with her focus on Kristina's mum and sister. And Charlie? Well, the phone call showed me that if I thought I knew him, I don't. He sounds like he's moved on. As to how he could do that, it just shows that I don't understand him at all. How could I? We were friends in school days. Thrown together again, forty years on, for an intense period, and now that the danger has passed, at least in Charlie's eyes, I'm being invited for *a bite to eat tonight.*

I get in my car and sit. Not quite sure what to do.

# TWENTY-TWO

## *'Being Played'*

Having struck out on any fresh ideas for tracing the dealer, I'm finding going to the pub for a mid-afternoon pint has proven to be a better idea than I'd expected. I'd pocketed a paperback for company, a battered, well-read copy of *The Mote in God's Eye*, a science fiction classic by two great authors: Larry Niven and Jerry Pournelle. It's an epic about first contact with an alien species. As an outsider from Glasgow, I see parallels in the pages of an alien encounter.

I've settled for a pub down near the football ground. My pint has a couple of inches off it. The cheese and onion crisps are already gone. I'm surfing on my phone. Looking for nothing in particular. I turn my thoughts to whether I'm going to stay in Fraserburgh and pull up a property site.

When Kam asked why I was back here, I'd thought of this place as my old home and also my new home. But the two are very different things. A memory versus a reality. What was, compared to what is.

I surf the property website. Prices have rocketed around here, admittedly from a low point, but the town has undergone something of a property resurgence in the last ten years. My house back in Glasgow has been mothballed. I'd considered renting it out, but I didn't like the idea of someone else staying in it while I was away. It also meant I could return to Glasgow quickly, if I felt the urge. I know I should get my home valued and then work out what I want from a place up here. What sort of house do I want?

After all that's gone on, the bigger question is, do I want a house up here? An ad on the website catches my eye.

*Noble Lets – Prime Property.*

Beneath is a picture of *my* block of flats. I click on the link, and I'm taken to the Noble Lets website. My letting agent isn't this one. I scroll down the site. It has a number of properties up for rent in the Fraserburgh/Peterhead area.

I click on the *About Us* section of the website.

*'Keith Noble started the Noble Lets business with his son Charlie twenty years ago to provide the best possible rental property in the area.'*

I switch to my email account to dig out a statement from my letting agent. At the bottom, in tiny type, it says 'acting on behalf of Noble Lets'. I'd never noticed that before.

Charlie is the owner of my flat?

My Fizz Buzz gurgles. I reach out for my pint, misplace my hand, knocking over the glass. I swear, jumping up as the liquid sloshes over the edge of the table and on to my shoes. The barman comes over with a cloth. I apologize.

He's seen it a thousand times before. 'Can I get you another one?'

'Is it free?'

'Sorry,' he says. 'I'll charge you a half pint for a pint. Will that do?'

It's a fair offer given I spilled the thing. 'Thanks.'

'Are you OK?'

I must look a little distracted.

He cleans up the fluid.

'I only ask because . . .' I don't listen to what else he has to say.

*I only ask . . . I only ask . . .*

Only Charlie didn't.

Charlie didn't ask.

Everyone asks.

*Everyone* asks.

Thirty years in the police, I should know: everyone asks.

When someone dies, everyone asks how it happened. What happened? How did they die? It's normal.

When I said that Kristina was dead, Charlie didn't ask how it had happened. He wasn't even curious. The one person who could place him up at Broch House with Lemby, and he didn't ask how she had died.

I stand up, leaving the barman confused. I exit the pub at speed.

If people don't ask, it's because they already know or don't care. Charlie said he didn't know she had died. Did he lie? Why would he lie?

My phone lights up. Kam.

'Hi, Kam. We used to speak less when I lived with you.'

For a short while, Kam and I had shared a down-at-heel flat in the Shawlands area of Glasgow.

He laughs. *'I can still smell the stench of your feet even now.'*

I don't bother with a response.

*'Anyway,'* he carries on. *'Remember you asked about a dealer in Fraserburgh.'*

'You have something?'

*'I have something you'll like. Are you ready for this?'* He pauses. *'They just nailed Mitch Campbell.'*

My world stops spinning. 'Jesus. Mitch Campbell. Do you mean nailed him or *really* nailed him?'

*'Stone cold.'*

'Fuck. When?'

*'Last night.'*

I'm at a loss as to what to say. Mitch Campbell, as well as being my friend in the past, was also the dealer I had tried to fit up in my last week on the force. For near on twenty years, I'd danced around him, and at the end had decided enough was enough.

*'I'm just out of the interrogation. I'm not telling you any of this. Is that clear? But given your relationship with Mitch, I thought you should know.'*

'I understand.'

*'Don't drop me in it, Blake.'*

'I won't, I promise.'

*'OK. We also caught a lowlife when we raided Campbell's office. A mule who was bound for Fraserburgh. I don't know who he was to contact there. He said he was supposed to call Campbell when he got up there for more instructions. I thought it might be of interest.'*

'What was he carrying?'

*'Weed.'*

So Mitch was Doddy's supplier. Surprise, surprise.

'Thanks, Kam.'

*'Blake, this doesn't wipe the slate clean of what you did. Even if Campbell goes down, you know that you shouldn't have tried to fit him up.'*

'I'm just glad the man's finally been caught.'

*'OK, see you, buddy. And please keep it all to yourself.'*

'I will.'

Mitch Campbell.

Unbelievable.

I almost smile.

The scalp to end them all in Glasgow, and scalp is the appropriate word. Mitch was known as the Tomahawk, because he was once rumoured to have used a genuine Native American tomahawk to scalp someone. Probably an urban myth, but one he'd perpetuated as it did his street credibility no harm at all.

The Tomahawk.

I freeze.

What was it Charlie had said when I asked about how he got started as we chatted in the pub? *'I work with a couple of people like the Tom . . .'* Then he had stopped, mid-word.

I yank my phone from my pocket and dial Charlie. I'm breathing hard. The Tomahawk. Was that what he had been about to say? How did I miss that?

Charlie answers.

'Charlie, is the offer of food tonight still on?'

*'Eh, sure.'*

He doesn't sound sure. 'What time?'

I hear him cover the phone to shout something. He comes back on. *'About eight o'clock.'*

'See you then.' I hang up.

If he knows Mitch, then that's how he knew about Spence when he called me out about not being squeaky clean.

My phone lights up. It's Terry.

'Hi, Terry.'

*'We just found out where the pills came from that Kristina took. Kyle told us.'*

'Where?'

*'In a teddy bear.'*

'Inside a teddy bear?' Incredulity in my voice.

*'Kyle told me it was delivered to the hospital early on the morning after you brought her in. It's Kristina's bear. Her mum recognized it. Kristina brought it over from Poland with her. It used to sit on the bedroom window in her flat. She threw it out of the hospital window after she took the pills. They only just found it.'*

'Who the hell would stuff a teddy full of pills and send it to someone?'

*'I don't know.'*

'Do they know what the pills are?'

*'Not that Kyle said.'*

I finish the call with a promise to pick her up if she needs me.

I walk to my flat to discover a new 'To Let' sign has gone up on the flat beneath mine.

The sign reads, 'Noble Lets – It's Better to Let the Noble Way.'

I enter my flat. Thoughts stand on thoughts. I work through what has gone down. Take it apart and put it back together. I take out an old police notebook, an empty one. Dropping on to the sofa, I start to scribble, wishing I had taken notes as I'd gone along. When I was an officer, I would have had a slew of pages filled with my scrawl by now. As I scribble, I spin back and forth through the pages, write some more and shake my head. I scrub stuff out, re-enter it, re-scrub it. I fire up my Mac and start surfing. I scribble some more.

I switch on the Bose. I search my music to find some late-nineties chilled music.

I settle back down and, two cups of tea later, I put my pad down. I give Google a final rummage and lie back.

I look at the final page of writing. My summation.

*Shit.*

The clock tells me it's nearing dining time with the Nobles.

I decide to smarten up. I shower and put on a light green shirt that I was told is *my colour.* I have one decent pair of jeans that don't look like old man's blues, a pair of Vans and a single-button sports jacket. It's as good as it gets.

I circle out to the Co-Op on Buchan Street to buy some chocolates and a bottle of wine. The Co-Op sits next to Lochpots. There's a queue of punters waiting on deep-fried heaven.

I arrive at Charlie's house five minutes late. Carol is standing at the door. Charlie's hanging back. Carol is blonde now.

I hand her the chocolates and the wine. 'Carol, you look good.'

'Not too bad yourself, Blake Glover.'

I rub my stomach. 'A bit more of me.'

'A bit more of all of us,' she says, stroking the chocolate box. Carol steps back. Charlie leads me into the living room.

It's huge. My flat would fit in here with space to spare. The décor is cool and classy. A massive TV dominates one wall. Carol sees me looking at it.

'Charlie's baby,' she says. 'He wants an even bigger one.'

I have a fifty-inch set in Glasgow. This one could eat mine for breakfast. Carol offers me a drink, and I ask for a cup of tea.

'No booze,' I explain. 'I promised Terry I'd be on call if she needs me.'

'Charlie told me about her Polish friend,' says Carol. 'Terrible news. How's young Terry?'

'Cut up.'

Carol launches into a series of who's doing what with who, where and when. She seems to know the story of every member of our old school class. An hour in and she's still going strong.

'Carol,' says Charlie, who hasn't uttered a word since Carol started talking. 'Food?'

She laughs. 'I nearly forgot. It'll take me half an hour.'

She leaves Charlie and me to our own devices.

'Carol doesn't half keep in touch with a lot of our school friends,' I point out.

Charlie nods.

'Did you hear that they found where Kristina got the pills from?'

'No.'

'A teddy bear.'

'Really?'

I wait for more.

Nothing?

'Is that all you're going to say?' I ask.

Charlie leans away from me. 'It's a bit odd, but so what?'

I sit, patting the leather suite with my palm.

'She overdosed,' I say.

'Did she?'

'You didn't ask earlier.'

'Ask what?'

'When I said she died, you didn't ask how she died. And when I mentioned pills just then, you didn't blink an eye. I'd have been asking something along the lines of "What pills? What teddy bear?"'

He looks to the kitchen. 'Would you?'

'Yes.'

'Blake, what's done is done. She's dead.'

'A girl's dead and where are you on it? Eh? "Let's sit down to eat? Why don't we chew, swallow, be merry? Let's forget the deceased, move on, talk about shit"? Is that it?'

Charlie turns to look at the kitchen door. I think he's willing Carol to come in.

'You didn't tell me you owned my flat.'

He keeps the kitchen door under observation. 'I do?'

'Noble Lets?'

'Dad and I run it.'

'Are you saying you didn't know you owned my flat?'

'No, I didn't. We own a bunch of flats.'

I've been here so often before. Asking the questions with answers I know. Cornering people. Tripping them up.

'Then,' I say, 'how the hell did you know where to drop me before you tried to do the run to Broch House without me? I never told you where I lived. Yet you headed straight for my flat? And you also knew my front door was as thin as paper when you asked about signs of a break-in when the box went walkabout. What was it you said – "hardly the vault door of the Bank of England". How would you know that?'

Carol comes back in. This stops Charlie answering.

'Won't be long,' she says.

'Carol, do you know a guy called Laurie Makewith?' I ask.

She crosses the room, begins to arrange some stuff on the dining table. 'He's not well,' she says. 'I'm on the school board with him. He was here a couple of nights ago. He looked terrible. Don't you think, Charlie?'

Charlie says zip.

'Charlie keeps in touch with a lot of people,' says Carol.

'So I hear. Always on the cutting edge is our Charlie. Especially with Glasgow friends.' I make a chopping motion with my hand.

Charlie's eyes widen a little. Carol vanishes into the kitchen.

Charlie stands up. 'I think you need to leave.'

'Why?'

'You just do.'

OK. Time to get serious.

'Charlie, let's not beat around the proverbial. You knew Kristina had died. And you knew how. That's why you didn't ask. Right?'

I feel the tension crackling across the room.

'And what about your dad and his connection to Broch House,' I add. 'You kept that quiet.'

'Blake, just leave.'

'And that will make this all OK?'

'Leave.'

His voice carries to the kitchen and Carol comes back in, 'What's going on?'

'Blake needs to go,' says Charlie. He looks at me. 'Don't you?'

I size up the situation. 'Yes. I just got a text from Terry. She needs a lift.'

Carol looks down-hearted. 'Dinner's nearly ready.'

'Sorry,' I say, 'I really need to go.'

Charlie doesn't move to show me out. Carol does the decent thing by escorting me to the door instead.

I leave.

As I walk across the gravel driveway, I turn and say, 'Bye, Carol.'

A keen breeze has swept in. Clouds are racing above, pockmarking the landscape with light as the moon vanishes and reappears.

'See you, Blake.' Carol looks confused. I'm not surprised.

As I slide into my car, I'm thinking of how naïve I've been. Charlie is no longer the lean strip of a boy I flew with. My police instinct had been clouded by our past friendship. I haven't seen clearly till now.

What I now know is that Charlie Noble has been playing me like a well-used, seasoned fiddle.

# TWENTY-THREE

## *'A Cure?'*

I drive to the end of Charlie's road and park up behind a truck. This is the only road out from his estate. A neatly trimmed hedge provides a pee stop for a stray mutt. It gives me a look as it wanders away.

I wait.

Charlie doesn't disappoint. Twenty minutes later, his Porsche appears. I pull out to follow him but keep far enough back not to be seen. Charlie doesn't drive far. His destination is not unexpected. Father and son are about to meet up.

Charlie parks his car directly outside his dad's house. I park further back, across from the nursery. I watch him disappear inside the house. As I get out of my car, a light flicks on in the front room. I walk towards the home.

There's no one singing atop the fountain.

The curtain for Keith's front room is drawn, but I can see shadows moving and I can hear voices. I wait until a couple walk past me. They stop talking as they draw level. Once they are a few yards away, I metaphorically grab my balls and walk down Keith's path.

Knocking on the door stops the voices from within. I wait in Keith's porch. With no response to my knock, I bend down and shout through his letterbox, 'Charlie. Keith. Let me in or I call the police.'

A shape appears through the frosted glass of the door. Keith opens the door to me. He still looks like death. If anything, he's worse than when I saw him last time.

He leads me, staggering more than walking, into the front room. Charlie is standing next to the ornate mantelpiece. An old leather three-piece suite with ripped arms takes up most of the floor space. Keith slumps on to the sofa.

Charlie places an arm on the mantelpiece. Trying to dominate the room.

He waits for me to speak. I oblige, 'Why, Charlie?'

'Why what?'

'Do you really want to do this? Play twenty questions? In front of your dad?'

'I'm not doing anything else at the moment. Let's see what you think you know.' Keith sprawls a little more on the sofa.

'Blake,' Keith says to me, his voice more tremble than not, 'say what you need to say, and then fuck off!'

I drop to my knees, grab Keith by his shirt. 'Me fuck off? *Me* fuck off? Let's get something clear here, *Keith.* You're the bastard that killed my mother. I've spent my life thinking I was the one that helped her die . . . most of my *fucking* life. So I'll fuck off only when I'm good and ready. *Understand?*'

Charlie rushes at me from behind and pulls me from his dad. He screams at me, 'Don't fucking touch him!'

I yank Charlie's fingers from my arm. 'Did you know your father killed my mum?'

'Blake,' he half shouts. 'You know fuck all. Fuck all. Dad nearly bankrupted us trying to save her.'

Keith croaks a reply, 'I shouldn't have, but I loved her.'

Charlie bends down. 'Dad, you don't have to say anything.'

'I want to.' He looks up at me. 'Blake, you should know.'

My anger is back. Red mist and all. 'I don't want to talk to you. You're a murderer.'

Keith lifts his head a few more inches. 'Aye. But I tried everything to help her. Even things I shouldn't have.'

'What are you talking about?' I spit.

'Your mum was dying. Treatment back then wasn't great. I knew a doctor who said he had a new drug. Untested, but he said it might work.'

'You gave my mother an untested drug?'

Keith falls forward.

'He spent nearly all our money on it,' says Charlie. 'I found out later that we nearly lost the house.'

I lean on the back of the sofa. 'And that makes what he did all right? Eh?'

'I promised Dad never to say anything,' Charlie says.

'No wonder. Your dad killed my mother.'

'I tried to save her,' mumbles Keith.

I ignore him. 'And, Charlie, how long have you been dealing drugs? Years?'

'No.'

'Aye, right. Have you heard of a guy called Mitch Campbell?'

His face ticks.

'Of course you have. You nearly mentioned him. Back when we first met in The Sailor's Rest. You started to say the Tom . . . then you stopped. You nearly said the Tomahawk. Didn't you? Mitch Campbell's nickname. Your partner in pubs. That's why you asked me to leave your house. When I made the chopping sign with my hand. You may as well have written me a confession. Mitch was the supplier to Doddy for his cannabis, wasn't he? Did you two work together? Are you Mitch's bitch up here? Some more cash to buy pubs?'

Charlie just stares at me.

'There was another load on the way up here today,' I say. I pray Kam will forgive me for the indiscretion. 'The police in Glasgow just lifted Campbell. Who knows what he'll say?'

Charlie is as still as a statue.

I ram home, 'And you never asked how Kristina died. That's because you knew.'

Keith interrupts, 'Charlie, what's he on about?'

He's only managing to hold himself upright by grabbing the chair arm.

'Pile of nonsense, Dad,' rumbles Charlie.

'A teddy bear,' I say. 'A teddy bear. You sent her drugs in a teddy bear?' Charlie's face twists a bit more.

'I checked a few things tonight, Charlie. You also own the flats that Broch House rent for their employees. I don't know how you got Kristina's teddy, but you did. You would have keys to the flats. Stuffed it with pills and sent it to her. Was there a note with it? "This is all you are getting." So she took the Lemby way out. Like father, like son – is that it? Killers!'

Keith moves again. 'Are you saying Charlie killed someone?' His voice is so low I almost miss it.

'Keith, don't you act the innocent!' I exclaim. 'You've been treating the poor bastards up at the annexe. Why else would you be up there? The main hotel is dead. Don't tell me you don't know exactly what that stuff does if you stop using it. And' – I cock my head at Charlie – 'your son sent a pile of that crap to Kristina.'

Charlie speaks. 'Blake, you're a real prick. You know nothing about this. Nothing about the drug. Nothing.'

'I know it kills.'

'It does and it's a bad way to go. That crap wants you to die badly. I wasn't trying to kill Kristina. They had her hooked on the stuff. All I did was send her enough of the drug to keep her going until she got out. I was trying to help her. I was trying to keep her alive.' Then, more quietly, 'She just decided to eat as much as she could. That wasn't what I wanted. But it's what she wanted. She knew what was coming when the supply ran out. Even with what I smuggled in – she knew that the end is hellish once you can't get more. She'd *seen* it.'

*Sweeties.*

'Up at Broch House, you said you didn't know who she was. It's just one lie after another with you,' I say. 'Charlie, you've played me.'

Keith slides face down into the chair arm. He says nothing. Charlie is glaring at me as if I'm crapping on his floor.

'And who took the box of Cost from my flat?' I ask. 'I know Lemby didn't. Why would he be crying out for it up at Broch House if he had it? Now that the people behind the House have bailed out, I'm guessing that box is all that is left of the drug around here. Wendy trashed Lemby's stock of it. He told us that much. So who knew I had the box? Three of us. Lemby. Wendy, *if* she knew what was in the box. And you, Charlie.' I point a finger at him. 'But who has a key to my flat? The letting agency – which you just happen to own. There was no sign of forced entry. Who did you send? A lacky from the agency? Not taking anything else was a mistake, Charlie. It meant whoever was in my flat knew about the box and wanted it and nothing else.'

'You've got this all figured,' says Charlie. 'And you have squat.'

Keith mutters something.

'What did you say, Dad?' asks Charlie.

He speaks up, 'I need some.'

I lean over to look at Keith. Sweat is soaking his clothes.

'Shit. Not you too, Keith? Are you a user?' I look up at Charlie, 'You put your dad on that crap?'

Charlie throws his arm up and shouts, 'Fuck off. Just fuck off! Dad's dying. The same disease your mum had. The exact same fucking cancer. Cost's the only thing that kills the pain. That's why he's on it. It was designed as a pain killer first and foremost. Nothing else works for him.'

Keith murmurs, 'Hurts. Really hurts. Blake, your mum went through this. It's so . . .'

Charlie reaches into his pocket and takes out a small plastic box. He opens it, extracts a white pill from the box, slips it into his dad's mouth and lifts a glass of water to his dad's lips.

'In the back.' He points to me as his dad rolls over.

We shift rooms.

'OK, so what do you want?' he asks me.

'Want?'

'How much to go away. To return to Glasgow and never come back.'

'Charlie, I'm not going anywhere.'

'You do know you've got nothing.' He sits on the edge of the oversized dining table. Looking like his dad in his heyday. 'You have no drugs, no witnesses. All you have is a bunch of speculation and a wild story that I'm a dealer.'

'It's enough to get Kyle Anderson interested.'

'And how will that help you? I can dump the drugs anytime I want. Then what do you have?'

'Did you give Laurie, Amy and Mohamed the drugs?'

'Yes.'

'So, you are a fucking dealer.'

'Blake, you know fuck all. Fuck all of fuck all. I'm not a dealer. I had to give them the stuff.'

'What do you mean, "had to"? Were they already on it?'

'Them and about a dozen others I know of. Have been for a while. I've no intention of selling the stuff to anyone new. I need all I have. Without it, they'll all die, and not in a nice way. I need to ration the shit amongst them now that the people up at Broch House have vanished.'

'Oh, so you're performing a public service now.'

'Blake, this is tiresome. I told you I didn't know what this shit was at first. I wasn't lying. I don't deal. Never have. Dad got the job as GP up at the house and thought it was a legit one. When he found out what was going on, he told me. That's how I got started with the runs. They threatened to kill my dad. Told me that if I didn't do what they wanted, they'd slice his throat open in front of me. When I knew things were going south and word was out on the internet about the whole thing, I knew the people behind it all would cut and run. Some of my best friends are on that crap, and their supply would be cut off. I told you that the people at the House had some local players hooked. Well, I know most of them. I had to get my hands on some Cost. And you had a box of the stuff. I had to take it.'

'At all costs?'

'Fucking funny, haha. But yes, at all costs.'

'OK, so what happens when the drug runs out?'

'They all die.'

'How long will the box last?'

'A couple of months, max. Without it, they'd all be dead in days. That's why I had to get the box. I'm trying to help. I've been trying to help for an age. I'm not the enemy here.'

'Why not tell the police?'

'Sure, that would work! The first thing they'll do is ask if I have any of the drug. Impound the stuff. And then what? My friends die.' He runs his hand across the table. 'I'm trying to fix this. I've been trying to fix it for an age. I know a private drug firm. I've given them a shedload of cash to find a way to get people off this shit. Spent nearly everything I have. They say they are close. Maybe a few weeks. I need the time. If they crack it, then I don't care who knows what. But if the police pile in on this, the drug company will shut up shop.'

'Will this cure work?'

'It's cost me most of my business, so I hope so.'

I'm trying to piece this back together. 'How long has this company been working on it?'

'Since I found out that my friends were on it.'

'When?'

'A long time back. More than a year and a half. It's been hell. I've had to sell most of my pubs to Mitch Campbell. I needed to sell to keep up the supply of cash for the research. We're so close to cracking it.'

'You just opened a new pub in Dundee.'

'Owned by Campbell. I'm a front.'

'Why were you working with Mitch in the first place?'

'He helped me at the outset. Way back. He knows how to run pubs. I knew his reputation, but he's been good to me.'

'I'm sure he has. But he's a bastard. A real hard nut. And he's snared Doddy. He's dealing weed.'

'Doddy met Mitch through me a while back. Doddy's a gambler. I knew he was betting with Mitch. I also knew Mitch offered to supply Doddy with dope when the debt spiralled. Conn told me all about it. So I leaned on Mitch to take it easy on Doddy for Conn's sake. If I hadn't, Doddy would be kissing the bottom of the harbour by now. I've been throwing everything I have at the drug company.'

'Then you threw Doddy and Conn into the whole mess.'

'They needed the money, and I still got a cut. I needed money to fund the research, but I couldn't be here for the runs. It worked for all of us.'

'And a couple of months sunning yourself in Spain helps.'

'Fuck off. I was never in Spain. I was down south with the drug company. I needed to be there. Given who I'm dealing with to find a cure, I need to keep an eye on them. That's why I couldn't do the runs. I told you, we are close to something that might help. So close.'

'So that's why you kept up the connection to the House. To steal the drug.'

He wraps his arms around his waist. 'I also needed the money, but Doddy needed it just as much. That's why I sent Lemby his way. I also needed to have a plan in case they stopped supplying my friends. It's what they do to you if you don't do what they say. They just cut you off and you die. Die bad.'

'Who else is on the stuff?'

'You don't need to know. But do you think they managed to keep people away from Broch House with a set of gates and a surly attitude? They used the drug with key people. Hooked them, then controlled them. I told you as much. Do as we want or there's no more Cost. It's a fucking effective way to control people.'

'Shit.' Then I ask the key question. 'You?'

'No. I won't touch it. If they'd wanted me to, they would just have force-fed it to me. It's what they do. They did that to Kristina. And she was low down on the food chain, just expected to keep the customers happy. It's what they did to anyone that they wanted to control. But they didn't do it to me. People are unpredictable on that shit. They need to keep an eye on them. I was reliable. No hassle in bringing in the customers.'

'What about Lemby?'

'He was an idiot. He tried the stuff for himself and got hooked.'

'But on your wee fishing boat, you could have given him some. You had the box. You could have saved him. You let him die.'

'No, I didn't have the box. One of the guys from the partner agency had it. I'd sent him into your flat for it. He took it home. Lemby flipped before I could get more for him.'

'You sent me back for it, knowing the box was gone.'

Charlie slides along the table and places his hand on the wall. 'I wasn't for telling you the story. I was hoping I could sweat it out with Lemby until I could get in touch with my man. I needed you out of the way.'

'So why did you get Doddy involved in all this? Conn told me you introduced Lemby to Doddy.'

'I told you, Doddy has money problems like no one's business. Conn was at her wits' end. And when I needed to be down south a lot with the drug company, I needed someone to cover the runs while we worked on a cure. Doddy needed the cash. I knew Conn. She knew what she was getting into. Doddy had Mitch on his arse. She almost begged me to let her in on the runs.'

'For a cut.'

He nods. 'I told you, I'm near on skint. Ironic, isn't it? Ferrying the rich to try the drug is helping me pay for some sort of cure.'

'And the people behind Cost won't try to find what was stolen?'

'It's too hot around here now. They'll just open up somewhere else. What I have is small potatoes to them. They cannae risk being caught.'

I try to pull the threads together.

Charlie hangs his head. 'Blake, I didn't want you in on this. That's why I tried to do the run the other night on my own. To keep you out of it. I don't think the people from Broch House will come back. They can set up anywhere. A box of the stuff is nothing to them. I've been trying to push you away all this time. You just wouldn't let it lie.'

'That's why you told me to drop it all when we were on the pier?'

'Yes. You're a stubborn bastard. All that counts right now is that my drug company tells me we are close to something that might help.'

'Then what?'

'I hope I can get everyone off Cost.'

'That easy?'

He shakes his head. 'No. Not that easy. They won't want off it. They all love it too much. But they all know the downside to staying on it. Lemby wasn't the first to kill himself. There've been others, and it's nasty as hell. Once my supply is gone, they know they are dead. They'll have to take whatever my drug company comes up with. Either that or die in agony.'

'Charlie, this is too wild. Too out there. This will all get out. Kyle Anderson won't let it drop.'

'Why? What does he have? There were no signs of drugs at Broch House, and those guys are long gone. Lemby drowned himself.'

'Kristina swallowed the pills. In hospital!'

'So what? Drugs get smuggled in all the time. Ask my old man. OK, so they don't know what the new drug is she took, but new shit hits the street every day.'

'And the other customers that didn't come back from Broch House?'

'If bodies turn up, then I'll worry, but they won't. Well hidden is my guess. Dad tried to help them, but some had a bad reaction to the drug. He said it was a bit like a warzone up there on his last visit. I don't think it needed the internet site or Kristina to shut that place down. They knew the end was coming. Had their exit well planned.'

'Someone will talk.'

'Not anyone who is on the drug that I know. They know that will kill the supply. Who else? The fishermen who brought in the suckers? I don't think so. Why fess up to that? And even if they did, what can they say without dropping themselves right in it? And who else can talk? Conn? Doddy? You? Me? Why would we? What's to be gained? And Terry knows nothing, not really. Mrs Lang? Add it all up and Kyle will have zip.'

'What about the people researching the cure? They know. Will they not talk?'

'Why would they? What kind of people do you think would do this kind of work? They might be good at what they do, but they are far from legit.'

'Don't tell me, they make illicit drugs.'

'Who else would touch this? They have people all over the world cooking up new narcotics. Pay them enough money and they turn their hand to being good guys.'

'Really?'

'They have some bloody good scientists on the team. OK, so they are all a little tarred with a bad brush, or on the take, but they know what they are doing, although they charge through the nose.'

'Pharmaceutical companies have massive budgets, but they haven't produced magic answers for junkies?'

'There's no money in it for them.'

'And your "scientists" have got it figured?'

'We got a break. It cost me a mint, but I managed to get some of the research from the original military drug creation project. It gave us clues as to how to manage people off.'

'You stole research from a military project?'

'It cost me most of my cash, but no one is going to come looking for us. The whole project was buried for good reason. They'll not want any connection to what is going on.'

'And that is that? We just ignore the deaths, the missing people?'

Charlie walks to the window. 'Blake, what else can I do? Can *we* do?'

'Hand it all over to the authorities.'

'Sure, and will they keep my friends alive? Will they keep funding the drug research run by some drug makers who are more used to making designer narcotics? My scientists would disappear like snow off a dike as soon as I went to the police. And I'd probably end up sucking mud in Fraserburgh harbour soon after. If I thought there was another way, I'd hand it all over to the authorities in an instant. I'm running low on cash, and now I've got next to nothing left to sell.'

'Charlie, how did you find the people that are working on the cure?'

'Mitch Campbell. He gets his stuff from them.'

'It figures. And will this cure for Cost work?' I ask.

'It has to.'

He stands up, walks over to me, places a hand on my shoulder and stares into my soul. 'Blake, it has to work.'

He places his other hand on my other shoulder.

'And' – the last three words leak from him like slow escaping gas – 'for everyone's sake.'

# TWENTY-FOUR

*'The End?'*

Kyle Anderson is sitting across from me. We're in the café near my flat. He called me. Asked to meet.

The woman with the iPad has defected to the BBC and is catching up on *EastEnders*. The café window is awash with steam and mist; a pool of water has formed on the bottom of the wooden frame. Beyond, Fraserburgh is in soft focus.

'I've just been to see Terry,' Kyle says. 'I thought I'd talk to you face to face rather than by phone.'

'What did you see her about?'

'They found Tomas.'

'Is he OK?'

'He's dead. His body washed up near Rosehearty. They're running tests, but it looks like he drowned.'

'Suicide?'

'We're not sure, but you were trying to help Terry Lang find him, so I thought you should know.'

'How is she?'

'What do you think? Blake, there's more to this, isn't there?'

'Kyle, you have three dead people – what more do you want?'

'The truth. Kristina, Lemby, Tomas. Three suicides don't sit well with me. You knew all three.'

I correct him. 'Kyle, I knew *of* all three. I only met Kristina when I found her wandering up at Broch House. I met Tomas for twenty minutes over a cup of tea. I picked up John Lemby's kids. There's a lot more people who know them a lot better than I did.'

'But there is more. Isn't there? We still haven't got to the bottom of the fire at Broch House. We've also had some odd calls from people enquiring after people they knew who may or may not have been at Broch House.'

'I thought you said you didn't find anyone in the fire?'

'We didn't.'

'And?'

'I also want to know who sent Kristina the pills she took. What kind of pills were they? It's not something we've come across before. Our tech guys don't recognize them.'

'Another designer drug?'

'Probably, but she wasn't alone in taking it.'

'No?'

'No. The tox screen for John Lemby had the same stuff on it as Kristina's. What's the betting that Tomas has the same stuff in his system?'

We sit in silence.

He eventually buttons up his coat and, through the steamed-up café window, glances at a plastic bag that skips along the street.

He's a good man and wants to do his job.

'Blake?'

'Yes.'

'Are you going to be staying in town for long?'

'I don't know yet. I'm still thinking on it. Why?'

'Just curious.'

With that, he leaves me to my tea.

# TWENTY-FIVE

## *'Keep Quiet'*

'*Blake, where the f' are ye?'*

'Doddy, I'm at Tesco waiting for Mrs Lang. Where else would I be?'

*'Ye should hiv drapped her aff by noo.'*

It's four weeks since Doddy's stroke. He came back on the microphone last night. Conn and I have been holding the fort between us, but Conn said Doddy was driving her insane in the house. Needed something to do.

There's a knock on my window. I look up. Charlie is standing there. I wind the window down. 'Stranger!'

'Do you have a minute?'

'I'm waiting on Mrs Lang.'

'I saw her inside. She's with her sister; I think they are arguing.'

'That might take a while.'

'I was going to call, but I saw your car. I just picked this up.'

He pushes the latest copy of the *Fraserburgh Siren* through the window.

'Get in,' I say. 'No point freezing out there.'

He rounds the car and drops into the passenger seat.

'Read page one,' he says.

I flick the paper over. The headline blares: 'Fraserburgh Drug Company Busted.'

AC Superiore, a multinational corporation, have had their head offices in Los Angeles, London and Madrid raided. An international task force consisting of US, European and UK police and drug forces carried out a simultaneous raid on three offices and other premises. The company is accused of manufacturing and selling illegal class A drugs through their network of high-end hotels and retreats.

AC Superiore were the owners of Broch House near Rosehearty

before part of the establishment was burnt down in a fire and the owners decided to close the premises. Although there is no firm evidence that drugs were sold at Broch House, we are led to believe that AC Superiore had distributed drugs through all of their global estate. Broch House was also linked to the two tragic suicides in the last month of Kristina and Tomas Kadlinski, cousins who both worked at Broch House.

Gail Till, until recently the head of housekeeping at Broch House, said that she had been unaware of anything in connection with drugs. Her boss, Jose Martinez, has left the country for a job in Spain and we have been unable to contact him. Other employees that we have contacted also denied any knowledge of drugs.

It is understood that over a hundred people have been arrested in connection with the drugs raid. A spokesperson for the National Crime Agency said, 'This is one of the most significant raids on a drugs cartel in recent years. The use of five-star hotels and retreats allowed the owners to distribute expensive and highly dangerous drugs, selling them almost as an extension of the hotel and retreats packages. It is believed that some of the world's richest people were regular customers, and we expect more arrests in the near future as the investigation proceeds.'

'Bloody hell,' I say. 'So Broch House wasn't a freak one-off?'

'And we were right to be scared of these people,' says Charlie. 'I've looked up some of the names of the people arrested and we are talking killers across the board.'

'And none of this will come back to bite us here?'

'What do you think?'

'That, in the scheme of things, Broch House was small fry. Although if one of the customers is brought in for questioning, they might remember the faces of the people who provided transport.'

'Unlikely.'

'Any news on a cure for Cost?'

Charlie checks the supermarket entrance. There is no sign of Mrs Lang.

'We got a break. And it looks good. You know what methadone is?'

'A synthetic opioid.'

'Very good. Amazing what a police education does for you.'

'Methadone is also used to treat heroin addicts.'

'By helping to wean them off it by replacing the heroin while they try to kick it. In itself, it's addictive and it has its own problems, but it can help.'

'And methadone helps with Cost?'

'A variant seems to. It looks like it staves off the worst part of the withdrawal. And that's a win. Lemby and Kristina both took their own lives rather than endure that.'

'And you've tested it? On whom? Who would try it out? Surely it can't be safe. Drug trials don't take years for no reason.'

'We haven't got years. And, yes, I found someone to try it. They've been on it for two weeks, and so far, so good.'

'Who?'

'Dad.'

'Your dad?'

'Who better? He's a doctor, so can assess the stuff. He's hooked and wants off, and his cancer isn't going to vanish. He knows he only has so long. He volunteered. The new drug helps with the cancer pain, but there's no high. He's even experimented with not taking it for a day or two. He says it's bad, but nothing like the withdrawal from Cost, and he would know. Before I got your box, he was without the drug for nearly a day. I just got to him in time. Funnily enough, he's actually a bit better, but I'm not stupid: he doesn't have long left to live.'

'Will you give it to the others?'

'They need to decide that. I'm going to run out of Cost, and they need to make a call.'

'What's to stop your scientists making Cost? Win, win if you ask me, in a dark way. You offer the best high ever, and the method to get the user off it.'

'They tried; I knew they would. But it's not just a case of putting all the ingredients in a bowl and mixing it up. Even with the research I got from the military, the manufacturing process is complicated. Our guys at AC Superiore may not have even cracked it. They might have just stolen a supply and were using it until it ran out. There are cheaper and more cost-effective drugs to be made than Cost – the guys I'm using told me that.'

'And they now have you over a barrel. These guys might have helped you, but they have their claws into you.'

'True, but what can I do for them? I'm near on skint as it is.'

'So that's that?'

'Nearly. Your man Mitch has reached out. He's got a date in court.'

'Mitch has been in touch with you?'

'A wee warning to keep my mouth shut. I hear he's told Doddy the same.'

'That's Mitch.'

I spot Mrs Lang at the supermarket door; she's struggling with her bags as the customers flow around her.

'That's my fare, Charlie.'

'To the horn and back, Blake.'

'To the horn and back,' I reply, and he gets out. I get out as well to help Mrs Lang. I can't help but glance at the cemetery as I do so. I still haven't been to visit my mother's grave. Conn has been. She told me she put some flowers near the stone and tidied around.

I just need a little more time.

I reach the store entrance, dodging a herd of kids heading for the snack aisle. The security guard shouts at them to stop running. They ignore him.

'Hi, Mrs Lang,' I say.

'Was that Charlie Noble in your car?'

'Yes, he said he saw you and Agnes in the supermarket.'

'She's a real old sow, is my sister.'

'So you've fallen out again?'

'She fell out with me! Now, are you going to take my bags?'

I take her shopping, and we walk back to the car. She gets in. Front seat. Belts it. Waits. I drop her shopping bags in the boot.

When we leave the car park, she talks. 'How is Keith Noble doing?'

'Charlie says he's doing a bit better, but long term it's not looking good.'

'In the long term, son, no one looks good.'

I set off.

'Terry told you that Keith pushed me down the stairs, didn't she?' says Mrs Lang.

I promised Terry I wouldn't reveal what she had said to me.

'Don't worry about Terry,' Mrs Lang says. 'She told me she'd warned you off Keith.'

'Mrs Lang, we don't need to talk about this.'

'We do. You need to know that Keith Noble never pushed me down any stairs. Yes, he was a bit rough, but he never hit me.'

'You said he hit others.'

'I'm not sure. I thought he had. I could be wrong. He never hit me, though.'

'So how did you fall?'

She laughs. A weird sound, like a horse braying. 'Keith was there that day all right. We were in bed together. My Ian was supposed to be in Edinburgh, but he came home early. The first thing he always did when he came home was to go up to our bedroom and pull on an old jumper, a pair of shorts and his favourite slippers. I couldn't let him do that, so I grabbed his stuff and, in my rush to stop him coming up to the bedroom, I tripped on his jumper and fell down the stairs. Keith escaped by shimmying down the drainpipe.'

It is my turn to laugh. I drop her at her house and am still refused entry. I decide that I need a break. I kill the radio and head for my flat. As I enter the main door, I turn to check my letterbox, one of eight on the wall next to the front door. It's usually good for nothing other than bills and flyers. This time amongst the junk is a postcard. I pull it clear of the rest.

On the front is a picture of His Majesty's Prison Barlinnie, in all its Victorian drabness. It's an aerial shot. You can see the M8 motorway to the right and the buildings enclosed in the wall of undetermined height; I say undetermined as I know someone who had asked how high the wall was under the Freedom of Information Act, only to be told that the information was classified under section 35(1)(f) of some other Act.

I flip the postcard over. It is blank save for four words and a name:

Wish You Were Here!
Mitch

# Acknowledgements

This novel was inspired by my father, Morgan Brown, who was born in Fraserburgh and grew up there (as did Blake). After his National Service my dad joined the police in Glasgow as a constable and served through the 1960s and 1970s, choosing the beat over promotion for his entire career (as did Blake).

My childhood holidays (and more) were spent in Fraserburgh and although I'm Glasgow born and bred, a precious part of me is attached to that town – bringing back memories of my grandfather and grandmother packing our family, six of us, into their miniscule, three-room flat on Cross Street when we rolled into Fraserburgh.

Some of the shops, pubs, cafes and places in this book exist, or existed, some don't. I'll admit there is no rhyme or reason to this. And if, along the way, I've got a little of my geography wrong, forgive me – sometimes my erroneous childhood memories get in the way of reality.

In writing this book I have several people to thank. First of all, I need to thank Francesca Riccardi, my agent, for all her help and advice. To Severn House and my editor Tina Pietron, to Editorial Director Rachel Slatter and to my copy editor Katherine Laidler, a big thanks for the input and direction. A special editorial thank you goes to Gwen Jones-Edwards (I now see the value of the exclamation mark). To John Corrigan who sense-checked my work for any glaring police errors (and do not blame him if any remain, they are mine). To my beta readers Irene Sutherland and Tracy Hall, who see my work in its rawest form. To Marion Todd for introducing me to Francesca. To Findlay Noble at Fraserburgh FC who assures me that Fraserburgh does not come out in too bad a light in this book. I'd also like to take the opportunity to thank Kevin Pocklington and Russel D. McLean for all their help when I started out writing about Blake Glover. And I am due a huge thank you to my wife Lesley for putting up with me every time I drag out my Mac, at various times of the day and night, and in so many different places – all of which gets in the way of so many parts of her life. And to my children Scott and Nicole, there's a special thanks for supporting their dad.

As a footnote I'd encourage readers to look up Thomas Blake Glover, whom Blake takes his name from. A man from Fraserburgh, forgotten by many, and a man who all but kick-started the industrial revolution in Japan.

Read on for chapter one of the next gripping instalment in the thrilling Blake Glover crime novels

# THE FRACTURE

# ONE

*'Goodbye'*

The pillbox is almost invisible, half covered in sand, squatting in a dip between dark dunes. The gun slits of the concrete octagon, constructed to counter the expected German invasion in the early years of World War II, look to the horizon, watching fishing boats plough their way into the North Sea. A hunter's moon picks out white horses in the bay flashing into life before dying back to black. The distant glow of a cigarette marks the bow of a boat as a fisherman on board contemplates the day ahead. Behind him, like a neon Cyclops eye, Kinnaird Head lighthouse strobes the world. The beam flashes across the water in a rhythmic pulse, as if trying to push the fishing fleet away.

When the light kisses the beach, it illuminates a man planning to take his own life.

Inside the pillbox, Callum Craig is sleeping, curled up next to his holdall, wrapped in a sleeping bag that's too thin for winter on the northeast shoulder of Scotland. Two empty bottles of tonic wine lie next to his head. He rolls over in the space where an anti-ricochet wall once stood.

Callum's dreams are lurid affairs that scare him, night terrors that no amount of booze is able to dull. Tonight is heinous. His dead son's hand reaching from the cot. The tiny fingers covered in blood. Hauled from sleep, Callum screams and throws himself at one of the gun slits, gasping for air. He grabs the concrete sill, pushing his head out into the night, his lungs inflating and deflating with steam hammer speed. The vision of the tiny, bloodied hand still floats in the night. Callum shakes his head to banish the vision.

This dream was hyper-real. Down to the minuscule ragged fingernails; each one needing a cut with the baby blunt scissors his wife never got to use. Callum cries out again, the sound deadened by the surrounding sand and gorse. He waits, his breath slowing, for the hand to fade.

As the last of the fishing boats disappear behind the harbour's main pier, Callum rests his chin on rough concrete. He's smart enough to know he has mental issues but has a pathological fear of doctors. He self-medicates with booze and wishes he had more medicine right now.

When the figure appears on the beach, Callum takes it to be a residue of the nightmare. He rubs his eyes to clear them, but when he looks again the figure is still there. Wrapped in a parka, the individual stops and looks out to sea. Callum raises his head from the sill as the person removes their hood to reveal a bald head sprouting a few wisps of greasy hair that flick in the night air. The man turns and stares in Callum's direction. Callum ducks, but there is no need, in the dark of the pillbox he is hidden from sight. The man is wearing heavy-duty glasses, lenses reflecting the beam of the lighthouse. He looks to the night sky before sweeping his glasses from his head, letting them fall to the sand. His eyes are hooded, black holes buried in a web of wrinkles.

Callum rises to get a better view. Behind the man, choppy water is being driven by a storm that's building out in the North Sea. A cold, cutting wind precedes it. With nothing between the coast and the Arctic Circle, the gusts are chilled by a deep winter breath.

There's something out of place about the man. Late-night walkers are not uncommon on the beach, but there's a sense of despair hanging around this figure like a tight-fitting cloak.

The man on the beach undoes his coat. He fights the last button and, after a few seconds, drops the coat next to the fallen glasses. He slumps down on to the coat, removing his shoes and socks. He rolls the socks into a ball and inserts them into the left shoe. He stands, slowly, as if his knees might not support him, inching back to upright. He slips the belt from his trousers, and Callum knows where this is going.

A few years back, Callum had been sitting up at the harbour, a bottle of whisky in his hand, when a car had driven up to park a few feet away. The radio in the car was loud and the driver was singing along. The words of the song caught Callum's attention – 'Swim until you can't see land.' A track by a band called Frightened Rabbit, he'd later discover. A band whose lead singer had taken his own life. More and more, Callum found himself singing the song title over and over.

The tune runs through his head now.

The man on the beach stands in his boxer shorts, fingering the waistband but he doesn't take them off. His body is wire-thin, skeletal, fat exorcised completely. Bending down, he arranges his clothing into a small, neat pile, placing the shoes on top, a groan escaping his lips as he stands up again.

The man starts to sing, loudly – not a tune that Callum knows.

Callum moves. He can't sit and watch the man kill himself. He scrambles up the mound of drifting sand that part blocks the entrance to the bunker and tumbles out into the night. As he rounds the corner of the bunker, bringing the beach back into sight, he sees the man, standing at the water's edge, the waves are rolling over his ankles, his lungs bursting with song.

Callum shouts, 'Stop!'

The man either doesn't hear or ignores the warning. He begins to wade out into the water. Callum tries to run, but the sand is soft and fights him.

The man, now waist deep in the ice-cold saltwater, raises his hands high and throws himself forward. The water engulfs him. As he vanishes from sight, Callum reaches the water's edge, screaming. The man resurfaces, beyond the breaking waves, long, slow strokes carrying him to the horizon, still singing. Callum is no swimmer, and his clothes are thick and heavy. Even so, he starts to kick off his boots, still shouting, looking around for help. The beach is deserted. The caravan site at the end of the bay shut up for winter, the beach café closed tight, the town lights of Fraserburgh too far away for anyone to hear him. Callum throws off his coat and looks out to sea.

Nothing. No sign of the man. No singing. Callum frantically scans the water. The dark hides the man completely. Callum stops stripping. He has no idea where the man is. He jumps into the air to try to catch a glimpse. Nothing. He thinks about diving in, swimming in the direction that the man had taken. But to what end? He hasn't swum since he was a kid. He looks up and down the beach, desperate.

There is no one.

He stands. Watching.

After half an hour of searching the beach in case the man came back ashore, Callum returns to the pathetic pile of clothes left by the man. A pitiful memorial to a human being. He wonders if he should search for ID while also asking himself if the clothes would fit him.

He walks to the water's edge one more time. Not to look for the man but to say goodbye to a weary soul.

He shakes his head and begins the walk to town.

To the police station.